Alice in Exile

PIERS PAUL READ

A PHOENIX PAPERBACK

First published in Great Britain in 2001
by Weidenfeld & Nicolson
This paperback edition published in 2002
by Phoenix,
an imprint of Orion Books Ltd,
Orion House, 5 Upper St Martin's Lane,
London WC2H 9EA

A CIP catalogue record for this book
is available from the British Library.

ISBN 0 75381 350 5

Printed and bound in Great Britain by
Clays Ltd, St Ives plc

Part One

One

In January 1913, a young army officer, Edward Cobb, passing through London on his way home after a tour of duty in South Africa, was taken by a friend to a party in Chelsea. There he found himself among people he had never encountered before – actors, artists, writers, publishers and young women who smoked cigarettes, drank gin and danced the Boston and the Tango. Edward was drawn to one young woman in particular who was dark and pretty and taught him the steps of the Turkey Trot, the latest craze. When they went out on to a narrow balcony to escape the heat and noise, she became more serious and asked him about South Africa: what were the differences between General Herzog and General Botha? Had he seen the effects of the recent drought?

With the gin coursing through his veins, Edward answered her questions at rather greater length than was appropriate at a party. The girl, Alice, listened patiently and smiled and seemed to like him. When they went back into the living room, the music from the phonograph had slowed and most of those dancing had reduced their step to no more than a swaying embrace. They did the same. Edward could feel her bosom against his chest and her hair tickled his nose. A pleasant scent came from her skin – a whiff that had something of spices and incense and the aroma he remembered from the cigars in his father's humidor.

In a dark corner of the room, they kissed. Edward had kissed few girls before: her embrace was gentle, her lips were soft and she seemed to know when it was the right moment to break for a breath of air. After a while, the thought entered Edward's head that they might go further – that in the world of actors and artists and writers girls thought little of going to bed with a man after a party, even a man they had never met before.

'Where do you live?' he whispered.

'In Markham Square,' she replied.

'On your own?'

'With my parents.'

He thought of his parents' house in Eaton Place where he was to stay overnight with Hamish, the friend who had brought him to the party. Could he take her there? Or to a hotel? What did she expect?

The girl gently pulled away from him and said: 'I think, in fact, since you mention it, the time has come to go home.'

'May I escort you?'

'If you like.'

While she found her coat, Edward told Hamish that he would have to make his own way back to Belgravia. He rejoined Alice and the two went out into the streets. The air was damp and the pavements wet but the rain had stopped. Edward looked for a cab but Alice said that her home was nearby and she would rather walk.

'How did you come to be at the party?' she asked.

'I came with a friend.'

'Who knew Erskine?' She gave a short laugh. 'It must have been Erskine.'

Edward frowned. 'What makes you so sure?'

'He paints portraits.'

'He has never painted mine.'

'No. But it means he meets people . . .' She hesitated. 'People one wouldn't normally meet.'

'Don't you like to extend your circle of acquaintance?' Edward asked.

'Yes, I do. And you?'

'It depends upon who the new people are,' he said.

'Of course.'

They walked on for a moment in silence. Then Edward asked: 'Will *we* meet again?'

She looked up and across at him, as if trying to judge from his expression what measure of feeling lay behind this question. The yellowish light from the street lamp, diffused through the damp air, made her face, framed by her dark hair, seem like an exquisite mask. He stopped, took hold of her shoulders and kissed her with a clumsy vigour.

4

She did not resist him but this embrace in the cold air seemed unwelcome. They walked on. She said nothing until they turned a corner into Markham Square.

'Thank you for seeing me home,' she said.

'Is this your house?' he asked, looking up at the front door.

'Yes.'

'Might we meet again?'

'At another party?' She went up the steps and put a key in the door.

'No. I mean, may I invite you for dinner or something like that?'

'Of course. You know where I live.'

'But I don't know your name – your family name, that is.'

'Fry. I'm called Alice Fry.'

Two

On the train to York the next morning, Edward was unable to concentrate on the newspaper he had bought at King's Cross station. Instead, he rested his head on the antimacassar, closed his eyes and thought about Alice Fry. Hamish, who was to spend a weekend with him in Yorkshire before returning to his family in Ireland, sat beside him in the first-class compartment.

After the train had passed through Peterborough, Edward opened his eyes and turned to Hamish. 'Did you talk to that girl called Alice Fry?'

'You hogged her. I didn't get a chance.'

'Do you know anything about her?'

'Apparently her mother's foreign.'

'Yes, she told me. Her mother's French.'

'How exotic.'

Edward frowned. 'She was very well informed.'

'I'd say so,' said Hamish. 'I bet she taught you a thing or two on your way home.'

Edward turned to look out of the window to hide his annoyance – an annoyance compounded by recalling that he had hoped, the night before, that she would be the kind of girl

Hamish took her to be. His head rose and fell as his eyes followed the telephone wires that were strung from pole to pole along the line. In the smutty glass he could see a faint reflection of his own lean face. What would his family make of him after two years away? Would they remark on the change? He thought of the *veldt*, of Natal, of Cape Town; then of the long voyage back in the troopship and the different ports of call: and as the sky darkened he wondered whether perhaps last night's encounter had been just the last of his adventures that would fade from his memory once he had returned to the affections and preoccupations of home.

At York, Edward and Hamish changed on to the branch line that took them across the Vale of York to the market town of Malton. A pale sun illuminated the landscape so familiar to Edward who, as a child, had often made this same journey returning home from boarding school in the south. As the train entered the valley of the River Derwent, the line following the twists and turns of the river, the same strong emotions that had always accompanied this homecoming arose in Edward once again. Passing the ruined abbey of Kirkham, he rose precipitately from his seat as if this would somehow hasten his arrival and, with Hamish behind him, stood looking out of the open window of the carriage door.

As the train drew in, the chauffeur from Nester Park was waiting on the platform with a young woman who, seeing Edward, ran towards him with a shout of 'Eddie!' and a look of delight. It took a moment for Edward to recognise his younger sister, Sylvia, who, when he had left for South Africa, had been a scrawny tomboy confined to the nursery. Now, her figure had filled out and her long blonde hair, once loose and straggling, had been pinned up in a grown-up fashion.

Running ahead of the chauffeur, Sylvia reached her brother and his friend. She did not kiss or even embrace Edward but took hold of his arm, saying: 'I nearly didn't recognise you. I thought you were an Indian, you're so brown.'

'And I thought you were ... someone else.'

'Someone enormously grown-up and sophisticated, I dare say?'

'Just that.'

Edward introduced her to Hamish. Sylvia shook him by the hand. Edward then turned to Jennings, the chauffeur, who welcomed him with the same mixture of deference and affection as he had shown when Edward had returned for the holidays from school.

'So you've come out?' Edward said to Sylvia as the three young people settled back in the seat of the car.

'Last summer. And you missed my ball, you pig,' said Sylvia.

'You could have waited.'

'How could I have waited? When one's out, one's out.'

'And have you hooked a husband?'

'Not yet. I'm being choosy.'

As they drove out of Malton and up into the Wolds, Edward questioned Sylvia about what had gone on at Nester in his absence, and Sylvia relayed the gossip about her debutante friends in London. Hamish joined in when a name came up of someone he knew and Edward would take advantage of his friend's intervention to glance out at the rolling countryside, his eye alighting on a familiar farmhouse or a horse-drawn plough until finally the well-trimmed hedges and stout fences marked the start of the Nester estate. Five miles on they came to the tall stone wall that surrounded the parkland and a mile after that they turned in past the south lodge of Nester Park.

Edward's home was a large four-square country house built in the middle of the nineteenth century in the Palladian style. Running up the steps ahead of Sylvia and Hamish, Edward found his parents, Sir Geoffrey and Lady Joyce Cobb, in the drawing room where, with their two younger children, they had been waiting for the hero's return. Lady Joyce stood to greet her elder son, and proffered her cheek for a kiss. She showed no more emotion than if Edward had been absent for a weekend; only a slight quiver of the muscles around her eyes suggested the effort required not to show any stronger emotions.

Edward's father, Sir Geoffrey, tried but failed to show the

same sangfroid: with a red face and moist eyes he embraced his elder son and heir, saying: 'Good to have you back.' He then stepped back to let the two younger children, Rose and Arthur, each grab one of Edward's hands. 'Come on,' said Rosie, dragging him towards the door. 'It's tea-time. We've been waiting and waiting and *waiting*.'

'Tell them we're ready for tea, will you, darling?' Lady Joyce said to Sylvia. Then, from a reflex politeness, she turned away from Edward to his friend Hamish to ask after his parents whom she had known in Ireland as a child.

Edward let himself be led by Arthur and Rosie up the shallow stone staircase and along the corridor to the nursery. They, like Sylvia, had grown while he was away but they were still indubitably children. What changes had come over the other members of his family? As they sat down at the nursery table, a shaft of sunlight from the fading winter sun fell on the face of Sir Geoffrey. Smaller than his son, and largely bald, his face had always been ruddy from heavy drinking and life in the open air; but now, as he leaned forward to take a cucumber sandwich and accept the cup of tea that had been poured out for him by Nanny Peake, Edward perceived a new fatigue in his manner and bleariness in his eyes.

Nanny Peake was unchanged – the same old crone – and Edward's mother remained much as Edward remembered her – tall, erect, reserved. The sight of her evoked the same tepid affection that Edward had felt for her before but now, after two years' absence and a greater knowledge of the world, his affection was tinged with a measure of pity. How constrained she was by her inhibitions; how blinkered her narrow concept of good form.

'Don't pester poor Edward,' Lady Joyce said to her younger children who were impatient to see the elephant tusk and zebra skin that Edward had told them were in his baggage; and then, to give them some distraction, added: 'Why don't you show Hamish to his room?'

During the days which followed, Edward basked in the comforts of his family home – not simply the physical comforts of a large, well-run country house but the psychological satisfaction of a new respect in those who had seen him leave as a child and now saw him return a man. Physically, all was the same – the linoleum of the nursery floor, the flaking limestone of the Temple in the landscaped gardens, the smell of dead vegetation; but these familiar things that had once marked the boundaries of his experience were now mere mementoes of his past.

It was in his mind, and in the minds of those around him, that a shift in perception had taken place. The plump cook, the grave butler, the jolly maidservants, the trainer, the gamekeeper, the groom, even old Nanny Peake, all deferred to him in a way they had not done before. The young Eddie whom they had once teased and even chastised was now Lieutenant Cobb of the Yorkshire Regiment, the Green Howards.

The attitude of his family had also changed. On the very evening of his return, when his mother and sisters had left the dining room and Geoffrey Cobb had called forward the two young men to sit down beside him to drink port and smoke cigars, the opportunities that were open to him, now that he had left the army, were set out by his father as if he had been waiting impatiently to launch his son on a political career.

'I think they'd adopt you at Knapley if you felt you were ready to stand,' he said. 'I saw Billy Berwick at Doncaster and he said that they're keen to get some young blood into the party.'

Edward, as he listened to his father's plans for his future, wondered for a fleeting moment whether standing as a Conservative might affect the feelings of the girl who had taught him the Turkey Trot; but the thought slipped away as, in a haze of cigar smoke, he and his father and his friend Hamish discussed how they would settle the somewhat chaotic state of the world. They talked with gravity, conscious that they belonged to the oligarchy that ruled a vast empire, and so that the conclusions they reached could have some bearing on the course of events.

Edward, at the age of twenty-eight, now had all the qualities and qualifications required to enter Britain's governing class.

His father was a baronet with a great deal of money and his mother the daughter of a peer. Certainly, the peer was only an Irish peer but the connection was old enough and good enough to provide cousins in some of the most influential families in Britain. There was also money to back his ambitions – money that came originally from coal in the West Riding of Yorkshire but had now lost its grimy provenance and was mostly invested in government stocks and agricultural land.

Like his father, Edward had gone to school at Eton; and then, unlike his father, had gone up to Oxford where he had studied Mods and Greats – classical Latin and Greek and the philosophy of the ancient world. He had won a second-class degree when he had hoped for a first, which was like drawing a Jack instead of a King; but he had been dealt a King from another source. Sir Geoffrey's membership of the Jockey Club had made him friends who were dukes and princes, and even a real king, a reigning monarch, King Edward VII himself.

After leaving university, Edward had drawn another card which turned out to be an ace. Against the advice of his parents and friends, he had joined the army and, while serving in South Africa, had distinguished himself in a minor action against a force of fractious Zulus. Accounts of this engagement had been printed in both *The Times* and the *Morning Post* and Edward Cobb had been mentioned in dispatches. His parents were proud; some friends were envious; but, to the kind of people in the counties who chose candidates for safe Conservative seats, here was a young man in the mould of Scott and Shackleton, an outstanding specimen of the British race.

It was, of course, an account of this adventure that Edward's family wanted to listen to over and over again – a version for his father with details of strategic deployment; another for his mother touching on the family connections of the colonel who had sent him on this hazardous mission; and, for the younger children in the nursery, some vivid details – the hide shields and long spears, the fierce face-paint and the wild war cries of the Zulus.

One afternoon, after telling the story yet again over tea in the nursery, Edward found himself alone with Sylvia. Hamish had gone home to Ireland; his parents had left and the two younger children had been dragged off by Nanny Peake to have their bath. Edward sat on the scuffed club fender by the nursery fire, Sylvia on the lumpy sofa.

'Weren't you awfully afraid?' asked Sylvia, referring to the fracas with the Zulus.

Edward shrugged. 'I'm pretty thick-skinned.'

'It would have been horrible if you'd been killed.'

He laughed. 'A spear in the belly?'

'I mean it would have been horrible for *us*.'

'For Mother and Father, of course. But once you find a husband, you'll manage quite well without a brother.'

Sylvia thought for a moment, then said: 'I'd hate to think that by marrying I'll somehow stop being part of our family.'

'It depends who you marry. If you marry a duke, you'll move into his orbit, but if you married Potts . . .'

'Oh shut up.' Potts was the gamekeeper.

'Even if you married someone like Hamish, you'd be off to Ireland and kept busy moving the buckets to catch the rain from the leaking roof.'

'I'm not going to marry Hamish.'

'That's rather harsh. I think he took a fancy to you.'

'He's not my type.'

'What is your type?'

'Someone able and ambitious and brave. In fifteen years' time I'd like to see you and the man I marry both in the Cabinet.'

'Ah, but who would be the Prime Minister – him or me?'

'That remains to be seen.'

The chimes of the nursery clock struck six.

'You mustn't marry with too great expectations,' said Edward, standing, arching his back and stretching his legs. 'The man might not measure up.'

'My main fear is that I might fall in love for all the wrong reasons.'

'I would have thought it unlikely.'

'If I do, I count on you to put me right.'

'Certainly, if you wanted to marry Potts, I would advise against it.'

She stretched out her hand as if to hit him. 'I don't want to marry Potts.'

'Nor Hamish.'

'No. But what about someone like Harry Baxter?'

'Has he shown an interest?'

'He's been ... attentive.'

'The parents would be pleased.'

'And you?'

'I haven't seen him for a while.'

'He's improved.'

'He was clever enough at Eton, and I gather that since then he's done pretty well.'

'He's a barrister, or will be, when he's finished eating his dinners. Lord Graveson said he was the most promising pupil he'd ever had in his chambers.'

'I'd like to take another look at him.'

'You will. He's coming for the shoot.'

That evening, as he changed for dinner, Edward found that he was dejected and, when he probed his mind to discover what might have lowered his spirits, he realised that it was the idea of Sylvia marrying Harry Baxter. It was not that Edward felt any animosity towards Baxter; indeed, if Sylvia had to marry someone, and there was no doubt but that she did, she might as well marry someone with a title, plenty of money and a fine country house: these were the things she was used to and they would no doubt ease the transition from childhood to married life.

But her choice was somehow predictable and therefore banal. The Cobbs and the Baxters came from the same circle; they were even remotely related. It was as if the marriage had been arranged by the older generation. It baffled him that Sylvia should contemplate such a conventional choice. It might not be in her nature to do something rebellious – to go to university or marry Potts; but all the same, she must have met men at her debutante dances and coming-out balls with qualities that would contribute something new to the Cobbs's genetic stock.

When Edward was alone with his father drinking port and smoking a cigar, talking about the war in the Balkans and then the Government's plans for Irish Home Rule, this line of thinking led him to suggest that there might be less strife in the world if people married outside their clan, class, nationality or religion. 'If only Bulgarians would marry Albanians and Turks marry Greeks and Catholics marry Protestants, then we wouldn't have wars.'

Geoffrey Cobb looked queerly at him. 'And Englishmen marry Zulus, perhaps?'

'Well, whites have married blacks, or at any rate had children by blacks, and there are several hundred thousand Cape coloureds to prove it. And they're a moderating influence, Father, because they're neither black nor white nor Boer nor British – that's just my point.'

'But they're not thoroughbred.'

'People aren't horses, Father.'

'I don't see the difference. You won't get a good racehorse if you cross-breed with a cart-horse.'

Edward stubbed out his cigar, irritated by the way his father could only see the world in terms of the Turf. He had been home for less than a fortnight and already the relief he had felt on discovering that so little had changed at Nester was giving way to exasperation. He felt that he was being drawn back into a mould and soon there would nothing to distinguish him from Harry Baxter and his friend Hamish: an outsider would be unable to tell them apart. The time had come to escape to London to catch up with some of his more stimulating friends.

Edward could not leave before the shoot, for which twelve guests had been invited to Nester. Most were friends of his parents, but among the young there was Harry Baxter, who was much as Edward remembered him: clever, courteous and almost deferential towards the brother of the girl he hoped to marry; and Elspeth Deverall, who was now Sylvia's closest friend. Edward remembered her from before – a thin, bookish girl – but now remarked on how nature had effected a change, not just in the girl's face and figure, but in her manner and bearing. 'She's incredibly brainy,' Sylvia had said; and it also became clear when the conversation turned to Ireland that Elspeth, the daughter of a Conservative peer, knew more than anyone else at Nester about the strategy the Conservatives intended to pursue to defeat the Government's plans for Irish Home Rule.

Standing by Edward in the line, Elspeth talked to him about his prospects for the seat at Knapley and the people she thought he should call on for help. 'You have to be careful because too much influence can sink the boat.' She was not tall but stood erect, a long, elegant neck rising to thick brown hair swept up into a bun: Edward could see why, as Sylvia had reported, she had been dubbed one of the great beauties of the season. Her manner was friendly and unaffected. She behaved as if it was quite natural, as perhaps it was, that as Sylvia's closest friend she should show an interest in Sylvia's brother's career. Edward was also impressed by her connections: Mr Bonar Law had been their guest in the country the weekend before, while on Tuesday, after dinner, Lord Curzon had shown her a draft of the speech he meant to give during the debate on Irish Home Rule in the House of Lords.

'You should meet Lord Curzon,' she said to him as they trudged towards the barn where the shooting party were to eat lunch. 'I think his support would be crucial. A letter from him would really impress the people at Knapley – much more, I would say, than a note from Mr Bonar Law.'

'How should I set about it?' asked Edward.

'I can arrange it.' She spoke with remarkable assurance for a girl of just eighteen. 'You'll have to tell me when you're next in London.'

'There's nothing in particular to keep me here in Yorkshire.'

'Then why not come down for the debate? I'll see if I can get you a seat. Even if I can't, we're planning a celebration afterwards and Curzon is sure to be there.'

Three

Elspeth's influence turned out to be sufficient to get a ticket for Edward in the Strangers' Gallery in the House of Lords for the debate on Irish Home Rule on 31 January. He heard Lord Curzon's eloquent defence of the bond between Ulster and Britain; and was able to congratulate the eminent statesman in person later that evening at the reception given by Elspeth's parents, the Earl and Countess of St Giles, at their town house on Belgrave Square.

Knowing of Curzon's reputation for arrogance, and having been told that he could be cold and intimidating, Edward was nervous in anticipation of this encounter; but Curzon, when introduced by Lady St Giles, was unusually friendly, saying 'Yes, indeed . . . Mr Cobb' as if he knew precisely who Edward was. 'You want to stand at Knapley? An excellent idea. We need young men like you in the Commons with knowledge of the Empire.'

Lord Curzon's encouragement, and the kindly interest shown to him by a number of the St Gileses' distinguished guests, put Edward in an exultant mood. He was sufficiently controlled and sober to hide his high spirits; he knew it would be fatal to his prospects to show any conceit; but to find himself in sumptuous surroundings, made welcome by a leading statesman of the Conservative Party, with the beautiful daughter of the house rarely leaving his side, effaced for that evening all the misgivings he had felt in Yorkshire about being drawn back into the mould. Was a great destiny to be despised simply because it was predictable? Why row against a current that carries you where you want it to go?

'Are you free tomorrow?' Elspeth asked him after he had said goodnight to her mother. 'There's a spare seat in our box at the opera.'

'Sadly, I have an engagement.'

'Never mind. We'll see you at the Danvers' on Friday.'

The engagement for the following evening was to dine with

Alice Fry. Edward had written to her from Nester – a short note to confirm that he would like to see her again and asking her to dine at the Café Royal.

Edward was at the table when Alice arrived. The head waiter stepped forward to escort her, and Edward saw that a number of those dining at other tables – women as well as men – looked up from their food to watch her as she crossed the room. She was dressed with simplicity and elegance in a blue Empire-style silk dress, gathered under the bust. It was clear that Alice had taken more trouble with her appearance than she had for the party at Chelsea.

The memories of Alice that Edward had savoured had been more of her touch and her smell than her appearance. The image of her face he had kept in his mind was that mask he had glimpsed under the street lamp as she turned to look up at him and was rewarded with the brutal kiss. Now the mask had been removed and, in the subtler light of the restaurant, he saw a softer, darker complexion, a short nose, and eyebrows and long eyelashes as dark as her hair. As she sat down, she avoided looking at him but once seated darted a quick glance in his direction, then again looked away.

'It is good of you to have come,' Edward said. 'I wasn't sure that you would.'

Alice blushed. 'I had hoped to see you again, if only to apologise for my behaviour . . . before. I'm afraid I had drunk too much.'

'Should I apologise for my behaviour too?'

'Yes,' she said fiercely. 'I think you were also . . . drunk.'

The waiter came forward to fill her glass with champagne. She held up her hand. 'I'd like lemonade.'

Edward sighed. 'Are we in for a dreary evening?'

'Very possibly.'

'I'm sorry. I apologise . . . for what I have just said . . . but not for the other evening. I don't regret what we did.'

She looked pensive and bit her lower lip. 'I felt embarrassed the next morning . . .'

'Embarrassed? But not ashamed?'

'I felt embarrassed because I thought you'd think . . .'

16

'That you were loose?'

'Yes.'

'And you're not?'

'I like to think not. Not by my standards, though I may be by yours.'

'But you know nothing of my standards.'

'No, but I can guess what they are.'

'Please tell me. I'd like to know.'

The waiter came with a glass of lemonade. Edward nodded to indicate that he should fill Alice's glass with champagne. She watched as he did so and did not stop him.

'You've got a sister,' she said. 'You may not remember, but you told me.'

'I have two.'

'Well, I don't imagine that they'd kiss a man at a party whom they'd never met before.'

'Rosie probably would but she's only nine. Sylvia wouldn't, I agree, but then she rarely meets men at parties whom she hasn't met before.'

'But if she did, and she did kiss him, you wouldn't approve, would you?'

Edward thought for a moment. 'No, I think I would. But the case is hypothetical. It's not the sort of thing Sylvia would do.'

Alice sighed and looked down at the menu. 'Anyway, I wanted to see you again to show you that I'm *not* loose.'

'Then we *are* in for a dreary evening.'

She smiled up at him. 'Not necessarily. After all, you're no longer a man I haven't met before.'

She turned back to the menu and read it earnestly as if looking for a word in a dictionary. The waiter hovered. Alice chose. Edward ordered. The courses came and went. She left her lemonade untouched and sipped at her glass of champagne. Conversation was continuous but not altogether easy. Edward wanted to know more about her but thought it would be impolite to subject her to an interrogation; nor did he particularly want to talk about himself. 'Imagine,' he said at one point, using a ploy he had developed at hunt balls and

17

debutante dances, 'that you were a character in one of Jane Austen's novels. How do you think she would describe you?'

'She couldn't describe me. I had yet to be invented.'

'I don't understand.'

'For one thing, no women went to university at the time of Jane Austen.'

'Are you at a university?'

'Yes. I am studying languages at Bedford College.'

'What languages?'

'German and French. My mother is French and I suspect that Jane Austen would have found it hard to portray a sympathetic character who was half-French because the French were the enemy, whereas now, thanks to the *entente cordiale*, they are our best friends. Also there were no suffragettes.'

'Are you a suffragette?' He sounded alarmed.

'I certainly think that women should have the vote.'

'But you don't chain yourself to railings.'

'Not yet.'

'What about your mother?'

'She's the model of an old-fashioned wife. But my father thinks that women should have the vote.'

'Is he a . . .' The word that was about to escape from Edward was 'gentleman' because that, in a sense, was what he was trying to find out.

'Is he a what?'

'A lawyer?'

'No.' She laughed. 'He'd be a hopeless lawyer. He's a publisher.'

'What sort of books does he publish?'

'You wouldn't like them. They're *seditious*.' She hissed the word in a mocking manner.

'In what way seditious?'

'Some are tracts.'

'Calling for equal rights for women?'

'That, and self-government for India. An end to the Empire. A republic. Socialism. And of course Irish Home Rule.'

'Are you convinced by his tracts?'

'Some and not others.'

'But the defeat in the Lords of the Irish bill . . .'

Her brow clouded. 'That was monstrous, and undemocratic. We should abolish the House of Lords.'

'And do away with baronets?'

'Most certainly. Put them out of their misery.'

'Are they miserable?'

'If they're not, they should be.'

'Why?

'Well, a peer has some power and a knight has earned his title.'

Edward sighed. 'Whereas a baronet, I know, has neither power nor merit.'

She looked at him severely. 'I believe your father is a baronet.'

'Yes, he is, and he has power and merit but the power comes from his money and the merit from his character and ability.'

'That's just what I mean. He doesn't need a title.'

'But he does love being a baronet.'

'And your mother?'

'She was born with a title. Her father's a peer.'

'It won't be very long,' said Alice, 'before it's all swept away by a government of the working class.'

'And you with it.'

'Why?'

'You've kissed the son of a baronet in front of witnesses.'

'I didn't know that you were the son of a baronet when I kissed you.'

'But you know now.'

Alice blushed. 'Political principles shouldn't be the only guide to one's behaviour.'

'What else?'

She lit a cigarette to cover her hesitation, then said: 'One's feelings.'

'Yes.'

'And . . .'

'What?'

She frowned as she exhaled the smoke of her cigarette and

said sharply: 'Why do I have to answer all the questions? After all, it was *you* who kissed *me.*'

'*C'est toujours la femme qui décide.*'

She smiled. 'Your accent is dreadful.'

'I think that's what drew me to you. I sensed that here was someone who could help me improve my French.'

'What nonsense. You kissed me because you took a fancy to me.'

'And you let me kiss you for the same reason.'

'Yes I did. I'm not ashamed to admit it. You were certainly a cut above all those foppish aesthetes like Julian and Erskine.'

'You aren't attracted to aesthetes?'

'No.'

'Only to rugged warriors?'

'So it would seem.'

'Women are mysterious.'

'We're all pawns of the process of natural selection.'

'Did you read that in one of your father's tracts?'

'No, in *The Origin of Species.*'

Edward called for the bill. 'What shall we do now?' he asked Alice.

'Would you like some more lessons in dancing?'

'I think I need them, don't you?'

'There's a place called the Colonnade. Shall we go there?'

They left the Café Royal and drove in Edward's shining new Hotchkiss to the club in Mayfair, where they drank more champagne and danced slowly to the voice of a crooning American. Holding Alice, Edward became reacquainted with the smell and touch of her body – the softness, the tickling hair and the aroma of the humidor. He drew her body closer; she did not resist. At three in the morning, they stumbled out into the cold, damp air. They walked back to the Hotchkiss hand in hand. 'Where now?' he asked gently.

'I'd better go home.'

'You wouldn't like to stop off at my parents' house in Eaton Place?'

'To meet your parents?'

'They're in Yorkshire.'

Alice was silent as they walked towards the car. Then, as Edward opened the door, she turned, smiled and rose on her toes to give him a short, soft kiss. 'I'd love to see their house sometime,' she whispered. 'But not now . . . not yet.'

Four

The next morning, after a lecture on Baudelaire at Bedford College, Alice Fry had lunch at an ABC restaurant with her two closest friends, Vivien Flesch and Maud Hanbury-Jones.

'I think I'm in love,' she said in as matter-of-fact a tone of voice as she could manage.

'Not with that soldier,' said Vivien, who had met Edward Cobb at the party in Chelsea.

'Yes, with the soldier, or, to be precise, since he has resigned his commission, with the former Lieutenant Edward Cobb.'

'That's impossible,' said Maud, who was the daughter of a High Court judge.

'It may be *improbable*,' said Alice, 'but it can't be impossible because it is a fact.'

'It can't be a fact if you merely *think* you are in love. It would only be a fact if you are sure.'

'I think I am sure,' said Alice.

'What is he like?' asked Vivien.

'You saw him. What did you think?'

Vivien frowned as she thought back. 'He was good-looking in that kind of way.'

'What kind of way?'

'Well, in the way a soldier would be good-looking.'

'An officer . . .' said Alice.

'Officers are soldiers,' said Maud, 'in the generic sense.'

'And what are ex-officers in a generic sense?'

'You would have to tell me more about him . . .'

'Well, he read Mods and Greats at Oxford.'

Maud nodded to acknowledge that this was a point in his favour. 'And before that?'

Alice glanced away. 'I don't know. Eton, I suppose.'

'An Etonian!' said Vivien. Unlike Maud, who had a solid face and figure – handsome, firm, almost monumental – Vivien was thin and her dark features, particularly when animated by curiosity, gave the impression of a mouse sniffing at a scrap of cheese.

'And what else?' asked Maud.

'I don't know much more about him.'

'Then how can you know you are in love?'

Alice looked puzzled as she prepared an answer. 'It is odd, I agree. But as soon as I saw him I felt something, and when we talked I felt something more, and when we danced I felt, well, everything I had always imagined feeling when one fell in love.'

'Where does he live?' asked Vivien.

'His family home is in Yorkshire.'

'A country house?'

'Something like that.'

'A title?' asked Maud.

Alice blushed. 'His father's a baronet.'

'A baronet!' Maud repeated with an ironical smile.

Alice frowned. 'You can't blame him for that.'

'I don't blame him for anything. I just wonder . . .' She hesitated.

'What?'

'I wonder how one can fall in love with a man who, on the face of it, would appear to embody everything you have hitherto regarded with contempt.'

'I don't know how one can but I did,' said Alice.

'What does he do now?' asked Vivien, her tone of voice friendlier than Maud's.

'Well, he doesn't do anything as such at the moment but he means to stand for Parliament.'

'As a Liberal?' asked Maud.

'No,' said Alice, blushing. 'As a Conservative.'

Maud shook her head sadly. 'Really, Alice, after all you've said about sticking to one's principles and living up to one's ideals.'

'At least he's grown-up,' said Alice crossly, 'unlike all those juveniles like Erskine and Eddie and Frank.'

'It's easy to seem grown-up if one's got plenty of money,' said Maud.

'I long to meet him again,' said Vivien.

'I'm sure you'll like him when you do.'

'And do you think . . .' began Vivien timidly. 'I mean, do you think *he's* in love with *you*?'

Alice smiled. 'He seems to like me.'

'But where will it lead?' asked Maud. 'He doesn't sound like the kind of man you would want to marry or who would want to marry someone like you.'

'So much the better, since I don't intend to marry.'

'Nor do I,' said Vivien.

'Nor do I,' said Maud. All three had long since agreed that marriage was an ignoble form of servitude whereby a woman bartered her body in exchange for food on the table and a roof over her head.

'But I can envisage,' said Alice, 'a free union of some duration . . .'

'Of course,' said Vivien. 'So can I.'

'But it doesn't seem to me,' said Maud, 'that the son of a baronet who went to Eton would have views of a similar kind.'

'Then I shall have to convert him,' said Alice slyly. 'And I am sure that I will, given time.'

Returning to Chelsea on the top of a bus, Alice frowned as she thought back to her friends' reaction to her momentous news. What rankled in particular was Maud's judgement that Edward Cobb was not the kind of man she would want to marry or who would want to marry her. As Maud knew quite well, it was irrelevant whether or not Edward was a man she might want to marry because she was against marriage as an institution; and at first sight it might seem equally irrelevant that he might be a man who would not want to marry Alice; but there was, Alice suspected, behind that second observation the implication that such a man would be more likely to want to marry Maud.

Alice had known Maud since their school days at St Paul's

Girls' School when the two girls had taken it in turns to come top of their class. As they had grown older, however, Alice had become aware that Maud was more firmly rooted in English society than she was. It was not just that her father was a High Court judge with a house in Kensington and another in the country; but rather that Maud had grandparents, uncles, aunts and cousins all with a recognised position in English society.

Of course Maud, like Vivien, professed a contempt for snobbery and bourgeois values; but Alice knew that life would be easier for Maud than it was for, say, Vivien because people knew who she was. Her father's name appeared every now and then in *The Times* Law Reports and he was listed in *Who's Who*. There was no entry for Vivien's father, Adam Flesch, a Jewish refugee from Russia, or for Alice's father, Maurice Fry; and Alice was aware that, had there been an entry, and had Edward Cobb looked it up, he might have been taken aback by what he read.

Alice's grandfather, William Fry, had been a Low Church Anglican parson and her grandmother, Esther, the daughter of a Methodist minister: both had died before Alice was born. Maurice's childhood had been spent in industrial cities in the Diocese of Lichfield; his schooling had been paid for by his mother's brother, who manufactured hats. From Lichfield Grammar School he had won a place to read history at Queens' College, Cambridge, where, after studying the French Enlightenment, he had lost his Christian faith. This had led to an estrangement with his parents but had delighted his uncle in trade who thought that all religion was bunk.

Leaving Cambridge with a second-class degree and no money, Maurice Fry had got a job teaching history at a minor public school. A master of the art of self-deprecation, Maurice had often entertained Alice with accounts of his time as a teacher. He had hated his hearty pupils and had failed to keep order in class. However, the post had enabled him to go on studying his favourite authors: Maurice had learned as he taught and taught as he learned.

One summer, to earn extra money, he had tutored the backward son of a Scottish grandee. In the same household there had been a French governess, Françoise Chambon. While their employers were on the moors shooting grouse, the tall, gangling tutor and the small, dark young woman, the daughter of an army officer, would stroll around the garden arguing fiercely about the past. Françoise was a Catholic and royalist who abominated socialism and liberalism and wished that the French Revolution had never taken place.

At the end of the summer, Françoise had returned to Paris and Maurice to his post at the minor public school, neither expecting to see the other again. Maurice Fry's reading had moved on to the nineteenth century: Proudhon, Sorel, and finally Marx. Desperately but uselessly he tried to teach his pupils to feel for the toiling masses, to express outrage at injustice, to denounce the inequity of the society in which they lived. Most of the boys day-dreamed through his classes: a few listened and learned but they were Maurice Fry's undoing. At the year-end examinations, they turned in essays calling for Red revolution. The Head of History became alarmed: Maurice Fry was told to look for another position.

Just at that moment, his mother's brother – the uncle in trade – died suddenly, leaving Maurice his sole heir. The hat factory in Coventry was sold and Maurice Fry found that, if his inheritance was shrewdly invested, he would never have to work again. He went to Paris, rented a flat, took lessons in French and visited the sites of all those revolutionary events that he had read about in books. He knew no one but had the address of the governess from Scotland, Françoise Chambon. A month after his first arrival, he wrote to her and was invited to lunch by her widowed mother. Six months later they were married, and Alice was their only child.

How did it happen that two people of radically different sympathies should decide to marry? As she had grown older, Alice had often put this question both to herself and to her parents. The conclusions she reached went as follows: Maurice had been lonely in Paris and his visits to Françoise and her widowed mother were his only source of human warmth. Also, Maurice loved to argue – to expound in a loud voice his various theories, to have them indignantly refuted by Françoise, to retreat, regroup, then renew the attack armed with some snippet from a newspaper or reference from a book. The arguments that had started in the castle in Scotland continued throughout their courtship and well into their married life.

Why did Françoise, who went to mass with her mother every Sunday at the Church of Notre Dame des Champs, marry this atheist, socialist and free-thinker? Almost certainly, Alice had decided, because she was on the shelf. Françoise had been in her late twenties and had no other suitors. Françoise had also decided that Maurice's views were mere froth beneath which was a decent, dependable and kindly man. And in this she had been proved right. Maurice had remained an armchair revolutionary, limiting his seditious activities to the publishing of tracts.

Returning to London when Alice was aged three, he had founded a publishing company, the Progressive Press, with a friend from his Cambridge days, George Greaves. The office was Maurice's study in the house he bought in Markham Square. Greaves received a salary from Maurice to come up with ideas. This he did in pubs. Greaves never came to the house in Markham Square: Françoise refused to receive him. Some of Alice's earliest memories were of her parents bickering about Greaves. According to Françoise, he was a bogus revolutionary who only moved in progressive circles because the women were easily seduced. He lived with one woman but made no secret of his liaisons with others. He also took laudanum and was often drunk.

Maurice defended Greaves for having the courage of his convictions; and he insisted that his salary as a director was a worthwhile investment. Greaves knew the leaders of the Independent Labour Party and the Jewish Labour League, and a number of the foreign revolutionaries living in London. Shortly before he died, Friedrich Engels, then living in Regent's Park, was persuaded by Greaves that an abridged version of his *The Origin of the Family, Private Property and the State* should be published in English translation by the Progressive Press.

It had become clear to Alice as she had grown older that

Greaves was her father's alter ego. Maurice would have liked to have shown the same disregard for bourgeois conventions; but he was by nature uxorious and felt ill at ease in the company of members of the British working class. To atone for this fastidiousness, he subsidised Greaves and donated money to radical causes. In 1907, at Greaves's request, he had given £300 towards the costs of Russian socialists who, having been thrown out of Denmark, held their congress at the Brotherhood Church in Whitechapel and later published a pamphlet by one of the delegates, Maxim Gorky.

Greaves was not the only source of authors. Maurice himself found them in the pages of the progressive periodicals to which he subscribed such as *The Labour Leader, The Nation* or *The New Age*. The radical hacks were mostly delighted to be offered money to expand their articles into pamphlets and meet an engaging and self-effacing publisher who would pay for their lunch. Maurice also dealt with the printer and kept the accounts. He had no secretary and dealt with the company's correspondence himself, writing long and amusing letters from his study in his house in Markham Square.

Returning home after her lunch with Vivien and Maud, Alice found the house empty. Her father, she knew, had gone to Oxford; her mother was as usual taking tea with one of her compatriots in Kensington; while the servants had no doubt taken advantage of their employers' absence to go absent themselves.

This suited Alice because she had been set an essay on Molière and so could take advantage of the peace and quiet to work in her father's study. Since she had been a child, she had been encouraged to make use of Maurice's library to consult the *Encyclopaedia Britannica* or *Le Petit Larousse* and, if Maurice was absent, she had been allowed to work at his wide mahogany desk. She loved this quiet room that looked out over the garden better than any other in the house. The books that lined the walls seemed like the closed shutters of windows which, if opened, would reveal vistas of unexplored areas of experience and thought.

Most of these she had yet to open but they testified to the voyage of intellectual discovery made by her father since his days at Oxford – books by Rousseau, Constant, Condorcet, Diderot, Voltaire, Proudhon, Hegel and Marx – some of which she had read, and others she merely had dipped into, such as Darwin's *Origin of Species*. There were also the untidy piles of the journals to which her father subscribed, with articles by progressive thinkers such as Havelock Ellis and George Bernard Shaw; and of course there was a full set of the pamphlets published by the Progressive Press.

On this occasion, sitting down at her father's desk, Alice saw among the disordered piles of papers the proofs of a future publication of the Progressive Press entitled *The Sexual Nature of Woman*. The author was a Dr Benjamin Parvis and there was a foreword by George Greaves. She glanced cursorily at the opening sentence of this foreword:

> Much suffering is caused by the ignorance and obfuscation that surrounds the subject of sex. It is the object of this concise and scientific treatise by Dr Parvis to dispel that ignorance in terms that the lay man or woman can understand.

Alice's eye ran on down the galley to the text of the work itself and immediately found that certain words and phrases intrigued her – 'the engorged penis of the man . . . the lips of the labia . . . the mucus lubricates the vulva to assist penetration . . . the woman's clitoris, too, becomes engorged and can properly claim to have an erection'. As she read on, Alice felt a tingling sensation in her loins. Here, in concise scientific language, was a description of the male and female genitalia and an account of how they functioned in intercourse.

The light was fading. She turned on the lamp on her father's desk. In just over an hour she had reached the last page and, as Dr Parvis had intended, her ignorance was dispelled. She now knew all there was to know about what was involved in making love with a man; she had even learned what homosexuals and lesbians actually did together; the veil was drawn from their sophisticated obfuscation. Masturbation, anal intercourse, dildoes (made of ivory!) – and all to attain orgasm, that explosion of ecstatic sensation that was the pleasure beyond all pleasures, the greatest physical joy known to mankind.

Alice sat back to reflect on what she had read. Dr Parvis, whoever he was, said little about love: clearly he thought that sex was something good in itself – best, perhaps, 'as it would seem that nature had intended', between a man and a woman, but good too between members of the same sex, or by a man or woman on his own. 'Can one say that masturbation is unnatural?' he had asked rhetorically.

> Look only in the jungles of Africa at the behaviour of the baboon. Not that men and women are baboons, but surely those hands and mouths which no doubt were evolved over the millennia to feed our aboriginal ancestors have since been used to paint frescos, carve statues, write poetry and play cantatas. Why should it be deemed wrong for those same members to play symphonies on the erogenous zones of another, or indeed solo cadenzas on their own?

Alice left the study and went up to her bedroom in a pensive mood, still with the buzzing in her loins. Lying back on her bed to rest before dinner, the image came into her mind of the tall fair soldier with whom she had dined the night before. As she imagined him touching and caressing the most intimate parts of her body, she touched and caressed them herself, finding that the sensations this engendered were as powerful as Dr Parvis had predicted, mounting in wave upon wave until, reaching a crisis, her whole body arched and shook and made the springs squeak beneath the mattress of her bed.

Five

Françoise Fry dreaded eating alone with her daughter Alice, who did not conceal the mild contempt she felt for her mother because of her limited education and religious beliefs. That evening, to her great relief, her husband Maurice returned from

Oxford in time for supper. Françoise and Alice listened to his account of the dinner he had attended the night before at the High Table of Magdalen College and Françoise smiled at his guileless praise of a young don whom he had persuaded to write an essay on John Stuart Mill.

'I would like you to meet him,' Maurice said to Alice. 'I mean I know you don't want us to push anyone in your direction, but he's a most amusing and intelligent fellow – bound to be a Regius Professor in due course. I know that life for the wife of a don isn't perfect, but you enjoy studying and, who knows, you might be the first woman to gain a fellowship yourself.'

'Did you offer him my hand?' Alice asked, smiling – her tone quite devoid of the sarcasm that such a direct reference to a husband usually provoked.

'No, of course not, dear, of course I didn't. But I did say that I had a daughter who was taking a degree at Bedford College and he was full of admiration and said that he hoped he'd be able to meet you when he was next in town.'

'I would be happy to meet him, Father, but I rather doubt that he would be the kind of man with whom I could fall in love.'

'But you're so *demanding*,' said Maurice. 'You're as bad as the Princess and the Pea.'

'Would you want me to give myself to a man I didn't love?'

'Of course not, of course not. But you mustn't set your sights too high.'

'Do you think I'm waiting for a duke?'

'A duke? God forbid. I don't mean high in that sense. I mean high in the sense of someone so exceptional that he may not exist, and if he does, you may not find him.'

'Oh, I'm sure he does exist,' Alice said gently. 'In fact, he may be just around the corner.'

The next morning, to Françoise's astonishment, Alice asked her if she would accompany her to help her choose some clothes. The two women took a bus to Knightsbridge and spent the morning in Debenham & Freebody's and Harrods. Françoise was only there to advise: since she had come of age, Alice had had her own allowance which she had rarely spent: now, at Debenham & Freebody's she drew on these reserves to acquire a well-cut, fur-collared winter coat and three dresses.

'This is too smart for going to college, isn't it?' she asked Françoise as the shop assistant held one costume up to the light; but then bought it all the same.

Later, Alice chose a pretty chiffon frock, saying, 'The time has come to raise the standards.' And finally, as they passed the display of debutantes' gowns, she said wistfully: 'I've missed the moment, haven't I, to wear dresses like that?'

This new interest in clothes, taken with Alice's remark that someone exceptional might be 'just around the corner', enabled Françoise to hope that her daughter had at last realised that the time had come to find a husband. She dared not say this: for a number of years now, both Maurice and Françoise had watched what they said in front of Alice, and of the several topics that they dared not discuss with their daughter, the most taboo had been that of marriage.

To Françoise, however, it was the one subject that mattered. Education was all very well but a woman's happiness would not be secured by taking a degree at London University. Alice must marry, as Françoise had married, a decent man; and a decent man, to Françoise, was not simply one who was honest and would be faithful; a decent man was also a man of means.

Two or three years before, a good marriage for Alice had seemed the least of Françoise's concerns. Her beauty, wit and intelligence had made her popular in the homes of 'good' families in Chelsea and Kensington. Her friends were the sons and daughters of barristers and academics, stockbrokers and higher civil servants. There had seemed no doubt but that in due course the son of a judge or a professor or a Permanent Secretary would fall in love with Alice and propose marriage.

In due course, a number of young men had indeed fallen in love with Alice but Alice had turned out to be choosy. Those qualities which her mother admired – steadiness, ambition, money – turned out to be just the qualities she despised. She accepted invitations to Commemoration Balls at Oxford and May Balls at Cambridge, but none of the young men who asked her survived the ordeal. Invariably they were dismissed as dull, inept, conceited – and there crept into Alice's terminology of disapprobation that dreaded word 'bourgeois', for which Françoise squarely put the blame on Maurice and the influence of his wretched tracts.

Of course, Françoise did not like to think of herself as bourgeois; but she would far rather be thought bourgeois than Bohemian and it was towards the Bohemians that, to her horror, she saw that Alice seemed to be inclined. The divide was not absolute: among the young writers and artists in Chelsea there were young men like the portrait painter, Erskine, who had been educated at Eton; indeed, even the most raffish sometimes turned out to have been to public schools. But Françoise knew the story of *La Traviata*: young men from respectable families did not marry Bohemian girls.

At the heart of Françoise's anxiety was the question of Alice's virginity. She knew that in Bohemian circles chastity was dismissed as outmoded, repressive and above all 'bourgeois': she was equally certain that the kind of husband she had in mind for her daughter would consider it of some importance. With little evidence to support her optimism, but with great confidence in her own feminine intuition, Françoise felt sure that Alice had yet to cross this threshold into adult life. True, on the shopping expedition to Debenham & Freebody's, Alice had bought new underclothes; but the care and attention she had paid to making her exterior appearance attractive suggested that her new plumage was to attract, not to hold, a mate.

To give weight to this hypothesis, Françoise noticed that as soon as they returned from their shopping expedition, Edith, the maid, was summoned by Alice to her bedroom to help unpack the new purchases, then sent down to inform Françoise that Alice would be dining out, then called back to help Alice pin up her hair. At half past seven, Edith was sent out on to the King's Road to find a cab, and when it was at the door,

Françoise had a fleeting glimpse of Alice in the hall wearing one of the most elegant of the dresses and her new fur-collared coat.

The next morning, Alice left at ten wearing the very dress she had said was too smart for college; and thereafter a pattern was established whereby Alice went out in her new finery, sometimes for lunch but more often for dinner, without telling her parents where she was going or with whom. This in itself did not concern Françoise; it was some years since her liberated daughter had felt she had to account for her actions to her mother; but she started to be concerned at the late hour at which Alice returned. Françoise was a light sleeper and now, night after night, she was woken by the rumble of a motor, the murmur of voices, the scratch of the key in the lock, the sound of the door being closed quietly, the soft steps on the staircase, and finally the squeak of the loose floorboards of Alice's bedroom on the floor above. The clock on the mantel of her bedroom, dimly illuminated by the gas light from the street, told her whether it was one or two or three in the morning – hours at which Alice had been known to return on odd occasions after a party or a ball, but never, as now, two or three times a week.

One morning, towards the end of February, Françoise was woken yet again by the sound of Alice returning home, not in the early hours of the morning but when daylight already shone through the curtains and the clock on the mantel showed that it was seven o'clock. This brought Françoise Fry to a pitch of anxiety, not from retrospective concern for her daughter's safety but from worry, the incessant worry, that Alice's disregard for propriety would jeopardise her prospects of finding a husband. What kind of reputation would she get if she went out so often unchaperoned and returned home so late?

Watching Maurice reading the paper over breakfast, Françoise opened her mouth to tell him about this unsettling development in their daughter's life but shut it again before any words came out. What purpose would it serve but to make him unhappy? In due course, Maurice left the dining room and went to his study. Françoise sat in the drawing room, pretending to wait for her daughter to wake up and, when Alice came down for breakfast wearing a dressing gown after only three hours' sleep, Françoise called down to the cook to send up some toast and tea. She then intercepted Edith at the top of the stairs to the basement and herself carried the tray into the dining room.

'Did you have a good time last night?' she asked Alice in as casual a tone as she could muster.

Alice, who had been reading the crumpled copy of the *Morning Post* that her father had left on the white tablecloth, looked up through bleary eyes – not at her mother but at a point straight ahead. Then, to Françoise's alarm, instead of the wrinkling of the brow into a frown and making the usual noncommittal reply, Alice smiled, turned, and reached up to give her mother a kiss. 'Yes.'

'Were you at the Arts Club?' Françoise asked, trying hard to keep the tone of worry out of her voice.

'No.' She was still smiling. 'I had dinner with a friend.'

'You seem to see him often.'

'Yes.'

'Is he anyone we know?'

Alice had returned her attention to the newspaper: now, once again, rather than frown and snap something at her mother, she looked up at that imprecise point in front of her, smiled and with unaccustomed gentleness said, 'No.' Then, with even more astonishing openness, and in an equally friendly tone, added: 'But I think you'd like him. You especially.'

'I hope we can meet him.'

'Oh yes, you shall.'

This wholly unusual sweetness in Alice's mood greatly increased her mother's alarm.

Nonchalantly, so as not to arouse Alice's suspicions, she drifted out of the dining room into the hall. She stood there, poised to go back into the drawing room to sit at her desk and pay the accounts, but instead turned towards the door at the end of the hall, intending to rouse Maurice out of his cosy isolation in his study and confront him with her suspicions about what might have happened to their daughter last night.

But what if her suspicions were misplaced? She turned back into the hallway and went upstairs. She hovered outside her bedroom: from inside she could hear Edith humming her common ditties as she dusted the dresser and waited for the cook to come and help her make the bed. Like a panther, Françoise bounded up the next flight of stairs and into her daughter's bedroom. There on a chair were the clothes she had worn the night before. Carefully, she raised the dress and the petticoats and saw, to her horror, marks on the underclothes that confirmed her suspicions.

Or did they? She slipped out of the room, terrified of being caught there by Alice. Perhaps it was just that time of the month. It was some time since she had known the timetable of such intimate events in her daughter's life. Edith might know, but how could she ask? Nor, in fact, did an intuition as powerful as that of Françoise Fry's require evidence of a material kind. It was not the blood that convinced her of the disaster, it was the smile.

Six

Alice's thoughts, as she read the paper and munched her toast, were far from her underwear or even the reports she was reading of the Balkan war, being wholly and exclusively and rapturously preoccupied with the charms of her lover, Edward Cobb.

It was now three weeks and five days since she had met him and a little less than twenty-four hours since they had consummated their love. Why had they waited? It now seemed to Alice that those three weeks and five days had been wasted. Had she not known as soon as she had seen him that Edward was destined to be her lover? Had he not invited her home to his parents' empty house?

She shook her head gently as if reproving herself for her mistrust of her own emotions and the tenacity of the bourgeois concept of respectability in even the most liberated mind. Had she really been so afraid that he would think her loose? Yet perhaps it had been wise to wait, because in the course of the time they had spent together – eating at restaurants, visiting galleries, going to the theatre, walking among the leafless trees in Hyde Park – all this had enabled her to see Edward as one might a friend – to recognise weaknesses, even, such as his pride in his new Hotchkiss car.

There had been no question from the start but that they would become lovers; Alice had made no bones about her contempt for 'bourgeois' morality in the sexual sphere. If anyone had been hesitant it had been Edward, which was, perhaps, only to be expected given his background. It was not that he was inhibited or inexperienced; Alice took it for granted that Edward had slept with women before.

At eleven, Alice left for a lecture at London University and after the lecture again had lunch with her friends Vivien and Maud.

'Well, it's done,' she said, hoping to sound happy, not triumphant.

Vivien gawped at her with wide-open eyes. 'It's done? The deed? The dreadful deed?'

'It's done,' Alice repeated. 'I'm now a fallen woman.'

'What was it like?' asked Maud.

'The rites of passage involve a modicum of pain.'

'Like circumcision . . .'

'There can't be much pleasure in circumcision.'

'And there was pleasure?'

'Pleasure is too weak a word.'

'You don't think that he'll now despise you?' asked Vivien.

'He can't despise me if he's in love.'

'Has he said he's in love?'

Alice smiled. 'No. He's not sentimental. But I know he loves me. I can tell.'

'And are you in love?' asked Vivien. 'Are you *really* in love?'

'Of course,' said Alice. 'Would I have gone to bed with him if I wasn't?'

'Some girls do,' said Maud drily.

'And you were desperate to go to bed with someone,' said Vivien.

'I most certainly wasn't,' said Alice. 'I just thought one should, perhaps, because repression is unhealthy, but I would never have done it with a man I didn't love.'

'But what if one never falls in love?' asked Vivien pensively.

'Oh, but you will.'

'Or what if no one falls in love with you?'

Alice glanced across the table at Vivien, thinking that this was a distinct possibility, but said: 'It's like looking for a cab in the rain. One always comes along.'

'I never take cabs,' said Vivien.

'Then the omnibus,' said Alice. 'You'll see a man on the omnibus . . .'

'Or at a party,' Maud interposed.

'And fall in love,' Alice went on.

'Oh, I'd love to,' said Vivien, 'but I wonder if I ever will.'

'You will, I'm certain,' said Alice. 'It's like a trap in the jungle covered with sticks and leaves. You can't see it but then suddenly you fall . . .'

'To be impaled on a stick,' said Maud.

Alice blushed. 'You fall before you are impaled.'

'Of course,' said Maud. 'But some might think that the fall should last a little longer than three weeks.'

'You don't calculate like that when you're in love,' said Alice.

'But don't you have to . . . up to a point? After all, there are certain biological consequences that can follow on from the emotional fact.'

'Of course,' said Alice, 'but fortunately in this case the lover is a man of some experience, not a callow youth.'

Vivien now left her friends, taking a bus to go north to Haverstock Hill while Alice and Maud found another to take them to Sloane Square. Both were silent for a while, Alice annoyed once again by Maud's cautious reaction to her momentous news. Had they not agreed after years of interminable discussion that women, like men, had sexual desires? That they should not be ashamed to express them? That to wait for marriage was a form of prostitution?

The two girls sat huddled in their coats on the front seats of the omnibus.

'You think I've been rash? Alice asked.

Maud hesitated. 'It just seems to me,' she said, 'that you haven't known him for very long.'

'How long does it take to know someone one loves? Romeo and Juliet, after all . . .'

'Writers invent.'

They were both silent as the bus proceeded down the Strand.

'To wait is to calculate,' said Alice. 'It makes love a kind of negotiation.'

'I think,' said Maud, 'that in fifty or a hundred years, when women *are* liberated, then one won't have to wait. The trouble with now is that so many men still have prejudices and think that women who sleep with them easily have probably slept with other men before and will sleep with other men again.'

'He can't think that,' said Alice. 'He knows that I haven't slept with anyone else before.'

'Did you tell him?'

'No, of course not. He didn't ask. But he must have noticed . . .'

'Yes, of course,' said Maud certainly. 'Unless, of course, he was drunk.'

Alice blushed deeply, remembering the champagne they had drunk the night before. 'He wasn't drunk.'

'No, I'm sorry.' Maud did not sound repentant. Then she asked: 'Has he told you about his family?'

'A little.'

'They live in Yorkshire?'

'Yes.'

'That will be the test. If he invites you up there to meet them, that means he loves you. But if he only wants to see you on your own, here in London . . .' Her voice tapered off.

'What will that mean?' asked Alice.

'That he only wants to use you to gratify his lust.'

The two girls parted at Sloane Square. Alice took a second bus along the King's Road, pondering what Maud had said. She realised that Maud possibly knew more about people like the Cobbs than she did. And she had to admit that Edward had said little about his family, but then she had told him little about hers. He had never spoken as if she might ever meet them and it had never occurred to Alice to ask herself whether or not she would be invited to stay at Nester Park.

Yet she could see the force of Maud's calculation. Would Edward introduce her to his family? Would he bring her into his circle of friends? Getting off the bus at Markham Square, Alice felt a sudden chill. There was a cold wind. She wrapped her coat more closely around her but the chill remained – even as she came into her parents' house and closed the door behind her.

'Oh, miss,' said Edith, 'there's a huge bunch of roses just been delivered. Cook's putting them in water and mum said to bring them up to the parlour. And there's a note, there on the table. No one opened it. It's for you.'

It was more than a note: it was a letter:

My dearest Alice,

When can I see you again? I'd like to be with you as often as you can bear it. I won't speak about last night because I'm afraid it would spoil the memory if I tried to put it into words. Do you know, I don't think I ever said that I loved you? Well, I say it now, in black and white. I truly do.

Edward

Alice was about to put the note back into its envelope – she did not want her parents to read it; but then saw that on the back there was a PS:

Would you ever consider coming to stay in Yorkshire? I'd love you to meet my family. It's awfully dank at this time of year but you'd do much to brighten it up. How about the weekend of March 9th?

Seven

After driving Alice back to Chelsea at seven that morning, Edward Cobb had returned to the flat he had taken in Duke Street, St James's, where he lay full length on the sofa and fell asleep.

He awoke at eleven with confused feelings and sat up. On the table in front of the sofa were two glasses and a half-empty bottle of champagne. He stared at them for a moment, then stood up and went into the kitchen to boil a kettle and make tea, which was all he could manage without a servant. The flat was small, with a bedroom off the living room, a kitchen, a bathroom and a small hall. He had rented it unfurnished, borrowing some items from his parents' house in Eaton Place, sending for some others from Nester, but going to Heals to buy a brand-new double box-sprung bed.

Edward sat at the kitchen table doing his best to digest the events of the night before. Part of him felt triumphant, as a man does when he first sleeps with a woman he has long desired, but part of him felt uneasy. He felt triumphant because, after a month's cautious courtship, taking Alice to the theatre, the opera, to dinner at the Savoy and the Berkeley Grill, as well as visits to art galleries, lunch at Pruniers and *thés dansants*, the moment had come, on leaving the Colonnade, when he had invited her not to his parents' house in Eaton Place but to the bachelor flat in Duke Street.

She had said she would come and, upon entering the living room, had looked around with the curious eyes of a child at the panelled walls, the large sofa, the leather chairs, and the gilded mirror and two finely framed paintings that had been sent down from Nester. Edward had stoked up the fire in the grate, then opened the bottle of champagne that lay in a silver bucket of melted ice.

Though it was clear to them both what was to happen, Edward had felt uneasy. He was not a practised seducer. At the age of twenty, he had been taken to a brothel in Paris by his uncle James and had subsequently returned there once or twice on his own. In Cape Town there had been a coloured woman, passed on to him by a fellow officer returning to England, who, though classified as Coloured and with a negroid physiognomy, had skin no darker than Alice's. Edward in turn had introduced her to another lieutenant in his regiment – a young man with sufficient means – when his tour of duty came to an end.

Alice, this girl of twenty-two, was the first woman he had not paid to enjoy and it was this that had made him uneasy. One knew where one stood when money changed hands; but, despite the time they had spent together, a number of pertinent questions remained unanswered because they were questions that could not be asked. What was Alice's experience? Had she been to bed with other men?

If these thoughts running through Edward's mind had amounted to misgivings, they were no match for the sweet, expectant look that he had seen in Alice's eyes; nor, when he embraced her, for that intoxicating scent of the humidor. They had kissed standing motionless for a moment in one another's arms. Then, after leading her to the bedroom, he had laid her on the wide box-sprung Heals bed. She had smiled and stroked his head. He had moved his mouth to her cheek, her ear, her neck; his hands moved down her back over her satin dress.

Now at this point his mistress in Cape Town had taken off her clothes in a methodical way; but Alice made no move to do the same. She held him and hugged him and kissed him; and when he finally grappled with her dress and corset, she squinted round to watch what he was doing as if she was the judge of some test of dexterity – a test which, to her amusement, he had failed.

She had smiled at his ineptitude and, when it came to her corsets and suspenders, she took charge, until finally they were both naked and, freed from the constraints of their clothes, able to make love. At the irrevocable moment, she gave a cry but clasped him closer; and when it was over, still clung to him but did not say a word.

It had been cool in the bedroom; Edward had pulled back the cover and they had climbed under the sheet and blankets into the bed. The glimpses that Edward had had of her body, and the feel of it in his arms, had put him into a state of drowsy rapture and he had fallen asleep thinking, 'What luck.' She too had slept, and though both were unaccustomed to sharing a bed, they had not woken until daylight came through the beige blinds. Then, with an ironic semblance of alarm at what her parents would say if they found her bed empty, Alice had gone to dress in the bathroom. Edward too had gathered up his clothes and as he did so had seen dark marks of blood on the sheets.

Now, sitting at the kitchen table drinking tea and reviewing the previous night's events, Edward felt obliged to accept the evidence that that first cry had not been of rapture but one of pain; that he had been Alice's first lover; that she had not been as 'experienced' as he had once presumed. This reality had many implications and cast doubt on the accuracy of the phrase 'what luck'.

Edward was not afraid of scandal. The social mores of his class put the onus on women to defend their chastity, and clearly a woman who had gone willingly in the early hours of the morning with a man to his bachelor flat was in breach of the accepted rules. What disturbed Edward was his own conscience: not the conscience of a scrupulous Christian – he was hardly that – but the conscience of a man of honour.

To Edward, the integrity of an Englishman of his class – the officer and gentleman – was what gave him the authority to govern half the world. It was the conviction that he possessed this precious quality that fired his political ambition. Fleetingly, in respect of the night before, he realised that he should perhaps have thought more about prudence and less about luck: but what was done was done, and in this, his first romantic encounter with a woman, he must preserve his self-respect. He therefore decided the feelings he had for Alice must be defined as love. If he did *not* love her, then he had seduced a virgin to satisfy his lust and was therefore a cad. It was out of the question for Edward Cobb to regard himself as a cad. He was not a cad and therefore he was in love.

The few misgivings that his mind put forward were

hypothetical and had no bite. Had it been wise to commit himself in love so soon after his return to England, before he had had a chance, as it were, to study the form in the enclosure? Had he slept with her with so little forethought because he had assumed ... Assumed what? That she was some kind of courtesan, a good-time girl? Certainly, there were older women in the *demi-monde* with whom one could be seen at parties or in restaurants but whom one would not bring into one's home; and certainly in this age of the liberated woman, it was not always easy to define who was respectable and who was not; but that was not the case with Alice Fry. She was a brave, intelligent, respectable young woman studying for a university degree who had slept with him only because she loved him, and had slept with no one else. She was not someone to be ashamed of or to keep away from his family. He therefore dispatched a note to his mother at Nester asking her peremptorily to send a formal invitation to a Miss Alice Fry for the weekend of 9 March.

It was inconceivable that his mother would refuse him – the eldest son so recently returned. However, he also realised that he would have to give Alice some provenance: he could hardly introduce her simply as the girl who had taught him the Turkey Trot. Could he make her the sister or cousin of a fellow-officer? That would need careful planning because his mother was a walking compendium of Burke's, Kelly's, Debrett's and the *Almanac de Gotha*. Nor did he like to lie to his parents: it was a matter of choosing a lesser evil to save awkwardness all round.

All that could be settled later: what mattered at that moment was to tell Alice that he loved her, 'now, in black and white'. He wrote the note and, having sealed the envelope, felt not just relieved but content. His memories of that night – not just the charm and fervour of her embraces but her cheerful conversation; her manner as *petillante* as the champagne – all this had made him enormously happy and he could think of nothing else but how and when he could arrange to see her again and again.

Edward could not see Alice that night because he had arranged to dine with his uncle James at White's. But they had lunch together the next day at Wiltons in Jermyn Street, arriving almost simultaneously, both slightly embarrassed at bumping into one another on the pavement as if they were strangers. They entered the restaurant; a waiter took Alice's coat – her fur-collared coat – then led them to a table in one of the booths.

Edward studied Alice as, for a brief moment, she glanced around the restaurant to see who else was there. Her expression was of someone trying to look worldly and suave but she could not sustain it, and as soon as her eyes met Edward's her face lit up and her eyes brimmed over with a look of happiness and love.

'Do you know,' said Edward, 'that this is only the fourth time we've seen each other by the light of day?'

She looked at him closely, as if studying a painting to judge whether or not it was a fake – his wiry fair hair, his sun-tanned neck, his straight nose, his clipped moustache.

'What do you think?'

She smiled. 'Oh, not bad.'

'You strike me as flawless.'

She smiled and pointed to her cheek. 'Can't you see where I've used powder to cover up a pimple?'

'I can't see any powder or any pimple. All I can see is the face of a girl I adore.'

She blushed. Edward glanced down at the menu. 'Don't order pheasant, you'll get that at Nester. What about some venison?'

'My father loves venison.'

'Perhaps he'd come to Scotland for some stalking.'

'He likes to eat them, not shoot them. I don't think he could tell a deer from a cow.'

'He's a publisher, I think you said?'

'Yes. But it's only a hobby, really.'

'And he's a radical?'

'He's more than a radical, he's a socialist, but he's very kind and gentle. He wouldn't hurt a fly.'

'And your mother?'

'Very conservative. A Catholic.'

'Are you a Catholic?'

Alice laughed. 'Most certainly not. I saw through all that when I was seven years old. You're Church of England, I suppose?'

Edward scrutinised her face to see if she had said this with a sneer, but Alice's expression remained matter-of-fact. 'I was brought up an Anglican,' he said. 'And I suppose the Ten Commandments have something to do with what I consider right and wrong.'

'Just as well, then,' said Alice with a sidelong smile, 'that they say nothing about fornication.'

Edward blushed. 'That's a horrid word.'

'Isn't it?' said Alice. 'For something so nice.'

'But I do think of myself as a Christian,' said Edward. Then he added, timidly, 'I hope you don't mind.'

She leaned towards him across the table and said, in little more than a whisper: 'A Christian. A Conservative. It doesn't matter what you are. What I love in you lies much deeper, so please don't change.'

Alice prattled on as they both ate first potted shrimps and then venison. She told him about her grandfather, the Low Church parson, and her great-uncle with the hat factory in Coventry who had left all his money to her father. Edward listened attentively, hoping to find at some point or other a genealogical loose end that would mean something to his mother. There was not so much as a thumb-nail's length of string.

Alice's mother's family, the Chambons, sounded a little more promising: there had been a grandmother called de Chastigny; and there was a coat of arms. He probed further. Was there an estate? A château, perhaps, belonging to a cousin however many times removed? Alice shook her head – only cousins in Bourges – and Edward saw that by probing the long-blocked channels to the aristocrats among Alice's maternal forebears he was jeopardising Alice's good mood. At one point she frowned and said grimly: 'So far as I know, they were all guillotined in the Revolution, and good riddance.'

Edward therefore abandoned the idea of subterfuge and changed the subject. He could simply say that he had met Alice at a party given by a friend of Hamish without saying anything about the Turkey Trot or the Progressive Press. And having decided on this strategy, he became relaxed and cheerful, and when Alice asked him what she would be expected to wear when she came to stay at Nester, he teased her with a list that included spats, waders, five different ball gowns and a pair of plus-fours.

Two days later, Edward received a note from his mother saying that she had written to 'Miss Fry' and wondering if Edward would like her to ask anyone else. Edward considered the matter carefully: he had deliberately chosen a weekend when there was no shoot or house party made up of his parents' friends. On the other hand, it might make things easier for Alice if there were others but he could not at first think of what others to ask. He had army friends, but they were hardly intellectuals and might lower his standing in Alice's eyes; and there was the brighter set from his time at Oxford whom he had not seen since he had left for South Africa, and who might think it odd to be asked all the way to Yorkshire at that time of year if there was no shoot.

Sylvia, who had gone to Florence, would by then have returned; and his mother had suggested, in her letter, 'some other young people – perhaps some of Sylvia's friends'. Edward knew that that would mean Elspeth Deverall, Harry Baxter and the younger political set who might either intimidate Alice or, worse, provoke her. He therefore wrote back to his mother suggesting a friend from Oxford, Thomas Garston, who had gone into the Treasury and married young: he had not seen him in eighteen months, and had met his wife only once, but he calculated that his good mind would impress Alice and – he was ashamed to make this kind of calculation – that his relatively modest background would make him appreciate an invitation to Nester at that time of year. He then gummed up the letter to his mother and sat back with a sigh: how straightforward things had been in the army, how complicated were the simplest matters in civilian life.

Passing through London on her way back from Italy, Edward's sister Sylvia insisted on taking a look at her brother's flat in Duke Street before going on to dine with him at the Berkeley Grill. While Edward mixed a cocktail, she peered into every room. '*Un letto maritale*,' she said, returning from his bedroom.

'It makes sense to think ahead,' he said.

'Of course.' And then: 'Who's this Alice Fry Mother says you've asked to stay at Nester?'

'Someone I met.'

'But no one I know?'

'Clearly,' he said irritably, 'you wouldn't have to ask who she was if you knew already.'

'What I meant was, is she someone one *might* know?'

'One might, perhaps, but since there are a good forty million people in the United Kingdom, and several hundred million in the Dominions and Empire, the odds are that there will be some girls who you won't know.'

'Oh, don't get so batey, Eddie. You know perfectly well what I mean.' But she did not pursue the matter and over dinner talked only about the wonders of Renaissance Art and the oiliness of Italian men.

Eight

The Garstons – Thomas and his wife Lydia – took the same train from London as Alice Fry. Edward had told both parties to look out for one another while waiting on the platform at York for the train to Malton; but since there were half a dozen others who seemed qualified with their first-class tickets and loud, drawling voices to be guests at a country house party, the friends of the Cobbs did no more than inspect one another out of the corner of their eyes. The train for Malton and Scarborough stopped at the small station that served Castle

Howard and it was here that the loud party of gentlefolk got off, leaving Alice and the Garstons at different ends of the train.

At Malton, they made one another's acquaintance and travelled together to Nester in the car sent by the Cobbs. When they reached the house, Edward came down the steps to meet them. As he introduced them to his mother in the small sitting room, he had a mental block as to the first name of his friend's wife and therefore could only call her 'Mrs Garston'. Since his mother was happy to call her Mrs Garston anyway, it perhaps did not matter, but he had used the name Thomas to present his friend.

'And this is Alice Fry,' he said.

'Miss Fry. How nice that you could come.'

Edward glanced at his mother to see if he could assess her reaction, but Joyce Cobb's expression would never vary, whether she was greeting a new acquaintance or her oldest friend.

Sylvia, who came up behind her, was different: she glanced only cursorily at the Garstons, greeted them with polite affability, then turned to subject Alice to a piercing scrutiny. 'Let me show you to your room,' she said to Alice. 'Harrison,' she said, turning to the butler. 'Mr and Mrs Garston are in the Westmoreland Room and Miss Fry is in the Pink Room.'

'Of course,' said Harrison gravely. 'Their baggage is being taken there now.'

'Tea is ready, isn't it, Harrison?' asked Lady Joyce.

'When you are, m'lady.'

'In the nursery?'

'No, in the dining room as Mr Edward suggested.'

'Give us five minutes,' said Sylvia, looking sideways at her brother to indicate that he should see to the Garstons, then taking Alice by the arm and leading her towards the wide, shallow staircase that rose gracefully from the hall.

Alice had been to stay at houses in the country before; Maud's family, for example, had a house near Guildford in Surrey and, when they had guests on a Saturday night, they would change for dinner. But compared to Nester, as Alice now realised, theirs was a suburban villa. It had no avenue leading up to the house, no pillars supporting a portico, no large hall with the busts of philosophers and statesmen from antiquity, no wide, shallow stairs with beautiful baroque balustrades; and no corridors so long that one could easily lose one's way.

Her bedroom, the Pink Room, had elegantly faded pink silk wall covering and a large eighteenth-century four-poster bed with heavy magenta hangings held back by ropes with golden tassels. Shown into the room by Sylvia, Alice had found a chamber maid in starched cap and apron already unpacking her suitcase; the maid turned and curtsied and was introduced by Sylvia as Mary.

Alice noticed that Sylvia gave a swift, sharp look over the clothes that Mary had laid on the bed prior to hanging them in the wardrobe. Rather than feel annoyed by this nosiness, Alice felt grateful and, turning deferentially to the younger girl, said: 'I hope you'll advise me on what to wear.'

'Isn't this a lovely gown, miss?' said Mary, the maid, holding up one of the new dresses bought from Debenham & Freebody made from dark red silk.

'Yes,' said Sylvia curtly. 'That'll do for dinner on Saturday night. And that,' she added, pointing to a dark green dress already hanging in the wardrobe, 'is a bit less showy, isn't it? That'll do for tonight.'

Alice blushed at the word 'showy' even though it was clear from the matter-of-fact way in which Sylvia had spoken that she did not mean it as a term of disparagement.

They went down to tea, walking down the long corridors and back down the stairs, Alice's eyes moving from left to right to look at the paintings and busts, wondering which could be the forebears of the Cobbs – not Octavius Caesar, surely, but perhaps the bewigged gentlemen painted by Romney or the ladies in long dresses with hair piled to an impossible height on the top of their heads.

At tea Alice sat between Edward and an empty chair. Then, when the guests had declined any more cucumber sandwiches or scones or slices of cake, the chair was filled by Edward's father who, Edward whispered to her, 'always comes to tea late'.

Sir Geoffrey was already seated before he realised that he was next to someone he had never met before. He immediately stood up, apologised, introduced himself, circled the table to greet the Garstons, then returned and sat down.

'Do you hunt?' he asked Alice.

'No.'

'Do you ride?'

'Not really.'

'Not really or not at all?'

His tone was not unpleasant: he simply wanted to get things straight.

'I have ridden horses,' said Alice, 'but not for some time.'

'Pity,' said Sir Geoffrey. 'There's a meet at Sledmere tomorrow.' He looked at his son. 'Will you go?'

'We might follow,' said Edward; then he turned to Alice. 'If that's what you'd like to do?'

'Of course.'

'You're going out, aren't you?' Sir Geoffrey said to Sylvia.

'Yes.'

'On Hyacinth?'

'She's lame. Newman thinks I should try Tracker.'

'Well, if you can't manage him, no one can.' He turned to Edward. 'What about your other friends? If Sylvia's taking Tracker . . .'

'They don't hunt,' said Edward.

'Pity,' said Sir Geoffrey. 'To come all this way at this time of year and not hunt.'

'There are other things,' said Edward.

'Oh yes?' asked his father.

'Fresh air, conversation . . .'

The older man looked sceptical.

'And with luck, some good food and drink.'

'Has Harrison decanted that '89 Dows?'

'Almost certainly.'

'It should be damned good.' Sir Geoffrey cast a quick look

around the table, then added, under his breath but heard by Alice: 'Too damned good.'

Alice wore the dress picked out for her by Sylvia – a Paul Poiret gown of dark green satin – and when she came into the drawing room there could be little doubt in anyone's mind as to what Edward saw in her, and he felt somehow vindicated to see the women as well as the men so struck by her appearance in evening clothes. The dowdy Lydia Garston was not in contention; but even Sylvia, unquestionably beautiful and a better colour after her month in Tuscany, seemed insipid alongside Alice.

Edward was equally proud of her at dinner. Conversation turned to a correspondence that had been running in *The Times*. 'Did you happen to see that, Miss Fry?' asked Lady Joyce. 'It started with a letter from someone who simply called herself "a peeress" – I have a suspicion who it might be – asking how a mother sending her daughter into society could ensure that she would not find herself at parties doing those dreadful modern dances.'

Alice looked puzzled. 'What dances could they be?'

'Well . . . perhaps you know better than I do, Mr Garston?'

'I am afraid not, Lady Joyce. Now that I'm married, I rarely go to balls.'

'Well, apparently there are these dances of negroid origin from the United States and South America that in some circles are all the rage. According to this peeress, one is called the Tango, another the Boston and a third the Turkey Trot.'

'The Turkey Trot?' asked Alice with a straight face. 'What kind of dance is that?'

'I have no idea. I thought you might know.'

'Do turkeys trot?'

'I wouldn't have thought so.'

'As for the Tango,' said Alice, 'I have seen someone dance what I think was the Tango.'

'And?'

'It's a dance popular in Buenos Aires.'

'In Buenos Aires! And is it . . . indecent?'

'It seemed to permit, even to oblige, a certain intimacy.'

'That's what they say. Oh dear, I do hope poor Sylvia won't find herself obliged to dance the Tango.'

This conversation followed the soup and carried through to the fish. When it came to the roast pheasant, Sir Geoffrey Cobb tackled Tom Garston on national insurance, about which he felt as strongly as his wife did about the Tango. 'It's a slippery slope,' he said, talking across Alice to Garston. 'Taxation for defence, law and order, that's one thing: but once you admit the principle that the state can legitimately take money from one set of citizens, those with property, to support another, those who don't, then where's the incentive for a labourer to do an honest day's work?'

'The view of the government, I believe,' said Thomas Garston, 'was that a modest level of welfare for the very poor would ultimately benefit us all.'

'Stuff and nonsense,' said Sir Geoffrey.

'You should consider Germany,' said Alice. 'They have a highly developed system of social welfare and as a result their socialist party is as quiet as a mouse.' She turned. 'Am I not right, Mr Garston?'

'Indeed. It was the genius of Bismarck to see that a combination of patriotism and welfare for the workers would spike the guns of the revolutionaries.'

'So,' said Alice playfully, turning back to Sir Geoffrey, 'social benefit is surely a small price to pay for sleeping safely in your bed.'

'The danger now, of course,' Garston went on, 'comes from nationalism, not socialism. Without Bismarck's shrewdness, I fear, the Kaiser may paint himself into a corner and only be able to escape through a war.'

Conversation now turned to Fashoda, the Triple Alliance, the uncertain sympathies of Italy, the role of the Turks, the siege of Adrianople and the likely outcome of the Balkan war. This was the kind of talk that normally waited for the ladies to withdraw. When they eventually did, and the men moved up the table to sit close to their host, Thomas Garston said to Edward, in tones of surprise: 'I find that Miss Fry is extraordinarily well informed.' And when the men's conversation came around to the Balkan war, Edward had the satisfaction of hearing from his clever friend from the Treasury, 'As Miss Fry was saying just now . . .' And later, 'Miss Fry's understanding of the situation was somewhat different.'

The next morning, Alice put on a new tweed walking suit, tailored by Redfern, with a wide flowing skirt, heavy hem and nip-waisted jacket – unquestionably elegant but perhaps, she realised when she came into the dining room for breakfast, too elegant for a Saturday morning in a Yorkshire country house. She passed over the silver dishes filled with kidneys, kedgeree, sausages, eggs and bacon and ate only toast and marmalade. Sylvia was already half dressed for the hunt in a riding skirt and a shirt and stock. Her hair was pinned up in a bun and her cheeks were caked with powder. 'You'll get awfully hungry,' she said, 'if you're going to follow the hunt.'

As they rose from breakfast, Edward took Alice aside. 'Do you mind skipping the hunt? We'll run into too many tedious neighbours who'll want to know all about the Zulus.'

'I don't mind what we do,' said Alice. 'I'm in your hands.'

She remarked, however, that Edward said nothing to discourage the Garstons and, placing them in the care of his younger sister and brother, Rosie and Arthur, saw them off in the large car that had brought them from the station. Edward then turned to his father. 'Would you have time to show Alice the stud?'

Sir Geoffrey brightened up at once. 'By all means.' He turned to Alice. 'You don't mind a bit of a walk?'

'There's nothing I'd like better.'

Ten minutes later Alice set out from the back door to Nester escorted by Sir Geoffrey and Edward Cobb. They walked through a huge walled garden, neatly hoed and raked, past great fruit cages and greenhouses to a door that led on to a track that led to the home farm. The sun was shining and although there was little sign of spring – the grass was grey, there were no buds on the trees – small clumps of snowdrops had pushed through the sodden ground. The air had that particular scent – a mixture of moss and the smoke from burning leaves – but it was pure and bracing: Alice felt physically exhilarated from this vigorous walking with Edward at her side.

They came to the stud – a series of brick buildings with pantiled roofs formed around a courtyard; stables on three sides, stores and saddle rooms on the fourth. To the south was a solid, well-built house, lodging for the Cobbs's trainer, Gilbert Raines; and to the east some cottages for the jockeys and stableboys: it was a small, autonomous settlement dedicated to raising horses that would be first past the post.

'We've two things for which to thank the Arabs,' said Sir Geoffrey as they started on the tour. 'Their numerals and their racehorses. Every racehorse in the world is descended from three Arabs – the Darley Arabian, the Godolphin Arabian and the Byerley Turk. Mind you, breeding's taken us a long way since then – for better or worse. Our modern racehorse is faster than his forefathers, but he's a damn sight less robust. He couldn't stay the kind of course they ran in the time of Charles II.'

There was certainly something magnificent about the horses that Alice saw when she peered over the lower stable doors. Sir Geoffrey knew the pedigree of each one and repeated them to Alice, often back two or three generations. She learned about famous trainers such as the Dawson brothers and William l'Anson, who had worked for the Cobbs, and, since Sir Geoffrey had taken in that Alice's mother was French, was told how the French blurred the line between steeplechasers and flat-racers, often using the same horses for both. 'In Britain,' said Sir Geoffrey, 'the jumps are too high for a flat-racer; you need a far tougher, stronger and more determined horse.'

'And rider, perhaps?' said Alice quietly.

'Oh, no, there are some damned good French jockeys and a lot of these American jockeys now live in France. I won't use them, but by God, they get results.'

'And this is Saladin,' said Edward as they reached the last of the loose boxes, 'the beauty who's going to win the Derby.'

Alice looked into the box at a fine horse with proud head, long neck, curved back and silken flanks.

'You're looking at a beast,' said Sir Geoffrey, 'that can run faster than any other creature on earth.'

'Except, perhaps, an ostrich,' asked Alice, 'or a cheetah?'

'You can't run an ostrich in the Derby,' said Sir Geoffrey, who appeared to accept this as a perfectly reasonable observation, 'and a cheetah couldn't carry a man.'

'He is magnificent,' said Alice.

'I named him Saladin,' said Sir Geoffrey. 'Owed it to the Arabs, I thought.'

'And will he really race in the Derby?' asked Alice.

'That's the plan. We ran him at the Bilbury Club meeting at Salisbury as a yearling; and we're trying him at Kempton next week, but after that, nothing until Epsom.' He turned to his son. 'Did I tell you that Baron Rettenberg wants to buy him? He was here last weekend.'

'Do you want to sell him?' asked Edward.

Sir Geoffrey laughed. 'Every horse has his price, and Rettenberg's awash with money. It depends on how he does in the Derby. Rettenberg knows that. He's willing to wait.'

With stableboys deferentially doffing their caps to their employers, Alice followed Edward and Sir Geoffrey across the yard, waiting quietly beside them while the two men stopped to talk to two of the jockeys; and she did her best to appear impressed when introduced to a shifty-looking man in a trilby hat, the celebrated trainer Gilbert Raines.

Sir Geoffrey now remained at the stud to talk business and Edward suggested that they return to the house making a detour through the park.

'Who is Baron Rettenberg?' Alice asked as they walked away from the stables down a muddy lane.

'A Russian with more money than sense.'

'I hope you don't sell Saladin.'

'You took to him?'

'Yes.'

'And I think my father took to you. It was good of you to show such an interest.'

'I shouldn't have said that about the ostrich and the cheetah,' she said, lighting a cigarette.

Edward smiled. 'He didn't mind.'

'I like the jargon,' said Alice. 'It's refreshingly blunt.'

'What do you mean?'

'If you were a racehorse, you'd be described as "Edward by Geoffrey out of Joyce".'

'And may I be refreshingly blunt?'

'Of course.'

'How would you feel if you received a visit in your bedroom later tonight?'

'It rather depends on who was visiting me. I wouldn't be altogether delighted if it was Mr Garston.'

'And if it was me?'

'That's another story. But . . .'

'What?'

'Would it be wise?'

'Isn't that what corridors are for – creeping along at night?'

'I don't know. There aren't any corridors in houses in Chelsea.'

'I can assure you that in country houses a bed's made up in the dressing room for the husband precisely for that reason.'

'I've heard that that sort of thing goes on, but as you say, it's usually a husband slipping out to visit someone else's wife.'

'It seems unfair to deny the privilege to the unmarried.'

She nodded. 'That's true. But if you were seen, say, by your mother, wouldn't it be as bad as catching me with a cigarette?'

'Their rooms are in the west wing.'

She turned towards him and took his hand. 'Then I'd be delighted to receive you. The Pink Room, remember? You don't want to find yourself creeping into bed with Lydia Garston.'

For dinner that night, Edward's mother, Lady Joyce, had invited some neighbours and the widowed rector of Nester with his unmarried daughter who were often brought in to fill in the gaps in the Cobbs's long table. Some had not seen Edward since his return from South Africa and so gathered around him in the drawing room, where he stood with his back to the fire. Edward greeted the guests politely but his eye kept glancing over their shoulders towards the door; and in due course Alice entered wearing her dark red gown and looking so lovely that Edward thought to himself, not with complacency but with amazement: 'To think that that girl is mine!'

Sylvia broke away from a group of newcomers and sidled up to her brother. 'I think that Mrs Garston is feeling neglected,' she said. 'You've hardly spoken to her since she arrived.'

Edward nodded and dutifully crossed the room. 'What did you think of the hunt?'

'Colourful,' she said abruptly. 'It was a pity that your friend Miss Fry did not come.'

'It left more room in the car.'

'Of course.' She said this with a touch of derision, as if Edward should have been able to come up with a better excuse. 'And perhaps she would have been pained by the fate of the fox.'

'One can never be sure which side she will take.' Edward looked anxiously towards the door, hoping to see Harrison come to call them into dinner.

'Tom thinks she is clever,' said Lydia.

'He's well equipped to judge.'

'She's also beautiful, of course, and that sometimes clouds men's judgement.'

'Not of intelligence, surely?'

'Pretty girls are rarely contradicted.'

'That doesn't mean they don't say silly things.'

Edward sensed that Lydia Garston was not enjoying her stay at Nester. She was one of those women who, because they are plain, promote other, sounder feminine qualities such as honesty, domesticity and, above all, common sense. Why had Tom married her? Edward wondered. To establish a secure home base – a wife who would devote herself to him and his children, wholly dependable and predictable, always ready to listen to the anxieties he brought home from the Treasury, always willing to console him, encourage him and renew his self-esteem? 'May fate save me from a wife like that,' he thought, and involuntarily looked across the room at Alice.

Lydia caught his glance. 'It was good of you to ask us to stay . . .' she said in a tone that was more interrogatory than emphatic.

'I had got out of touch with Tom.'

'Yes, of course.' She seemed unconvinced.

'I mean to go into politics.'

'So I've heard. You're to stand at Knapley.'

'If I'm selected.'

'Of course.'

'And I thought that Tom might give me some advice.'

'His sympathies tend to be with the Government.'

'I know. They always were. But while I've been away in South Africa, he's been working in the heart of Whitehall. He surely knows what's going on.'

'Yes, he does, and I'm sure he'll tell you – if your other obligations leave you time.' And with that remark, she too looked across the room at Alice Fry.

As Edward filed into the dining room with a neighbour's wife on his arm, he resolved to keep his eyes off Alice and tell the story of his adventures in South Africa yet again with the dedication of an actor who, after a thousand performances, still looks at ways to improve the delivery of his lines. But Edward was not an actor and, as course followed course, he could not prevent himself every now and then from glancing at Alice through the orchids and oleander entwined between the silver candelabra and the silver racehorses: all the table pieces had a racing theme.

Every now and then, Alice too caught his eye and smiled and then raised her eyebrows as if to ask: 'How am I doing?' And Edward would either smile with a slight nod, as if to say 'Fine' or, when he saw that she had failed to follow his mother's lead to shift her attention from left to right, indicate with his eyes that she should stop talking to Tom Garston and turn to the rector instead.

Occasionally, Edward also glanced across at Sylvia, who,

when she caught his eye, gave one of those looks with which brothers and sisters can flash messages such as 'Poor you, I bet he's a bore' or 'Don't let Father keep you too long over the port.' But he also saw something else in Sylvia's expression, only too familiar from their days in the nursery, which suggested that she was up to some mischief. And sure enough, as they were being served with sorbet and meringues, after a quick defiant look at Edward, and taking advantage of the lull in the general conversation, she leaned past the Rector and said in a quiet but carrying voice: 'Have you asked Miss Fry, Dr Osborne, whether she will be coming with us tomorrow to your church?'

'No, dear me,' said the Rector, confused, 'of course I haven't asked her. But I very much hope, perhaps, that if she felt so inclined . . .'

'But you wouldn't want her to feel obliged to come,' said Sylvia, 'if it isn't something she would normally do?'

There was silence at Alice's end of the table. Edward saw her brow wrinkle into a frown. 'No,' she said firmly. 'It isn't something I normally do.'

'Are you not a Christian, then?' asked Sylvia.

'No, I'm not a Christian.'

'Are you Jewish, perhaps?'

'Sylvia!' said Lady Joyce.

'I'm afraid there's no synagogue,' said Sylvia, ignoring her mother, 'not even in York. They killed all the Jews in the Middle Ages.'

'I'm not Jewish,' said Alice. She paused, then turned to Dr Osborne. 'My grandfather was a vicar but I was baptised a Roman Catholic because my mother is a Roman Catholic.'

'There's a Catholic church in Malton,' said the Rector.

'Thank you,' said Alice, 'but I don't go to church at all.'

'Ah, a free-thinker,' said Lydia Garston, her eyes alert at this chance to exact some kind of revenge.

'It is quite wrong to talk like this at dinner,' said Lady Joyce.

'That suggests, my dear mother, that you're no true Christian, because here we have Dr Osborne sitting next to a lost soul and surely he should try to save it.'

'I would not say that Miss Fry is a lost soul,' said the Rector.

'Doesn't one have to believe to be saved?' Sylvia turned to Alice with a wide, disingenuous smile. 'Of course, you're at university so you probably know some theology.'

'It's very convenient, isn't it,' said Alice, 'to think that you are justified by faith alone. Isn't that the right theological formula, Dr Osborne?'

'Indeed, Luther, and of course Calvin . . .'

'It enables you to dispense with good works.'

'Well, not entirely, of course,' the Rector mumbled. 'We are commanded to love our neighbour as our self.'

'And who is our neighbour, Dr Osborne?' Alice went on. 'Is he just someone who lives in a large house nearby? Does it show sufficient love of one's neighbour to ask him to dinner on a Saturday night?'

'Dear me no,' said the Rector. 'One must always think of the poor.'

Alice turned to Lady Joyce. 'You mentioned the correspondence in *The Times* about the dangers of the Tango and the Turkey Trot. You may also have seen a report about the work of the Slum Sisters of the Salvation Army who go each day to help the wretched people living a subhuman existence in Notting Dale, only half a mile from the grand mansions of Holland Park?'

'I saw the piece,' said the Rector.

'Well, to me,' said Alice, 'they are the true Christians, not people who build palaces for their racehorses and leave human beings to rot.'

There was a protracted moment of silence at one end of the table: neither Edward nor the Rector nor even Sylvia, let alone Joyce Cobb, to whom Alice's question had been addressed, produced a response. Edward glanced at his father and saw that, engaged in conversation, he could not have heard Alice's last remark. But it had unquestionably reached the ears of his mother who, though some of the guests had not yet finished their sorbets and meringue, rose from the table and led the ladies out.

When the gentlemen rejoined the ladies in the drawing room

half an hour later, Edward was met by Sylvia with an impudent smirk. 'I'm awfully sorry, Eddie, I didn't mean to set her off like that.'

'Where's Alice?'

'She said she had a headache. She went to bed.'

Trapped by his role as the elder son, Edward could not leave the drawing room until the neighbours had left and the Garstons had retired to bed. Then, ignoring his sister, he said good night to his parents and went upstairs. On the landing, rather than turn towards his own bedroom, he went down the long corridor and tapped gently on the door to the Pink Room.

Alice came to open the door. Her hair was down; she was wearing her nightdress and he could see, from the drawn-back blankets, that she had already gone to bed. He put his arms around her, then leaned back against the door to close it. 'Were you asleep?'

'I'm so sorry,' she said.

He drew back to look at her and could see from the redness around her eyes that she had been crying. 'You did nothing wrong.'

'It was so rude, after your father's kindness . . .'

'He didn't hear.'

'But your mother . . . '

He kissed her. 'Don't worry about my mother.'

'And Sylvia . . .'

'Sylvia is jealous.'

'Of me?'

'She was always possessive. Sisters often are.'

For a moment it felt as if her agitation, and his wish to console her, would subdue the passion he had felt mounting throughout the day; but her scent, her warmth and the feel of her body through his evening clothes acted like a poultice that drew out all his anger and frustration. 'Do you want to sleep?'

'To sleep? Oh no.'

'Do you mind if I stay?'

'I was waiting. I was afraid you wouldn't come.'

Some hours later, Edward was woken by a dream of the kind

that is powerful but only half remembered. He lay for a moment trying to reconstruct the fragments; then, feeling Alice's body next to his, he realised where he was. The room was cold. The bed was warm. He told himself that he must leave the bed, put on his clothes and go back to his own room. He could not bring himself to do so; his will was no match for his sense of contentment. He drifted back to sleep.

Later it was Alice who woke him. 'It's past seven,' she whispered.

He leaped from the bed, put on his underclothes, shirt and trousers, his socks and his shoes. 'I'll see you at breakfast,' he said as he leaned forward to kiss her.

'Be careful.'

As he walked back down the corridor, carrying his jacket and tie, the door of one of the other guest rooms opened and he found himself face to face with Lydia Garston. He nodded, as one might to an acquaintance one passes in the street. She looked at him first with astonishment; then her eyes darted back along the corridor towards the room from which he had come. She looked back at Edward with an expression of grim vindication. She said nothing but it was not difficult for Edward to read her thoughts: 'Now I see why we were asked here – a cloak of respectability to cover your tawdry affair!'

Edward walked past her to return to his room.

The guests left Nester after lunch: to Edward their departure was the end of an ordeal. Tea, as always on a Sunday afternoon, was served in the nursery. There he was alone with his mother, Sylvia, Nanny Peake and the two younger children.

'A most unusual young lady,' said Nanny Peake.

'Do you mean Miss Fry?' asked Lady Joyce.

'The dark young lady, yes. Not Mrs Garston.'

'There are lots of girls like that in London,' said Sylvia, 'but you usually find them chained to lamp posts.'

'Whatever you may think of her opinions,' said Edward, 'it is inexcusable to be rude to a guest in your father's house.'

'How was I rude to her?' asked Sylvia with feigned innocence. 'I only asked her if she wanted to go to church.'

'No one has to go to church,' said their mother.

'I didn't say she had to . . . and anyway, she was the one who was rude. Palaces for racehorses, indeed.'

'She was provoked,' said Edward.

'Well, I certainly didn't mean to provoke her. But if you ask me . . .'

'I don't.'

'She was rather pleased with herself, and a little too forward with her opinions.'

'She's been properly educated, that's all.'

' "A little learning is a dangerous thing",' said Sylvia. 'Don't you think so, Mother?'

'Only if it makes young women disregard conventions,' said Lady Joyce.

'It suits some young men, Mother, if some young women disregard conventions,' said Sylvia, darting one of her mischievous looks at her older brother.

Edward blushed. 'You're being intolerable . . .'

She leaned forward and patted his arm. 'Then I'll shut up. I don't want to make you angry, Eddie. If she's nice to you, that's all that matters, and any friend of yours is a friend of mine.'

Nine

The next day, Edward Cobb went south, not to London but to the market town of Knapley in Northamptonshire where the members of the Conservative and Unionist Party were looking for a candidate to represent them at the next election. His speech to the selection committee that evening went down well; and the excitement he felt on the train to London on the Tuesday morning at being back in the swim pushed into the back of his mind the irritation he felt after the weekend at Nester.

This irritation did not extend to Alice; quite to the contrary, he felt that he had been right to invite her and that she had brought just the kind of vitality and originality that Nester required. It was the other women who had annoyed him: not so much his mother, who had remained aloof, as Sylvia, with her mischief-making, and above all, the vile Lydia Garston. The dislike she now inspired was exacerbated by a twinge of bad conscience: perhaps he had only asked the Garstons to Nester to sanction the presence of his mistress from the *demi-monde*. And was there not some truth in what Sylvia had said – that conventional men took advantage of unconventional girls?

When Edward reached London and was swept into the crowd at King's Cross station, his anxieties were left to fester at the back of his mind and he became busy. He saw Alice frequently – not just in the evening, taking her to concerts, to the theatre and to the Royal Opera at Covent Garden; but also for lunch, to visit art galleries and, as the weather improved, to walk in Hyde Park. He bought her small gifts and she, in return, turned up with things she had found to brighten up his flat – cushions, tablecloths, vases, even a painting. She seemed even more determined than he was to show that there was more to life than love.

And there *was* more to their lives than love. Alice was to take her final examinations in June; she spent long hours in the library at Bedford College; and sometimes, after making love, would recite passages from *Phèdre* which Edward only half understood. Edward was preoccupied not just with politics but also money: his father had been impatient for him to return from South Africa and resign his commission so that he could take on some of the responsibilities that a large fortune entailed. There were meetings in the City with stockbrokers, bankers, accountants; a burgeoning number of directorships in companies in which the Cobbs had an interest; and decisions to be made about their investments both at home and abroad. Although unconventional in some ways, and determined to be different from the run-of-the-mill baronet's elder son, Edward never doubted that it was the duty of the rich to grow richer; and, surveying the host of the Cobbs's holdings, he was pleased to be in command.

Making money, however, was not an end in itself but simply a means to different kinds of glory. Sir Geoffrey Cobb's ambitions were limited to the Turf, and concentrated still further on his racehorse, Saladin. Edward's were grander; he felt destined to serve the nation, the Empire and the world. He was selected as the Conservative Parliamentary candidate for Knapley, and, since the constituency always returned a Conservative, could now be sure of a seat in the House of Commons after the next election

But if Edward was to make his mark on the party and come to the notice of the party leaders, he would have to make speeches in other parts of England and write articles on issues such as women's suffrage and Home Rule for Ireland. Here he needed some help, and help was provided by Sylvia's friend Elspeth Deverall. She knew the workings of the Conservative and Unionist Party inside out and told Edward who to cultivate – who would be pleased to be asked to lunch at White's, who had wives who would be flattered to receive an invitation to dine at Eaton Place; or who, like Lord Curzon or Mr Bonar Law, should simply be engaged in conversation when Elspeth's mother, the Countess of St Giles, was at home in her house in Belgrave Square. 'Don't be too earnest,' she would advise Edward, 'and above all don't bore them. Not that you would, but you know what I mean.'

Edward was not so naïve as not to realise that Elspeth's interest in his future came not just from her friendship with Sylvia, but from the possibility that in due course it might be linked to hers. Seeing the value of her support, Edward did nothing to disabuse her. He also did nothing to encourage her either – that would have been dishonourable; and he did not envisage, when the time came to marry, marrying a woman he did not love. At that time the woman he loved was Alice, and though Alice was never mentioned by Elspeth, he felt sure that Sylvia would have told her about the weekend at Nester.

Perhaps – the idea occurred to him, but he had no way of knowing whether or not it was sound – Elspeth's expressions of contempt for the suffragettes were animated by knowing that Alice was in favour of giving women the vote. 'There are some very stupid arguments against women's suffrage,' she said one day when Edward had taken her to lunch at the Berkeley Grill. 'Did you read that tract by that idiot Blakeney saying that, because there were more women than men, it would be undemocratic? As if women would vote only according to the interests of their sex.'

'So what are the intelligent arguments against it?'

'Oh, there are a number. First of all, most women are simply not interested in politics and quite rightly see their proper sphere of power and influence in the home.'

'But there are women like you,' said Edward, 'who know as much if not more than most men about what is going on in the world.'

'Of course, but first of all we are a small minority and always will be; and secondly our influence is more effective if it is exercised through men. Violet Asquith has much more power as the Prime Minister's daughter than she would have if she were an MP or even a Minister, and there are any number of highly influential political wives.'

'You don't think it is demeaning to women to deny them the vote?'

'You are demeaned only if you feel demeaned and until now it never occurred to women that their dignity depended upon voting for a Member of Parliament. It was only when a few self-important blue-stockings started to tell them so that they began to wonder; but even now, you wouldn't find that a majority of women actually want it. They realise quite rightly that it's part of a much wider plan to drive a wedge between men and women. It sounds fine to say that women should be independent of their fathers and husbands; some idiots even make it sound like the emancipation of slaves; but in reality it's a Gradgrind's and Casanova's charter that will make working-class women into wage-slaves and middle-class girls into sluts.'

Elspeth spat out the word 'slut' with a particular vehemence and glanced sharply at Edward as if to say that he should know whom she had in mind. Or did he imagine it? Edward may have been sensitive to the charge that he was behaving dishonourably in sleeping with Alice Fry, but he was surprised to find in Elspeth so strong an apologist for a strict sexual morality, since it was well known that her mother, Lady St

Giles, had conducted several adulterous liaisons with her husband's friends.

Elspeth was beautiful: indeed, she had been judged by the duennas as among the most handsome young women of her season. The sharp features that Edward remembered from when she was a child had been softened as she had filled out – her slim figure made only slightly top-heavy by a large bosom. She carried her physical attributes with a certain nonchalance and, though capable of flirtatious looks and sultry glances, was clearly more comfortable with the straight manner she adopted when talking politics with Edward.

Thinking of Alice's slim figure and dusky skin, Edward wondered what Elspeth would be like naked. The thought of her large breasts provoked no desire. He could see that she was beautiful, but so was Sylvia. One could recognise the loveliness of a woman without wanting to possess it. Or did he feel unmoved by Elspeth's beauty because he had been so frequently and thoroughly satisfied by Alice?

Hamish, who also knew Elspeth, and who came to London from Ireland in mid-April, said that she had the mind of a man. 'That's why you like her, Eddie. You don't know how to deal with womany women.'

'Isn't Alice a womany woman?'

'She's a blue-stocking, isn't she? She'd talk the head off a rat.'

'We don't just talk.'

'I'm sure you don't. But I tell you, if I felt a woman was only half as clever as me, I'd run a mile.'

'Then it's just as well there's a good supply of stupid women,' said Edward.

'Thanks for the compliment, Eddie.'

'That doesn't mean that you're stupid, but surely a woman who was *half* as clever as you are . . .'

'You're quite right. She *would* be stupid.' Hamish sighed. 'One has to get married, I suppose.'

'In due course, I think one does.'

'You ought to take care, though,' said Hamish.

'Why?'

'Well, quite a few people know about you and Alice Fry.'

'I haven't made any attempt to conceal it.'

'So I heard. But some of the mothers don't like it.'

'I haven't noticed the flow of invitations drying up.'

'No, of course not, not yet. You're so damned eligible. But mothers don't like the idea of their daughters marrying men with other women in their lives.'

Edward frowned. 'I've known a number who have got married even though it was known that they'd had affairs with other women.'

'Other *married* women, perhaps. That's one thing. But with an unmarried woman . . . I mean, it's not as if she's someone you're keeping in a house in Brighton. She may not be someone one would marry, but . . .'

'Why isn't she someone one would marry?'

Hamish looked confused. 'Well, she isn't, is she? At least, she's not someone *you* would marry.'

'Why not?'

'Well, I can see that she's a lot of fun and all that, but . . .' His voice tailed off. 'I say, I'm awfully sorry. I've blundered into something . . . I really didn't mean to. God, Eddie, I'd better marry a clever woman or my children will be real duffers.'

Although they had agreed at Nester that they should meet in London, Edward did not arrange to have lunch with Tom Garston until the end of April. The ostensible reason was to familiarise himself with the workings of the Treasury and to pick Tom's brain on the question of tariff reform, on which Edward had been invited to express an opinion by the editor of the *Morning Post*. They met at the Carlton Club, of which Edward was now a member, and a fortnight later, after Tom had read a draft of Edward's article, they met again for lunch, this time at Garston's club, the Reform.

When they had finished lunch and were drinking coffee in the club's atrium, Edward leaned forward and said: 'I wonder if I could ask your advice on a personal matter?'

'Of course.'

'Do you remember meeting Alice Fry at Nester?'

'Of course.' A tone of caution crept into Garston's voice. 'Your wife took against her, I think?'

'Lydia . . .' he began. Then: 'I thought Miss Fry was exceptional. That may explain why Lydia took against her.'

'I also think that Lydia, perhaps quite rightly, thought herself compromised, somehow, by Alice being at Nester.'

'Lydia believes strongly in the sanctity of marriage.'

'And she's right to do so, which is why I am thinking of asking Alice to be my wife.'

'Ah!' The civil servant was clearly astonished. 'Is this because . . . ?'

'Because I love her, yes.'

'And one should marry the woman one loves.' He said this as if it was not a self-evident truth but a proposition that might be profitably discussed.

'Not necessarily,' said Edward. 'And that's where I need your advice. Do you think that, if I married Alice, I should give up the idea of a political career?'

Tom considered the question before he answered. 'No, not necessarily. Clearly, she is not the ideal wife for a Conservative politician; she would fit better on the radical side; but the Prime Minister's wife, after all, is fairly outspoken, and there was Lady Caroline Lamb . . .' And Tom then drew up a list, in a methodical fashion, of all the statesmen who had had eccentric or flamboyant wives.

'I would be grateful,' said Edward, 'if you could keep this to yourself. I haven't yet asked her and am by no means certain that she'll have me.'

Tom smiled – a rare smile. 'Certainly, from what I observed at Nester, one could not predict which way she would jump.'

'And my parents know nothing about it.'

'I don't suppose they will be altogether delighted.'

'No. She's not at all the kind of bride they have in mind.'

Tom hesitated, as if considering whether he should express a thought that had come into his mind. 'I had heard,' he said, 'that there was talk of a match between you and Elspeth Deverall.'

Edward blushed. 'She's a very good friend,' he said, 'but I don't love her.'

'No,' said Tom.

'And we are agreed, are we not, that it is better to marry someone you love?'

'Of course, but . . .'

'What?'

'It's simple for me to say that. One isn't expected to make a dynastic marriage if one is a member of the professional class.'

'I am not a king,' said Edward.

'No, of course not.'

'And even kings make morganatic marriages.'

'Indeed they do.'

'It would be wrong, wouldn't it,' Edward said, 'to promote and praise liberty in the political arena if one does not oneself exercise the liberty of marrying the woman of one's choice?'

'It might certainly be deemed . . . inconsistent,' Tom Garston replied. He was a man who used words with precision in the drafting of laws.

Ten

Since Edward had asked her to Nester to meet his family, Alice thought that she would reciprocate and invite him to dinner at Markham Square to meet hers. She had told him on a number of occasions that she had this in mind; he always said that he would very much like to meet her mother and father; that he would make sure that he was available on any date she should happen to choose; that he would be delighted if the party included some of her friends; or, on another occasion, equally delighted if it was just the Frys. Week followed week; February turned into March and March into April without Edward having met Maurice and Françoise Fry.

When Alice asked herself why she had not put her plan into effect, she made a number of different excuses: that she had not had time because her finals were imminent; that it would be too embarrassing without her friends; but would he get on with her friends? And which friends? And finally that she could not spare him for the company of others – she wanted him all to herself.

In reality, Alice knew she was afraid that he would take against her parents and as a result might fall out of love. She had studied closely a book on love by one of her set authors, Stendhal; he had described how a twig immersed for a time in the pools of the salt mines in Salzburg becomes covered with sparkling crystals. Love followed the same process: the most humdrum characteristics of the beloved became jewels in the eyes of the lover. However, Stendhal also talked about the process of *decrystallisation*: the salt crystals crumble and drop off to reveal the dull bark of the twig.

Alice was now obliged to recognise that she was wholly in thrall to Edward. She could still apply her mind to her studies; she could still talk to Maud and Vivien about other things; but she could find no way to anaesthetise the painful yearning she felt when not in his presence, or to subdue her joy when he was there. She tried to analyse her feelings. Were they an offshoot of vanity? Was it simply that she saw reflected in his eyes, as he sat facing her across a restaurant, a beautiful, attractive, amusing woman? Or was she merely gratified by the passion she saw in his face when he hovered over her naked body? Was love selfish, as Vivien tried to persuade her – an '*égoïsme à deux*'? Did she simply feel flattered that one of London's most popular young men said he was in love with her? Was it just that she was intoxicated with his attention and admiration?

Or was her mental attachment to Edward simply the consequence of her sexual fulfilment – the overwhelming sensations he induced in her when making love? How totally and utterly she had been misled by Dr Parvis's *The Sexual Nature of Woman*. She now thought back to her reading of the proofs of that work with some embarrassment, and what she had done in consequence with some shame. How fraudulent to describe the mechanics of intercourse and recommend sexual sensation without admitting that the first was banal and the second insignificant compared to the magnificence of love.

There was, of course, a mechanical aspect that Alice could

not ignore. She did not want to find herself pregnant and so she now douched herself after making love, which meant that Edward did not have to withdraw – a disagreeable but necessary precaution he had adopted after their first encounter and before Alice had sought advice.

By the end of April Alice felt that she could procrastinate no longer and so she chose a date in the middle of May when Edward would come to dinner at her home in Markham Square. As the day approached, Alice's unease about what Edward might think of her parents infected her mother. Terrified that she might inadvertently offend or disgust Alice's admirer, Françoise became so agitated in her countless conferences with the cook about what to serve at the dinner that the anxiety, like a contagious disease, spread to the basement. Edith, the maid, was to be seen practising her curtsy and plaguing the cook, already distracted, about how she should serve the soup.

Maud and Vivien were not so much anxious as apprehensive at the prospect of meeting their friend's admirer. Both wanted to be loyal to Alice but could not imagine liking the son of a baronet who had been to Eton, served in the army and was to stand for Parliament in the Conservative interest. Since Alice did not know other young men of a similar kind, they had to make do with Erskine, the Etonian portrait painter, and a young journalist, Julian Marlow.

When Edward arrived and was shown into the drawing room by the butler who, at the last moment, the Frys had hired for the evening, he seemed to Alice somehow preoccupied. He greeted her mother as if she were a duchess and spoke to her father with respect. The younger guests, too, Edward treated with the kind of familiarity that suggested that, if they were not already friends, they soon would be. Erskine he knew from the party in Chelsea and they were both Etonians; they could talk about their school days and about Hamish, the friend they had in common.

The aspiring journalist, Marlow, would be trickier to charm: the cape he had removed with a swirl in the hall before handing it to Edith in her new apron and cap, and his green velvet jacket, proclaimed his Bohemian allegiance; and the look of disdain he directed at Edward, dressed like Maurice in conventional evening clothes, suggested a prejudice to be overcome. Vivien, too, when she was introduced to Edward, showed by the set of her jaw that she was ready to go into battle to defend her radical ideas. She wore a plain grey dress, modelled on a Grecian tunic; Maud, her plump body somewhat constricted by a straight-line corset, moved as gracefully as she could in a grander, blue silk gown.

Alice's father was unusually genial, bustling around the butler to make sure that his young guests' glasses were kept filled with champagne. When dinner was announced, they moved down to the dining room where Edward was placed to the right of Françoise with Maud and Vivien on either side of Maurice Fry. The table was not so large that conversation was confined to those sitting on one's right or one's left, and after the usual exchanges about nothing in particular had taken them through the first two courses – consommé and poached salmon with mousseline sauce – Julian Marlow leaned across Alice to address Edward. 'Do you read *The New Age*, Mr Cobb?'

'I have been introduced to it by Alice.'

'And do you find that you approve of what you find there?'

'It seems to express a variety of opinions.'

'Not all to your liking, I dare say?'

'Contrary views sharpen one's wits.'

'But raise the blood pressure, perhaps?'

'That's no bad thing.'

'Did you read the poem by Strindberg in this week's edition?'

'No. I haven't yet seen it.'

'He curses England.'

'Does he?'

'He calls her a "whited sepulchre".'

'And what does Mr Strindberg think we have done wrong?'

'Oh, there's quite a list. He says our sins are as blood-red as our roast beef.'

'Our sins?'

'Our African crimes. Our Irish outrages. But he forgives them.'

'I'm relieved to hear it. I would not want England to be damned – even by a Swede.'

'Doesn't it disturb you that we are so much disliked for so many reasons?'

'A successful nation is bound to arouse the envy of a less successful nation.'

'You see it as the voice of envy, not the voice of conscience?'

'Nietzsche, so I understand, believes that conscience is a weapon of last resort used by the weak against the strong.'

'So you read Nietzsche?'

'I have to admit that I don't, but I am learning about him from Alice.'

Alice blushed: this was the kind of exchange she had dreaded. 'I believe one can appreciate Nietzsche,' she said, 'and Strindberg, without necessarily agreeing with what they say.'

'One might say the same of *The New Age*, perhaps,' said Edward.

'Of course,' said Alice. 'Its position on women's suffrage is absurd.'

'That must mean that it is against it.'

'For the most unconvincing reasons.'

'What are those unconvincing reasons?' asked Edward.

Vivien, who had been talking to Maurice, turned away from him to join in the conversation across the table. 'They say that women are not by nature political, and that they don't want the vote.'

'How patronising,' said Maud.

'And they say that the interests of women are best left in the hands of men,' Vivien went on. 'That if we had political power we would forfeit the right to chivalry – seriously, that was the word they used, *chivalry*. As if we were living in the Middle Ages!'

'Perhaps Mr Cobb thinks that we are,' said the sneering Julian Marlow.

Edward smiled. 'It is difficult to define the middle of anything until we have come to the end.'

'I like that,' said Erskine, who hoped that Edward Cobb might introduce him to some patrons. 'How *can* one know what's the middle until you've reached the end?'

Julian Marlow's eyes were still fixed on Edward. 'You don't wish to be drawn, I think, into giving your own opinion on the woman question?'

Edward glanced at Alice. 'I still have an open mind. But I wouldn't dismiss so readily the *New Age* view that, so long as men are the stronger sex, and so long as women depend on men, women should beware of spurning the sense of responsibility that men feel for women. That, I suppose, is what is meant by chivalry.'

The conversation continued, moving on from the woman question to the Marconi affair, poverty, Ulster and the Balkans until finally Maurice Fry raised his hands and said: 'We won't solve these problems this evening. Or, indeed, tomorrow. In fact, I wouldn't be at all surprised if people are still talking about Ulster, the Balkans and the status of women in a hundred years' time.' And at that Françoise stood up to signify that the time had come for the ladies to withdraw.

Edward hoped that Maurice would not let the gentlemen linger over their port and cigars. Julian Marlow had the look of a frustrated gladiator whose opponent refuses to fight, while Erskine, turning his chair to trap Edward and give him no way of escape, was lecturing him on the superiority of the painted portrait over the photograph. Photography would never replace art – not, at any rate, when it came to recording the subtle beauty of the human physiognomy. Edward had surely noticed that when comparing pictures of his sister Sylvia taken by a camera and a painted portrait. He hadn't seen her painted portrait? Did that mean Sylvia's portrait hadn't been painted? He would have thought that Sargent or perhaps Lazlo . . . They hadn't? Had they thought of commissioning a lesser painter?

'My sister does not think of herself as a beauty.'

'Ah, but she is. Harry Baxter thinks so, and so do I.'

'Then perhaps Harry should commission a portrait.'

'Husbands rarely do. They have the real thing. They don't need a memento.'

'He isn't her husband.'

'But soon will be, or so I understand. And once she has gone, your father might like her portrait hanging on the wall.'

'My father is more interested in his horses.'

'Oh, I paint horses too.'

After the decanter had made a second journey around the table, Maurice Fry rose from his chair saying: 'Shouldn't we join the ladies? The girls, after all, see one another all the time.' His guests stood up but Edward hung back and, after the three younger men had been ushered out of the room by their host, turned to Maurice and said: 'I wonder, sir, if I could detain you for a moment?'

'Of course, of course.'

Edward closed the dining room door and returned to the table. He did not sit down. Neither did Maurice. Edward looked at the glass from which he had been drinking, then at the decanter, still two-thirds full, wondering whether to refill his glass. He decided against it but now sat down on the chair next to the one Maurice had occupied, leaving Maurice no choice but to sit down too. Edward did not move in to the table; he sat at an angle on the edge of the chair, gently gesticulated for a moment as if moving his hands would bring out the words, then clasped his hands together and said: 'I would like your permission, sir, to propose marriage to your daughter.'

Maurice gaped at his guest. 'You want to marry Alice?'

This response left Edward momentarily confused. Was there another daughter? 'Alice, yes. I love her and I would like to marry her.'

'Has she ... has she ... What does she think of this idea?'

'I haven't put it to her. I thought I should ask your permission first.'

'I appreciate that, of course, but Alice is old enough ... I mean, even if she wasn't old enough, she is someone who knows her own mind.'

'That's one of the qualities I admire in her.'

'She wouldn't feel that you required my permission.'

'I realise that. But she is your only daughter and . . . I am perhaps not the kind of husband you had in mind.'

'I . . . we . . . I'm not sure what kind of husband we had in mind, or whether we had one in mind at all. Alice, after all, has never talked as if she intended to get married.'

'But would you object if she did?'

'Good heavens, no. I'm married after all.'

'So do I have your permission to propose to her?'

'By all means. Of course. Good luck to you. But shouldn't you consider . . .' Maurice hesitated.

'Consider what?'

'You are aware of what I do?'

'Yes.'

'Your parents might not consider her a suitable choice.'

Edward smiled. 'Though I may seem to some to live in the Middle Ages, I am sufficiently modern, I think, to feel that a man should make this choice for himself.'

'Yes, indeed,' said Maurice, 'and Alice has qualities they might come to appreciate. She speaks perfect French, good German and some Russian.'

'She is very beautiful, highly intelligent and utterly charming,' said Edward.

'You don't have to sell her to me, Mr Cobb, but you might have to sell her to them.'

'How can they not come to love her if I love her?' asked Edward.

'Perhaps, perhaps,' said Maurice Fry in a doubtful tone of voice.

When Edward returned to the drawing room with her father, Alice saw at once that his mood had changed. Until then, she had felt that the evening had been a failure. It had been a great mistake to invite Julian Marlow; she should have known that he would show off, snapping at Edward's heels like a terrier. Vivien, too, had been wholly predictable in going on about women's rights. She was also so exceptionally plain – almost ugly – with her large nose and bandy legs. Alice had never thought that looks mattered that much, but seeing her through Edward's eyes, she decided that they did. But then she had been almost equally irritated by Maud, who had said little but, in her fancy new corset, looked wonderful and seductive and had never taken her eyes off Edward. Erskine, too, was obnoxious – little better than a commercial traveller in the way he touted his talents; but then Edward had already known Erskine, so she was hardly to blame.

Her mother had been self-effacing, which was perhaps for the best. There was nothing wrong with her mother but there was nothing much right either. Alice had been afraid that she might embark on one of her inconsequential stories; or, worse, start gossiping about people she did not really know: would Edward, perhaps, seeing Françoise through his mother's eyes, decide that she was one of those foreigners 'who tried too hard'?

Only her father, her beloved father, had behaved perfectly: he had not tried at all. As always, he had been courteous and hospitable, treating Edward no better and no worse than he treated her other friends. She had watched Edward's expression as, earlier in the evening, Maurice had described some of the authors on his list in much the same way as Edward's father had listed the racehorses in his stud – some of them familiar, such as Shaw, Belloc and Chesterton; others unfamiliar, but possessing minds that were sharp, original and ahead of their time.

The ten minutes or so during which Alice's father and her lover had lingered over the port, and the look on Edward's face when he returned to the drawing room, suggested to Alice that some kind of affinity must have arisen between the two men. Her father's expression was harder to read; he busied himself with the mechanics of hospitality and, if she caught a look of slight perplexity, it was surely because there were glasses still to be filled.

Alice could not ask Edward before he left what had been discussed, not even when taking leave of him in the hall, because he had promised to drop Maud off in Cadogan Gardens on his way home. She would therefore have to rely on her father's account, but here too she was frustrated: neither Vivien, Erskine nor Julian made any move to leave, whereas Maurice and Françoise, soon after midnight, made their excuses and went to bed.

Nor could Alice question her father the next morning, because by the time she got up he had left for Clerkenwell to see his printers. Edward, she knew, had gone to Knapley and she herself had an appointment with her tutor at Bedford College. She saw Vivien and Maud only briefly; both said that they had liked Edward, though Vivien added that it was always difficult to know what lay behind the reserve of 'people like that'.

When Alice got home that evening, her mother asked her daughter anxiously whether she had been pleased with her party. 'And you, Mother,' Alice replied, 'what did you think?'

'It all seemed to go well.'

'But what did you think of . . . the guests?'

'Edward was so well behaved, certainly when compared with the other young men.'

'Is that all you can think to say about him?' asked Alice. 'That he was well behaved?'

'No, no, my dear. He was very handsome and seemed intelligent.'

Edith was more expressive. 'I thought he was a stunner, miss. And he's really taken a shine to you, I'd say.'

Finally Maurice returned home, but he gave Alice little chance to talk to him alone, going straight into his study, then to his dressing room to change for dinner. It was only when the three of them were at table that Alice, disregarding her mother as she so often did, asked her father what he and Edward had talked about after dinner the night before.

Maurice looked confused. 'Oh, this and that. I really can't remember.'

Alice frowned, her curiosity thwarted. 'Were you impressed with what he said?' she asked.

'Impressed? I don't understand.'

'You can't have sat in silence. He must have said something.'

'Of course.'

'And you must have formed an opinion of him.'

'Yes, indeed. I liked him. He has, I think, a more open mind than one might suppose.'

'Did he talk about me?'

'He said something, yes, something complimentary, of course, but I can't quite remember what it was.'

Alice sensed that her father was being evasive. 'And did he ask about you?'

'About me? What about me?'

'About your ideas, and the Progressive Press?'

'No, he seemed remarkably incurious about my list. He had heard of some of our authors, and he asked about some others but I didn't gain the impression that he was especially interested in new ideas.'

'He is more interested than he was,' said Alice.

'Yes, indeed, now that he has started reading *The New Age*.'

A letter of thanks to Françoise from Edward arrived the next morning written on the thick headed writing paper of Nester Park. In the same post there was a note to Alice saying that he had had to go from Knapley to Nester but that he would be back on Friday in time to take Alice to the ballet: they had tickets to see Rimsky-Korsakov's ballet *Scheherazade* at the Coliseum. This production of the Russian Imperial Ballet had been transferred from Paris and was something Alice had looked forward to with some eagerness; but now the anticipation of what she would see on stage was subordinate to her curiosity about that ten-minute conversation between Edward and her father.

They met in the foyer. Edward was late and they had no time to talk, reaching their seats only moments before the lights were lowered and the conductor took charge of the orchestra. The curtain was raised; the ballet began: but Alice's impatience spoiled her enjoyment. The great leaps and pas de deux of the dancers only served to irritate her. Even the costumes seemed absurdly exaggerated – almost vulgar in their flamboyance.

In the first interval, after taking a sip from a glass of champagne and some perfunctory exchanges about his trip to his constituency, she asked Edward how he had liked the dinner at Markham Square.

'I liked it very much. Didn't I say so in my note?'

'I hoped you might expand a little.'

'Well, your mother seemed charming, your father intelligent and considerate, and your friends – well, I took to some more than others. I have to say that the young journalist slightly annoyed me.'

'He was tiresome. He often is. But he's actually very clever and can write well.'

'I'm sure.'

'You liked my parents?'

'Very much. Your father was very far from the wild revolutionary I had been led to expect.'

'He was on his best behaviour.'

'He can be wild?'

'Never wild, no, but he can get angry.'

'He did not get angry with me.'

'You gave him no reason. In fact, you must have got on well together because you lingered over the port.'

'Yes, we did.'

'What did you talk about?'

He smiled. 'This and that.'

Alice was obliged to sit through the second half of the ballet with her curiosity unsatisfied. After the final curtain call, they went out into St Martin's Lane, and then, because the evening was reasonably mild and there were no cabs to be seen, they walked along the Strand to the Savoy Hotel. In the Grill Room, as soon as they had been served with a cocktail and had chosen what they wanted to eat, Edward leaned forward and said: 'I think we should get married.'

Alice frowned, was silent for a moment, then said: 'Is this a proposal? Are you asking me to marry you?'

Edward blushed. 'Yes, yes, I am. I am putting it badly. I wanted to wait until we were somewhere ... somewhere special, but now I feel it can't wait.' He stretched across the table and took hold of her hand. 'I love you, Alice, and it would make me very happy if you would agree to be my wife.'

Alice withdrew her hand and looked into Edward's eyes. 'Was that what you discussed with my father?'

Edward seemed confused. 'Your father? When?'

'Over the port.'

'I thought . . . I thought I should ask his permission . . .'

'To marry his daughter?'

'Yes.'

She pondered what he had said for a moment, then asked: 'And what if he had refused his permission?'

Edward looked perplexed. 'It never occurred to me that he would.'

'No, of course not. You're so eligible.'

'I don't see myself as particularly eligible. I see myself as a man who loves a woman and believes that he will always love her and that he will love no one else.'

'Yet must consult the present owner before making off with his chattel?'

'I did not . . . I do not think of you as his chattel,' he said quietly. 'But it is customary to ask a father for the hand of his daughter . . .'

'It *was* customary and no doubt still is among the Hottentots and the Zulus . . .'

'It isn't that you belong to your father any more than you would belong to me if we were to marry, but the love a father feels for a daughter surely gives him some right to a say over her future.'

'And what of the mother?'

'I assumed that he could speak for her . . .'

'In the same way as he votes for her.'

Edward sighed and looked down, dejected. 'Perhaps I should have asked her too.'

Now Alice felt sorry for Edward because things had not gone the way he had planned. He had hoped that the Imperial Ballet would put Alice, who loved all things Russian, into a romantic frame of mind. He had also thought, no doubt, that a marriage proposal to a modern, educated woman should be made in this way; no kneeling before one's beloved in the moonlight but simply a pragmatic recommendation put forward over dinner at the Savoy: they *should* get married. She could see how all this had come about; she would even concede with her head that he was right, that this *was* the way to propose to a modern, rational woman, and she felt almost ashamed of the twinge of sadness that Edward had asked for her hand in such a matter-of-fact way.

On the other hand, that *should*, though it betrayed a calculation, was very much better than a *should not*, and *should not* could so easily have been a position he might have taken; it would certainly be that of his family and most of his friends. And now that he had put his request in a more appropriate way, Alice realised that she had to come up with an answer.

Should she say yes or should she say no? Except as a most idle speculation, the thought of marrying Edward had never occurred to Alice; and even now that it was a concrete project, she felt no kind of triumph or excitement but only a sense of joy that he wanted to authenticate his love in this conventional way.

The two were silent as they were served with their food. When the waiter had left them, neither picked up a knife and fork to eat for several minutes, although Alice was hungry and liked the look of the pink *crevettes* laid out with lettuce and mayonnaise on her plate. Finally Edward started eating – no doubt because he felt that he should – and after a mouthful of smoked eel and brown bread and butter said, in an easier tone of voice: 'You don't have to answer now, you know. You can take your time.'

Alice spiked a prawn with her fork. 'You know that I love you,' she said. 'I've shown that, haven't I, in the best way a woman can? And in that sense, I feel that I'm married to you already. As to the institution – a ceremony in a church when I don't believe in God, with your family, my family, your friends, my friends, all that . . .'

'It would be an ordeal, I know,' said Edward, 'but for only one day out of a lifetime.'

'I can't believe that I'm the kind of daughter-in-law that your parents have in mind.'

'That can't be helped.'

'They would expect things from me ... so would you.'

'I would expect nothing, and I would hope for nothing other than that you continue to love me and remain as you are.'

'I would have to promise to obey you.'

He laughed. 'I wouldn't hold you to it if you did.'

'Not now, perhaps, but later . . .'

'Listen,' said Edward, 'if we lived on an island in the Pacific it would be different, but we live in Britain at the beginning of the twentieth century where love outside marriage is thought wrong, particularly for women. We may not think it is wrong but we can't ignore indefinitely the views of people around us, and if we love one another and feel that we will go on loving one another, then it seems obtuse not to do what is normally done in such a situation – that is to get married.'

Alice was given time to consider her reply by the waiters, who came with plates covered with silver domes, laid them on the table and then, with a flourish, removed the covers to reveal a Dover sole on her plate and lamb cutlets on Edward's. And then there were vegetables to be served, the claret to be tasted by Edward and Alice's glass refilled with Meursault; and while she was waiting for the waiters to finish these ministrations, the thought popped into Alice's mind that, if she were to marry Edward, she would be able to eat at the Savoy whenever she chose. She would be able to invite her father and mother; even Vivien and Maud. And, at the thought of Maud, another consideration came to her – that if she did not marry Edward, then he might turn to someone else.

Alice looked across at Edward's expectant face and said: 'Don't let your cutlets get cold.'

'I've lost my appetite.'

She took a mouthful of Dover sole and said, with a trace of mockery: 'Shouldn't we do what is expected of us, whatever our personal inclinations might be?'

He cut a piece of meat from his chop.

'If you sent back your food uneaten, the chef would assume it was because you didn't like the way he had cooked it. He couldn't know that your lack of appetite came from a broken heart.'

He looked at her with an expression that showed the first traces of exasperation. 'And is my heart to be broken?'

The time had come to stop teasing. Alice shook her head. 'No. I love you and I can't envisage ever loving any other man. I will do anything that will make you happy, but . . .' She hesitated, then went on: 'But I may need a little time for my thinking to catch up with my feelings, because until now, as you know, I thought of marriage as a form of serfdom for women, and that women should have the chance to have amorous adventures, just like men. And even if I had, surreptitiously, the idea – even the hope – that I would love one man so much that I would want to spend the rest of my life with him and have his children, I never thought he would be . . .' She hesitated.

'A Conservative politician?'

'Someone from such a different world.'

'It's because you're from a different world that I love you, Alice. I couldn't love any of those girls who my mother and sister are always pushing at me.'

'But that's what worries me. Could I be a good wife to a Conservative politician?'

'I think you could be whatever you chose to be. People are sick of stereotypes. They love originality.'

'Have you thought and thought and thought about this? Are you really sure you know what you're doing?'

'I have thought and thought – more than I should have done, perhaps. And I am absolutely sure that I know what I am doing.'

'Then I say yes. I will marry you and do all I can to make you happy as your wife.'

After they had finished dinner, Edward and Alice walked down through the Savoy and out on to the Thames Embankment.

The evening remained unusually warm. They crossed the road and sauntered arm-in-arm along beside the river. They stopped by Cleopatra's Needle and considered its antiquity and discussed the rise and fall of civilisations and agreed on their good fortune in living in such a prosperous and stable age. Alice said that she was glad that Edward was to become a politician because there was still so much to be done in the world. They talked about the two nations, the rich and the poor, and then about Disraeli, first as a statesman, then as a novelist; and sometimes they agreed and sometimes they disagreed but none of the disagreements mattered because Edward never once let go of Alice's hand and Alice never once tried to remove her hand from his. And then, though there were others around them standing by Cleopatra's Needle, they embraced and kissed and felt at peace.

Eleven

The day after Alice had accepted his proposal of marriage, Edward Cobb returned to Yorkshire to break the news to his parents. He knew that it would not be welcome and he had meant to prepare the ground the weekend before but, still uncertain as to whether Alice would accept him, had decided to wait until he could present them with a fait accompli.

He first told his mother, finding her alone in the morning room after breakfast on the Saturday morning.

'She is expecting a child, I suppose,' she said coldly.

'Most certainly not.'

'Then the engagement must be a long one so that people don't come to that conclusion.'

'It can last as long as you like.'

His mother looked out of the window at Nester Park.

'I think that once you get to know her . . .' Edward began.

'I don't need to get to know her,' said Lady Joyce. 'One knows the type at a glance.'

'What type is that?'

She did not answer. 'You will greatly upset your father,' she said.

'Surely he will not disapprove of my choosing to marry the woman I love.'

She looked at him sharply, as if trying to gauge whether what he had said was a comment on her own marriage. 'Love, as you will discover, involves more than physical attraction.'

'I have discovered that already, Mother.'

'It only survives if there are shared interests, a mutual respect . . .'

'We have all that, Mother.'

'So, she's become a Conservative, has she, to hook you?'

Edward turned and left the room. He passed Harrison, the butler, in the hall.

'Have you seen Miss Sylvia, Harrison?'

'She's gone riding with Miss Rose.'

'And my father?'

'He'll be with the horses, Mr Edward.'

Edward walked out of the house and set off, with angry strides, towards the stud. Spring had finally reached Yorkshire and all the majestic trees of Nester Park were a feathery green. The crumbling statues, the tempietta, the cleanly cropped grass, the solid five-bar gates, the long stretches of strong stone walls, all those features of what was both his home and his inheritance, flickered indistinctly on the edge of his vision. Edward was blinkered by his rage and thought only of the confrontation that he was determined to win. If his father would disinherit him, then so be it: he would not have the course of his life decided by others.

He found his father leaning over the lower door of Saladin's loose box. Raines, the trainer, stood beside him. Edward waited, not wanting to interrupt; but they had heard his footsteps on the gravel and both turned to greet him.

'Take a look at Saladin,' Geoffrey Cobb said to his son.

Edward moved in between the two men and looked in at the fine horse with its great sleek flanks and noble head.

'He's going to run at the Derby,' said Sir Geoffrey, 'and there's a damn good chance that he'll win.'

'He's on form?' Edward asked the trainer.

'Top form,' said Raines.

The father and son now left the stables and walked back towards the house.

'I've something to tell you, Father.'

'I could see you'd something on your mind.'

'I'm going to get married.'

'To Elspeth?'

'No, Father. To Alice Fry.'

For a while, Sir Geoffrey said nothing. 'Alice. Was that the dark-haired girl who came to stay?'

'Yes. She was here with the Garstons.'

'I remember. Why are you marrying her?'

'Because I love her.'

'You love her . . .'

'Yes.'

They walked for a while in silence. Then Sir Geoffrey asked: 'Who is she? Who are her people?'

'Her father's a publisher called Maurice Fry. Her mother's French. Alice is very intelligent. She speaks three languages.'

'But her father's in trade?'

'So to speak. His publishing is more like a hobby.'

'But they aren't rich?'

'I'm rich enough, Father.'

'*We* are, yes.' He emphasised the 'we' as if it might not include Edward.

Twenty more paces in silence, then Sir Geoffrey asked: 'Have you thought about how it might affect your chances in the House?'

'I have thought about that, yes. She might not be to the taste of all the old ladies in the constituency, but she'll be a great asset . . . in time.'

'Is she a suffragette?'

'By conviction, but she doesn't chain herself to railings.'

'She won't embarrass you in that respect?'

'I am confident she loves me and will do her best to make me happy.'

'Of course. But, well, there's all this . . .' He waved his hand in the direction of the parkland and the house.

'I know.'

'It's difficult to run a house like this unless one's bred to it.'

'I dare say that Mother will be mistress here for quite a while to come.'

Another spell of silent rumination, then: 'Have you told your mother?'

'Yes. She wasn't pleased.'

Sir Geoffrey gave a grunt that was half a laugh. 'I don't suppose she was. She had put all her money on that girl Elspeth. Sylvia, too.'

'One can't choose whom one loves,' said Edward.

'Perhaps not.'

They were approaching the house. 'It isn't just that I love her, Father, and feel that she would make me happy. I also feel . . .' Edward searched for a way to express what was hardly articulated in his own mind. 'I sense that the world is changing, quickly, perhaps dangerously, and that a family such as ours needs new blood.'

'Perhaps that's true, but one usually chooses new blood on the basis of the pedigree of the dam or the sire.'

Edward frowned. 'We're talking about people, Father, not horses.'

'You're right. People are perverse.'

They had reached the house. 'Do I have your . . . sanction?' Edward baulked at the use of the word 'blessing'.

'You're of age, Edward. You don't need my sanction. You must choose your own wife. It'll be the devil to bring round the women and I'll do what I can to help you with that. Your mother will have to receive her mother, I suppose? And you say she's French? Well, that's better than a Jew or a German. And with all your new-fangled ideas, you might have brought home a Zulu. That's the line to take, I think. Thank God for small mercies: a suffragette is better than a Zulu. And the father's a gentleman . . . He *is* a gentleman, isn't he? No, don't tell me. I don't want to know if he's not.'

The women: it was the women who had to be won round, not just his mother, but his maternal grandmother, the Countess of Mawe, his aunts, his cousins and, most formidable of all the likely opponents to the match, his sister Sylvia. He walked back towards the house, hoping to meet Sylvia on her way home from her ride – no longer striding in the manner of the angry man of that morning, but dawdling with heavy steps. He felt grateful to his father: he may not have received the news with any enthusiasm but he had accepted his son's right to choose his own wife. There had been no talk of disinheriting him or banishing him from Nester Park.

Edward did not see his younger brother or his sisters until lunch. From the expression on their faces, it was clear that the secret was out. Arthur looked embarrassed; Rosie's mouth was turned down in an expression of severe disapproval, but when she saw Edward, she rushed towards him, embraced him and burst into tears.

'If you don't stop crying at once,' Lady Joyce said to her younger daughter, 'you'll have your lunch in the nursery.'

Rosie sniffed and sat down.

Sylvia, too, sat down, her eyes looking anywhere but at her older brother. Edward could see from the set of her jaw that she was angry. Only when the butler started to fill their glasses with water did she turn to him and say: 'What's this, Harrison? Water? Didn't you know we have something to celebrate?' She turned to Sir Geoffrey. 'Surely, Father, Edward's news merits a bottle of champagne. Or perhaps just cider. Or better still, a bottle of pop.'

'Sylvia,' said Lady Joyce, 'I will not have a word of this matter at table.'

'Very well, Mother. Let's talk about the weather. Or perhaps Edward will tell us about his week in London?'

'I went to the Russian ballet at the Coliseum.'

'How exotic. Not alone, I hope.'

'No, with Alice.'

'Alice . . . ? Of course, Alice Fry, your . . . No, I'm sorry, *pas devant.*'

'I know what that means,' said Rosie. 'It means not in front of the children.'

'Or the servants,' said Sylvia. Harrison had left the room.

'Fry's a funny name,' said Arthur.

'Better than boil,' said Rosie.

'Boyle is a perfectly proper name,' said Edward.

'And what about roast?' asked Arthur. 'Do you know anyone called roast?'

'There are some distinguished Frys,' said Sir Geoffrey.

'Do you mean the Frys who make chocolate?' asked Sylvia.

'Gosh,' said Arthur, turning to Edward. 'Does her father make chocolate? Will we get lots for nothing?'

'I have told you, Arthur, that I do not wish to discuss this matter at table.'

'He doesn't make chocolate,' Edward whispered to his brother. 'He publishes books.'

After that, all the Cobbs obeyed the ruling of Lady Joyce that Edward's engagement was not to be discussed at table. After lunch, they all went their own way – Sylvia more swiftly than the others, so that it took Edward a moment to realise that she was no longer among them. He went to look for her, first in the library, then the nursery, and finally knocked at the door of her room.

She opened it. Her eyes were red. She had been crying and now she returned, sniffing, to lie on her bed. 'I'm sorry,' she said, 'I'm being horrible. I should be happy, I want to be happy, but I just can't help feeling, well, sad.'

'You didn't like her?' said Edward, sitting down on the blue-upholstered button-back chair.

Sylvia shrugged.

'If you got to know her better . . .'

'Perhaps. I hope so. But I can't envisage ever being *really* good friends.'

'You never know.'

'I'm sure she's clever, much cleverer than I am, but she comes from such a different world. She has such different values. I can't see how she'll ever fit in; and if she won't fit in, then she'll pull you out into her circle. I know. I've seen it happen. Wives always do.'

'I don't believe that she has a circle as such.'

'Perhaps not now. But she won't feel comfortable among the kind of people you will have to mix with in politics, whereas Elspeth . . .'

'I don't love Elspeth.'

'Oh, Eddie, you men don't know what love is. You go to bed with a beautiful woman and you think *that's* love.'

Edward blushed. 'There's much more to it than that.'

'But you have been to bed with her, haven't you?'

'She believes that if you love a man . . .'

'Of course, I know the arguments. If you love a man, you don't hold anything back. And I don't want to say that she's immoral or anything like that, but there is much, much more to love than sex.'

Edward now began to feel irritated by this lecture from his younger sister. 'Of course there's more to love than sex. I don't love Alice simply for her beauty. She is amusing, original, cultured and extremely intelligent. She has opened my mind to any number of things that I was quite unaware of before. She has shown me that there is world beyond the army, politics and the Turf.'

'Does that mean that you're going to give up a political career?'

'No. And she wouldn't want me to.'

'And would you if she did?'

'No. She hasn't bewitched me, Sylvia, as you seem to think. I gave the whole question a good deal of thought; I even took advice.'

'From whom?'

'Tom Garston.'

'He thought Alice would pass as the wife of a Conservative politician?'

'Yes.'

'Well, we'll see.'

Edward stood to go, but when he reached the door, he

turned round to face his sister. 'Are you going to marry Harry Baxter?'

'I should think so, yes. Unless . . .'

'My *mésalliance* puts him off?'

'I don't suppose it will.' She sounded uncertain.

'Will you tell Elspeth? I'd like her to know before it appears in *The Times*.'

'Don't you think you should tell her?'

'I'd rather she heard it from you.'

Twelve

Before he left Nester, Edward agreed with his parents that the engagement would not be announced until after the Derby on 5 June. Sir Geoffrey could not apply his mind to anything else until the race was run and Lady Joyce said that she required time 'to prepare the ground'. The Derby itself would be a good opportunity to introduce Alice into society as one of the guests in the Cobbs's box.

Two days before the race, having lunch at the Carlton Club, Edward was approached by an acquaintance from Oxford, Peter Stanfield-Johnson. 'Is it true that you're getting married?' he asked Edward.

'Yes. To Alice Fry.'

'That's what I heard. And I was also told that she's the daughter of a man called Maurice Fry.'

'She is.'

With almost a smirk on his face, Stanfield-Johnson asked: 'The publisher?'

'Yes.'

'The Progressive Press?'

'That's right. Do you know of it?'

'Well, I didn't until last week. But then some papers passed over my desk for my chief's approval . . .'

'Who's your chief?'

'The Attorney General.'

'I don't understand the connection.'

Stanfield-Edwardson hesitated. 'I shouldn't . . . no, I might as well tell you, since it'll be in the papers tomorrow or the day after. Your future father-in-law is to be prosecuted for obscenity and the corruption of public morals.'

Edward frowned. 'There must be a mistake. His books may be seditious but I can't believe that they're obscene.'

'Have you seen his list?'

'No.'

'Look out for a pamphlet called *The Sexual Nature of Woman.* And if you want to read it, better buy it today. You won't find it in the shops tomorrow.'

Edward left his club and walked across Trafalgar Square and up St Martin's Lane to the Charing Cross Road. To buy a book, he would usually have gone to Hatchards in Piccadilly; but even if Hatchards had stocked what he wanted, he would not want to be seen buying it by the staff, who knew him well. On the Charing Cross Road, however, there were shops selling more esoteric works, and in the third he found the full range of books published by the Progressive Press. Edward bought three – *Guild Socialism and the State, Beyond Empire* and *The Sexual Nature of Woman.* He then hailed a cab and returned to his flat in Duke Street.

By seven that evening, he had glanced through the first of the two pamphlets and read the third from cover to cover, from the epigraph, '*Fay ce que voudras*', to the last full stop on the final page. The work of Dr Parvis filled him with dismay. If it had been no more than a guide to the mechanics of intercourse to prepare a young couple for their honeymoon, then the descriptions of the sexual organs and their functions might have been justified. But Dr Parvis made no mention of marriage or conjugal love. He extolled sexual pleasure as an end in itself; as valid if self-induced or in an exchange between persons of a different or even the same sex. 'Masturbation, fornication, adultery and sodomy,' wrote Parvis, 'are all pejorative terms derived from our superstitious past . . . Nature has never made unlawful any form of sexual satisfaction; it is only the priests and rabbis of repressive religions who imposed their code of so-called morality as a means to exert power over the people.'

It was also clear that Dr Parvis, by describing so vividly and in such detail the reaction of the male and female sexual organs to stimulus and suggestion, wanted his words to prove his point. The message was in the medium and it was precisely because he was aroused by reading this supposedly scientific tract – in particular the anatomy of the female genitalia – that Edward finished it with a sense of disgust.

That disgust was compounded by the knowledge that the tract had been published by Alice's father. All at once the vague, distracted but inoffensive middle-aged man whom Edward had asked for the hand of his daughter became someone corrupt, even debauched. And Alice – what did this say about Alice? Did she share her father's views? And if she did, how could it be possible that she had remained a virgin until the age of twenty-three? His mind was suddenly filled with suspicions: perhaps the blood on the sheet had not come from a ruptured hymen but was a residue from menstruation or even the by-product of some fissure or abscess or venereal disease.

He shook his head. That was surely impossible. He could not be so poor a judge of character, even the character of a woman, as to be wholly deceived by Alice's air of innocence and the sincerity of her love. And yet, and yet . . . Had she ever said that he was her first lover? Had he ever asked? She had led him to suppose that he was, or so he remembered, but were not women adept at deceiving not just their lovers but themselves? He thought of the coloured woman in Cape Town, passed on from one officer to another; then of his mother and his sister Sylvia; then of all the heroines in opera and fiction. What was the common judgement of the novelists and librettists? *La donna è mobile, Così fan tutte*: we weep for Violetta in *La Traviata*, but was not Violetta a whore?

Edward stood at the window of his living room looking down at the people passing by on the pavement on the other side of Duke Street. He thought back to his first encounter with

Alice. Had he seduced Alice or had she seduced him? At the time it had seemed that he was the predator and she the prey; but now, in the light of the book that lay on the small table between an armchair and the mantel, he began to wonder whether it had been the other way around. Did not the enthusiasm she had shown for love making from the early days of their affair suggest some measure of experience? Had another man broken her in? Or even a woman? A lesbian suffragette?

Edward turned back into the room and listened to the counsel for Alice's defence. How could he be sure that Alice had read the pernicious pamphlet by Dr Parvis? And if she had, that she agreed with what he said? And was not Edward being somewhat duplicitous? Was he simply concerned with the light the pamphlet cast, retrospectively, on Alice; or was there not something more calculating behind his doubts – a worry about the damage that would be done to his political prospects if he was to marry the daughter of a man charged with obscenity and corruption? Until now honour and self-interest had marched in step; he could marry Alice and still pursue his career. But if she was to become tainted by scandal . . . Well, then he would have to choose.

Edward was to dine out that evening with his uncle, his mother's brother, the Earl of Mawe. He knew that the invitation had been instigated by Lady Joyce and was part of her campaign to prevent his marriage to Alice Fry. He had not been asked to bring Alice, but Alice had promised to come to his flat on her way back from Bedford College.

She arrived at six in high spirits: she had sat her final exam. 'No more German, no more French, no more sitting on the hard school bench,' she chanted as she kissed him. Then, noticing at once that his response was lifeless, even cold, she stepped back and said: 'What's the matter?'

Edward picked up his copy of *The Sexual Nature of Woman*. 'Have you seen this?' He handed her the book.

Alice glanced at the title and blushed. 'Yes.'

'Did you read it?'

She did not answer his question. 'Where did you get it?'

'From a bookshop in the Charing Cross Road.'

'And why did you buy it?' she asked. 'I would have thought you knew enough on this subject already.' She smiled.

'I bought it,' said Edward acidly, 'because from tomorrow it will become a collector's item.'

'I don't understand. Why a collector's item?'

'All stocks are to be seized by the police, and the author, publisher, printer and book sellers are to be prosecuted for obscenity.'

Alice turned pale. 'Who told you this?'

'A friend who works for the Attorney General.'

'Does Father know?'

'If he doesn't, he soon will.'

'Will he be arrested?'

'Yes.'

Alice had been standing, but now she staggered as if she had received a blow and only saved herself from falling by leaning against the back of the sofa.

'Let me get you a drink,' said Edward.

'Thank you.'

'A glass of brandy?'

'No, a glass of water.'

When Edward returned from the kitchen, he saw that Alice had moved round to sit on the sofa. She was still holding his copy of *The Sexual Nature of Woman.* 'What can have possessed him,' Edward asked Alice as he handed her the glass of water, 'to publish a pamphlet of such a scurrilous kind?'

'It was recommended by his partner, George Greaves,' said Alice. 'Father probably didn't even read it.'

'Then he's a fool.'

Alice looked at him severely. 'My father is not a fool. He may be gullible, and naïve, and over-idealistic, but he is not a fool.'

Edward sat down beside her and took hold of her hand. 'I'm sorry. I shouldn't have said that. But I can't see what ideal is served by publishing pornography of this kind.'

'I think,' said Alice, clearly choosing the words she used with care, 'that the intention was to do away with the phobias and inhibitions that so often spoil women's enjoyment of sex.'

'That's a feeble defence,' said Edward. 'It won't stand up in court.'

'Perhaps not. But that doesn't mean ...'

'What?'

'That Father didn't mean well.'

'How could he have meant anything if he had not read it?'

'He may have been persuaded by others ...'

'Do you mean Greaves?'

'Yes. Father may have felt that George knew more about this sort of thing than he did.'

Edward now remembered the question she had evaded earlier.

'Have you read it?'

Alice looked at him squarely. 'Yes.'

'Didn't it strike you as pornographic?'

Alice thought for a moment, then said: 'Yes, in a way it did. Its chief fault is that it says nothing about love, and sex without love is ... pornographic. But overall, I should have thought, it can be defended.'

'I'd like to know how.'

'It shows that women are designed to enjoy sex quite as much as men.'

'But it doesn't circumscribe that enjoyment. It approves of every kind of perversion.'

'It goes too far. But if the book helps women lose their inhibitions, that also benefits men.'

'But how is a man to know whether his wife's lack of inhibition comes from reading Dr Parvis or from sleeping with other men?'

Alice looked at him sharply, then blushed. 'He can always ask her,' she said, 'or, if he loves her enough, decide that it doesn't particularly matter.'

'It would matter to me.'

'Then you should ask.'

Edward looked into her eyes. 'Did you ... have you ...'

'No.'

He took her in his arms. 'I knew, of course I knew, but that damned book put the most terrible thoughts into my head.'

Alice did not respond to his embrace, but added: 'Not quite.'

'Not quite?'

'Not quite would be a more truthful answer than no. I have been kissed and caressed by other men, and at times I went to the edge, but never over the edge, if you see what I mean.'

'Well, of course at parties when one's had a few drinks ...'

'That kind of thing.' She paused, then asked: 'And you?'

'Me?'

'Had you been to bed with other women before you went to bed with me?'

'But I'm a man.'

'Is that so different?'

'I think it is.'

'I think it isn't. I should like to know.'

'There was a woman in Paris ...'

'A whore?'

'You could call her that. And in South Africa I had ... an encounter with ... well, a coloured woman ... one might call it a liaison.'

'A love affair?'

'No, I didn't love her.'

'Did money change hands?'

'Yes.'

'Another whore.'

'A kept woman.'

'More like a wife?'

'This was temporary. It was understood on both sides.'

'So your sexual experience comes from whores, while mine comes from a book.'

'And the kissing.'

'Yes, of course. The kissing.'

Edward sat down on the sofa.

Alice remained standing. 'Aren't you going out?'

'Yes, I am,' said Edward.

'Shouldn't you change?'

He looked at the clock on the mantel. 'I should.'

On similar occasions, when Edward had been going out to dinner without Alice, she had remained in his flat until the last moment, sometimes scrubbing his back as he lay in the bath. Such an intimacy now seemed out of the question. 'I must go home to warn Father,' said Alice.

'He should go abroad,' said Edward.

'It's too late for the night train to Paris,' said Alice. 'And anyway, he wouldn't leave the others in the lurch.'

'Expect some nasty stories in the newspapers.'

'And you? How will it affect you?'

'That remains to be seen.'

She turned towards him. 'And what about the Derby? And the ball at the St Gileses? Am I still to go with you?'

'Of course. It's your father who faces charges, not you.'

'Wouldn't it be an act of kindness to your parents if I stayed away?'

'No, no,' he said. 'We must see this thing through.'

Edward saw her to the door. As she reached it, Alice turned, put her hands on his shoulders and kissed him lightly. 'If you decide that ... because of this ... it would be better not to marry me, you have only to say so. I could never be happy if you were unhappy, and I know that there are things that matter to you besides our love.'

Edward was about to protest but before he could do so she had slipped through the door and was gone.

The next morning, as Stanfield-Johnson had predicted, all copies of *The Sexual Nature of Woman* were seized by the police, and the directors of the Progressive Press, Maurice Fry and George Greaves, the printer in Clerkenwell and the book seller on the Charing Cross Road were all arrested and charged with publishing an obscene work and conspiring to corrupt public morals. A warrant was also issued for the arrest of the author, Dr Benjamin Parvis, until George Greaves told the authorities that he himself had written the offending pamphlet: Benjamin Parvis was his *nom de plume*.

The accused were released on bail, put up by Maurice Fry, and ordered to appear before Bow Street Magistrates for a preliminary hearing in one week's time. The day after their arrest, 4 June, the matter was reported in the press. There were leaders in four newspapers. Three – *The Times*, the *Morning Post* and the *Daily Mail* – supported the prosecution: 'It is right,' thundered *The Times* leader, 'that those who publish and disseminate such corrupt and lascivious works under the guise of scientific enlightenment should be held to account. To recommend sexual pleasure as an end in itself, with no reference to marriage or procreation, is indeed a prescription for social disintegration.' The *Morning Post* also criticised the author and publisher for the pseudo-scientific tone of the work. 'How many gullible persons of the female sex, supposing this to be the work of a doctor, would accept its recommendations as a prescription for mental health?' Only the *Manchester Guardian* came out against the prosecution on the grounds that it was an infringement of the citizen's right to free speech. 'One may regret the lascivious tone of this work, and one may disagree with its libertine theme, but one should note that research into neurasthenia undertaken by serious scientists such as Dr Freud in Vienna has shown a link between this condition and sexual repression. This prosecution can only inhibit a similar line of research in Great Britain.'

The only paper to make the connection between Maurice Fry and the Cobbs was the *Daily Mail*. In an article on 5 June headed 'Who will be at the Derby today?' the paper told its race-going readers that in the royal box with the King they should look out for the Crown Prince and Princess of Sweden, the Duke of Connaught, Prince Arthur of Connaught, Princess Victoria of Schleswig-Holstein and the Hereditary Grand Duke of Mecklenburg-Schwerin. The Earl of Rosebery and Mr Leopold de Rothschild each had a private box. The readers should also expect to see the Earls of Derby, Portsmouth and Essex; the Maharaja of Cooch Behar; Mrs Featherstonehaugh, the Honourable Mrs Rochfort and the Russian Ambassador, Count Lützow; Sir Geoffrey Cobb, the owner of Saladin, and Lady Joyce Cobb, in whose box they would find another eminent Russian, Baron Rettenberg, the Earl and Countess of Mawe, the Earl and Countess of St Giles, the Honourable Henry Baxter, Lady Elspeth Deverall, 'and also Miss Alice Fry, daughter of Mr Maurice Fry, charged yesterday with the corruption of public morals. The announcement of her engagement to Mr Edward Cobb is thought to be imminent.'

Since Alice had told her father of what lay in store, the mood in her home in Markham Square had been one of despair and distraction. Maurice's first thought was for his daughter: it was only too clear what impression the news would make on the Cobbs. But soon his daughter's place in society became the least of his worries. Forewarned, Maurice was able to retain a solicitor to defend him before the arrest was made; but the solicitor was far from sanguine about the outcome of a trial. Maurice's defence – that he had only glanced through the pamphlet and had published it on George Greaves's recommendation – was, said the solicitor, no defence at all. The court would take the view that a publisher should always know what he publishes, and not to have read it compounds the crime.

The solicitor's advice was that Maurice should take the moral high ground, claim the right to free speech and mention the researches of Dr Freud in Vienna – something neither the solicitor, Maurice nor any of his friends had heard about until reading of it in the *Manchester Guardian*. Maurice assured his daughter – and Alice believed him – that he had had no idea that it was in fact Greaves who had written *The Sexual Nature of Woman*. Greaves epitomised dissipation; he would make a poor impression in court. His choice of pen name was also unfortunate – not the name Parvis as such, but the use of the title Doctor, clearly to lend authority to the work. In the view of the solicitor, a conviction was more than likely and the probable sentence a hefty fine.

It became clear, after the protracted discussions that took place that day in the Frys' house in Markham Square, that the whole family and all those associated with the Progressive Press should be seen to have the courage of their convictions. If they were to claim the moral high ground, then they must hold it, not run for cover and hide in shame. Alice saw this with great clarity and, though she dreaded the ordeal and would have begged a God if she had believed in one to let this bitter chalice pass from her lips, she determined to go with the Cobbs to the Derby as planned, and also to the ball given by the St Gileses that night.

Thirteen

The Cobbs's party was to meet up at Victoria station and go to Epsom by train. However, twenty-four hours before, a note arrived from the Lord Chamberlain inviting Sir Geoffrey, an official of the Jockey Club, and Lady Joyce to join King George on the royal train. The rest of the party therefore took an earlier train, while Edward and Alice boarded the train that followed.

Alice deliberated for some time as to what to wear at the Derby, and finally chose a wide-brimmed hat and a blue V-necked dress made as a crossover with a turned-down collar and a fill-in fichu beneath. Oddly, since she had bought it only a month before, it seemed slightly tight. Though by no means immodest, and the height of fashion, it was a departure from the high-boned choker style still adopted by Edward's mother and sister. It caught the eye of other women on the platform and was admired in the first-class compartment by the wife of an acquaintance of Edward's who betrayed, by her friendliness, that she had not read that morning's papers.

The weather on that Derby Day of 1913 was clear and fine. The sun shone on a multitude that already covered the Epsom racecourse. Since no charge was made for entry, it was a chance for the poor as well as the rich to enjoy a good day out. Londoners of every class and kind clustered around the bookies' stands, the gypsy fortune-tellers' booths, the coconut stalls and the beer tents. A barrier lay between those parts of the racecourse open to the common man and the royal enclosure, the private boxes and the facilities reserved for members of the Jockey Club. Edward, with Alice at his side, was waved through this barrier. They climbed the steps and were shown into Sir Geoffrey Cobb's box by Harrison, the butler from Nester, who had been brought south for the occasion.

Conversation stopped as they entered. Edward greeted his mother but Lady Joyce stood as if paralysed by the sight of Alice Fry. It was her duty to introduce Alice to her other guests but she seemed unable to bring herself to do so. Her face, normally without any expression, betrayed a barely suppressed rage. Sir Geoffrey was not there. Sylvia, who might have greeted Alice, remained silent, standing at the edge of the box. There was a touch of mockery in the look that she gave her brother, as if to say: 'Don't expect me to pull your chestnuts out of the fire.'

The silence, which seemed so long, lasted less than a minute and was broken by Elspeth Deverall, who stepped forward saying: 'You must be Alice.'

'Yes.'

'We've all been so impatient to meet you...' She turned towards her parents. 'Isn't that so, Father?' She snapped it out, like a military order.

'Indeed,' said the Earl of St Giles, shaking Alice by the hand.

'And this is my mother,' said Elspeth; and again, Lady St Giles came forward to greet Alice. 'We hope you'll be able to come to our party this evening.'

'Yes, indeed. It was kind of you to invite me.'

'Any friend of Edward's is a friend of ours,' said the Countess.

Elspeth now took Alice by the arm, as if the box was hers, not the Cobbs's, and introduced her to the other guests. 'You know Sylvia, don't you? Of course you do, you've been to stay at Nester. Lord and Lady Mawe. And Harry Baxter. But you won't have met Baron Rettenberg...' A tall, middle-aged man bowed as he shook hands. 'He's Russian, not German, as you might think.'

'From the Baltic, perhaps?' said Alice.

Baron Rettenberg nodded. 'Precisely.'

'Don't you speak some Russian?' Elspeth asked Alice.

'Very little,' said Alice, blushing.

'My compliments,' said the Baron in Russian.

'Thank you,' said Alice in the same tongue.

'And of course you know Edward's mother, don't you?' said Elspeth.

'Yes, I do.'

Having had these few moments to regain her composure, Lady Joyce managed a tone of icy civility: 'We were so glad you could come.'

'Yes, indeed,' said Sylvia, who stood next to her mother. 'Have you been to the races before?'

'No.'

'Well, let me tell you what it's all about. A group of horses gallop from one end of the course to the other and the one that gets there first is the winner.'

'You make it sound damned stupid,' said Sir Geoffrey, who had returned to his box.

'Simple, Father, not stupid.'

Sir Geoffrey looked at Alice with perplexity.

'You remember Alice, don't you, Father?'

'Of course.'

'She's never been to the races,' said Sylvia.

'The Derby's a good place to begin.' Sir Geoffrey led Alice forward to the edge of the box. 'The course is a hard-going one and a half miles. For the first two furlongs' – he pointed as he spoke – 'it runs uphill, then bends to the left as it runs downhill, gets steeper again as it comes up to Tattenham Corner, turns the corner, and after two more furlongs on the straight, starts uphill again to the post. You have to have a horse with stamina and a jockey who will keep some of it in reserve for that last climb to the post.'

'And Saladin is running?' asked Alice.

'He's running and he'll win.'

'Craganour's the favourite,' said Sylvia.

'The favourite doesn't always win,' said Sir Geoffrey.

'And Shogun's second favourite at 6–1.'

'They haven't seen Saladin run, that's all,' said Sir Geoffrey.

'What do you think, Rettenberg?' he asked, turning to his Russian guest.

'I am afraid that my money is on Aboyeur, Sir Geoffrey.'

'You want to buy Saladin but you won't back him?'

'I would have backed him with another jockey.' The Russian spoke English with the merest trace of an accent.

'An American, I dare say.'

'I am afraid you will pay for your patriotism, Sir Geoffrey. With an American jockey, Saladin would win.'

'Patterson will do fine, you'll see.

'For your sake, I hope you're right.'

Sir Geoffrey laughed. 'You don't want him to win because you know that if he does you'll have to pay double the price.'

'If he wins, you won't want to sell him.'

'That's true.' Sir Geoffrey turned to Edward. 'You've backed Saladin, I hope?'

'Of course.'

'And this young lady?' He turned to Alice. 'Have you placed a bet?'

'Not as yet,' said Alice.

'Well, you've missed your chance,' said Sir Geoffrey. 'The race is about to start.'

The whole party now moved to the edge of the box, the ladies in the front, craning their necks or standing on tiptoe to catch a glimpse of the horses on starter's orders. With the fall of the flag, they were off, Aboyeur in the lead with Craganour close behind. After Craganour came Shogun, then the French colt Nimbus, then Saladin, Louvois and the King's colt, Anmer. Edward, realising that Alice was unfamiliar with both the horses and the colours worn by the jockeys, whispered a commentary into her ear. The roaring crowd below, and the harsh cries of encouragement coming from the owners in the boxes, rose to the apex of a crescendo as the horses reached Tattenham Corner. Then, within sight of the Cobbs's box, a woman slipped under the railings, ran on to the track and grabbed hold of the reins of the King's horse, Anmer. The horse stumbled and fell on top of her; the jockey tumbled free.

'What the devil was that?' asked Sir Geoffrey.

'Anmer's down,' said Lord Mawe.

'And Aboyeur's in the lead,' said Lord St Giles.

As the horses entered the straight, Craganour caught up with Aboyeur, with Nimbus, Louvois, Day Comet and Shogun close behind. Saladin had dropped back. 'Dammit,' shouted Sir Geoffrey. 'What's got into Patterson? Saladin can do better than that.'

All the attention was now on the leaders. The great roar of the crowd swelled again as Shogun clashed with Day Comet; the noise subsided, then rose again when Rief, the American jockey riding Craganour, barged his horse into Aboyeur, who, under the impact, veered left into Shogun. Craganour, rico-cheting off the rails, now collided with Aboyeur and the two horses went past the post virtually in tandem, with Craganour a few inches ahead.

'You've lost your money, Rettenberg,' said Sir Geoffrey.

The Russian seemed unruffled. 'There may be an objection,' he said.

'What happened to Saladin?' asked Sylvia.

'God knows,' said Sir Geoffrey. 'I'll go down and find out.'

The next half-hour saw much coming and going from the Cobbs's box, each person returning with a new snippet of information on the assault on the King's horse, Anmer, and the foul play by Rief. The objection flag was raised but shortly afterwards Craganour's number was placed in the frame. A great cheer went up from the crowd at Epsom and the bookies started to pay out to those who had backed the favourite.

But this drama was not over. The stewards themselves – Lord Rosebery, Lord Wolverton and Major Eustace Loder – had objected to the decision on the grounds that Craganour had jostled Aboyeur, the runner-up, and even as the horse was being led away from the winner's enclosure, he was ordered to be brought back. An impartial judge was called to adjudicate and finally the stewards' objections were upheld. Craganour was disqualified and Aboyeur declared the winner.

While the outcome of the race was being decided, Edward had

taken Alice down to the enclosure. When they came across any of his friends or acquaintances, he introduced her, and few behaved as if her presence was unusual. The occasional reserve in a woman or concealed amusement in a man revealed the readers of that morning's *Daily Mail*. And it was not as if Alice was a complete outsider, for she came upon Maud and Maud's parents, Mr Justice Hanbury-Jones and his wife. While Edward talked to the judge, Maud drew Alice aside and said: 'Did you see what happened at Tattenham Corner?'

'A woman ran on to the course.'

'It was Emily Davison.'

Alice put her hands to her mouth as if to smother a cry. 'The suffragette? Did she do it for us?'

'As a protest. Yes.'

'And is she all right?'

'No. The horse fell on top of her. She has fractured her skull.'

'Will she live?'

Maud shook her head. 'They think not.'

Alice returned with Edward to the Cobbs's box. There they were served with cold salads, lobster, chicken, pasties and champagne. Alice was given a glass which she quickly emptied, and emptied again when it was refilled. The wine did not sweeten her mood. What was she doing, she asked herself, among all these relics of a feudal age who cared so much more about horses than they did about human beings?

'Well, Father's sold Saladin,' said Edward, unaware as yet of Alice's change of mood. 'Rettenberg's come up with twenty thousand pounds.'

Alice said nothing.

'Father hates to hang on to a loser,' Edward went on, 'but Rettenberg seems to think that with a different jockey ...'

Just at that moment, Sylvia returned to the box with her mother. 'You'll be pleased to hear that both Anmer and Herbert Jones are fine. The King has been to see them.'

'And the woman?' asked Elspeth.

'In hospital with a cracked skull.'

'Serves her right,' said Sir Geoffrey.

Alice turned to him. 'That is a cruel and callous thing to say.'

Sir Geoffrey went red in the face. 'I'll say what I damn well like and what I like to say is this: that if some damn-fool suffragette throws herself in front of a horse, risking the life of the jockey and the jockeys riding behind, then she damn well deserves to get her skull cracked, and if she dies, then so be it.'

'So be it indeed,' said Alice, 'because, after all, she's only a woman, not a horse, and so it won't cost anyone twenty thousand pounds!'

Sir Geoffrey, still red in the face, turned on his son. 'For God's sake, Edward, get this woman out of here. I won't have a suffragist in my box on Derby day.'

They spoke little on the short train journey back to London. Neither was angry with the other but both seemed to want, for the time being, to keep their thoughts to themselves. They sat side by side in the compartment, Alice next to the window. Edward could see Alice's reflection in the glass and he looked fondly on what he saw: she was no less beautiful when indignant – and she was still indignant – than when she was loving and calm.

And yet if he refocused his eyes he could see, beyond her reflection, the rows of mean houses that backed on to the railway embankment. There lived the British people, the teeming mass that he had seen beyond the barrier at Epsom. Was it his destiny to serve them or would that destiny be thwarted by his choice of a wife? Was it perhaps true, as Alice herself had said, that there was more to a man's life than love?

His eyes refocused on Alice's reflection and this time she caught his eye in the glass. 'I should stay away from the ball tonight, don't you think?' She put the question quietly to his reflection in the window.

'No, you must go. We must see this thing through.'

'Will you come for me? I don't think I could bring myself to go alone.'

'Of course.'

Now she turned to him. 'I was rude to your father. I'm sorry.'

'He's not one to hold a grudge.'

'I was upset by the thought of Emily Davison...'

'Of course.'

They remained silent for a while longer: then she said, 'I worry, Edward. I worry even when I am sleeping. I wake every morning feeling sick.'

'About our marrying?'

'Yes, about that. And other things.'

'If it's too much...' Edward began, then frowned as if unsure as to how he should finish the sentence. Nor did Alice press him to do so. To the relief of both, the train drew into Victoria station, where Alice took a cab to Chelsea and Edward to St James's.

As Edward entered the carpeted hall of his block of flats, the porter handed him a telegram that had been delivered earlier in the day. Edward opened it as he climbed the stairs. It was from the Conservative agent at Knapley.

MANY ENQUIRIES CONCERNING STORY IN DAILY MAIL STOP PLEASE CONFIRM OR DENY ENGAGEMENT TO DAUGHTER OF MAURICE FRY.

Alice found her parents sitting silently in the drawing room of their house in Markham Square. From the rings of inflamed skin around her eyes, Alice could see that her mother had been crying. Her father, who had been sitting staring at nothing in particular in the middle distance, looked up as Alice came into the room.

'Ah, dear Alice, was it all right? Did they treat you well?'

'Well enough,' she said.

'They won't want you to marry him,' said Maurice.

'It's not up to them.'

'So you say, dear girl, so you say. But they can put pressure on your young man.'

'Edward has a mind of his own,' said Alice.

'I dare say, I dare say.'

'And will you go to the ball?' asked Françoise.

'Yes, I will,' said Alice. 'There's no reason not to.'

'They can be so cruel,' said Françoise, sniffing to hold back her tears.

'And here we've made some decisions,' said Maurice. 'Your mother will go to France. She cannot be here in London during the trial and we shall have to let this house, and perhaps even sell it.'

Alice was disconcerted. 'But surely you have enough money to pay a fine?'

'That may be so, but there are the fees of the solicitor and a barrister, and that won't be cheap because I am told we should have a King's Counsel, which means paying for a junior as well.'

'Shouldn't we wait until we know the outcome?'

'Of course, I may be acquitted, but it is unlikely. The papers are comparing me to Oscar Wilde.'

Alice sat down. 'And where am I to live?'

'This won't happen at once, dear girl. You will have a home here until you marry; and if you don't marry Edward . . .'

'I am to marry him, Father.'

'But if, for any reason, the wedding should fall through, then you will join your mother in Bourges.'

'Bourges?'

'Paris will be too expensive,' said Françoise, 'and we have relatives in Bourges.'

Alice turned to her father. 'And where will *you* live? Can't I stay with you?'

'I shall stay with friends until the whole thing's over, and then I'll join your mother in France. I've done with England. Win or lose, I shall move to France.'

Fourteen

Alice had only an hour to prepare herself for the ball. She lay on her bed for twenty minutes, then summoned Edith to help her dress. Edith too had been crying. 'It's such a pity, miss, I've been so happy here.'

'Have you been given notice?' asked Alice.

'A month's notice, yes, miss, and so has Cook. Mr Fry, your father, has said he will have to let the house.'

'He says that, Edith, but it may never happen. And if it does, then you can come with me.'

'Are you really to get married, then, miss?'

'Of course I'm to get married. I have done nothing, after all, to give anyone any reason to call it off.'

'Oh, you're so lucky, miss,' said Edith, puffing as she pulled the strings on Alice's corset, 'to find a man like that.'

'Yes,' said Alice uncertainly, 'I dare say I am.'

'What've you been eating, miss?' said Edith, still straining at the strings of the corset.

'I've grown fatter, haven't I?' said Alice.

'Well you have, if I may say so,' said Edith.

'Your sisters are married, aren't they, Edith?'

'Yes, miss, they are.'

'Do you know, then, what it means if you miss the curse?'

'Oh, miss, you haven't missed, have you?'

'What does it mean?'

'Well, if you're married, miss, it means you're expectin', but you aren't married, miss, at least not yet.'

'Expecting a baby, you mean?'

'Yes, miss. What else?'

'And if you feel sick in the morning?'

'That too, miss. Our Eleanor, when she's expectin', always feels sick in the morning.'

Alice pursed her lips and said nothing more. Edith too was quiet apart from the occasional sniff as she helped Alice into the most dazzling of all her gowns – a dress copied by her dressmaker from a design by Paul Poiret that Alice had seen in the *Gazette de Bon Ton* – colourful and wild like the costumes by Léon Bakst for the Ballet Russe.

The sight of Alice, so radiant, set her mother weeping once again and her father looking heavenward as if pleading with a God in which he too did not believe. Edward arrived in his Hotchkiss. He stepped out but did not mount the steps to come into the house. Alice said goodbye to her parents and looked to see what impression her dress made on Edward. He saw it but said nothing: he helped her into his car. As they made their way down the King's Road towards Belgrave Square, Edward took hold of her hand. She looked towards him; he turned and smiled – a weak, almost formal smile, as if this were what good manners demanded.

As she entered Deverall House, Alice was given a card with the programme of dances and a space in which to enter the names of her partners. Edward asked her to put him down for the first dance, the last waltz and a polka in between. He remained at her side throughout the supper and introduced her to friends and acquaintances here and there. None asked for their names to be put on her card. Edward's mother, his sister Sylvia and Lord and Lady St Giles all greeted her with a cold reserve. Alice could read, or thought she could read, in Sylvia's expression compassion – not for Alice, the wallflower, but for her brother. 'You have promised me the first polka, haven't you?' she said to him. 'Don't you dare let me down.'

After the first dance, a quadrille, Edward sat with Alice at a table with two old dowagers, friends of his mother, Lady Joyce. They sat out the second dance, a waltz, and when the music started again, Edward left Alice with the two old ladies to dance the polka with Sylvia.

The two old ladies made no move to draw Alice into their conversation. Alice stood and moved towards the landing at the top of the stairs, either to smoke a cigarette or to retreat to the cloakroom. She decided on the retreat to the cloakroom but this meant going down the stairs; and when she reached the bottom a third possibility came to her: she would relieve Edward of his burden and leave the party altogether. She stepped forward to ask for her gown.

'Miss Fry?'

Alice turned and saw the middle-aged Russian who had been in the Cobbs's box at Epsom.

'You remember me? I am Baron Rettenberg.' He leaned forward, took hold of her hand and kissed it.

'Of course.'

The footman came forward with her gown.

'Are you leaving?' asked the Baron.

'I am feeling unwell.'

'That is a pity. I left dinner early to get here before your card was filled.' The footman held up the gown to place it over Alice's shoulders: Rettenberg held up his hand to suggest that he should wait.

'Where were you dining?' asked Alice.

'At Buckingham Palace.'

'With the King?'

'A dinner for members of the Jockey Club, of which I happen to be an honorary member.' He spoke his carefully modulated sentences in an old-fashioned English.

'Isn't it a breach of etiquette to leave early?' asked Alice.

'It is,' said Rettenberg. 'It may mean I shall never be asked again. And it would all be for nothing if you were to leave, although I dare say I will be only one among a number of disappointed men.'

Alice handed him her dance card. 'As you can see, there is only one, and I suspect he will be relieved rather than disappointed.'

Rettenberg glanced at the card. 'Perhaps these empty spaces have something to do with your indisposition?'

'One never knows how the mind affects the body.'

Alice felt Rettenberg study her in her radiant dress before holding out his arm, which she took without quite knowing why, letting him lead her back up the stairs. 'Your dress reminds me of our Imperial Ballet,' he said.

'It is modelled on one of Bakst's designs.'

'You have seen the Ballet Russe?'

'Here in London. Not in Paris.'

'You should see it in St Petersburg.'

'I should like to. One day, perhaps.'

They came to the ballroom as the orchestra played the first bars of a waltz. Rettenberg led her on to the floor as if, having brought her back to the party, he had jurisdiction over the blank spaces in her programme. Alice, seeing Edward dancing with Elspeth and Sylvia with Harry Baxter, spoke with a cheerful animation about her love of all things Russian – the novels of Dostoevsky and the plays of Chekhov.

When the waltz came to an end, Rettenberg led her towards the buffet where they were quickly surrounded by his friends and acquaintances, whom he presented to Alice. Among them was Count Lützow, the Russian Ambassador, and a secretary from the Russian Embassy, a young Pole, Count Zamoyski, who asked Alice if, by any chance, she was free to dance.

Had he done so at the Baron's suggestion? Alice did not care. Without even looking at her card, she gave him her arm. They danced first a vigorous polka, then a gliding waltz. The young Pole then took her back to the buffet, where they were both given a glass of champagne. 'You are a friend of Baron Rettenberg?' he asked.

'I don't know him well,' said Alice.

Zamoyski smiled. 'He is much admired in Russia. He should be a minister, at the very least.'

'And why is he not?'

The diplomat shrugged. 'He speaks his mind a little too easily and they say that some of his qualities offend the Tsar.'

'What qualities?'

'Baron Rettenberg is a connoisseur.'

'Of what?'

'Of whatever he values.'

'Horses?'

'Of course. But also art, literature and, of course, women.'

Alice blushed. 'But surely he is married?'

'He is. But . . .' The young diplomat gave a smirk. 'If a connoisseur is to remain a connoisseur . . . It is said, for example, that he once went to dine at a house in Paris and left at the end of the evening with the maid who had opened the door.'

They rejoined Baron Rettenberg and the Russian Ambassador, Count Lützow, who presented Alice to his wife.

'*On m'a dit que vous parlez français, mademoiselle,*' she said.

'*Ma mère est Française.*'

'*Quelle bonheur. Je trouve la langue anglaise bien fatigante.*'

And then, with a candour quite un-English, the Russian Countess told Alice how she had heard about '*le scandale autour de votre père*' and how it could never have happened in Russia, where the censor saw a book before it was published.

From the ballroom came the opening chords of the polka that Alice was to dance with Edward. She glanced over the shoulder of Countess Lützow to see if he would seek her out to claim the dance; and sure enough he appeared in the doorway and raised his eyes as if to say, 'I've found you at last.'

They did not talk as they galloped around the ballroom, but Alice could sense that the mood of her partner did not match the cheerfulness of the music. 'Better at marching than dancing,' she thought to herself, remembering the smooth mastery of her Slavic partners, the Russian Baron Rettenberg and the Polish Count Zamoyski.

When the dance was over, Edward led her out of the ballroom into the garden. 'I see you've made friends with Baron Rettenberg,' he said.

'One finds one's friends where one can,' said Alice.

'I can't stand the man.'

'He's an excellent dancer,' said Alice.

'Oh, women like him,' said Edward, as if that in itself was a reason for disliking Rettenberg.

They sat down on a bench in the garden and Edward took hold of her hand in a lifeless way.

'We don't agree on much, do we?' said Alice.

He took her question more seriously than she had intended. 'It is difficult to know,' he said, 'when qualities are complementary and when contradictory.'

Alice glanced across at his pale, troubled face, and with a growing sense of doom that made itself felt in the pit of her stomach, she asked: 'Is one beginning to seem more like the other?'

Edward did not meet her glance but looked down at his knees, his brow wrinkled as if he were trying to solve some intractable mathematical problem. 'I think when one marries,' he said, 'one should feel reasonably confident that one is going to be pulling in the same direction.'

'Pulling what?' asked Alice.

He frowned again but still did not face her. 'I think you know what I mean.'

'I am not as familiar with equestrian metaphors as you are.'

'Until today,' he said, letting her jibe pass, 'I thought that one's feelings for a person, because they were so strong, must be enough. But perhaps they are not enough if, despite loving one another, a man and a woman would always be at cross-purposes as man and wife.'

'Perhaps they could learn from one another and grow together – if they loved one another, that is?'

'Perhaps.' He sighed and then added: 'And perhaps not.'

For a moment they sat in silence. In Alice the feeling of doom in the pit of her stomach grew increasingly acute, yet she felt a reckless urge to confront it. 'You feel, do you, that it *is* all too much?'

'I feel . . . I feel that if we were to marry I could not lead the kind of life I had envisaged . . .'

'The life of a politician?'

'Of a statesman, yes. I couldn't serve my king or my country as I would like to serve them, and I would . . . fester.'

'To fester at Nester,' said Alice with an abrupt, crazed giggle. 'That wouldn't be much of a life.'

Now he turned to face her. 'You must see that if one has so many advantages, as I have, one must do something with them, but that one can only do something with them in terms of who one is and what one has got. Even if I was to switch parties like Churchill . . .' He shook his head. 'But I couldn't. The die is cast in that respect.'

'I would always support you,' said Alice, 'but I am who I am.'

'Precisely,' said Edward. 'And it would be wrong for me to expect you to change.'

'But you knew what I was like . . .'

'I did. But I didn't really know what *I* was like.'

Again, a moment of silence: then, gently, Alice removed her hand from his flaccid grasp. 'I never asked or expected you to marry me,' she said.

'I know. The whole thing . . . is my fault. But, thank God, it has remained a private matter . . .'

'You mean it has only been mentioned in the *Daily Mail*, not announced in *The Times*?'

Edward frowned. 'You have the right, of course, to hold me to my word . . .'

'Do you really imagine that I would do that?'

'No.' He shook his head sadly. 'You have been consistent . . . from start to finish.'

'And it is finished, is it?'

'Yes, I'm afraid it is.'

Alice stood. She felt unsure as to whether she could stop herself crying – or whether the tears, when they came, would be tears of sadness or tears of rage. 'I think I shall go home,' she said to Edward.

'I'll take you.'

'No. I'd rather go on my own.'

Alice turned and went back through the French windows into the crowded drawing room and made her way towards the stairs. With irrational paranoia, she felt that a dozen eyes were on her, and now, seeing her leave alone, would know what had transpired in the garden. Pride saved her from tears. She had not asked to marry Edward: it was he who had asked her; and it was only if she was to judge herself by their standards that she should feel humiliated by his rejection. She managed a smile as she sauntered towards the hall, behaving as if she was making for the cloakroom. But, as she asked for her gown, this bravado left her, and though she bit her lower lip in an attempt to stop the flow of tears, she felt them well up into her eyes and one burst the dam of her lower lids to run down her cheek.

'Please call a cab,' she said to the liveried footman at the door.

She waited for the cab beneath the portico at the entrance to Deverall House, sensing that the footmen and chauffeurs were wondering why she was leaving early and alone. Then another guest came and stood beside her, waiting for his carriage or car. It was Baron Rettenberg.

'Again indisposed?' he asked with a trace of humour in his

tone of voice. 'That young man, Zamoyski,' Rettenberg went on without waiting for Alice to answer, 'was hoping, I think, for another dance – perhaps even that last waltz, if it had become vacant . . . But the moment comes, doesn't it, when enough is enough?'

Alice, feeling that Rettenberg, like the footmen and chauffeurs, must be privy to her humiliation, said nothing.

Rettenberg's limousine drew up in front of them. 'Where do you live?' he asked.

'I have asked for a cab.'

Rettenberg turned to the footman and said: 'It won't be required.'

'I live in Chelsea,' said Alice. 'I would not want to take you out of your way.'

The footman hesitated for a moment but then, at a glance from Rettenberg, turned to intercept the cab. Feeling too helpless to object, Alice sat beside Rettenberg in his car.

'Where do you live?' he asked again.

'Markham Square in Chelsea.'

Rettenberg took the mouthpiece and gave new directions to the chauffeur, then sat back in the leather seat. 'And what about Edward Cobb?' he asked. 'Won't he be looking for you for that last waltz?'

'No.'

'You have quarrelled?'

Alice wondered, before she answered, whether she should be offended by the intimacy of this question, but Rettenberg's kindly manner made it seem natural to confide in him; and, anyway, he was a foreigner who would soon be gone. 'We didn't quarrel,' she said, 'but we were engaged to be married, and now we are not.'

'He has broken off the engagement?'

'Yes.'

'You will no doubt find someone better.'

She laughed. 'In Bourges?'

'Why in Bourges?'

'I am sure you know about my father.'

'I have heard something about his . . . troubles.'

'We shall have to leave England. My mother's family live in Bourges.'

'Do you have to go with your parents?'

'I am not in a position to provide for myself in London.' Then she added, in a bitter tone: 'Women in England, as you may know, are very poorly paid.'

'Then come to Russia.'

'To Russia?'

'We need a governess for my children.'

'Is that why you're here?' she asked. 'To find a governess?'

'And to buy a horse.'

'You've bought your horse.'

'Yes. Saladin.'

'A governess will cost you less.'

'I would hope so.'

'There are agencies that will find you a governess.'

'I have interviewed a number but none of them has the right . . . combination of qualities.'

'They could surely speak English?'

'Yes, but I am looking for more than that. I would like to find someone who could also open the minds of my children. And, I should add, someone whose company one would appreciate. The winters are long in Russia, as you probably know.'

Long winters in Russia. Thoughts of Chekhov, Tolstoy, Turgenev, Dostoevsky flitted through Alice's mind, and were put in the scales against her anticipation of life with her parents in Bourges.

'I would like to visit Russia,' she said cautiously.

'If you should be interested in the appointment,' said Rettenberg, 'we should discuss it further. You can find me at Claridges Hotel.'

The next morning, Alice sent Edith to make an appointment with the Frys' family doctor, Dr Ramsey. It was arranged for four in the afternoon.

That evening, at supper, Alice told her parents that she would not now be marrying Edward Cobb.

'Oh dear, oh dear,' groaned Maurice Fry. 'I knew this would happen. They cannot countenance scandal, people like that. And it's all my doing, my poor girl, your own father has destroyed your happiness.'

'It was as much my doing as his,' Alice said with slowly spoken but emphatic words. 'I felt I could not be happy with ... people like that.'

'But he was so ... fine,' said Françoise, utterly dejected.

'He appeared to be, Maman,' said Alice. 'But underneath they're all the same.'

'What will you do?' said Maurice. 'The trial will be a torment, and I may well lose all my means.'

'We shall go to France,' said Françoise.

'And I to Russia,' said Alice.

'To Russia?' asked Maurice.

'Baron Rettenberg, whom I met at Epsom, is looking for a governess for his children, and I feel inclined to apply for the post.'

'A governess!' said Françoise. 'It has come to that!'

'But you were a governess,' said Maurice Fry to his wife.

'I had hoped for better for my daughter.'

'Oh, so had I, so had I,' said Maurice. 'But to be away for just a year or so, to be away for the trial, and to see another country, to learn another language, that wouldn't be time wasted, and no one would see it as a disgrace.'

'All in all,' said Alice, 'if you could manage without me, I think it would be best if I went somewhere strange and far away.'

'Yes, go,' said Maurice, 'and go with my blessing, my dear child, my dear child.' He stood and, coming up behind her chair, kissed the top of her head and embraced her and could not hold back his tears.

Françoise, who knew of Alice's visit to the doctor, directed a cool, penetrating look across the table at her daughter. Their eyes met. 'Is it for the best?' asked Françoise.

'Yes, Mother,' said Alice quietly, 'in every way it is for the best.'

Part Two

One

On a hot day in early July 1913, Baron Rettenberg left London for Paris on the first leg of his journey to Russia. He sat by the window of a first-class compartment of the Golden Arrow. Next to him, sitting bolt upright and staring straight ahead, sat his valet Pytor, a young man with close-cropped hair and immobile features. Facing Rettenberg, also by the window, sat Alice, reading, or at least pretending to read, Maurice Baring's *The Mainsprings of Russia*. Rettenberg watched her over the rim of his newspaper. Every now and then her eyes left the page, her head turned, and she looked out of the window, first at the rows of dingy houses, then at the pretty Kentish countryside. Occasionally, Rettenberg noticed, Alice would steal a glance at Pytor: perhaps she was ill-at-ease seated in the same compartment as a valet. She did not look at Rettenberg; she had never, since the start of their acquaintance, given him more than a cursory glance.

Rettenberg had reason to feel content. He had set out from Russia to buy a stallion for his stud and hire a governess for his children; he now had both. Saladin was being shipped from Tilbury to Riga and Miss Fry was on the train. He was also glad to be going home. Though Rettenberg wore suits made in Savile Row and shirts tailored in Jermyn Street, he disliked the English, particularly the English upper class. He was constantly astonished that the kind of Englishmen he came across at race meetings – people like the St Gileses, the Maweses or the Cobbs – should be so self-satisfied when they were, in Rettenberg's estimation, ignorant of the rudiments of philosophy, history and art.

It also irritated Rettenberg that his English friends were so ready to lecture him on the backwardness of his country and criticise its system of government – the autocracy of the Tsar. If only Russia would become a parliamentary democracy with a constitutional monarch, he was told, then it could join the community of civilised nations and all would be well.

But was Britain a democracy? Did it not rule, without consent, a large part of the world's population? Had not Britain exploited its maritime supremacy to conquer, annex, seize and sequester any port or patch of land that might serve its vanity and interest? Was it not to keep up with his neighbour that the Kaiser now built battleships and rattled his sabre? Was it not the example of Britain that Austria was following when it annexed Bosnia and Herzegovina, leading to its present confrontation with Serbia? It was Britain, Rettenberg considered, that was largely responsible for the present dangerous state of the world.

Of course, Russia too had tried to follow Britain's example, seizing an empire in Siberia and attempting to assert itself in the Far East, ending with its catastrophic defeat in the recent war with Japan. Nor was Rettenberg blind to the Russians' mistreatment of their national minorities – the Georgians, the Armenians, the Poles, the Ukrainians and above all the Jews. The Baltic German nobility to which he belonged were the only minority to have flourished under the Russian tsars; but he nonetheless believed that, for all their failings, the Russians had qualities of faith, generosity and compassion that raised them on to a higher moral plane than the peoples of other European nations.

There was also a sense of fraternity to be found in Russians that the English could never understand. The regimentation of Russian society, imposed by Peter the Great, was an import from Prussia that had not affected the soul of the *moujik*: to him there was God and the Tsar, and there were their subjects, with no intermediary gradations: this was why Pytor, Rettenberg's manservant, was never relegated to a third-class compartment.

It also explained why Rettenberg's first appreciation of Alice at Epsom had been tinged with compassion: here was not simply an attractive young woman but, as it were, a damsel in distress. He had heard the gossip and had read the *Daily Mail*: he knew before he saw her that she was the subject of the

Cobbs's disdain. When she had entered the Cobbs's box, the contrast between the radiance of her appearance and the disdain shown to her by her hosts had been noted by Rettenberg. He had seen at a glance what was at play and, after her outburst over the fate of the suffragette, noted the look on the face of young Edward Cobb. The man was weak: he would not go through with his marriage to Alice Fry.

It was therefore to take another look at Alice that Rettenberg had, in breach of all etiquette, left the dinner given for members of the Jockey Club by King George V at Buckingham Palace. Certainly, he had been told to find a governess in London and Alice would do as a governess; but he at once saw, with his experienced eye, that here was a girl who would alleviate the tedium of life on his estate at Soligorsk. The Cobbs had sold him Saladin and in time would regret it: now Rettenberg had relieved them of Alice and he felt sure that, in due course, they would come to regret that too.

Two

The air in Paris was stagnant and hot. Rettenberg took a cab from the Gare du Nord to the Hotel St James and Albany on the rue de Rivoli: Pytor sat with the driver while Alice sat beside Rettenberg in the back. Rettenberg judged from the introspective look in her eyes, that her thoughts were still on matters in England; that she was scarcely aware that she was in Paris. He interrupted these thoughts to ask her whether she had been to Paris before. She replied that she had, a number of times. The question seemed to break the brooding and she started to look around her with something of the wonder of a child.

At the hotel, they were shown to the suite that was always reserved for Baron Rettenberg – an elegant sitting room with two bedrooms. The manager, Monsieur Potain, escorting Rettenberg to these rooms in person, asked after the Baron's two older children, Alexander and Ekaterina, who had been with him in Paris the autumn before. Rettenberg explained that Alice was to be the governess for his younger children.

Monsieur Potain asked if she should be put in the second bedroom in the Baron's suite or in a room of her own.

Rettenberg turned to Alice. 'Which would you prefer?'

Alice frowned as if irritated at having her thoughts about other things disturbed. 'I don't mind.'

'It would be simpler, I think, if you took the children's room.'

The children's room. This meant that Pytor, who clearly could not share a room with the governess, should sleep in an attic. Potain bowed in acquiescence.

Pytor unpacked Rettenberg's suitcases. A maid came to do the same for Alice. Rettenberg waited in the sitting room for Alice's unpacking to be complete and then, when the maid had left, asked Alice to join him.

'We are here until Thursday night,' he said. 'I have a number of engagements, but since you know Paris, I imagine that you will be quite happy to be left to your own resources.'

Alice nodded. 'Yes.'

'Are there friends here you would like to see? Cousins, perhaps?'

'Maybe.'

'You are welcome to entertain them here at the hotel, if you would like that.'

'That's very kind.'

Rettenberg could tell that she had no intention of seeing anyone.

'I must dine out this evening. If you are tired, you could ask for supper to be brought here to this room.'

'Thank you. I am tired. I should like to go to bed early.'

'Of course.'

'Will it be as hot as this in Russia?'

'Quite possibly, yes.'

'Then tomorrow I should perhaps buy some lighter clothes.'

'We have an account in a number of stores.'

'That is kind, but I have my own money.'

'I have ordered some school books to be delivered to the hotel,' said Rettenberg. 'If you think them unsuitable, then you should change them.'

'You know, I have little experience . . . of teaching children.'

'That doesn't matter.'

He turned towards his room.

'Could you tell me, perhaps . . .'

He stopped and turned.

Alice's expression was one of embarrassment, almost mortification. 'I should have asked in London . . .'

'Asked what?'

'What sort of clothes I will be expected to wear, as your children's governess.'

Rettenberg smiled. 'The clothes you might normally wear at a house in the country . . . Not a grand house. A simple house. But a house where one dresses up a little for dinner and where you might be asked to a party, even a ball.'

'I might be asked . . . ?'

'Yes. Of course. You will live as a member of the family.'

At eight Rettenberg left for the Russian Embassy, where he dined in the company of the Ambassador and Ratchkovsky, the head of operations in western Europe of the Tsar's secret police, the Okhrana. In the course of a discursive conversation about the state of public opinion among Russia's allies, Rettenberg reported on what he had observed in England.

To say that Rettenberg worked as a spy would be false or, at any rate, an exaggeration. He received no payment for his services: he acted from patriotism and from a desire to involve himself in something more interesting than horse racing and the rotation of crops. He did not have to put himself out to perform these duties: his friends and relations in the capitals of Europe were also the friends and relations of high officials or were high officials themselves who would happily discuss state secrets with their *cher cousin* from Russia; and his long-standing liaison with Lilli von Kombach had less to do with her husband's position in the Ministry of War than the scent of tube rose that came from her silken skin.

Nor did Rettenberg feel demeaned by working informally for the infamous Okhrana; little distinction was made in Russia at the time between a soldier and a civilian. Even civilians had a rank and Rettenberg, who had been a captain in the Chevalier Garde, was now the equivalent to a colonel and had been rewarded for his services with the Order of Vladimir.

Despite Rettenberg's dislike of the English, he recognised that Austria was now Russia's rival in the Balkans and it was likely that those friends and relations with whom he mixed so easily in Vienna could at any moment become his antagonists in a war. The question that Ratchkovsky and the Ambassador wanted him to answer was whether Britain, in the event of a war on the continent of Europe over the Balkans, would honour its obligations under the Triple Entente.

Rettenberg reported that he had found little understanding in Britain for the solidarity of Slav nations, so if the war was between Austria and Russia alone, then Britain might stand back: however, feeling against Germany was strong, and so if Germany came in to support Austria, and France to support Russia, then Britain would back its allies: it could not afford to let Germany win a Continental war.

The next day, since it was still unpleasantly hot, Rettenberg ate his breakfast in the courtyard of the hotel. When he returned to the suite, he found Alice drinking tea and reading her book on Russia. She blushed and made as if to stand when he came in; he told her to remain seated. If she was going to have lunch at the hotel, he recommended the courtyard because it was cooler. She thanked him. Rettenberg collected his Gladstone bag, then left to keep a ten o'clock appointment at Rothschild's Bank.

Rettenberg was rich, or he seemed to be rich: no one who bought a racehorse for twenty thousand pounds could be considered poor. Before the liberation of the serfs, the estate at Soligorsk, which covered fifteen thousand hectares, was valued at over a thousand souls. His wife, Tatyana Andreiovna, might not have been an heiress, but his mother, Olga Pavlovna, was the daughter of a crafty profiteer of the Crimean War, Pavlov Filipovich Budarov, and had brought a vast dowry to her marriage with Fedor Mikhailovich Rettenberg, part of which was the estate of Soligorsk.

It was not appreciated in western Europe that women in

Russia could own property, and therefore it did not occur to Rettenberg's Jockey Club friends that he did not himself own the stud at Soligorsk or that he had not bought Saladin with his own money. In reality, Rettenberg had bought the horse with his mother's money and on his mother's behalf. His only inheritance might have been the Rettenbergs' ancestral estate in Latvia but this had been sold by his father before his marriage to Olga Pavlovna, to pay off his debts.

It puzzled many who knew him slightly that a man as able and intelligent as Pavel Fedorovich Rettenberg, now well into his middle age, should be willing to act as his mother's bailiff; but it was no mystery to those who knew him well. From his infancy, Pavel Fedorovich had been his mother's favourite and he had subsequently rewarded her for this preference by falling in with her plans.

His mother, on her marriage to his father, had settled his gambling debts and indulged his passion for the Turf. Even after Fedor Mikhailovich's death, Olga Pavlovna had continued to pour money into the stud at Soligorsk, not to indulge her son but because she saw that a stud was an aristocratic accessory that, like the pedigree of her son's wife, raised the social standing of the Rettenbergs in Russian society. For the same reason, she had refused to buy back the estate in Latvia because, despite the ruins of a medieval keep which proved the antiquity of the Rettenbergs, its modesty showed that they were not Lievens or Benkendorffs but came from the minor Baltic gentry.

Rothschild's Bank in Paris was the conduit used by Rettenberg to meet his expenses in western Europe. The twenty thousand pounds for Saladin had been advanced by the London branch and now Rettenberg called to make sure that this had been covered by the transfer of roubles to Rothschild's agents in Russia. He had another matter that he wanted to raise with the banker. How could he move some of his mother's money abroad? The nub of the problem was not any government prohibition, but the adamant refusal of Olga Pavlovna to permit her son to invest her money in anything other than Russian government bonds. The reasons for her implacable opposition to any kind of foreign investment were various, some openly stated and therefore susceptible to reasoned argument, some rooted in preferences and prejudices in her unconscious mind.

Olga Pavlovna was convinced, for example, that to invest in foreign companies, or even the bonds of foreign governments, was to hand money over to the Jews. She knew few Jews, since Soligorsk was outside the Pale of Settlement, and those she came across she tended to like, even when she realised that they were Jews; but she had read *The Protocols of the Elders of Zion* and accepted the view common among priests and reactionary politicians that the Jews were the enemies of Christianity and, either as capitalists or revolutionaries, were working for the downfall of Holy Russia. She was convinced of the guilt of the Ukrainian Jew Mendel Beiliss, then on trial for the ritual murder of a Christian child in a cave outside Kiev.

Rettenberg believed that Beiliss was innocent and dismissed his mother's anti-Semitic paranoia as absurd, but he was obliged to recognise that her prejudices were to be found, to a greater or lesser degree, in his wife Tatyana, his sister Varvana, most of his mother's friends and neighbours, the Imperial Government, the Imperial Synod and the Tsar himself; and found expression in the laws that forbade Jews to own land, join the civil service, hold commissions in the army, or reside outside the Pale of Settlement in the western provinces of Russia. Jews were subjected to more than a thousand discriminatory regulations and, as the Beiliss case showed, were ready scapegoats when anything went wrong.

Linked in the mind of Olga Pavlovna to this mistrust of the Jews, and therefore to all financial institutions in western Europe or the United States, was a vague sense of guilt at the source of her fortune – the exorbitant profits made by her merchant father supplying the Russian Army during the Crimean War. At least, she would say to Rettenberg, the money stays in Russia and supports the throne. God forbid that it should go to Russia's enemies, by which she meant not just

Russia's present potential enemies, the Austrians and Germans, but also her enemies from the siege of Sevastopol, the British, the French and the Turks.

Very early on, soon after Rettenberg had been given charge of his mother's affairs, she had grudgingly agreed to invest twenty thousand roubles in an Argentinian mining enterprise after assurances from everyone she knew that the Argentinians were neither French nor English nor Americans nor Germans nor Austrians nor Jews. The company had collapsed; the entire investment had been lost; and that fiasco had remained ever since the ace of trumps played by Olga Pavlovna: 'There, you see, really, Pavel dear, these places are a long way away, you know nothing about them. Remember the gold mine in Argentina? Twenty thousand roubles ... poof! Up in smoke. Here, at least, we know what's happening to our money. It is in the safe keeping of the Tsar.'

It was precisely this thought that worried Rettenberg and took him to Rothschild's: how safe was the Tsar? If, as now seemed likely, there was to be a European war, how sanguine could anyone be about the outcome? Rettenberg had served in the Chevalier Garde for five years. He knew the strengths and the weaknesses of the Russian Army, and felt confident that, if it had only to take on the forces of the Austro-Hungarian Empire, then it could hold its own. However, there were the Germans, and here the outcome of a conflict was less certain. It seemed possible, even likely, that events would follow the same pattern as 1905, when an over-optimistic Russian government had gone to war with Japan, leading to a humiliating defeat and then social revolution. A wise man would make plans for such a contingency; he would, if he had money, place some of it abroad.

It would have been impossible for Rettenberg to reason in this way with his mother, his wife or even his son. To them, it would have seemed unpatriotic, even irreligious, to contemplate a Russian defeat. Edouard de Rothschild, on the other hand, sitting in his Paris bank, agreed that a prescient investor would not leave all his eggs in one basket, particularly if that basket was the Imperial Government of Russia. He was a racing acquaintance of Rettenberg's and was eager to help. Rettenberg described his mother's intransigence: he ascribed it to her patriotism and did not mention her animosity towards the Jews. Rothschild pondered the question. It was unfortunate that Rettenberg did not have power of attorney. But the problem might be resolved by some sleight of hand. If the Russian government were to raise a loan on the Paris market, and that loan were to be guaranteed by the government of France, then Rettenberg might be able to persuade his mother that it would be as patriotic to invest, say, a million roubles in that loan as it would be to leave the same sum in Imperial Russian bonds.

Rettenberg did not wholly understand the mechanics of what Rothschild proposed but, other than by buying a string of fictitious racehorses, it seemed the best way to send some of his mother's money out of Russia. Rothschild promised that he would present a proposal in due course and, after settling the question of the transfer of funds for purchase of Saladin with a minion in the outer office, Rettenberg left the bank in time to arrive punctually for lunch with the author Armand Gerard at his house on the Ile St-Louis.

After lunch the two men, despite the heat, walked to the Left Bank of the Seine. They looked into some of the smaller galleries displaying avant-garde works of art. What did they make of the work of this young Spaniard, Picasso? Even if one acknowledged his originality, could one live with one of his paintings on one's wall? And in the final analysis, if one had to choose between a Cubist painting such as Picasso's *Demoiselles d'Avignon* or the Vuillard Gerard had in his house, would one not prefer the Vuillard?

After parting from Gerard, Rettenberg went to buy gifts for his wife, his mother and his children. At six, he returned to the Hotel St James and Albany to change for dinner. Alice Fry was not in the suite and Pytor, when asked by Rettenberg, replied that he did not know where she had gone. Rettenberg looked into her room and saw a number of packages with the names of well-known couturiers, suggesting that she had bought new clothes for Soligorsk. Her trunk was half open on the luggage stand and there were signs that she or the maid had been packing in preparation for their departure the next morning.

Rettenberg went further into the room to look at the clothes in the suitcase, and those piled neatly on her bed. A delicate scent arose from the blouses and bust-bodices, the skirts and stockings and corsets, which, to Rettenberg, was the aroma of youth. He did not think that it would have been the same had the clothes been those of his sister or his mother.

Rettenberg went to his room, where Pytor had laid out his evening clothes. Thinking that Alice might return before he left for dinner, Rettenberg ordered a bottle of champagne with two glasses to be brought to his room. He drank first one glass, then another, alone; and then lingered past the time when he should have left the hotel, and drank a third, also alone. At ten past eight, disappointed, and irritated at himself for being disappointed, he took the lift down to the lobby, still hoping that Alice might come in as he was leaving. But she did not and, after reminding Monsieur Potain that they would be leaving the next morning, he took a cab to the Invalides to dine with his friends the Comte and Comtesse de Vareilles.

The Vareilles were racing friends. 'Bobby' de Vareilles had heard of Rettenberg's purchase of Saladin and gently mocked him throughout the evening for buying a horse that had come tenth in the Derby. 'Of course, if you run Saladin at Chantilly, he might well win because there will be no silly suffragist to bring down the King's horse because we don't have a king. Ha! Ha! Saladin's gone to Russia? Well, perhaps in Russia he'll do better. In the cold! Ha! Ha!'

Why was Rettenberg wasting a valuable evening with such a buffoon? Because some years ago he had taken a fancy to Antoinette de Vareilles. It had been a passing fancy, a flirtatious suggestion that he had never followed through: but women never forget a compliment of that kind, and in this case, and as they grow older – loose and fat, he thought, as he glanced at

Antoinette's shoulders in a low-cut dress – they savour the memory and in the savouring perhaps exaggerate the significance of what may have been envisaged but was never done.

Rettenberg was bored, and to mitigate his boredom, he emptied his wine glass as soon as it was filled. He drank brandy after dinner and returned to the St James and Albany with his heart pounding and his senses in a state of illusory alert. He let himself into the suite. A parcel of books was on the table that had not been there before. They would not have been purchased by Pytor and so showed that Alice had returned. Or had she gone out again? Rettenberg was easily persuaded that he should look into her room to find out; and if, in so doing, the image of the withering skin of Antoinette de Vareilles' bosom might be effaced by a glimpse of the firmer flesh of the sleeping Alice Fry, then so much the better.

Gently, he turned the handle of her bedroom door. It opened without a squeak. Pale light came through a gap in the curtains from the street lamps on the rue de Rivoli. He stepped into the room and saw at once not just an ankle or a wrist or a neck, but the whole naked body of the girl who in the heat had removed her nightdress and then, unconscious in slumber, had kicked off the sheet.

Rettenberg was drunk, and in his drunkenness thought he would make love to her there and then. Why wait to wear her down over the months at Soligorsk? Why not slip into the bed, gently part her slender legs and take her before she knew what was being done? When she awoke, it would be too late, and when it was done, it was done. No protests would repair her broken hymen. And if she was outraged, what could she do? Who would believe that she had not been willing, the daughter of an indicted pornographer sharing a suite with a man with Rettenberg's reputation?

He loosened his tie and removed his jacket, then moved towards the bed, but in doing so he unblocked the light that shone in from the room behind him and saw, now quite clearly, the outline of Alice's body as it lay on its side. He saw that her stomach was not flat but protruding and that her breasts were not slender but swollen, marbled with blue veins, the nipples engorged. Alice slept. She did not stir. Rettenberg looked closer. The stomach. The breasts. The nipples. He had seen this condition on another woman – his wife. The girl was pregnant. Cobb had been there before him. The governess he had hired for his children was well on her way to bearing Cobb's child.

A sudden sobriety came upon Rettenberg. He drew the sheet over her body, as if covering a corpse with a shroud, then left the hotel for an address near the Etoile.

Three

Alice Fry had set out for Russia with two hundred pounds in large white five-pound notes and a banker's draft for two hundred pounds more, pressed on her by her father before she left. On her first day in Paris she changed ten of her notes into French francs to buy clothes. The skirts and frocks and petticoats were not simply chosen to deal with the anticipated heat of a Russian summer, but were rather the kind of loose and ample garment that would both take account of and conceal her new girth.

Alice regarded her pregnancy as if it was a disease – something she might have avoided if she had taken the kind of precautions that a traveller might take if it was known that there was typhoid or malaria in the region of his voyage. But she had not been, after all, an experienced traveller; before setting off with her only guidebook *The Sexual Nature of Woman*, which had made no mention of the danger of conception. At times she felt some resentment that her mother had not told her more about such things; but then she had known well enough about her mother's inhibitions, and to have asked her specific questions would have been to admit that she was sleeping with Edward Cobb. In any case, it was now clear that the precautions they had taken had been ineffectual, or that she had become pregnant after the very first time they had made love.

Why had she not realised that she was pregnant? Her

periods, which had only started at the age of seventeen, had always been irregular and so she could excuse herself for failing to see any significance when they stopped. But the morning sickness? And, more recently, the swelling stomach? Again, Alice felt exasperated but also puzzled by her own obtuseness. Had she simply refused to recognise the symptoms because she was unwilling to face up to their significance? Or had she felt that, since Edward loved her and wanted to marry her, it would not matter if she was pregnant with his child?

Whatever the reason – whatever the degree of innocence, ignorance, gullibility and self-deception – Alice was now determined that she would never make such a fool of herself again. She would be practical. She would face facts. The disease would run its course; she would have the child; then give it up for adoption and rejoin her parents in England or France. She had heard that there were doctors who could end pregnancies but, like most others at the time, she thought that that would be both dangerous and gravely wrong.

The first step in this new life based on common sense had already been taken: Alice had distanced herself, and would distance herself further, from the scene of her disgrace and humiliation. Of the three things that had brought her down – her pregnancy, her father's arrest and the end of her engagement – it was the jilting by Edward that she minded most. She minded because she had loved him without calculation and without reserve. She had not thought of marrying him as such but simply of being with him throughout life; and when he had argued, so cogently, that marriage was the best way to effect such a commitment, she had happily agreed to be his wife.

Certainly, once Alice had accepted his proposal, she had played pleasurably in her mind with the idea – she blushed to remember it – that she might one day be mistress of Nester and invite her friend Maud and her future husband to stay. But that had never been her ambition or a source of her love for Edward. Or so she insisted to herself as she looked at her own reflection in the mirror at Mme Lepusier's millinery. Not all

Alice's purchases were for maternity clothes: it would be mad to pass through Paris without buying at least one new hat.

Why not stay in Paris? It was too close to London. Word would get back about the baby. It would also humiliate Françoise if her French relatives were to learn that Alice had given birth to an illegitimate child. She could, perhaps, go to Berlin: she spoke some German and could probably give English lessons or get a post as governess with a German family. But Alice shared the general prejudice against the Germans; and why look for a post when she already had one in a country so vast and far away?

Of course, Alice would not hold the post for long: it was clear that even with the loose and voluminous clothes that she was now buying in Paris, she could not conceal her pregnancy for more than another month or so. And when it did become apparent, she would certainly be dismissed. But at least she would be in Russia and once there would surely find some kind of employment. She knew from reading Dostoevsky that there were feminists and free-thinkers in Moscow and St Petersburg; she might find friends among them; or she could envisage teaching English in a school deep in the Russian provinces run by the kind of disillusioned idealists that she felt she knew from Chekhov's plays and short stories.

Alice felt some exhilaration at the thought of taking that second step into the unknown. The first step – the step she had already taken – seemed predictable and so dull. As Rettenberg himself had realised, Alice had not thought much about her employer; he was simply a middle-aged foreigner with plenty of money who had conveniently proposed a way of escape. The few things that had been said about him at the St Gileses' ball had scarcely been retained in her memory, so dramatic were the other events on the same occasion. She had left London in his company knowing only that he had bought a racehorse for twenty thousand pounds and had dined with the King at Buckingham Palace.

Neither of these facts were marks in his favour so far as Alice was concerned. But did she need to know more if, after a month or so at his house in Soligorsk, she would be off to one of the big Russian cities? Until the morning of their departure she had thought not; but when, at around eight, as she was being served with her breakfast of tea and toast in the suite at the St James and Albany, Rettenberg had come in behind the waiter, unshaven and still wearing his evening clothes, she had realised that there might be sides to him that she had not appreciated, and she tried but failed to remember what the young Polish diplomat had told her about Rettenberg at the St Gileses' ball.

Rettenberg, apparently quite unembarrassed at his state of dress, sat down at the table next to Alice, told the waiter to bring him some coffee, and then took a piece of her toast. It was quite clear to Alice, as she smiled coldly at her employer, that his evening clothes must have been taken off before being put back on because there was a button undone on his shirt and the ends of the black tie were uneven. Even more distasteful than this state of disarray was the faint scent of violets and roses that came from his clothes. She also felt slightly indignant that he neither apologised for nor sought to explain his condition, but sat munching her toast and reading the paper that the waiter had brought into the room with Alice's breakfast.

Rettenberg's coffee was delivered with a basket of French croissants and brioche. '*L'appétit vient en mangeant*,' he said to Alice, as with a silver knife he picked up a twirl of butter and spread it on to the horn of a croissant. He nodded towards the basket. 'Please, help yourself.'

'Thank you, but I won't.'

'Don't you feel hungry?'

'I have had some toast.'

'I would have thought you would feel *particularly* hungry.'

Alice blushed. What could he mean?

'But you must please yourself.' He picked up his newspaper, which Alice took as a sign that she might rise from the table and go to her bedroom.

When Alice walked into the concourse of the Gare de l'Est at Rettenberg's side, with Pytor behind them directing four porters, the trolleys piled high with their luggage, she felt for the first time a surge of excitement at the idea of travelling to an unknown far-off country. Smuts from the coal and steam from the boilers of the locomotives mixed with the smells of scent and sweat from the crowd of passengers, and the wisps of smoke from innumerable pipes, cigarettes and cigars. Boards proclaiming the destinations of the different trains of the Compagnie Internationale des Wagons-Lits et des Grands Express Européens conjured up the exotic cities themselves – the Orient Express to Venice, Belgrade and Istanbul; the Ost Express to Vienna, Bratislava and Budapest; and their train, the Nord Express, to Berlin, Warsaw and Moscow.

Rettenberg's party was shown to two twin-berthed first-class compartments – one shared by Rettenberg and Pytor, the other by Alice and a Russian woman of around fifty who, speaking poor French, had been made almost hysterical by the drama of her departure. Alice, though she understood nothing of her companion's gabble, managed to calm her down and learned from the slowed torrent of words that a suitcase she wanted with her on the journey had gone to the luggage van. Alice explained this to the porter; the porter retrieved the suitcase; and the two women settled down facing one another by the window. Before the train left, Rettenberg made sure that Alice was satisfactorily installed in her spacious compartment, then returned to his.

The Nord Express drew out of the platform of the Gare de l'Est and started its long journey across eastern France towards central Europe. Having had a light lunch in Paris before they left, Alice had no reason to see Rettenberg, and either read her book or listened to her travelling companion who, when she had recovered her self-possession, expressed her gratitude to Alice for recovering her suitcase and then proceeded to reward her with her life story in a mixture of rapid Russian and broken French.

At around seven, there was a knock on the door of the ladies' compartment. It was Pytor, speaking slowly as he struggled with each word in French: 'Monsieur le baron vous invite à dîner vers huit heures.'

Alice nodded to acknowledge the invitation.

Pytor hesitated by the door. '*Vous acceptez?*'

'*Oui.*'

'*Il vient vous chercher.*'

At eight there was another tap on the compartment door. Alice, who had changed into a simple evening dress, found Rettenberg in the corridor in evening clothes. He led her to the dining car, where they were seated at a table for two. The head waiter, who seemed to know Rettenberg from earlier journeys and, to judge from his affable yet respectful manner, remembered the generosity of his tips, went through the menu with him, making his recommendations *sotto voce* as if the fact that the turbot was not quite fresh but the *cailles aux cerises* were superb was privileged information for Rettenberg alone.

It was the same with the wine waiter, already familiar with Rettenberg and ready to furnish a particularly fine Burgundy that did not appear on the list. All this Alice enjoyed. She had travelled before, to France and to Germany; and she had eaten in expensive restaurants in London where the waiters had fawned on Edward in a similar way: but here clearly she was in the company of a man of unusual refinement, respected by the staff of the restaurant car as not just a man with money but a man with taste. And as Alice made this observation she suddenly remembered what the young Pole had said about Rettenberg: that he was a connoisseur of art, literature and racehorses, of food and drink, and of women.

She frowned at the thought of this last category as a class for his delectation and the exercise of his good taste: she had assumed that his appearance in their suite that morning still dressed in his evening clothes had followed a night of dissipation.

'Don't you like smoked salmon?' Rettenberg, who had just suggested this as an entrée since the turbot was not fresh, had misinterpreted her scowl.

'I do like smoked salmon.'

'And quail, or an entrecôte? Or even the *crème de volailles*? They usually do that well.'

Alice chose the quail and left it to Rettenberg to decide what wine should go with it. But even as the smoked salmon was served, and she drank half a glass of Chablis, she could not shake off the line of thought that had begun with her recalling that Rettenberg had been described as a connoisseur of women. Was it possible that he contemplated ... that he was taking her to Russia ... in the expectation that ...? No. The idea was absurd. A man as old as Rettenberg would surely never envisage a love affair with a girl of her age. And yet, men *married* much younger women and those women bore children, which suggested that what seemed on the face of it utterly repugnant did sometimes occur.

With a look of slight puzzlement, Rettenberg made conversation of a light and desultory kind. He asked her what she made of Maurice Baring's book on Russia, then told her about Baring, whom he knew, and his brother Everard, whose wife Ursula came from Yorkshire. 'Perhaps you came across him when staying at Nester? Sleightholmedale's not so very far.'

Alice shook her head. 'No.' Then she added, tartly, 'I admire Maurice Baring despite his social connections.'

Rettenberg smiled. 'Of course. A writer's talent can flourish in any class of society. We have Turgenev and Tolstoy and then Chekhov, whose grandfather was a serf, and Maxim Gorky. Do you know Gorky's work?'

Alice nodded. 'Yes. My father published a short story by Gorky.'

'His work is not entirely to my taste but I can see that it might interest you. He's very radical in his political views.'

'Does that spoil his writing ... as art?'

'It might enhance it. Our Russian intelligentsia only value art that serves to improve society.'

Alice's suspicions had subsided and in consequence her mood cleared. Perhaps Rettenberg's only ulterior motive in choosing her for his children's governess was the need for someone to talk to about books. 'You don't share that view?'

'No. I think one can admire a novel by a writer whose political opinions one deplores. Zola, for example.'

Rettenberg continued to make conversation in this vein as the Nord Express sped across the plains of Champagne towards

Germany. The dusk turned to night; the smoked salmon to quail; the quail to peaches in Chartreuse jelly. The effect on Alice of the food, the wine and Rettenberg's easy-going chatter about books and ideas was to lull her into a sense of well-being. The train reached Metz. They were offered coffee which Rettenberg accepted but Alice declined; and chocolates which Alice accepted and Rettenberg declined. He also sent for a glass of brandy and then offered Alice one of his Boguslavsky Russian cigarettes. She took one and, as she did so, to her own irritation, blushed.

Rettenberg leaned across the table and lit Alice's cigarette with his silver lighter. 'Have you ever thought of writing a novel?' he asked her. 'Or perhaps a short story?'

'I have thought of it, yes, but while I was studying there wasn't time to try.'

'You will have plenty of time at Soligorsk.'

'It would seem presumptuous to try and write in the land of Tolstoy and Dostoevsky.'

'One should never be afraid to presume.'

Alice took a puff of her cigarette, which was stronger than she was used to, and thought of what she might write. The train clattered over the points at junctions and clicked rhythmically as it passed over the joints in the rails.

'Do you think one's stories should be rooted in one's own experience?' asked Rettenberg.

She took another puff. 'Yes, perhaps. Up to a point.'

'Then let me suggest a plot for your first story.' He sat back in his chair. 'A young woman, an American perhaps, or English, with progressive ideas, falls in love with a young man. He is ardent; they talk about marrying; but she has always despised women who barter their bodies for a wedding ring; and she feels it would be reprehensibly bourgeois and old-fashioned to deny her favours to the man she loves. But either he or she, or perhaps both, is a little careless, and the girl, this modern girl, discovers that she is expecting a child.'

Alice felt her face become suddenly scorching hot, and prickles ran all down her body.

Rettenberg did not look at her. He stubbed out his cigarette.

'That doesn't matter to the girl, of course, because, for all her progressive views, she has assumed that she will in fact end up married to this man whom she loves. But then, alas, the young man decides – one can come up with the reasons later – that he does not want to marry her after all.' He stopped and now he did look at her. 'What do you think of the plot so far?'

'It seems a little banal.'

'Most human dramas are banal to those who are not involved in them.'

'And what does this girl do in her ... predicament?'

'She goes abroad to have her child and avoid the scandal of giving birth to a bastard.'

Again Alice felt herself blush. 'That seems plausible.'

'She has some money but not quite enough to provide for herself.'

'What do her parents think of all this?'

'She does not tell them. They have troubles enough of their own.'

'And her lover?'

'She doesn't tell him either.'

'Why not?'

'She is too ... proud.'

'Would a proud girl have given herself so easily?'

'It is, I think, precisely because she was proud that she gave herself. She thought she was above the petty constraints of conventional morality.'

'And now she gets her comeuppance.'

'How do you mean?'

'Even abroad, I don't see how she can escape the stigma of having a child but no husband.'

'You are underestimating our heroine. She is very inventive. She takes a boat – to Australia, perhaps, or the United States – or a long railway journey, perhaps to Russia; and while on her way she changes her identity. She is transformed from a jilted lover into a widow.'

'A widow? How?'

'Simply by deciding that that's what she is and finding someone who will vouch for her.'

145

'Why should someone do that?'

'Well, it might be someone who has hired the girl to be the governess for his children.'

'Americans don't have governesses.'

'All right.' Rettenberg drew in the smoke from his cigarette. 'Let's say that this man is a Russian; that he lives in the middle of nowhere; that he finds out about the young woman's condition on their way to Russia; that it surprises him because he knew the young man, but it does not shock him, in particular, let alone outrage him, because, well, the man's not a bigot or a prig. Moreover, he has not chosen her for her virtue but for her intelligence and originality. He knows that it would be the devil of a job to find another governess with qualifications of the same kind; he knows that his wife, for various reasons, would not take on the search; that he himself has other more important things to do, and even if he hasn't, he can't be bothered to start looking for a governess all over again.'

Alice watched her own fingers as they twiddled with a spoon: she knew that Rettenberg was watching her closely. 'Wouldn't it be irresponsible of him to bring his children under the influence of a governess with no morals?' she asked.

'I don't think that our heroine getting pregnant proves that she has no morals, just morals of an unconventional kind. And perhaps her employer thinks that it would stimulate his children to be taught by someone who has thought things out for herself. But it doesn't really matter what he thinks. If your readers know the work of Gogol, they'll know that rural Russia is filled with eccentrics. Almost anything you said about them would be true.'

Alice was silent for a while. She did not want to look at Rettenberg for fear of what she might see expressed in his eyes. Clearly he knew she was pregnant, otherwise why would he concoct a plot of this kind. But how did he know? She was a little fatter, certainly, but contained by a corset the bulge in her belly surely did not show. But if she worked on the presumption that he did know, and was prepared to help her, then she would be foolish not to take advantage of his offer. It would be better to bear her child in a comfortable country house than in a tenement in Moscow or St Petersburg.

Now she looked at Rettenberg. Their eyes met. His expression was amused but not mocking. He held out his silver cigarette case and offered her another cigarette. 'What do you think?'

Alice took the cigarette and leaned forward to let Rettenberg light it. 'What would the Russian – the employer – tell his wife?'

'He would have to deceive her. And his sister. And his mother. And his friends.'

'Wouldn't that be . . . dishonourable?'

'Perhaps, like the girl, he has an unconventional sense of what is honourable and what is not.'

Alice puffed at her cigarette. 'She would be a widow?'

'Yes.'

'And change her name?'

'Perhaps even her nationality. That is, if she was fluent in another language, such as French.'

'A French widow?'

'Yes. Can you think of a name?'

'Alice.'

'Your name. Why not? And her family name?'

'Chambon. My mother's name.'

'Alice Chambon. That sounds convincing. And her husband – may we call him Claude?'

'Whatever you like.'

'How did he die?'

'A heart attack?'

'In someone so young?'

'An accident?'

'Let's say he was a soldier. A young officer serving in Morocco who was killed in a skirmish with the Bedouin.'

Alice drew on her cigarette, and as she blew out the smoke said: 'Poor Claude. And I was just going to join him when I was given the tragic news. But why didn't I go back to live with my parents?'

'Your father is dead and your mother married to a man who molested you as a child.'

'One can hardly say that.'

'One can put it about.'

'And Claude's parents?'

'They never accepted you.'

'What was wrong with me?'

'They thought you weren't good enough for their beloved son.'

'That, at least, has the ring of truth.'

'And to punish them, you didn't tell them that you were pregnant with their grandchild.'

'They didn't deserve to know.'

'Most certainly they didn't.'

'But if they are so snobbish, shouldn't we give them a prefix?'

'Aren't there snobs among the bourgeoisie?'

'I dare say. But I like the idea of being Alice *de* Chambon.'

'As you liked the idea of being Lady Cobb?'

Alice scowled and stubbed out her cigarette. 'I think it's time I went to bed.'

Rettenberg drank what remained in his brandy glass, then, having signed the bill, escorted Alice down the corridor to her compartment.

Alice had recovered her composure by the time they reached it. She turned to her employer. 'Thank you, Baron Rettenberg, for a most interesting evening.'

'It is *I* who thank *you* for keeping me company. Good night, Madame de Chambon.'

The next morning, when Alice awoke, she climbed down from her bunk and opened the window to air the compartment and clear it of the strong odour of scent and sweat given off from the lower bunk. From the landscape and the names of the stations that they passed through at some speed, she saw that they were now well into Germany. She did not wait to be summoned by Baron Rettenberg to join him for breakfast but went with Madame Rosskosskaya, her travelling companion, to the dining car. There she saw the Baron sitting alone, reading a German newspaper and drinking coffee. He nodded courteously both to her and to Madame Rosskosskaya as they passed.

'*Tout à fait comme il faut*,' said Madame Rosskosskaya of the Baron as she sat down with Alice, '*mais plus Allemand que Russe.*'

More German than Russian? A man who proposed that she live under an assumed name and pretend to have been married when she had not been? Alice hardly thought so but could not argue the point with Madame Rosskosskaya. Nor was there any need for her either to agree or disagree with what she had said because Madame Rosskosskaya was an interminable talker who did not expect any response. While her companion babbled on about the trials and tribulations of her life, Alice could think of other things.

It was not so easy when they returned to their compartment. Alice sat by the window and took up her book. So too did Madame Rosskosskaya; but either she was not interested in what she was reading, or she simply preferred to talk, for, as on the day before, whenever Alice looked up from her book Madame Rosskosskaya seized the chance to engage her in conversation.

As a result, following an invitation relayed by Pytor, when Alice left the compartment for the dining car to have lunch with the Baron, she felt greatly relieved. She remembered, of course, his crack about Lady Cobb but the danger of a repeat of some such witticism weighed lightly against the torrent of talk from Madame Rosskosskaya.

The Baron was easy to talk to; lunch went in a flash. They amused themselves embroidering on the life story of Madame de Chambon. Rettenberg advised her to drop the prefix. 'You will meet Russians who know *Almanac de Gotha* almost by heart. As soon as they hear the prefix, the *de*, they'll run to it to look you up. Far better to remain an anonymous bourgeoise.'

'And it would certainly be easier to play the role, since that's what I am,' said Alice tartly, still smarting from the jibe of the night before.

At the Russian frontier station of Verzbolovo-Eydtkuhnen, all the passengers disembarked from the coaches that had run on the fifty-six-and-a-half-inch gauge of the west European railways, changing on to the superficially similar coaches of the Nord Express that ran on the wider Russian tracks; and which were pulled by a locomotive fuelled not by coal but by lengths of birch.

Passports were examined by both the German and Russian officials, and when she took hers back and put it in her handbag, Alice felt that she was burying for the moment her identity as Alice Fry. In Russia – and they were now in Russia – the only person to whom she had introduced herself by that name and with an English identity was Madame Rosskosskaya; and she was easily persuaded that she had misunderstood that first introduction; that Alice was in fact a widow and was French.

Four

There was a moment on the two-hour journey by car from the station closest to Soligorsk when the road, having followed the undulations of some low hills and crossed a stream by a wooden bridge, climbed through a forest on the other side and came to the crest of a hill. Here, by custom, the Rettenbergs had always stopped – to rest the horses, stretch their legs and stand before the far-reaching view. Even when the coach and horses had been replaced by the dust-covered Renault, the custom remained, because not only was the view pleasant in itself but it also displayed before the eye the many acres of the Soligorsk estate, with the two-storeyed white house just visible in the middle distance like a palace at the heart of a secret kingdom.

Rettenberg, always moved after a journey abroad by this first glimpse of his childhood home, directed Alice's eyes towards their final destination. Ever since their arrival in Russia, Rettenberg had noticed Alice's alert fascination at everything she observed, and though he himself disliked many aspects of Russian life, he found, to his own irritation, that he wished her to gain a good impression. On the train from Moscow she had stared silently out of the window, but over lunch at the railway restaurant at Riajsk where they had changed trains, she had bombarded Rettenberg with questions in the manner of a curious child. Why were there the husks of sunflower seeds on the platform? What was the significance of the different bells that rang out from time to time? What was *kvass* that was sold on the platform? And why did the bookstalls stock a translation of Milton's *Paradise Lost*? What was signified by this or that uniform or costume? Why were there people with no shoes?

Rettenberg found that his answers were defensive: certainly, the peasants' habit of spitting out the husk of the sunflower seeds before eating the kernel was perhaps primitive, but it combined a useful form of nutrition with a particularly Russian form of contemplation, and the husks were to be preferred, perhaps, to the stubs of cigarettes. The bells – they were a signal that a train was about to depart. *Kvass* was a kind of beer made with rye, barley and rye bread. *Paradise Lost* was extremely popular among Russians, and a uniform did not necessarily mean a man was a soldier or a sailor; they were also worn by civil servants. Different costumes were worn by different nationalities – there were Muslims and Asians in the Russian Empire. And the lack of shoes? Well, though Russia was more prosperous now than perhaps ever before, the peasants remained poor.

Why was Rettenberg taking such trouble with his children's new governess? Why did he care whether or not she gained a good impression of Russia? It was, perhaps, because she was both intelligent and dispassionate; not the kind to think that material prosperity was all that mattered and everything British was best. He also felt that he could learn something by seeing his own country through Alice's eyes: most Russians had long since ceased to notice the husks of sunflower seeds on the platforms and in the waiting rooms of their railway stations.

Yet often the strongest feelings we have about our own country are difficult to convey; and it was with a sense of uncertainty that Rettenberg took Alice to the crest of the hill and pointed to Soligorsk in the hazy middle distance, then to the nearby monastery and the churches, the villages, the river, and the forests on the far frontier of the estate. Would she compare it with the majestic scenery found in western Europe and find it insignificant, even dull? Alice said nothing, but she sighed, and that sigh Rettenberg took as a better token of her appreciation than any compliment paid in words. They returned to the Renault and set off on the last lap of their journey.

A long drive flanked by poplars led up to the house at Soligorsk. The driver, Leonid, gave three short blasts on the horn as he brought the Renault to a stop by the shallow flight of steps that led up to the front door. Pytor leaped out to open the door of the car for Rettenberg and Alice – both tired, both dusty, both apprehensive. First to greet them were two Labradors who came bounding round the side of the house, catching up with their master as he mounted the first step, wagging their tails and nuzzling him in delight at his return. Then, having heard the horn of the car at the same time as the dogs, but slower than the animals, came two children, the younger of whom – a girl of ten – ran up to Rettenberg and jumped into his arms. The boy – a year or two older – waited for his father to make a move to embrace him. 'Come,' said the girl to her father in Russian, after a quick curious look at Alice. 'Babushka's waiting with the samovar. And Mother's there too.'

'This is Madame Chambon, your new governess,' said Rettenberg; and then, turning to Alice, he introduced first his daughter Nina, then his son Fedor. The two children shook hands and politely greeted her in French.

'You must speak to her in English,' said Rettenberg.

'But is you English?' Fedor asked Alice in English.

'*Are* you English,' said Alice kindly. 'No, I'm French.'

Rettenberg and Alice, now flanked by Fedor and Nina, moved into the house, where they were met by a light-haired middle-aged woman, Tatyana Andreiovna, Rettenberg's wife. She embraced her husband with a certain formality and, after a sharp initial glance at Alice, welcomed her in a way that was correct but oddly indifferent, as if she had no curiosity about who was to be governess to her children. There were no courteous questions about the journey: after shaking hands, she simply turned and led the way back through double doors into the large, light room from which she had come.

Here the windows looked out on to lawns on the other side of the house. The room was sparsely furnished with solid pieces from the early nineteenth century, the time when the house had been built, and on the walls were pretty eighteenth-century French paintings of pastoral scenes in gilt frames. The walls were yellow; the skirting boards and plasterwork white. There were heavy, slightly faded curtains and, in one corner of the room, a large tiled stove.

At a round table by the window, almost hidden by a large silver samovar, sat a small old woman, Olga Pavlovna, Rettenberg's mother. She did not rise as they came into the room but met her son with a look of grim satisfaction. 'So, you're home at last,' she said to Rettenberg.

'Indeed I am.' Rettenberg went round the table and stooped to embrace his mother from behind.

Olga Pavlovna leaned back and half turned her head. 'And you've bought a horse?'

'I have.'

'One that lost the Derby, or so I hear.'

'The jockey was no good.'

'I hope it will win races for us.'

'Saladin will win races and father winners.'

Olga nodded, apparently satisfied, and only now turned towards Alice. 'And this is Madame Chambon?'

'Yes,' said Alice, holding out her hand.

The old lady ignored her and turned back to her son. 'I thought you were going to find someone to teach the children English?'

'My mother was English,' said Alice firmly, 'and I was educated in England.'

'Madame Chambon is far better educated than most governesses,' said Rettenberg as they all now sat down at the table. 'She has a degree from London University.'

Olga Pavlovna shrugged as if to say, 'That's something.' She turned the tap on the samovar and handed out cups filled with tea. The children offered Alice brown bread and butter with

Tate & Lyle's golden syrup, brioches covered with sugar and almonds, Huntley & Palmer biscuits and slices of plum cake. Olga Pavlovna, too, urged her to eat. 'Go on, take something, you must be hungry after your journey.'

Alice took a brioche.

'I understand that you are a widow,' said Olga Pavlovna.

Alice lowered her eyes. 'Yes. My husband was an officer in the French Army. He died three months ago in Morocco.'

'Was he eaten by a tiger?' asked Nina.

'Nina!' This was the first word spoken by Tatyana Andreiovna since she had sat down at the table.

Alice hid her face in her handkerchief, as if trying to suppress tears.

'He was killed by the Bedouin,' said Rettenberg.

'What's a Bedouin?' Fedor asked Alice.

Alice turned to Rettenberg.

'The Bedouin are a tribe who live in the desert and ride camels,' said Rettenberg. 'And they don't like the French.'

For Rettenberg, Soligorsk had a particular smell – of coolness on a hot summer day coming from the flagstones of the passages, mingling with the scent of roses and tobacco plants drifting in from the garden through the open windows. It was a smell that evoked the happiness but also the dramas of his childhood, and, like a magic or narcotic inhalation, always used to reduce him on his return to a state of happy paralysis.

Until well into his middle age, to be at Soligorsk was sufficient; the world outside might as well not exist. Ideals, ambitions, passions and rivalries could all be shelved. But this sense of invulnerability when at Soligorsk had been changed irrevocably by the troubles that had swept over the Russian Empire after 1905. The belief that the peasants were content with their lot – happy children of their matriarchal mistress, Olga Pavlovna – was shown to be largely an illusion. Though the troubles had been far worse at her estates in the Ukraine – the house looted and burned, the sugar beet factory destroyed – there had been a series of attempted 'expropriations' at Soligorsk, mainly by peasants from other villages, and there had been some unpleasant confrontations with the Soligorsk peasants over the share of the harvest. At night, after the troubles, Rettenberg had made sure that the shutters were closed and the doors locked – something that had never been considered necessary before. And of course, home itself had its own troubles – or the fossils of past troubles, evident in particular in the melancholy, slightly neurasthenic manner of Tatyana Andreiovna, his wife.

Tatyana Andreiovna Pashkova came from a family that was noble but poor, and it was because she was noble and poor that she had married Pavel Fedorovich Rettenberg. This had not been made explicit at the time; both had believed that they loved one another as much as a betrothed couple should. Tatyana Andreiovna had been beautiful in an 'aristocratic' way – her hair was softer, her features sharper and her face longer than one found in a peasant beauty. She had also had the bloom of youth, and had certainly been considered attractive by a number of young men, while Rettenberg had been able, intelligent and handsome, particularly in the uniform of the Chevalier Garde.

If, subsequently, both had come to realise that Tatyana had been delicately steered towards a marriage with Rettenberg by her parents because he was rich; and Rettenberg prepared by innumerable imperceptible influences throughout his youth to choose as a bride a girl whose distinguished pedigree was that of a Russian aristocrat, not a Baltic German, which would give some lustre to the dull metal of his mother's Budarov fortune, it did not make them feel that their marriage had been invalid. Such marriages were not uncommon in their class at that time. The solid benefits each had brought to the other were more durable than dizzy love.

At that time the young Rettenbergs had lived mostly in St Petersburg, going to Soligorsk only for a month or so in the summer and for the festivals of Christmas and Easter. They went to dances and parties and to dinner with their friends. Both flirted gently with those friends they found attractive, and the friends, in turn, flirted with them. They were frequent guests at the Winter Palace and for two years Tatyana acted as a lady-in-waiting to the Grand Duchess Vladimir. Rettenberg wrote occasional articles for newspapers putting forward cautiously liberal ideas; and when, after the defeat by Japan, Tsar Nicholas II reluctantly agreed to summon a Duma, Rettenberg had been elected as the representative for his home province, joined the Octobrist faction, and made a fine maiden speech.

Rettenberg, as one of the younger members of the Duma, seemed to be a coming man. Stolypin, the Prime Minister, was said to think highly of him, and word came from Tsarskoe Selo that in due course Rettenberg might be a minister if only he were to temper some of his more liberal ideas. Rettenberg had become giddy with self-glorification, and nowhere was his heroic image reflected more clearly than in the eyes of beautiful women.

Not that Rettenberg liked a coquette: quite to the contrary, he considered himself morally fastidious and avoided the company of anyone who might be considered depraved. But there were one or two women – one in particular, whom he had always admired because she was beautiful, intelligent and reserved. Rettenberg had met her through her husband, Prince Karsky, with whom he had served in the Chevalier Garde.

Rettenberg had always considered Karsky a buffoon. So too, it turned out, did his wife Angelica. One evening, at a ball, this reserved young woman, already a mother of two children, confessed her unhappiness to Rettenberg – an indiscretion, given her temperament, that amounted to an invitation to Rettenberg to start a discreet courtship in the months which followed. As it turned out, the Princess Angelica had found it far easier to bare her soul than her body: she had scruples and, if she did not fear damnation as a punishment for sin, she understood quite clearly that if it became known that she was conducting a liaison she would be exiled from court by the prudish Tsar and Tsarina.

Yet she did not let Rettenberg off the hook. His illicit attentions became essential to her sense of self-worth. Her beauty, her social connections, above all her mind deserved to be acknowledged by a man like Rettenberg. Was she really to grow old with her oafish husband as her only lover? Did not nature demand the conjunction of two such fine specimens of the species? And was she not in love?

Angelica would have been happiest, Rettenberg later realised, to have held him in thrall simply with the promise that at some indefinite time in the future – a moment that for ever receded – she would be his. But Rettenberg was a man; what was the point of the hunt if you never caught the quarry? He grew impatient, even exasperated, and finally cornered her, discreetly, at a time and in a place which made it reasonably certain that no one would ever know. Then she surrendered and, soon after, surrendered again until their encounters became quite routine.

It had been fanciful, of course, for either to imagine that their liaison would not be discovered, or at least suspected: why else should Rettenberg spend so much time in the company of an idiot like Prince Karsky? Angelica could insist, to those who discreetly questioned her, that there was often smoke without fire: but it was precisely because she had hitherto been so reserved and demure that she gave herself away. The men, among them her husband, might not notice, but there were women who saw how her eyes lit up whenever Rettenberg entered the room.

In due course, Rettenberg's affair with Angelica Dimitrovna came to an end: rumours had finally reached her husband, who insisted that Angelica accompany him for an indefinite period to Baden-Baden. This ultimatum came as a relief to all parties concerned. The parting of the two lovers was poignant – worthy of Pushkin – but both were play-acting to give a retrospective nobility to their affair. Angelica, remembering the fate of Anna Karenina, had made a cool little calculation of what mattered to her most. The time had come to retrieve her position in society before it was too late; while Rettenberg had discovered that after a certain period of time, making love to a mistress becomes as banal as making love to a wife.

There could be no doubt but that Angelica Dimitrovna was a beautiful woman, and when she had lain naked in his arms,

Rettenberg would sometimes think how fortunate he was. Yet after a time, he had realised that the keenest pleasure had come at that first moment when this proud woman had finally surrendered to his advances. The thrill, then, was not in eating the beast, it was in the chase and the kill. Rettenberg had therefore moved on to other women of Angelica's kind.

Then he became bored of more of the same. A challenge was not enough; there must be curiosity too. He knew women of his own class inside out; but what would it be like to sleep with a schoolteacher or a German doctor's wife? Did Austrian women behave differently in bed to Russian women? How would it be with a gypsy girl or a French whore? Rettenberg's travels gave him the opportunity to sample the women of the world.

Even at Soligorsk there were neighbours with wives and daughters; but it was harder to conduct an affair in the country with the same discretion one could exercise in town or abroad. Each house had its body of servants who could not fail to notice the visits of a neighbour to their mistress when their master was away. Moreover, the countryside was teeming with peasants, so trysts on horseback, under trees or behind barns all carried the risk that a head of matted hair would pop up out of a hedgerow and report back to the village what had been seen.

There were women closer to home such as the village schoolteacher, Vera, who, though not pretty, was of a species that Rettenberg had not studied before; and under his own roof there were women who were neither his mother, his sister, his daughters or his wife – fresh girls from the village who worked as maids in the kitchen or the laundry; or even the poorer, barefoot girls who hung around the stud. It was not unknown – indeed it was quite common – for young men to gain their first sexual experience from peasant girls on the estate. Older men, too, took mistresses from their own village: a neighbour of the Rettenbergs', Vassily Nikolaivich, had two daughters by his laundress and now lived with his gardener's daughter; but Vassily Nikolaivich was unmarried and eccentric; he was not a deputy in the Duma; not even a member of his local Zemstvo. Rettenberg had always had to remember that his authority rested on his reputation as a man of probity: even in his own home, he had to be discreet.

It was therefore with discretion that Rettenberg had seduced first Vera, the village schoolmistress, and then Mademoiselle Lafay, the children's governess. Neither had been easy: Vera was politically radical and despised Rettenberg's Octobrist views; while Mademoiselle Lafay had been a thin and nervous young woman, proper in her upbringing and hard to wear down. Yet she too had finally given in to Rettenberg's persistent attentions and for some six weeks one summer she would come to his study or they would go for walks, supposedly to help Rettenberg perfect his French.

In due course Rettenberg's interest in the school curriculum waned and he lost interest in improving his French. The older children were sent to boarding schools in St Petersburg – Alexander to the Ecole des Pages, Ekaterina to the Smolny Institute – and Mademoiselle Lafay returned to France. For a time, Rettenberg was distracted from lechery by political events. There was a change of ministry: the Duma was prorogued. When Rettenberg stood again, he lost his seat. There was a wave of anti-German feeling that touched everyone with a German name, even the Baltic barons. It was then that Rettenberg, with time on his hands, set off for England to find a new stallion for his stud and a new governess for his children.

After rising from the tea table, Tatyana Andreiovna accompanied her husband up to his bedroom, calling on Nikifor, the old manservant who had served Rettenberg's father, to attend to the Baron, and herself taking his dusty coat as he removed it, then leaving him as he washed and changed.

Tatyana Andreiovna had determined from the very start of her marriage that it would never be said that she was a bad wife. A husband returns from a journey; it is the duty of his wife to be there, to express an interest, to ask after his health – even if she knows that anything of importance will wait until he is also in the company of his mother, and that a true account of his adventures will wound her as she has so often been wounded before.

Tatyana Andreiovna was a woman who was pious, wise, but also lethargic, and she herself was never able to make a clear distinction between the three. When, after four or five years of marriage, she had noticed that Rettenberg's attentions to her had become less ardent, she had accepted this as a phase that many couples passed through before settling down to an agreeable companionship enhanced, for want of anything better, by a less ecstatic but nonetheless pleasant enjoyment of physical love. And when she had seen how her husband smirked and grew alert in the company of Princess Angelica Karsky, she had been saddened largely because the gossip that he brought back from the Duma, once retailed to Tatyana in their bedroom, was now kept for the drawing room of Angelica Dimitrovna or, Tatyana soon supposed, some place where the two met to make love.

Tatyana had said nothing and her behaviour towards Rettenberg did not change: she had been content to keep the company of the Karskys and even treat her rival, Angelica, as a friend. Never for a moment did she consider paying him back in the same coin by taking a lover herself. The *starets* from the monastery five miles or so from Soligorsk, Tatyana's spiritual adviser, ascribed this resignation to the Grace of God; but it was not only love of God or fear of divine retribution that kept her chaste.

There had also been some worldly considerations. First and foremost, there was the cruel fact that no candidate came forward as a lover. Time had passed. Her bloom had faded. Her face was now described as 'distinguished' and her figure, though graceful enough, showed the wear and tear of two miscarriages and four live births. Nor did Tatyana encourage any advances. She did not want to be seen naked by a man other than her husband; or suffer the humiliation that she had seen in other women who, deceived by their husbands, offered themselves on the adulterous market but raised no bids.

Why did Tatyana not divorce her husband, Pavel Fedoro-vich, as was permitted to the deceived party by the Orthodox Church? Her brother and some of her friends frequently urged her to do so. Her answer was always the same. What then?

Would she be happier living alone? Rettenberg might have a weakness for women but he was never violent and rarely drunk. He was an entertaining companion and a good father. She loved the children she had had by him; she did not want to take them away from their father; and she loved Soligorsk. Sometimes, idly, she would imagine what her life would have been like if she had married someone else: she ran through the list of their male friends and always concluded that on balance, if she could live her life over again, she would still marry Pavel Fedorovich Rettenberg.

Tatyana's only miscalculation had been the assumption that she would suffer most from his first infidelity; that if others were to follow, she would suffer less. She never asked and did not want to know if, after the departure of Angelica Dimitrovna, some other woman had stepped into her shoes. She spent more time at Soligorsk and less in St Petersburg, partly because she loved the quiet rhythm of country life, but also to avoid occasions of possible humiliation: she had come to suspect that any woman who approached her in a friendly way was her husband's mistress, and that people looked at her with pity whenever she entered a room.

At Soligorsk there were the children, there was the garden and there were the neighbours to keep her amused. But there was also the schoolteacher and the governess and Rettenberg's sudden interest in the school curriculum and later his declared intention to improve his already flawless French. Would he have pursued the same interests if Vera and Mademoiselle Lafay had been men? Rettenberg's mother, Olga, seemed to see nothing, but Tatyana, though she might have liked to do the same, could not fail to notice the moments when Rettenberg was absent; and these affairs with the governess and the schoolteacher, going on under her own nose, were far more painful to her than his infidelities with Princess Karsky and unknown others away from home.

Tatyana did not suffer simply as a deceived wife: she suffered on Rettenberg's behalf. How would such weakness be perceived if it became known? How could he retain the respect of his children or his authority among the peasants or his standing in the province if he came to be seen as a man who chased after any and every girl? How degrading to make love to the schoolmistress, with her bandy legs, wire-rimmed spectacles and banal revolutionary views! And the scrawny Mademoiselle Lafay with the torso of a chicken and breasts the size of scones?

Given this past history of the Rettenbergs' marriage, it was only to be expected that Tatyana Andreiovna should have regarded the advent of Alice with some dismay. It had perhaps been foolhardy to give her husband the task of finding a governess in London, but since he was to be there, it would have seemed unreasonable to give it to anyone else. A wire from London had stated simply that he was returning with an English governess; and only a further wire from the Friedrichstrasse station in Berlin had added that the governess was a widow and in fact French.

The first look at Alice had filled Tatyana with dread. What possible reason could Rettenberg have had for bringing such a beautiful woman into the house other than to seduce her – that is, if he had not seduced her already? Quite clearly, she was not even a governess. She could no doubt speak English, and Tatyana knew that a woman with a university degree was less common in England than in Russia; but she seemed altogether too *mondaine* to sit in the schoolroom at Soligorsk day after day teaching English grammar to Fedor and Nina and explaining the works of Shakespeare, Byron and Oscar Wilde.

Instead of tackling her husband on this subject, and making her own feelings known, Tatyana waited while he washed and changed. When he emerged from his bedroom he gave her the gifts he had bought for her, among them a jigsaw puzzle – Tatyana Andreiovna spent much of her time doing jigsaw puzzles – and sheet music from Paris. Then, together, they walked down the corridor to visit Rettenberg's mother, Olga Pavlovna.

Rettenberg's mother still slept in the principal bedroom at Soligorsk. It was a large, light room with a balcony that looked on to the garden. Next to it, almost as large, and connected by double doors, was another room, filled with bric-a-brac and clutter. In his lifetime, this had been the dressing room of Olga's husband, Fedor Mikhailovich. Now it was here that Olga Pavlovna spent most of her day. If she chose not to come down for meals, food would be brought to her here by her companion Zlata, a woman from the village almost as old as Olga Pavlovna herself.

Rettenberg and Tatyana found Olga Pavlovna seated in an armchair with Zlata on a stool beside her. Olga was trying to do petit point for a cushion cover, but even with spectacles, her eyes were frail, and every now and then she had to hand the frame to Zlata. Zlata would then put the needle through the cloth and hand the set back to Olga Pavlovna, who would then draw the wool through with a short grunt of satisfaction. Every now and then, Olga Pavlovna would drop the needle or break the thread and snap at Zlata as if it was her fault. Zlata would grumble back. Neither paid any attention to what the other was saying but both looked up with pleasure when Pavel and Tatyana entered the room.

'So, Zlata, you're still alive,' said Rettenberg in a bantering tone.

'Only just,' said Zlata.

'You'll outlive us all.'

'It's for the Lord to decide.'

'As if he didn't have more important things to think about,' said Olga Pavlovna, putting aside her embroidery. Though ostensibly religious, constantly confessing, attending every rite and ritual at the monastery, and plaguing the Abbot with her demands, a mischievous glint came into her eye whenever anyone talked about God. 'Now come,' she said, 'come and sit down . . .' She pointed to the shabby Empire sofa that faced her. 'Tell me about London and the racehorse, Saladin. I don't like that name at all. An infidel. No good Christian will back him with a name like that. And you paid twenty thousand pounds. Can I really afford a sum like that?'

'You can't buy a stallion with a good pedigree for less.'

'I only hope that you weren't throwing my money around simply to impress your friends in the Jockey Club.'

'What other reason could there be?'

'I hear you dined with the King.'

'Not alone, Mother. There were a great many others.'

'Varvana had a letter from the Lützow woman. Apparently you left early.'

'I was feeling unwell.'

Olga Pavlovna looked sceptically at her son. 'All that Brown Windsor soup?'

Rettenberg smiled.

'And who else did you see besides the Cobbs? What about the Gravesends and the St Gileses?' Olga Pavlovna went through a list of names of people from the racing world who had been friends or acquaintances of her husband.

Rettenberg gave an account of his stay in England – listing the country houses where he had spent the weekend, the studs he had visited, the dinners he had attended in London, including a more detailed description of the evening at Buckingham Palace – which his mother listened to with a slight frown on her face as if at any moment he might make a mistake in reciting a poem he was supposed to have learned by heart. When his report was finished, however, the frown turned to a look of satisfaction. On the face of it, her son had done well.

'And this governess?' Olga Pavlovna said finally. 'I thought we were to have an English woman, not another French girl.'

'Yes,' said Rettenberg, picking up his mother's embroidery frame as if suddenly interested in the stitching. 'I went to all the agencies and asked if anyone knew of someone who would suit us; but to be honest, the women I interviewed were all so prim . . . and dull.'

'Prim,' said Olga Pavlovna. 'We don't mind "prim", do we, Tatyana?'

'And dull,' Rettenberg repeated before his wife could reply. 'There's no point bringing a woman to Russia who would put the children off English altogether.'

'And what about a young man? Fedor might have preferred a young man whom he could take shooting.'

'Again, I asked if there was anyone suitable, and there were one or two possibilities, but then I met Madame Chambon and she seemed to be just the thing. She is fluent in English, speaks some German and is learning Russian.'

'I don't pay a governess to come and learn Russian,' said Olga Pavlovna.

'Of course not, Mother, but you know what a burden these women become if they can't speak a word of it.'

'Hmm.' Olga Pavlovna turned to her daughter-in-law. 'What do you think?

Tatyana glanced at her husband. 'I do not quite understand why someone with Madame Chambon's ... abilities should want to bury herself in Russia.'

'No,' said Olga Pavlovna, turning sharply towards her son. 'She's extremely attractive, after all. Why on earth would she want to live here in the middle of nowhere?'

'She's very recently widowed, Mother.'

'Well, it's unlikely that she'll find a new husband here.'

'She wants to get over her grief.'

'Her grief?' Again, Olga Pavlovna darted a sceptical look at her son.

'And give birth to her child.'

Rettenberg imparted this news in a most casual tone of voice as if it was a wholly unexceptional reason for someone to want to stay at Soligorsk, but if he had hoped that in this way it would pass without notice, he was disabused by a muted cry from Tatyana, followed by a long silence as his mother's face darkened and became set with a look of rage. Even Zlata, who normally sat among them as if she was a piece of furniture with no eyes or ears, looked briefly at Rettenberg as if to say, 'Now you've gone too far.'

Rettenberg glanced at Tatyana. She turned sharply away to hide her tears. 'It did not seem a good enough reason not to employ her,' said Rettenberg.

'And when is the child due?' asked Olga Pavlovna, a terrible menace in her voice.

'Towards the end of the year, I believe,' said Rettenberg casually. 'In late November or early December.' He then watched his mother as she began to count back nine months. Tatyana made the calculation more quickly than her mother-in-law:

there came from her another suppressed sob, this time of relief. Rettenberg had not left Russia until May.

Olga Pavlovna, too, had finally understood that the governess's child could not be Rettenberg's: the look of fury abated. 'Even so,' she said, 'has the girl no parents who could have looked after her?'

'They are facing difficult times. She has to earn her own living.'

'And what about her husband's family?'

'They disowned their son when he married ... Madame Chambon.'

'Why?'

'They were snobs.'

'Ah.' This was a shrewd card to have played, because Olga Pavlovna, coming herself from the merchant class, disliked snobs.

'But how will it look?' She turned to Tatyana to add with a glance a question that remained unspoken: 'What will people think?'

Tatyana had not yet recovered from her sense of relief. 'I can quite see,' she said, 'that it would have been un-Christian to refuse to employ Madame Chambon simply because she is expecting a child. Widows and orphans, after all, have first call on our charity.'

Olga Pavlovna seemed satisfied with this formula. 'I shall ask Father Yosef, but I am sure that what you say is true.' She turned to her son. 'And she *is* a widow, is she?'

'So it would seem,' said Rettenberg.

'So it would seem? Hmm. Well, that's good enough, I suppose.' She turned to Zlata. 'Madame Chambon is a widow, Zlata, and I don't want any of the servants saying anything else.'

'I dare say they'll call her mamzel as they did the last one all the same.'

Rettenberg now left his mother and his wife to go to his study in a summerhouse tucked away at the corner of the garden. He had made the move from the library in the house to escape interruption at a time when he had to work hard on speeches for the Duma, or on articles for newspapers and political reviews. That this summerhouse had also been used to discuss school curricula and practise his French, and would, he hoped, in due course be a place to discuss philosophy and literature with Alice Fry, did not detract from its original function – a haven where Rettenberg could concentrate on anything from his correspondence to the estate accounts.

This summerhouse, built in the form of a Doric temple, had been deliberately left by Rettenberg in a poor state of repair. Paint flaked from the damp that came through the walls in patches, and there were gaps between some of the panes of glass and the rotting wood of the window frame which held them. The stone-flagged floor was covered with an old rug that had been thrown out of the house because it had been chewed by the dogs; and the furniture – a heavy oak desk, a swivel chair, a button-backed sofa – had all been taken from the attics where it had been stored. Rettenberg had not wanted to risk any valuable pieces in the summerhouse in its current condition, and though he had had it in mind for a number of years to restore and redecorate this tempietta, the thought of the disruption had been enough to put him off. Even if the work had been done while he was abroad, he would have had to sort through his notebooks and papers and lock some of them away.

Also, this was a corner where he could escape from his own fastidiousness – be a slovenly Russian rather than a pedantic German. Catching the breezes, the summerhouse was cool in summer and, with a large stove, warm in winter. Occasionally Pytor or old Nikifor – but only one of these two men – was permitted to sweep up the dead insects from under the windows and shake the rug on the lawns. It was above all a place to escape from all pervading influence of women at Soligorsk – a male haven with the smell of cigars in the folds of the old curtains, and the chesterfield, with its scuffed leather and broken buttons, like the couch in a doctor's surgery, on which Rettenberg could entertain women who were not his mother, his sister, his daughter or his wife.

Though at such times Rettenberg took some pleasure in the

different contrasts – the smell of tobacco and a woman's scent; the bristle of the rug and smooth white cotton; and finally scuffed brown leather and soft pink skin – the summerhouse was more often used as a place to think and to work. Now, newly returned from western Europe, there were a number of matters awaiting Rettenberg's attention – letters from relatives, friends and former political colleagues; decisions to be made about the estate and the stud here in Soligorsk, and the saw mill and sugar beet factory in which he had invested his mother's money.

There were also requests from the peasants to buy certain tracts of land – a right given by Stolypin's reforms which Rettenberg had supported, but which were opposed by the village elders, who preferred the communal ownership of land. Rettenberg was the final arbiter on every case and, since the peasants could rarely read or write, he had to deal with them face to face. Even as he sat in the summerhouse sifting through the papers that he had brought from the house, he knew that, waiting for a summons, were the manager of the estate and the stud, a deputation of three from the village elders, and a number of other supplicants who wanted him to use his influence in some petty wrangle with a neighbour, the local Land Captain or the police.

With all these matters, great and small, calling for his attention, and the demands made on him by his family after such a long absence, Rettenberg had no time to consider how the new governess was settling in. He saw Alice at meals but she sat where the governesses always sat, beyond the children at the far end of the table. Moreover, the conversation at table was mostly in Russian and her fluency was not yet sufficient to enable her to join in. When Rettenberg asked his wife Tatyana how the first lessons had gone with Madame Chambon, Tatyana said, almost grudgingly: 'The children seem to like her.' And his mother, Olga Pavlovna, said of Alice, 'She isn't a chatterer, is she, your Madame Chambon' – leaving Rettenberg uncertain, as so often, as to whether this was a compliment or a complaint.

Less than a month after Rettenberg had returned to Russia with Alice, his second purchase, Saladin, arrived at Soligorsk. Pytor had gone to meet the horse at Riga and had brought him by train to the station at Morsansk. From here he had ridden Saladin at an easy pace to Soligorsk, arriving at five in the afternoon.

When the news reached the house, the whole household ran to the stud to greet the grand stallion. A pony and trap had been brought from the stables to take Olga Pavlovna and Zlata. The rest walked, Rettenberg leading, with Fedor at his side, Tatyana following with Nina and Alice – Nina now familiar enough with her governess to drag her across the lawns by the hand.

There, in the courtyard of the stud, stood Saladin, held proudly by Pytor and circled by an admiring group of stable boys and grooms. The horse's narrow head turned as if to greet its new owners, who stood to admire it with Olga Pavlovna in the trap behind. They all marvelled at the fine neck and sleek flanks of the stallion. Even Olga Pavlovna, though she did not leave the trap, grunted with satisfaction. Rettenberg himself was well satisfied, first that Saladin had made the long journey without mishap; and second that both his mother and the stud manager, Maxim Markov, approved of his choice. 'A really fine horse,' said Maxim Lvovich. 'He'll father a race of champions.'

Tatyana and the two children also seemed delighted, and they followed as Saladin was led away to a loose box. The trap, driven by old Nikifor, turned to take Olga Pavlovna and Zlata back to the house and Rettenberg found himself standing next to Alice.

'What do you think?'

'He's a fine horse,' said Alice. 'But then I thought so before.'

'Of course. You saw him at Epsom.'

'And at Nester,' said Alice. 'We're really quite old friends.' She then turned away from the racehorse, and as she did so, Rettenberg could see that tears had come into her eyes.

Five

From the very first, despite its strangeness, Alice felt content at Soligorsk. She was not happy; she had not expected to be happy or, for that matter, ever to be happy again; but she was less unhappy than she might have been and it was only the sight of Saladin that had made her feel sufficiently sorry for herself to cry. It was not that she was sorry about Edward: here her fury numbed the pain. It was rather that Saladin had reminded her of England and England of her parents. She had not realised, until she reached Soligorsk, how very much she loved them; how patient and kind they had been to her; and how, other things being equal, she might have been able to support them in their present ordeal.

Had she acted selfishly in running away? No. Though nothing had been said, her mother had known the true reason, the wretched unborn child. The disgrace would have compounded the scandal; the newspapers would have portrayed her as a slut; and the prosecuting counsel at her father's trial would have produced her predicament as proof that *The Sexual Nature of Woman* had a tendency to corrupt and deprave.

Yet she *had* run away, giving little thought as to where she was going and with whom. Might it not have been better to hide in one of those grim convents in France where fallen women went to have their babies, which were then given up for adoption? Or should she have gone to study in Leipzig, or emigrated to Australia, or the United States? All these things might have been possible but they would have taken time to prepare; and at that awful moment, when everything wretched seemed to be happening to her at once, Alice did not feel that she had any time. She had to go far away and at once.

So she had set off with Rettenberg to Russia. What had she thought of her employer? She had not thought of him at all. She had, perhaps naïvely, taken him at face value – a middle-aged Baltic baron who had come to England to buy a racehorse and hire a governess for his children. At first he had seemed slightly dull; he was a tall man with a thick neck and slightly receding hair. Then, to her surprise, the Baron had shown a different, slightly seamy side, when he had returned that morning to the suite in the St James and Albany still wearing his evening clothes. But that odd impression had been effaced by the easy-going way in which he had let her know that he knew she was pregnant, and his audacious proposal to change her identity from the English spinster, Miss Alice Fry, to the French widow, Madame Chambon.

As soon as the Nord Express had reached Moscow, Alice had send a telegram to her parents.

HAVE ARRIVED SAFELY STOP TELL NO ONE WHERE I HAVE GONE STOP ALL LETTERS TO BE ADDRESSED TO MADAME ALICE CHAMBON STOP WILL WRITE STOP ALICE.

Alice liked the idea of disappearing off the face of the earth. It made things simpler but also more dramatic and mysterious. One day, perhaps, when the baby was off her hands, she might tell Vivien and Maud where she was; or she might simply reappear in London speaking Russian like a native: that rather depended on the outcome of her father's trial. In her first letter home she asked them to tell her every detail of the case.

Please don't spare me any of the horrors: I would much rather know what vile things are being said than imagine them; and it will make it easier to bear not being with you if I can feel I am sharing in your suffering, even from so far away. But you must promise me one thing: when the whole thing is over, never again have anything to do with your treacherous friend George Greaves. He is to blame for all that happened. He deceived you and took advantage of your trust.

I am known here as Madame Chambon. Baron Rettenberg felt it would be more suitable to employ a governess who was a pregnant widow than a spinster about to give birth to an illegitimate child. How he knew of my condition, I do not know; but the fact is that he did and, rather than leave me in Paris or turn me off the train in Berlin, he came up with this solution. Madame Chambon's husband, Lieutenant Chambon, was killed by Bedouin rebels in Morocco. The role suits me fine. I do not have to pretend to feel sad.

Soligorsk is a beautiful house with large light rooms on the ground floor and a dozen bedrooms above. All sorts of outbuildings form a courtyard behind the house, among them a shed for an electrical generator and a bathhouse where you sit virtually naked in piping-hot steam and then are beaten lightly with birch twigs by one of the maids, which has a most exhilarating effect.

There must be a dozen servants around the house but it is difficult to discover who does what. There is an old man called Nikifor who wears a shabby tail coat and pours the wine at dinner but I would hesitate to call him a butler: he is more a kind of major-domo. Another old retainer seems to have the single task of seeing to the candles that burn in front of the icons on the ground floor. There are a number of cheerful girls who work as maids; they clean my room and wash my clothes and seem highly amused by some of my wardrobe which is, of course, unsuitable for country life. I have yet to work out where all these servants sleep; some, undoubtedly, sleep in the house and perhaps others come up from the village, but I doubt it because the peasants in the village are extraordinarily dirty whereas the servants in the house are clean. But the maids go barefoot. Apparently they prefer it!

Once they've done their mopping and dusting, they scuttle back to the kitchen, where clearly the main life of the house goes on. Elizaveta the cook (who is married to Nikifor) was trained by the Rettenbergs' old chef. He died only last year aged eighty-two! Apparently as a young man he was sent to be trained in Paris! Elizaveta has unquestionably learned some of his skills: the food is delicious. She takes enormous trouble in preparing it; and Soligorsk has its own bakery so there is fresh bread for breakfast, and at other times during the day the most delicious smells waft into the house – of pastry, cinnamon and icing sugar – and at tea you see the results – wonderful cakes and biscuits and brioches covered with almonds and sugar. And they eat jam with spoons without spreading it on bread and butter!

My 'employer', strictly speaking, is Baroness Rettenberg,

Tatyana Andreiovna. She is friendly enough but somewhat distant. She plays the piano beautifully – mostly melancholy pieces by Chopin and Schumann. Sometimes she summons me to play a duet. When not playing she is to be found bent over a jigsaw on a table in the salon. She sometimes looks wistful, even sad, and perhaps is bored but is too lazy to do anything about it. She shows very little interest in what I am to teach the children. Every time we discuss it, her eyes glaze over and she ends up saying, 'I'm sure you know best.' How can I know best? I've never taught children before.

But it is just as well that Tatyana Andreiovna is fairly passive because she would otherwise come into constant conflict with the dowager baroness, Olga Pavlovna. She is everything Tatyana is not. Tatyana is fair, Olga Pavlovna is dark; Tatyana is tall, Olga Pavlovna is short; Tatyana is thin, Olga Pavlovna is – well, not fat but dense. One might say that the Baron had chosen a wife who was as unlike his mother as possible! Olga Pavlovna must be aged around seventy but she has bursts of tremendous energy and a will of iron. Everyone is terrified of her. When she emerges from her upstairs boudoir, the maids who have been lounging around giggling and chatting suddenly busy themselves with their mops and feather dusters. Olga Pavlovna, as she passes, runs her finger along the tops of the furniture to make sure they have been properly cleaned. She hates to see anyone idle – once when addressed by Olga Pavlovna a girl in the bakery stopped kneading the dough. 'Come along,' said Olga Pavlovna, 'you can talk and work.'

I don't see much of the Baron. He is often away at race meetings or on business in St Petersburg. When he is here, he is kept busy running the estate. He works either in the library or he escapes to a folly in the garden – a kind of stone summerhouse – where no one is allowed to disturb him. Neither Tatyana Andreiovna nor Olga Pavlovna shows much interest in me: I think both are puzzled by my presence and somehow suspicious – and who can blame them? The only thing to get Tatyana Andreiovna to bestir herself is tennis. There is a wonderful new court built last year by workmen from East Prussia; and since the Baron and Maxim Lvovich, who manages the estate and the stud, are mostly too busy (and anyway, Tatyana told me that she hates playing with her husband), and the children not up to her standard, she plays with me, *faute de mieux*. We are quite evenly matched: but despite the handicap of my condition, I beat her today!

I have a beautiful large room overlooking the garden and I am happy to spend much of my time alone. There are many French books in the library; and I have set myself a target of learning ten new Russian words every day. But the most pleasant surprise is the children – Fedor, aged twelve, and Nina, aged ten. Nina is particularly enchanting; she has taken it upon herself to show me every nook and cranny of the estate. She is small and dark – a little like her grandmother, perhaps, but with lovely brown eyes. I have become her 'property'; she doesn't like me to do anything with anyone else. Fedor, her brother, is allowed to tag along if we go for a walk, and he will assert himself when it comes to manly things like the gun room or the stud. He has a fiery disposition but adores his father, and his father seems to adore him. There is none of the stiffness between father and son that you find in England. The Baron is unembarrassed to lift Fedor up into his arms and hug him. They tell me that it is unheard of to beat boys in Russian schools.

All in all, dear Maman and Papa, I feel I have been magically transported on to the stage of a Chekhov play. I have yet to meet the doctor, or an Uncle Vanya, though Maxim Lvovich may turn out to play a similar role: he is some sort of poor relation of Tatyana Andreiovna. There is a village schoolteacher called Vera whom I have yet to meet. I mean to suggest that we exchange lessons in conversational Russian and conversational English or French. Baron Rettenberg is against this idea but he doesn't explain why.

I will write again as soon as I reach Act I, Scene 2. In the mean time, all my love.

Alice

The first difference of opinion witnessed by Alice between Baron Rettenberg and his mother was over which neighbours should be invited to dine at Soligorsk. It opened with Olga Pavlovna saying, 'We must have the Troganovs. And the Boborokins – their daughter's playing is now really very good; and I think you know that Father Boris and Aroadna Mikhailovna are coming this afternoon.' She turned to her son. 'I do hope you won't shut yourself away.'

Alice noticed a look of contained irritation come on to Rettenberg's face. 'I am extremely busy at the moment, Mother.'

'At the moment! You're always busy, but no amount of business can excuse incivility.'

'But I have nothing to say to Father Boris, or the Troganovs and the Boborokins, and I am sure they have nothing to say to me.'

'But of course you have plenty to say to the Bieletskys! It won't be long, I dare say, before we see some of them at Soligorsk.'

'The Bieletskys are part of the family, Mother.'

'Not of my family!' She darted a look of fury at Tatyana.

'They're my cousins by marriage.'

'And the Troganovs and the Boborokins are my friends!'

In due course, when the short bearded priest, Father Boris, and his dull, plain wife, Aroadna, had come to tea and Olga Pavlovna was seated by the samovar, Rettenberg did indeed emerge from his summerhouse and talk politely to his mother's guests. It was the same when the Troganovs and the Boborokins came to dinner; the former, the local lawyer who dealt with some of the Rettenbergs' minor affairs, the latter, a merchant who owned a saw mill and the franchise for Singer Sewing Machines. The lawyer was a small, meek man with a wife who was also small but far from meek; she talked continuously in a shrill voice, retailing all the local gossip with a malicious delight, but larding her spite with unctuous flattery of Olga Pavlovna.

In the drawing room after dinner, the merchant's fourteen-year-old daughter played her violin, accompanied on the piano by Tatyana Andreiovna. Olga Pavlovna sat in her armchair with a look of immense satisfaction, as if she were an empress holding court surrounded by colourful boyars. The Boborokins, like the Troganovs, seemed ill-at-ease throughout the evening, as if they were not quite sure of how to behave in a house as grand as Soligorsk. They took any opening in the conversation to flatter Olga Pavlovna – 'Oh, the child's talent is nothing to someone who must have heard all the greatest violinists play in St Petersburg . . .' giving the old lady a chance to reminisce about how she had been present when Tchaikovsky himself had conducted the first performance of his Symphony No. 6 in St Petersburg.

No doubt the Troganovs and the Boborokins had heard all this before. Certainly, it seemed familiar to Pavel and Tatyana. They did not look bored. They went along with Olga Pavlovna's pretence that the company was as fine as the food and wine that had been served at her table; Rettenberg even pressed his mother's guests to linger when Olga Pavlovna seemed to want them to go; and when they had gone, joined his mother and Tatyana in a 'post-mortem' which concluded that the whole evening had been a great success.

As a quid pro quo, the younger Rettenbergs were allowed to invite their own friends to Soligorsk, and on these occasions, Alice noticed, the Baron found that the demands of his work had become less pressing. They came sometimes for the day, sometimes for the weekend, or they would join the Rettenbergs for picnics or swimming parties on a nearby lake. They were all civil to Alice and a number took advantage of her to practise their English, or show off their fluency in the language to their friends. She was sometimes summoned to make up a four at tennis, and while no one was unfriendly, there were some whose manner seemed designed to remind Alice that she was the Rettenbergs' governess, not one of their friends.

This was not true of Maxim Lvovich Markov, the poor relative of Tatyana Andreiovna who managed the stud and the estate, and Sophie Kyrillovna, his wife. Maxim was a decent, straightforward man with an open, almost naïve look on his face. He was well built, with dark curly hair: he loved and lived for the country, preferring animals to human beings 'because with animals you know where you are'. Sophie, his wife, as if to make up for her husband's simplicity, was cunning and cynical. She was suitably deferential to Olga Pavlovna and Tatyana Andreiovna, and was always cheerful in the company of her grand relatives and the Rettenbergs' friends; but in her heart, Alice was to discover, she could not forgive them for being so rich when she and Maxim were so poor.

Treating Alice at first with caution, Sophie Kyrillovna soon seemed to decide that she might make a friend. She invited her to tea in their modest single-storey house close to the stud; introduced her to her own two small children – a girl and a boy – and said that Alice was welcome to come there whenever she chose. 'Have you yet come across Olga Pavlovna in one of her rages? It's like a tornado – she flattens anything that comes in her path. But she never comes here; it's too far for her to walk and not far enough to harness up the pony and trap. She's not really interested in the stud. She sinks her money into it simply for the prestige. She thinks quite rightly that it gives Pavel Fedorovich an entrée into the smartest circles. Did you know that he had dinner with the King of England?

'She's probably rather wary of you because she can't quite place you and you have a university degree,' Sophie went on. 'She's wary of Tatyana, too, because she comes from a grand family, while the Budarovs, Olga Pavlovna's parents, as you probably know, were simply merchants. Really quite vulgar. And she's bourgeois at heart. That's why she lives in that horrible room next to her bedroom. Have you seen inside it? It's got all the clutter and vulgarity of the little house where she lived as a child. But then her father bought Soligorsk, and she's proud of Soligorsk and she won't allow Zlata to forget that she was born a serf. Did you know that Zlata is paid nothing? Not a kopek. Maxim once suggested that she should receive something and Olga Pavlovna flew into a rage. And of course, Zlata dare not ask for anything. Olga Pavlovna gives her her old clothes and has paid for her nephew Yakov to be trained as a priest. She loves to play the *grande dame* but in her heart she knows it's just a sham and she's quite aware that people see through her. That's why she feels quite ill-at-ease with people like the Bieletskys. She likes the idea of having a prince in her house, but she can't escape the feeling that they look down on her, which indeed they do. She only really feels at ease with people she can patronise, like the Troganovs and the Boborokins; and of course the priests, she loves the priests. Have you been to the monastery? Well, the abbot there's her closest friend. And the *starets*, Father Yosef. She bores him to death with her sins. But she gives generously to the monks, so they don't complain.'

Maxim looked pained if he heard Sophie speak of Olga Pavlovna in this way. 'You're unfair to her, Sophie. If it wasn't for her . . .'

'Oh, I know,' said Sophie. 'One shouldn't bite the hand that feeds one.' She turned to Alice. 'You'll find that too. But I advise you to keep your distance. She'll make all sorts of friendly gestures but then decide that you are getting too familiar and slap you down.'

Alice first met the oldest and grandest of the Rettenbergs' friends, Prince Vassily Bieletsky, at dinner at Soligorsk in late August. As she had learned from Sophie, the Bieletskys' neighbouring estate was three times the size of the Rettenbergs' and the present Prince's grandfather, before the liberation of the serfs, was the owner of over five thousand souls. So great was the Bieletsky fortune that Prince Vassily's dissipated youth had made only insignificant inroads: he had had to sell an estate that had belonged to his mother to pay off his debts. He was a cheerful, affable man – now aged around sixty – who exercised his charm on all around him. But he viewed the world *de haut en bas* and was quickly irritated if things did not go according to plan. His arrogance was expressed as a form of puzzlement: after being introduced to Alice at Soligorsk, and seeing her accompany them into the dining room, he bent over and said in an audible whisper to Rettenberg: 'So governesses dine with us nowadays, do they? Well, I suppose we have to move with the times.'

Prince Bieletsky's wife, Irina Yurevna, was the first cousin of Tatyana Andreiovna's mother – this was the link that enabled

Rettenberg to claim them as kin. Her father had been a minister under Nicholas I and her brother was an equerry to the Tsar. When Alice was introduced to her, she leaned forward and peered at her through her lorgnette. 'Is that gown French?'

'Yes. It was made by Worth.'

'Hmph.' She turned to Tatyana Andreiovna. 'A governess dressed by Worth! Really, what will we see next?'

Ekaterina Grigorievna, married to the Bieletskys' eldest son Grigory, also seemed disturbed to see a governess so elegantly dressed. A sturdy woman of around thirty, with a restless, bustling energy, she had also noticed the sudden vivacity in her husband Grisha, who was placed next to Alice at dinner. With an endearing disdain for duplicity, she leaned across the table and said to Tatyana in a loud whisper: 'Why couldn't Pavel Fedorovich have found someone a little more plain?' She then turned to Rettenberg, who was sitting next to her. 'One of those frumpy English spinsters? Weren't there any of those around? She'll cause trouble, mark my words, that French widow of yours.'

Grigory Bieletsky, her husband, turned to Alice. 'I understand that you have a university degree?'

'Yes.'

'From the Sorbonne?'

'From London University.'

'But I thought you were French?'

'I am, but my mother is English.'

'And you married a French officer?'

'He was killed in Morocco only a few months ago.'

'I am so sorry.'

Alice lowered her head to acknowledge his condolences.

'Our Caucasus, what?'

'I beg your pardon?'

'Morocco. Our Caucasus.'

'I dare say.'

Sitting on the other side of Alice at this dinner was Pytor Loputkin who, after one or two attempts to engage Alice in conversation – or, more precisely, to disengage her from Grigory Bieletsky – finally succeeded and, as if to prove Katya

Bieletsky right, looked at Alice with greedy eyes. He was, he explained, a government inspector of schools but his wife Dora – he nodded towards a woman sitting opposite him who had attracted Alice's attention for the frumpiness of her dress and her unkempt hair – was the younger sister of Natasha Alexovna.

'Perhaps you haven't met her yet?' said Loputkin. 'She has the estate adjoining the Bieletskys' – ten thousand hectares or more, a really substantial holding – and of course my wife Dora had her portion which enabled us – because I admit quite freely that I come from a less illustrious family – but with this portion behind us we were able to take our honeymoon in Paris. And that is why I am so delighted to make your acquaintance because you know, you surely know, that small restaurant on the corner of the Boulevard St Germain and the rue Grégoire which serves roast duckling with a Calvados glaze? You don't know it? You *must* know it! I can't believe that anyone who lives in Paris ... ah, you have lived in London. I see. Well, we also went to London and there, one has to admit, the food is not as good but I do remember, at the Savoy – yes, we really treated ourselves very well, but one only marries once! Oysters à la Russe, consommé Olga, filets mignon Lili, asparagus with a champagne and saffron vinaigrette and, of course, Waldorf pudding!' Loputkin's eyes gazed into the middle distance as he relived in reverie these gastronomic delights.

In due course, the school inspector's sister-in-law, Natasha Alexovna Voyeikov, came to Soligorsk with her husband, a retired but high-ranking civil servant; and another land-owning lady, Evgenia Purichievitch, with her husband, the local Land Captain, Leonid. At first Alice was confused by the advent of these new acquaintances with unpronounceable names, but after a while it became clear that there were no more than half a dozen households within the ambit of Soligorsk and that, with some minor variations, the guests were always the same.

There were, of course, visits by the Rettenbergs to the other houses to which Alice was not asked. On these occasions she remained at Soligorsk with Olga Pavlovna, who, though invited, invariably excused herself on the grounds of her age. There were occasions, however, when Olga Pavlovna, with a malicious look in her eyes, announced that she *would* come after all. 'She knows quite well she's not wanted,' Sophie told Alice, 'and she hates the Bieletskys, but she goes just to spoil everybody else's fun.'

By tradition, in mid-September, on the feast of St Alexander Nevsky, the local land-owning families gathered for the last picnic of the season by the small lake on the borders of the Rettenbergs' and the Bieletskys' estates. Alice noted an unusual bustle in the kitchen at Soligorsk the day before as pastries and cold meats were prepared for the picnic. At ten the next morning, the servants loaded three light wicker carts – *teleshki* – with the awnings, the samovar, the food and wine, and those who chose to walk to the lake set off followed by the bounding dogs.

Alice, because of her now quite evident condition, rode with Nina and the Markovs' small children on cushions placed at the back of one of the *teleshki*. As the sunlight filtered through the leaves of the trees and she inhaled the air scented with pine and herbs, still cool from the night, she felt a great sense of well-being. Nina chattered away; the child occasionally kicked in her womb as Alice brushed away the few flies that buzzed around her with a switch cut from elderflower by the taciturn Pytor who drove the cart.

When they reached the clearing, while Nina scampered off to meet the walkers, Alice sat down on a mound at some distance from the trestle tables, where she was joined by Sophie, who arrived on a horse.

'Here we go again,' said Sophie.

'But don't you enjoy it?' said Alice, looking up at the sunlight where it broke through the leaves of the tall trees.

'It's always the same people, over and over again. You'd think they'd get sick of one another, but they never do.'

'It is surprising,' said Alice, 'that all the relatives seem to be neighbours and all the neighbours relatives. Is it just a coincidence that Pytor Loputkin is a school inspector and Leonid Purichievitch a Land Captain in the province where their wives own estates?'

'And Lev Pavlovich Donat . . . You haven't met him yet, but he's coming today. He had a good post teaching philosophy at Kiev; he would certainly have become a professor in due course; but he no sooner marries Anna Vassilyevna than he comes to live here in a small house on his father-in-law's estate, supposedly writing a book that in fact never gets written. They continually humiliate him but he puts up with it for the joy of being the son-in-law of a prince. And that's true of all of them. They cluster round their family estates because it inflates their sense of self-importance . . . But here's one who got away, or we thought had got away, but even he's back . . .'

A genial young man, looking younger than he was, perhaps, because of the fatuous smile on his face, came towards them, greeted Sophie Kyrillovna, and after introducing himself to Alice as Georg, the youngest son of Prince Bieletsky, talked about this and that, and then ambled away.

'He's a disciple of Gurdjieff,' said Sophie Kyrillovna. 'He was about to marry a perfectly nice girl when suddenly he found truth or enlightenment or whatever you like to call it. All completely incomprehensible, but he'll bore you with it if you give him half a chance.'

'And what do his parents think?'

'Whisper the word "Gurdjieff" into the ear of Prince Bieletsky and you'll see. He explodes every time he's mentioned. "That damned charlatan" – that sort of thing. He's afraid Georg will give all his money to "the movement" and that later they'll have to bail him out. Irina Yurevna, of course, is more understanding. Georg always was his mother's boy. In her eyes, he can do no wrong. She even pretends to be interested in Gurdjieff herself but she's far too intelligent to fall for that mumbo-jumbo.'

Alice listened, amused, as Sophie prattled away in excellent French. When they were called to the trestle tables, now laid with a variety of cold meats, pies, pasties, salads, tarts and cakes, Sophie helped Alice to get to her feet. 'The last six weeks are the worst,' she said, looking at Alice's belly, 'but it's worse when it's hot and by the end of September it should have cooled down.'

'*Ah, die Gouvernante,*' said a scrawny man crossing the glade to meet Alice. '*Und man sagt dass Sie sind Magister der Literatur . . .*' He introduced himself as Lev Pavlovich Donat. 'Donat's a Baltic name,' he went on in German. 'We were the poor pagans converted at the point of a sword by the Rettenbergs and Benkendorffs and Rennenkampfs of this world. And then we married Russians – you've met my wife, haven't you?' A small, delicate woman was busying herself with seating the children. 'Anna, my dear,' he said in French, 'you must meet Madame Chambon.'

Anna Vassilyevna turned. 'Ah, yes. The governess. We've heard so much about you. You are French and yet lived in England, is that right? And your husband – how dreadful, how cruel . . . and yet we must see it as an honour that the Lord permits us to share His suffering . . .'

'No theology, dearest, not now, please.'

Anna Vassilyevna swallowed as if this was the best way to hold back what she *might* have said. 'You must sit down, my dear,' she said to Alice. 'I know what it's like – where are you, the seventh month? I've had five of them and I can tell you . . .' – she sat down at the table next to Alice and lowered her voice – 'you must make sure you have Dr Schimpfel to attend to you. Olga Pavlovna's come down against him because he's a German, but Dr Kukolnik is really no use at all. An amiable fellow, but he knows no medicine, so pay no attention if Olga Pavlovna tries to send you to him. You can be sure that if there was anything seriously wrong with *her*, she'd call on Schimpfel.'

'Yes,' said Alice. 'That was Baron Rettenberg's advice.'

'Of course. Pavel Fedorovich is sound on things like that. And I have to say that I'm pleasantly surprised that he found someone like you for Fedor and Nina. The older two – you won't have met them yet – they had the run-of-the mill governesses who taught them to speak French all right, but didn't open their minds. That's what Pavel hopes for from you, I think? That you will open their minds?'

'I shall do my best.'

'You must open them wide,' said Anna. 'The real problem here in Russia is that people's minds are opened so far, and in pour all the silly ideas of the Encyclopaedists, John Stuart Mill, Darwin, Hegel and Karl Marx . . .'

'A little learning is a dangerous thing,' interposed Lev Pavlovich, draining his vodka glass and moving on to wine.

'And out goes faith in the Christian religion,' Anna went on, ignoring her husband. 'Open the mind fully, however, and you become aware of the sublime truths of religion.'

' "Mysticism is but a transcendent form of common sense",' said Lev. 'Oscar Wilde, I believe.'

'No, dearest, Thomas Carlyle,' said Anna. 'Mysticism was hardly a subject to interest Oscar Wilde.'

Alice felt that she might come to like the Donats. Lev Pavlovich showed great interest in her studies – 'Ah, Stendhal, yes, a wonderful writer, but a treacherous guide to life, wouldn't you agree, my dear?' – and seemed indifferent to the fact that she was merely a governess; and Anna Vassilyevna, though she had always to be right, was genuinely solicitous and sympathetic about Alice's fictitious predicament. 'It seems so sad,' she said, 'that you can't be with your parents . . . Your mother's an invalid? And your father weak in the mind? Yes, that's what I heard. And your husband's family?' Here Alice was more eloquent, because she made a simple substitute in her mind of Claude for Edward and so could describe in detail the dreadful snobbery of the coal-owning Chambons.

'Yes,' said Anna with a sigh. 'It's always the same with the *nouveau riche*. At least the old aristocracy have some vestige of *noblesse oblige* – but the Gradgrinds of this world – I do so love the novels of Dickens, don't you? – the Gradgrinds of this world are really worse than the landowners. That was the flaw in Stolypin's reforms. He wanted to create a middle class, but the peasants hate the *kulaks* and the bourgeois far more than they do us.'

A little further down the table, the Land Captain, Leonid Purichievitch, took this observation about the Russian peasant as a cue to give his views. 'It's all very well to generalise about the peasants, Anna Vassilyevna, but if I may say so, the peasants you see are those on your father's estate who smile and tug their forelocks and give you a false sense of what they're really like. My duties take me down to the grass roots, as it were, and there you could say a hundred different things about the peasants, all of them contradictory and all of them true. On the one hand, the peasant's a rascal. He doesn't really believe in private property; certainly not one man having more than the rest. He'll set his cows on to your father's pasture and fell your father's trees because in his heart of hearts he doesn't believe that the Prince has any more right to them than he does. But he's also generous to an insane degree. Ask any peasant for alms in the name of God and he'll give you his last kopek. And if he hasn't got that kopek, he'll borrow it from a friend. He thinks: "That man could be me. He's down on his luck and one day I'll be down on my luck."'

'True compassion,' said Anna Vassilyevna.

'True compassion, maybe, but it becomes a real problem when it comes to law and order because to the peasant a criminal is just someone who's down on his luck who God loves more than the high and mighty. He's too damned religious, our peasant. That's the problem. If he went to the sacrament in a drunken stupor the morning after murdering a man, he'd feel more guilty about the blasphemy than the crime. So I ask you, how can you bring a country into the modern world with peasants who don't believe in private property or that the law has anything much to do with right and wrong?'

'They say that Rasputin,' said Lev Pavlovich to Alice in a quiet voice, not wanting to be drawn into an argument with Leonid Purichievitch, 'believes that sin actually brings one *closer* to God than virtue. He indulges in all those monstrous orgies that one hears about and then wallows in repentance.'

'It's St Augustine's notion of the *felix culpa*,' said Anna Vassilyevna, 'but vulgarised by a scoundrel.'

'No theology, please, my dear.'

Purichievitch, finding no interest in his discourse at Alice's end of the table, turned back to Maxim Lvovich Markov, who had heard it all before but was too amiable to say so.

The lunch tapered off into the warm afternoon. The older children went to swim, the younger children ran after them and the nursemaids followed the younger children, warning them to wait or else they would get stomach cramps and drown. Alice walked with Sophie to the shore of the lake and saw, to her embarrassment, two or three of the maids who had come to prepare and serve the lunch splashing about naked in the water.

'Don't they have bathing costumes?' she asked Sophie.

Sophie glanced at the naked bathers. 'They don't even have shoes. And modesty means nothing to them. They live like beasts.'

There was little shade by the side of the lake so Alice, feeling sleepy after drinking two glasses of wine, left Sophie with her children and walked back alone to the clearing where they had had lunch. The old manservant, Nikifor, who was always solicitous about her condition, took two cushions off the back of the cart and placed one on the mound where Alice had been sitting before, and one against the tree. This was not far from the end of the table where Prince Vassily Bieletsky, his son Grisha, Alexis Voyeikov – the civil servant married to Natasha Alexovna – and Baron Rettenberg sat discussing the fate of the world.

The four men did not appear to notice Alice, which suited her fine since she hoped to doze; but in the case of Rettenberg, it also mildly annoyed her. She did not expect the Bieletskys to bring the French governess into their conversation, but the Baron, on the journey to Russia, had appeared to regard her as both a social and intellectual equal: yet since reaching Soligorsk he had hardly talked to her at all. Had his initial familiarity been simply to alleviate the tedium of the Nord Express? Or did he feel that now she was simply a governess she could not also be a friend?

Alice closed her eyes and listened: fortunately, no doubt because of the servants, they spoke mostly in French. They seemed to be considering the prospect of war. 'Inevitable,' said Prince Bieletsky, 'inevitable, inevitable, *inevitable*, and because it's inevitable, the sooner the better – over and done with, there!' He hit his fist on the table; the bottles of vodka and wine, which he had done much to empty, jumped on the planks of wood. 'The Teuton has replaced the Turk as Russia's natural antagonist. That gaga old Franz Joseph, pushed by Berlin, is moving into areas that by race and faith belong to the Slav.'

'Certainly,' said Alexis Voyeikov, the cautious civil servant, 'Russia must stand by Serbia. If we give an inch, they'll take a mile.'

'There is a view,' said Grigory Vassilyvich, 'that we shouldn't let the Serbian tail wag the Russian dog.'

'Oh, damn the Serbs,' said Grigory's father, Prince Vassily. 'It's not that little runt of a country that I care about, it's Russia and the Orthodox Church. The Turks are done for, don't you see? There's a vacuum which either the Slav or the Teuton will fill. Why did Austria annex Bosnia and Herzegovina? To give the Teutons access to the Mediterranean Sea. Why do they want to neutralise Serbia? To protect their rear. If we don't stop them now, they'll snatch Constantinople from under our nose.'

Having heard nothing from Baron Rettenberg, Alice half opened her eyes to see if he was still seated at the table. He was, but seemed content to leave the discussion to others. But now Alexis Voyeikov drew him in. 'What do you think, Pavel Fedorovich? You've been to London and to Paris. What's the feeling there?'

'That's precisely the point,' said the intoxicated Prince Bieletsky before Rettenberg could answer. 'Paris and London. The Triple Entente. There's never been a better time to deal with the Germans; they'd face a war on two fronts; and the British would deal with their navy.'

'That would be true,' said Rettenberg, 'if you think we can rely on Britain. But remember – Britain has no vital interest of her own in the Balkans and would be as unhappy to see Russia as Austria in Constantinople.'

'*Perfide Albion*,' said Grisha.

'Then to hell with the English,' said Prince Bieletsky. 'We'll fight them with the French.'

'Yes,' said Rettenberg uncertainly. 'Germany and Austria would undoubtedly be vulnerable if they were fighting a war on two fronts. A Russian attack in the east should prevent them from overrunning the French, as they did in 1870; but I am not sure for how long such an attack could be sustained. The Germans have many more railways behind their lines which would give them significant advantages in manoeuvrability and supply.'

'Are you suggesting that we aren't a match for the Germans?' asked Prince Bieletsky, growing pink in the face.

'In terms of courage, more than a match. In terms of the technology of modern warfare, I fear we lag behind.'

'So the war would have to end within six months?'

'If it lasted longer, I wouldn't guarantee the result.'

'There is a view,' said Grigory Bieletsky, 'that it would be in the best interest of Russia to come to terms with the Germans.'

'And whose view is that?' Prince Bieletsky asked his son.

'People at court. Our Tsarina's a German, after all, and the Tsar himself has more German than Russian blood.'

'Are you saying that the Tsar is a traitor?'

'Of course not, Father. But one fears he is weak. How else can we account for the influence of Rasputin? And the way the Tsar tolerates the pro-German party in the Council of the Empire and the Duma – people like Prince Mestchersky, Stcheglovitov and Baron Rosen . . .'

'Rosen, of course,' said Prince Bieletsky, 'but also Fredericks, Korff, Grunewald, Benkendorff and all the other damned Baltic Germans that hang around the court.'

'Not forgetting the Rettenbergs,' said Baron Rettenberg.

'Pavel Fedorovich, forgive me,' said Prince Bieletsky. 'Of course I don't include you. After all, you're a Russian in all but name.'

'I don't think we need to worry about the patriotism of the

Baltic Germans,' said Rettenberg. 'They ... we'll fight for Russia to the death. Far more problematical is the competence of those in control of Russia's destiny – those friends of Rasputin like Sukhomlinov.'

'His wife is thirty years younger than he is,' said Grisha. 'I dare say she takes up most of his time.'

'Oh God, poor Russia,' wailed Prince Bieletsky. 'To be run by such scoundrels at a time like this.' And, slumping forward on to the table, he hid his face in his hands to hide his tears.

Six

Confined to Soligorsk, Alice had little opportunity to meet Russians outside the circle of the Rettenbergs' friends. There were other governesses in the neighbourhood whom Tatyana Andreiovna offered, in a lukewarm way, to invite to Soligorsk; but the passivity at the core of Tatyana's character meant that she did nothing about it and Alice did not take up her offer. She was largely content. She enjoyed the company of the children; as her Russian improved, she could converse with the servants and even pay visits to their families in the nearby villages. Dr Schimpfel, who came to the house when Fedor fell ill, was delighted to converse in German and invited Alice to his house.

On Sunday mornings the whole Rettenberg family, together with their servants, went to church. At first Alice went with them; she did not take communion but there was a particularly fine choir and she enjoyed the liturgy for its aesthetic and folkloric value. However, the smell of incense and melting candle-wax made her feel faint, and the congregation remained standing throughout the long ceremony, so Alice decided that she could no longer endure it and made the burden of her baby the pretext to go for a walk instead.

One Sunday, while the Rettenbergs were at church, Alice decided to call on the schoolteacher, Vera, who lived in a small house on the edge of the village. Alice had been told that, as a proclaimed atheist, Vera never attended the liturgy; also that she lived alone without any servant to cook her food or wash her clothes. 'The stupid girl is too high-minded to have anyone sweep her floor,' Olga Pavlovna had told Alice, 'but she doesn't sweep it herself. Apparently, the place is a pigsty. That makes her feel close to the peasants, I dare say.'

It turned out that Olga Pavlovna had never visited Vera Mikhailovna in her cottage, and when Alice first went there, she found that while there was a certain amount of disorder, the house itself was not dirty and the schoolteacher's appearance was tidy and clean.

Alice was greeted with suspicion by a small, dark-haired young woman wearing wire-rimmed spectacles, a form of peasant smock and cloth slippers. She must have been around thirty, perhaps a little older. With apparent reluctance, she invited Alice into her cottage and made tea. Alice explained who she was. Vera nodded; she had heard of Alice's arrival. She avoided looking Alice in the eye, and when Alice made her proposal – that Vera should help with her Russian in exchange for Alice's help with Vera's English or French – she said nothing for quite some time, and then only remarked with some reluctance that she could not speak any English but might benefit from conversing with Alice in French. 'Not all Russians, you must realise, have French governesses.'

Alice said that she understood that perfectly well. She could easily understand how a woman who taught the peasants' children should resent the privileged education of the Retten-bergs. She wanted Vera to understand that; she wanted her to know that she was not quite what Vera seemed to think she was: that her father was a radical publisher and she herself a suffragette. Yet she also wanted to preserve her incognito as Madame Chambon, recently widowed, so at that first visit to Vera's cottage she said nothing about herself but asked Vera how she had come to be the schoolteacher at Soligorsk.

Vera's father had been a minor civil servant in Perm. Vera had a brother who had started to study engineering at St Petersburg but had fallen into bad company and dropped out.

'What do you mean by bad company?' Alice asked flippantly. 'Drunkards or revolutionaries?'

'I wouldn't call revolutionaries bad company,' Vera replied sharply.

'Oh, nor would I,' said Alice apologetically.

'No, Ivan was befriended by other students who were far richer than he was. They all drank and so he drank too. He spent far more money than my parents could afford and in the end they could send him no more, so he abandoned university and went to work for a mining company in the Urals. We never hear from him. I dare say he's ashamed.'

'Were you able to go to university?'

'There is a charitable foundation that gives scholarships to future schoolteachers. You have to commit yourself to teaching for five years after graduation in some out-of-the-way place. It's a form of indentured labour.'

'And Soligorsk qualified as an out-of-the-way place?'

'It isn't a great metropolis.'

'I had noticed.'

'I have done four years. I have one year to go.'

'And will you then move somewhere else?'

Vera hesitated. 'I'm not sure. I've become attached to many of my pupils. It's wonderful to see their horizons widen when you teach them to read and write. But the company is limited.'

'So I've noticed.'

'You at least can mix with the friends of the Rettenbergs.'

'So long as I know my place.'

Vera looked at Alice – dressed modestly but elegantly in a light dress she had bought on the rue de Rivoli – and said, almost scornfully: 'Oh, you may be just a governess but you come from France and that lot grovel before anything foreign.'

'I feel . . .' Alice began. 'I would far rather dress as you do. Perhaps you'll help me find some similar clothes.'

'There's a seamstress in the village who will make you anything you choose. And you'll find it cheaper than Paris.' Again, there was a note of contempt in Vera's voice.

A seamstress – that was a word in Russian that Alice did not know. As they had been talking – Alice stumbling every now and then over words such as 'indentured' or 'horizons' – she had been jotting down the meaning of words and phrases.

Later, when they switched to French, Vera did the same. Vera's French was not bad and in this unfamiliar language she spoke more carefully; there were no flashes of sarcasm or contempt. She now asked Alice why she had come to this 'out-of-the-way' place – Alice could think of no better translation than '*en province*', since to the French anywhere more than fifty kilometres from Paris was out-of-the-way; and Alice told yet again the story of her engagement against the wishes of his family to Claude Chambon; their elopement; his death in north Africa; her return to France to find her parents decrepit, and her child and herself rejected by her husband's family, the Chambons.

As she told her story – stopped by Vera every now and then – the young Russian woman's expression became grave – and when she had finished it Vera's attitude towards her seemed to have changed. 'So you too know what it is to suffer from the bourgeoisie.'

'Indeed I do,' said Alice meekly.

'Have you by any chance read *The Origin of the Family* by Friedrich Engels?'

'Oh yes, my father pub—' She hesitated as if searching for the right word, but then could see no reason why her father should not be a publisher of radical pamphlets in France. So she continued: 'My father published it in France.'

Vera seemed dumbfounded. 'Your father published a book by Engels?'

'Yes. He even met Engels before he died.'

Vera trembled. The thought that here in her cottage in out-of-the-way Soligorsk was someone whose father had met Engels seemed to paralyse her. A look of deep incredulity came on to her face as if she thought that Alice was making fun of her; but since that was clearly not the case, she simply sat back and hid her face in her hands.

'I would be most grateful,' said Alice, 'if you would keep this to yourself. It is not something, I fear, that would please the Rettenbergs.'

'Of course, of course,' said Vera. 'They don't care who teaches the children of the peasants, but they wouldn't be pleased to think that *their* children were being taught by someone whose father had published Friedrich Engels.'

'And others,' said Alice, 'such as August Bebel and Paul Lafargue, who, as you probably know, was the son-in-law of Karl Marx.'

Vera seemed to have recovered some of her composure, and having been flattened by Alice's revelation, she now tried to reflate herself by saying: 'Of course I don't go along with all that Engels said – it's his writing on marriage that I find most interesting; and I wouldn't describe myself as a Marxist, either, though of course I've read Marx.'

'You're not a Bolshevik?'

'I'm a Social Revolutionary.'

'We know less about the Social Revolutionaries in England ... I mean to say, in France ... than we do about the Bolsheviks and Mensheviks.'

'Ours is the party of the rural proletariat – the revolutionary peasants. Marx, you see, thought that a revolution could only follow industrialisation and the creation of an industrial proletariat, but as you know, Russia has very far to go before it reaches that stage of economic development...' And so Vera continued, abandoning her French and continuing inexorably in Russian to give an exposition that Alice only half understood. When she parted from Vera later that day, Alice was hardly better informed than she had been before on the complexities of Russian revolutionary politics, but she felt that she had made a new friend.

When Alice told the Rettenbergs, at tea that afternoon, that she had been to see Vera and that they were to tutor one another in their respective languages, their reactions were mixed. Olga Pavlovna simply grunted – a grunt of disdain; the Baron frowned; while a strange smile came on to the lips of Tatyana Andreiovna's otherwise melancholy face. 'What a good idea,' she said with a sideways glance at her husband. Rettenberg was about to say something more but seemed to think better of it. He stood up and went off in the direction of his summerhouse study.

Alice felt that now she was well set up with two friends who, if they did not replace her two best friends in London, Maud and Vivien, did to some extent replicate their roles. Of course Sophie and Maud were different; Sophie spoke without thinking whereas Maud, like her father the judge, delivered only considered judgements; but there was much in Vera that reminded Alice of Vivien. Maud and Vivien. Would she ever see them again? Would they ever forgive her for disappearing without a word? The thought of her two English friends, like the sight of Saladin, brought on an attack of homesickness: Alice sat at the table in her bedroom which she used as a desk, looking out over the garden towards the west, thinking of the thousands of miles that lay between Soligorsk and England.

Alice thought as little as she could about Edward Cobb. This was not just because he was the man she had loved and then lost; but because what had happened had left her confused. She could not rid herself of a feeling of grievance yet could not explain to herself, in terms of her own principles, what Edward had done wrong. They had both been free agents; his greatest foolishness had been to propose marriage and perhaps her greatest foolishness had been to accept him. The baby, well, that was foolishness too. She blushed to think how each had made assumptions about the other's past. But could she really blame him for making those assumptions? Had she not encouraged him to think that she was a thoroughly modern young woman who thought little about going to bed with a man and would know how to avoid having a child?

Why, then, did she feel aggrieved? It was because through Edward she had been obliged to learn the lesson that love has its limits; that when a man says he loves you he may mean it, but not that that love will take precedence over everything else. Edward had thought that he could have his cake and eat it; that he could marry Alice on his terms. He had been attracted by her physical appearance and amused by her 'advanced' views; but he had never taken her seriously, never contemplated, through loving her, seeing the world in a different light. In the end, as Engels had said, he thought of a wife as a chattel.

Edward was what he had always been; a run-of-the-mill member of the British upper class.

Then why had she loved him? That was the question that vexed Alice as her belly bulged ever larger with the child within. She had loved him, she felt obliged to recognise, because she herself was not as emancipated from bourgeois attitudes and aspirations as she had supposed. She felt mortified, now, to remember her daydreams about being mistress of Nester. How vile to have looked forward to gloating over her 'catch' before Maud. Or were these attitudes not her own but her parents', unconsciously absorbed? Her father's? Most certainly not. But her mother's? Had not Françoise always longed for her to make a good marriage? Had it not been to please her, perhaps, that Alice had fallen in love with Edward?

Or had it, after all, been simply a matter of lust? Whatever the unconscious impulses behind her desires, had she not been impatient to experience the pleasures of physical love? Again, with mortification, she remembered the afternoon when she had read that vile book and the powerful sensations it had provoked in her body. Was it simply for sexual satisfaction that she had persuaded herself that she was in love with Edward? She thought back to those ecstatic encounters but found it difficult to conjure them up in her mind. It was as if they had been the experience of someone else. Certainly, they evoked no such feelings now. With the child pressing on her bladder and kicking in her womb, Alice could not envisage ever finding a man desirable again.

Seven

Alice was able to test this numb condition with the arrival at Soligorsk of an extremely good-looking young man, the Rettenbergs' eldest son, Alexander Pavlovich. Alexander, whom they called Sasha, physically resembled his mother. He was not as tall as his father but with fine features and an elegant figure was better looking. He had much the same reception at Soligorsk as Rettenberg and Alice: the dogs were the first to reach him; and then came the two younger children who, as Sasha came into the drawing room, rushed at their older brother and threw themselves into his arms. Olga Pavlovna, though she did not rise from her chair, had a particular look of triumph as Sasha came to embrace her as if she felt she could take full credit for this personable young man. And it seemed that, alone in the family, Sasha was licensed to tease her. 'Now, Babushka,' he said, 'what have you and Zlata been up to? Running races, perhaps? Swimming in the lake? Or . . . no, not petit point! I can't believe it. Look, everyone. Babushka's making a cushion cover!'

Alexander greeted Alice courteously with a glance down at her protruding belly. At dinner he was gently interrogated by his mother about his social life in St Petersburg. Olga Pavlovna was more direct. 'You should be married, Sasha. Is there no one who has taken your fancy?'

'It's not a time to marry, Babushka, if there's to be a war.'

'Don't assume the worst,' said Tatyana.

'But it's likely, isn't it, Father?'

'It's certainly possible . . .' And father and son started to discuss the international situation with the slightly self-important manner that men adopt when they are settling, between them, the fate of the world. If Austria and Russia went to war over the Balkans, would Germany join Austria and would France join Russia? Could Russia rely on a republic run by Freemasons and Jews to support a Christian autocracy? And what about Britain? Rettenberg described to his son his views on the state of opinion among the English ruling class.

Alice only half listened to what was said. She let her mind wander and put questions to herself that had nothing as such to do with the conversation. Why, though he was around the same age as she was, did Alexander Pavlovich seem so young? If she was to be marooned on a desert island, which would she rather as a male companion, the father or the son? Certainly the son was better looking, but one glance was enough to persuade Alice that he was one of a type – the dashing young officer, cheerful, bombastic, with reactionary views. The father, on the other hand, remained enigmatic: even now, after three months at Soligorsk, Alice had not the least idea of what thoughts passed through Rettenberg's mind.

'And Katya?' Alexander said, turning to his mother. 'Is there any news of her?'

'She's back soon, I think,' said Tatyana Andreiovna.

Alexander turned to Alice and said in French: 'You won't have met my sister, Katya?'

'No.'

'She's doing a Grand Tour of Italy with the Loborovskys – they're cousins of ours.'

'You seem to be well endowed with cousins,' said Alice.

Alexander laughed. 'Ah, you've met the Bieletskys, I suppose. Well, it's true. We've plenty of cousins . . .'

'On your mother's side,' said Olga Pavlovna drily.

'And there must be some on your side, Babushka, surely, selling pots and pans in Rostov?'

A cloud passed over Olga Pavlovna's face; the jibe was close to the bone; but since it came from Sasha, she let it pass. 'You will find, young man, that people have to sell pots and pans or do something of the kind if they haven't got parents and grandparents to pay them a handsome allowance and settle their debts.'

'Indeed, Babushka. The world is full of such unfortunate people. I think about them every day.'

The next day, a Sunday, Alice went to visit Vera, the schoolteacher, while the Rettenberg family were at church. It would not be long before the walk would be too much for her, and she wondered whether Vera, during her confinement, would overcome her dislike of the Rettenbergs and visit her.

A few weeks before, the two had agreed to give some system to their lessons and follow, in an informal way, one of the textbooks that Alice had bought in London to teach the younger children. Each lesson had a theme: 'In the Town', 'In the Country', 'At the Seaside' – and this week, 'About the House'. When Alice arrived, Vera had her samovar ready and she took from a tin some biscuits which she had baked herself.

'So you can not only teach,' said Alice, 'you can also cook?'

Vera blushed. 'Most of our intelligentsia, you should understand, are the children or grandchildren of peasants. I was given the recipe for these biscuits by my babushka.'

The two women now started their conversational exercises – speaking alternately in Russian and French. Going 'About the House', they went from room to room – Alice had to explain the difference between *salle* and *chambre*. When they reached the *salle à manger*, Alice was reminded of dinner the night before and asked Vera whether she had met Alexander Rettenberg.

Vera frowned. 'Yes. Yes, I have.'

'What do you think of him?'

'He's what you might expect.'

'Made in a mould?'

'Yes,' said Vera, a note of scorn in her voice. 'A very pretty mould, no doubt – the Alexander Lycée or was it the Corps des Pages? Then the Chevalier Garde – all paid for by the rent of the wretched *moujiks*, here at Soligorsk; but I don't believe he has ever had an original thought in his life.'

'And Ekaterina?' asked Alice. 'I haven't yet met her.'

Vera hesitated, then said: 'I liked her.'

'Like, surely? The present tense.'

Vera looked away. 'I haven't seen her for some time.'

'What puzzles me,' said Alice, 'is that the Baron's children are, as you say, what you might expect in an aristocratic family; and they are certainly what you might expect in the children of Tatyana Andreiovna, but the Baron himself – is *he* what you might expect?'

Vera said nothing.

'There seems to me to be something different – even unconventional – about him. Or perhaps it's just that he comes from a mould that's particular to Baltic Germans – a mould I haven't come across before.'

Still Vera said nothing.

'Don't you like the Baron?' asked Alice, noticing a strange look on Vera's face.

'You must . . . you must . . .' – the words came out slowly – 'you must take care of Baron Rettenberg.'

'Take care of him? Why?'

'He is not to be trusted.'

'Not to be trusted? You mean, he might steal my purse?'

'He is not to be trusted ... with women.'

'Why ever not?'

'He seduces them.'

'Ah!' Alice smiled. 'Now, that's a word – *séduire* – that I would not expect to hear from a liberated woman. It's surely on the brink of extinction.'

'I think,' said Vera, speaking slowly, 'that it still has a meaning.'

'In the context of men's relations with women?'

'Yes.'

Alice frowned. 'But that seems so demeaning to women – in fact, to both sexes. Surely adults can decide for themselves whether or not they want to make love or not?'

'Sometimes we can be ... deceived.'

'Deceived? I wonder. Certainly, one can have illusions and therefore be disillusioned ...' Alice was thinking of her passion for Edward. 'But I wouldn't say that is the same thing as being deceived.'

'But what if a man,' said Vera, looking strangely at Alice through her wire-rimmed glasses, 'what if a man deliberately pretended to love a woman simply to ...'

'To "enjoy her favours"?'

'Yes.'

'Well, I can conceive of some silly peasant girl being fooled by a dashing young officer like Alexander Pavlovich,' said Alice, 'but surely a woman of any intelligence would see through a man like that?'

'Some men are very cunning,' said Vera, 'and some women ... inexperienced.' And as she came out with that last word, she burst into tears.

Puzzled, Alice crossed to the sofa where Vera was sitting and put her arm around her shoulder to comfort her. 'I am sorry,' she said. 'I didn't mean to say anything to upset you.'

'Oh no,' moaned Vera, 'you're quite right, quite right. Some silly peasant girl, isn't that what you said? But there are silly schoolteachers, too.'

'Oh, Vera,' said Alice, 'dear Vera. But who? Not Sasha, surely?'

Vera sniffed and shook her head.

'The Baron?'

A further outburst of tears.

'The Baron?' Alice repeated with an incredulity that Vera fortunately seemed not to notice: for Alice's first reaction was, indeed, incredulity that a man as distinguished as Baron Rettenberg – an honorary member of the Jockey Club, after all – should have bothered with a woman as insignificant as Vera. She squinted down at her sobbing friend. She was young, of course, and fresh but that negligible bosom, those short, slightly bandy legs; the frizzy hair; the wire-rimmed spectacles! Was it just because she was there at Soligorsk? But then so was Sophie Kyrillovna and she was a hundred times better looking.

'When was this?' she asked Vera.

'Two summers ago.'

'And how did it happen? Did he just come and . . . sweep you off your feet?'

'No, no.' Vera sniffed and wiped her nose with her handkerchief. 'He . . . well, he . . . It was soon after I had taken up this post. He invited me to Soligorsk to discuss the curriculum. We sat in the library. He showed great interest in my ideas and said that he thought teaching the children of the peasants to read and write was all-important but how did I propose, the only teacher, to portion out my time between the slow learners and those who showed promise? He told me how, as a young man, he had had great ambitions for the village school but had always been thwarted by his parents and by Tatyana Andreiovna who, he said, wanted things to stay as they were. And then there was the influence of the village priest, who feared for his living if the peasants, through their children, should see through their superstitions. But now he felt he had an ally and together we could do great things.'

'Perhaps he was sincere,' said Alice.

'Oh, I dare say he had such ideas at one time. He certainly

remembered them well enough to play the part. And I believed him, and I believed *in* him, and I even believed that I was his inspiration to help his peasants. This curriculum . . . I used to come whenever he called to discuss it – first in the library and then in that summerhouse that he uses as a study. We would pore over our charts and the textbooks together – close together, all alone. No one ever disturbed us. The days grew shorter, and in the dusk . . .'

'But Tatyana Andreiovna . . .' said Alice.

'Yes, she was there in the house. But she had held him back, she had weighed him down. If only he had been married to someone who shared his aspirations. If only now he could find someone who was willing to devote herself, mind and body, to the great endeavour he had in mind. That is what he said.'

'Mind and body?'

'He said that the two went together.'

'There was no talk of love?'

'No. He talked of . . . affinity and freedom. He said true freedom meant the breaking of the fetters of constraint. No one belonged to one another simply because the law had made them man and wife . . .'

'And, of course, you had read Engels and so believed the same sort of thing.'

'I did, yes, I did. But once it was done . . . once I had consented to anything he wished . . . he seemed to lose all interest in the curriculum – he did not even conceal his yawns when I brought it up – and was only interested to teach me things which . . .' Vera blushed. 'Which filled me with shame.'

'So he had only pretended to have those high ideals?'

'He may have had them once but he revived them only to . . . seduce me.' She sniffed. 'And then he got tired of me. He no longer pretended to have the least interest in my mind and only summoned me to the summerhouse to humiliate me.'

'Yet you went.'

'Yes, I went.' Vera clasped her hands together and looked at Alice with a look of defiance. 'I went, and I went again and again until . . .' She baulked at the memory.

'Until what?'

'We were seen . . .'

'By whom?'

'By Katya, his daughter. She had just come home. She ran to the summerhouse and . . .'

'She saw you . . . together?'

'She saw enough. And that was the end of it. She never forgave me and she never forgave him. That is his punishment. She stays away from Soligorsk, haven't you noticed? She's at school at the Smolny and then goes on a Grand Tour with her friends.'

Alice took one of Vera's hands but did not look at her, saying instead: 'Seduce, reduce, induce, produce, all with the same root word – *ducere*, from the Latin, meaning to lead; to lead through, to lead with, as if when two people come together, one has to lead, the other to follow, and the Jews and Christians would say that that's how it was ever since God created Eve, who was seduced by the serpent and then seduced Adam into eating the forbidden fruit. But we mustn't fall for that superstition, must we? You mustn't consider yourself a "fallen" woman.'

'No, no,' said Vera. 'That's a bourgeois category.'

'And if there were a God, one could thank him for small mercies. At least you aren't left expecting a child.'

'No, no. Of course not. And I am not asking for pity. As you say, "seduce" is an old-fashioned word. But all the same, I felt I should warn you.'

Alice smiled and pointed at her belly. 'Do you think that Baron Rettenberg means to seduce *me*? In this condition?'

'Not now, perhaps, but in the future. He's a man of great patience. He's biding his time.'

Eight

In early October, there were mornings when Alice looked out of her bedroom window and saw that a white mist obscured the view of the garden. The grass was damp; the leaves on the trees and shrubs had lost their fresh look, turning a darker green and, finally, brown. Minute drops of water clung to the webs spun by spiders in the rose bushes. The constant hum of insects ceased; so too the chirping of the crickets and the croaking of the frogs. The fresh scent of wet vegetation rose from the ground as the inebriation of summer gave way to the sobriety of autumn.

Alice liked to walk alone in the garden where a rough lawn sloped down from the stone terrace in front of the house to the carp pond at the bottom. On each side there were shrubs and beds of annuals, and behind them lilac bushes. In front of the carp pond there was another paved terrace with a wooden bench placed in front of a sun dial. Beyond the pond was a copse of oak, lime and birch trees ensuring the privacy of the garden.

If Alice felt energetic she would walk farther afield, touring the greenhouses where peaches and apricots were grown. There were four gardeners, who would bow respectfully as she passed them, and at any one time half a dozen barefoot girls from the village who curtsied and giggled and then got on with their work. Beyond the greenhouses was the apple orchard and beyond that the road that led to the village. Alice lacked the courage to walk to the village in the evenings: the barefoot peasants, the men with long beards and matted straggly hair, the women in their long colourful skirts and headscarves, made her feel uneasy. But frequently, on these still warm autumn evenings, Alice would lean against the wooden fence at the edge of the orchard, and listen to the sound of song and the balalaika wafting over the scented air. At moments like these, she was filled with a sense of great serenity and contentment and did not wish to be anywhere else.

The shooting season had started in September and new guests came to stay at Soligorsk from outside the province. For Maxim Lvovich who organised the shoots it was almost the busiest time of the year. The main game were water fowl – snipe, mallard ducks and teal. In the woods were partridge and woodcock and an attempt had been made to raise pheasants with little success.

Olga Pavlovna, who disliked her son's sporting friends,

withdrew to her parlour on the first floor of the house. Alice, too, because her time was near, excused herself from the shooting lunches. She spent much of her time in her room, feeling removed in spirit as well as in body from the activities below. She had entered that stage in her pregnancy when her mind, quite unconsciously, had become absorbed by the care and nurture of the child as yet in her womb. Sitting in her armchair looking out of the window was not to do nothing; as with the earth, her very stillness was essential to the cycle of life.

From time to time, Dr Schimpfel came to call on her; so too did Sophie Kyrillovna to relay gossip about the shooting lunches, and Nina popped in two or three times a day with regular bulletins of what had been going on downstairs. Alice was able, in the mornings, to give Fedor and Nina their lessons; and she came down for dinner in the evening; otherwise, she was content to laze away the day. And this role – the role of the still earth in which a plant has been sown, has germinated, and is about to push through to the light of the day – made her feel that she now belonged to Soligorsk and that Soligorsk belonged to her. The girl who had dashed from Markham Square to Bedford College seemed someone quite different; so too did the young woman on the Nord Express who intended to give up her child for adoption. The little creature that every now and then heaved or kicked within her was now someone she could almost feel lying on her; then growing and standing and taking its place in the household at Soligorsk, with Nina, Fedor, Tatyana Andreiovna and Olga Pavlovna; with Zlata and the cook and the kitchen maids and the chamber maids; with the lugubrious Nikifor and the inscrutable Pytor; with Vera and Sophie and Maxim; with the Bieletskys, the Donats and the other neighbours; with no particular father, of course, but a number of men around – Maxim and Sasha and even the incongruous paterfamilias, Baron Rettenberg.

Towards the end of October, Alice received a letter from Bourges in France.

My dearest daughter; the ordeal is over. I stood in the dock at the Old Bailey with Greaves and the wretched printer, Kirsch.

We were found guilty, but given that we had no previous convictions, we were not sent to prison but merely fined. I say merely: the fines were heavy and I felt obliged to pay those of both Greaves and Kirsch since neither had any money. However, we are not bankrupt, only poorer than before, but rich enough to live here in France. You will understand why we have come to live here; it was too painful for your mother to remain in England married to a man whom the courts had found guilty of attempting to 'corrupt and deprave'. Here in France, even in Bourges, people seem to care less about that kind of thing. And your mother has her cousins, who seem mostly amused by the whole affair and ensure that she is a fairly large fish in this very small pond.

Dear Alice: we would be happy if you were not so far away. You cannot imagine how we miss you, our only consolation, our only joy. But the reasons you had for going still stand. The time will certainly come when you could come here, if you chose to; easier, of course, if you were a single woman without a child. We have a pleasant house in the town with a view of the cathedral. There is a garden – a walled garden – and sometimes I imagine how, should you choose to keep the child, it could play safely there.

Please write whenever you can. We so look forward to your letters. No detail of your daily life is too trivial; and we love your portraits of all those neighbours with unpronounceable names. And, of course, we would hope to have news at once of the birth of the child. Oh, that we could be there with you. But we must accept what providence sends our way. How lucky are those Christian believers who believe that a prayer can affect the course of events. I am sometimes inclined to pray on the chance that there *might* be someone, rather like a man marooned on a desert island who puts a message into a bottle and throws it into the sea. Don't despise me for that weakness; it is hard for parents to live separated from their only child.

As she was reading this letter sitting in her bedroom, Alice felt a brief spasm in her belly and then a trickle of liquid between her legs. She staggered to the door and called to the maid Sura to send a message to Sophie Kyrillovna to come at once and then to bring some hot water to her room. Twenty minutes later Sophie came, and on hearing what had happened, went to find Tatyana Andreiovna. Alice lay on her bed. The two women returned. Tatyana wanted to send for Dr Schimpfel; Sophie thought it was premature. 'It could be a day or more before the contractions begin and then there will be time enough to send for Schimpfel.'

Sophie's predictions proved right. Alice resumed the routine of her daily life, closely watched by all the women of the household and watching herself. Then, at nine one night, the first fierce contraction came upon her and, leaning on the arm of Tatyana Andreiovna, she went to lie on the bed in her room. Dr Schimpfel arrived at eleven, briefly examined her, then issued his orders to Sophie Kyrillovna, Elizaveta the cook and the midwife from the village, who all showed from their expression that they knew just as well as he did what to do.

Dr Schimpfel then went down to play billiards with Baron Rettenberg. Elizaveta, helped by Sura, assembled the towels and bowls of hot water, the midwife prepared a cot, while Sophie Kyrillovna sat on a stool beside Alice who, at every contraction, gripped tightly the hand of her friend. Waves of terrible pain came, then receded, then rose again as her body, with a will of its own, clenched and squeezed while she groaned. At one in the morning Dr Schimpfel looked in. '*Ach, ja,*' he muttered to himself, '*es wird mindenstens sechs studenden mehr*'; and Alice, the only one to understand German, knew that this meant the end of her life because six more hours of such suffering would be impossible to endure.

At seven in the morning, the midwife went down to the billiard room to wake Dr Schimpfel, asleep on the leather sofa. He returned to Alice's bedroom and this time he stayed until, half an hour later, he delivered Alice of a boy.

A week later, Alice replied to her father's letter.

Dearest Papa and Maman,
    You are now grandparents! Madame Chambon has given birth to a boy weighing just over three kilos. Both mother and

child are well (the mother well enough to sit up in bed and write a letter!). Dr Schimpfel who delivered him said that he had never seen such a fine baby. I am feeding him myself but have a nurse from the village – a peasant woman who has had eight children and thinks she knows best about everything. Fortunately, Dr Schimpfel keeps an eye on her and it is good to have someone to watch the baby when I rest.

The Rettenbergs have been unusually kind. Olga Pavlovna – that's the Baron's old mother – tottered into my room and poked the baby with her finger while making what were meant to be endearing baby noises but sounded like the death rattle of a horse. Tatyana Andreiovna calls in twice a day; little Nina comes whenever she is allowed to; she seems to think that the baby is as much hers as mine. Fedor (my male pupil, aged thirteen) looked at the baby, then turned to me and said, in English, 'Jolly good, well done.' My friend Sophie calls every day and even Vera, the schoolteacher, paid a visit with a bunch of flowers from her garden.

Baron Rettenberg also called on me the day after the baby was born. He said that he had sent you a telegram. Did you receive it? He also gave what I can only call an end-of-term report – favourable on all counts! He said the family liked me and that the children had learned more from me than from all their previous governesses put together. They would therefore like me to stay on if that suited me, and that my son would be treated as a member of the family.

He also showed me a cutting from *The Times* which had been sent to him from London (and which you may have seen?) announcing the engagement of Edward to Elspeth Deverall. You will be pleased to hear that I felt nothing but relief. It has to be said, however, that the baby has the unmistakable look of a Cobb. But I shan't name him Edward or Geoffrey! He will be called Claude after his poor dead father, Claude Chambon.

Part Three

One

On the first morning of their honeymoon on Lake Como, Edward and Elspeth Cobb ate their breakfast at a table placed by the window of their room. It looked out over the lake to the sheer mountains behind. There was a sheen on the still water below and a ground mist that made it seem as if the mountains were detached from the earth. However, neither Edward nor Elspeth looked at the view. Both their heads were bent over newspapers, one a local paper published that morning in Como that had been delivered with their breakfast, the other the *Corriere della Sera* bought at Milan's Termini station where they had changed trains the day before.

Elspeth wore a light peignoir over her nightdress. This was the first time she had worn it – it was part of her trousseau – and she looked dazzling, like a great amaryllis or a cluster of double-lilac in flower. It was clear, however, from the way in which she concentrated, with a slight frown, on what she was reading that Elspeth was not thinking about how dazzling she looked; and it was also apparent that Edward, her husband, when he shifted his chair to face the shadow, did so to escape not the radiance of his bride but the glare that came from the sunlight and its reflection on the lake. His expression, like Elspeth's, was serious because the dispatches they were reading were grave: the Archduke Ferdinand of Austria had been assassinated in Sarajevo.

Elspeth understood Italian imperfectly and Edward hardly at all. By applying his schoolboy knowledge of Latin and French, Edward managed to decipher some of the Italian text; every now and then he turned to Elspeth and asked her the meaning of a word. More often than not, she simply said, 'No,' meaning that she did not know it. Edward showed no irritation or disappointment: he had not married Elspeth for her knowledge of foreign tongues.

*

Why had he married Elspeth? The simple answer he gave when he asked himself this question was that it had been the obvious thing to do – obvious to the Cobbs, particularly Sylvia, to Elspeth's parents, the St Gileses, to all his relatives and to most of his friends. The course was set for his meteoric career as a statesman, for which he needed a suitable wife. Alice Fry had been an aberration, all the more easily forgotten because she had disappeared off the face of the earth.

Elspeth was more than a suitable wife for a prospective Parliamentary candidate; he was to a large extent her creation. Edward recognised that he would not be where he was without her and that with her he would go further and faster than if he remained on his own. She loved him – that was never in doubt; and they got on together exceptionally well. They had a similar background, shared interests, the same sense of humour; and, to top it all, Elspeth was generally acknowledged to be one of the great beauties of her year.

They had not made love before they were married; they had done things by the book. They had held hands; they had kissed and Edward had told himself how fortunate he was to be engaged to someone so lovely; but he had not in fact felt impatient to make love to her, nor, it would seem, she to make love to him. They had also been distracted by the frantic preparations for their wedding at Castle Desche, the largest and finest of the country seats of the Earl and Countess of St Giles. Making up the guest list had been a challenge in itself: it grew to absurd proportions, then shrank as names were ruthlessly removed (Edward's friends, the Garstons); then grew again as a B list was kept in readiness for expected refusals from busy men like Lord Curzon or the Prince of Wales.

The wedding had been a triumph and the bride and bridegroom, covered in confetti, had been whisked back to London by the Earl's chauffeur in his Rolls-Royce. The wedding night was spent in the bridal suite of the Savoy Hotel; and there, after a light supper, they had retired to the bedroom and kissed; but it was a tight-lipped kiss, and when Edward had started to move beyond kissing, Elspeth had said in her abrupt, matter-of-fact voice: 'I'm exhausted, aren't you? Let's wait.'

Edward had been happy to comply. He too was tired. They spent the night side by side like brother and sister. Early the next morning they had taken the Golden Arrow to Paris and, passing straight from the Gare du Nord to the Gare de Lyon, were installed in a first-class compartment on the Orient Express. Here again, they both agreed that the bunks were too narrow for two; and so it was not until they were installed in their large room overlooking Lake Como that the circumstances were suitable for the newly married couple to consummate their marriage.

Both had remained tired; they had not slept well on the Orient Express; there had been a slow journey from Milan to Como on the branch line; and a two-hour ride on the paddle-steamer to bring them from Como to the Grand Hotel Villa Serbelloni in Bellagio. However, the evening had been warm; the dinner served under a vine on the terrace overlooking the lake as romantic a location as one could find. The food was excellent and, after drinking two-thirds of a bottle of champagne, they mellowed under the effects of local Italian wine.

They had bathed before dinner; they now undressed and redressed, Elspeth in a beautiful lace nightdress, Edward in his pyjamas. The two kissed and embraced and for the first time Edward felt the shape of her body freed from corsets and stays. They moved to the large comfortable bed with its blue hangings and white mosquito net. Elspeth lay back, her eyes half closed. Edward kissed her body, marvelling at her great white breasts and her fine, slender legs. He told himself how fortunate he was to have such a woman for his wife; and his body responded as it should; but even as he ran his hand over the smooth surfaces of her skin and smothered her with kisses; even as he did all these things, he could not drive from his mind the memory of the dark, slender figure of Alice Fry.

That morning, sitting on the balcony of their bedroom overlooking Lake Como, and watching Elspeth spread a brioche with honey, and then return to *La Repubblica* and the *Corriere della Sera* as she ate it, Edward told himself how lucky he was to have a wife who was so open and frank. He thought back to the girl he had unwittingly deflowered the year before, recalling the rapturous way in which she had lain clinging to his body. Had that been sincere? Or had she been following the advice of the author of *The Sexual Nature of Woman*? He still could not decide.

Edward also told himself that he was fortunate to have a wife who, on the first morning of her honeymoon, did not expect her husband to sit holding her hand looking at the view. Of course, if the times had been less critical there might have been scope for a more sentimental approach; but the times were critical; there was now a real prospect of war; and even if the two had felt inclined to ignore the outside world for the duration of their honeymoon, such an attitude would have been irresponsible for a prospective Parliamentary candidate who was also an officer in the Reserve.

In fact – Edward hardly like to admit it, even to himself – the date of their wedding and hence of their honeymoon could not have come at a worse time. He had seen in advance that it would be unfortunate for a prospective candidate to go abroad during an international crisis; but he had also recognised that he could hardly expect to marry the only daughter of the Earl and Countess of St Giles without a grand society wedding which, like a war, required careful planning, complex logistics and the mobilisation of an army of lawyers, dressmakers, hairdressers, vintners, caterers, a vicar and the guests.

Once the process had started, there was little Edward could do but perform the duties expected of the bridegroom. He had observed with increasing admiration how Elspeth, clearly exasperated by her mother, still gave her attention to the guest lists and menus, and submitted to the dressmakers for the fittings of her trousseau and her bridal grown. And then, as they left England for Italy, so did the Archduke Ferdinand set off for Sarajevo.

Edward stood to refill his cup with the black and now tepid Italian coffee. It was hot. Out on the lake he could see a paddle-steamer setting out from Bellagio. 'Sylvia . . .' he began.

Elspeth looked up from the *Corriere della Sera*. 'I'm Elspeth. Sylvia's your sister.'

Edward frowned. 'Of course. I'm sorry.'

Elspeth smiled. 'It's the heat.'

'What shall we do? Shall we go out on the lake?'

She looked doubtfully at the paddle-steamer. 'We could.'

'Do you think we'd find an English newspaper at Como?'

'Only yesterday's or the day before's.'

'Even a French paper would be something.'

'Later in the day, perhaps.'

'It's so frustrating, not knowing what's going on.'

'I know. And, to go sightseeing if there's going to be a war . . .'

'But what else is there to do?'

Elspeth hesitated, then said: 'We could go back.'

Edward also hesitated, then said: 'We wouldn't have had much of a honeymoon.'

'I was just thinking of how it would look – the prospective Member for Knapley on a paddle-steamer in Italy on the day that war was declared.'

Edward felt a wave of relief and gratitude break over him.

'And it isn't clear,' Elspeth continued, looking back at the newspaper, 'what position Italy means to adopt. It would be tiresome to be trapped here, and even interned.'

'You're right.' Edward stood and stooped to kiss her – the taste of coffee on her lips. 'I'll get dressed and go down and get hold of Cook's. When shall we leave?'

'The sooner the better, don't you think?'

He hesitated. 'You aren't disappointed?'

'Of course. Aren't you?'

'Yes.'

'But you have a duty to the country and I have a duty to you.'

'Elspeth . . . ' Still he hesitated.

'What?'

'I love you dearly.'

She took hold of his hand and squeezed it. 'And I love you.'

Two

On returning to London, Edward found a letter summoning him to rejoin his regiment as an officer in the Reserve. He left the next morning, apprehensive but also exhilarated, and seeing in the eyes of his parents, his sister and, above all, in the eyes of Elspeth, his wife, an irrepressible pride in him as their hero going to war.

War was not yet certain. It was known that at least a third of the Cabinet Ministers felt that Britain should remain aloof from Continental imbroglios. Edward, like most members of the Conservative and Unionist Party, felt that the time had come to stand up to the Kaiser. He had no particular sympathy for Serbia, and he could see that Britain had no vital interests in the Balkans; but if France and Belgium were to be overwhelmed, and their fleets and colonies pass into German hands, then Britain would lose the advantage of its naval supremacy and its Empire would be put at risk.

When, on the train north the next morning, Edward had read that the German army had invaded neutral Belgium, the patriotic calculation gave way to fury. The Germans were brutes and bullies who felt that they could dispose of the world as they pleased through the use of Bismarck's *Blut und Eisen*. Well, Britain too had blood and steel. When he reached Rugeley Camp in Staffordshire he found the same sentiments in the old friends from his army days. Britain had done all that it could to avoid war but now, as the Prime Minister, Asquith, had put it, there was no honourable alternative. The only anxiety expressed in the officers' mess was that their regiment would not be in the vanguard of the British Expeditionary Force crossing the Channel to France.

Inexorably, over the months that followed, that first enthusiasm was extinguished by the realities of the war. Edward did not delude himself about the dangers: alone among the armies on the Western Front, the British Expeditionary Force was composed entirely of professional soldiers who, like Edward, had experienced action in colonial wars. The older among them had learned from the conflict with the Boers in South Africa how to deal with rifle fire from entrenched positions. They now used their skills to resist the first German assaults in northern France.

But further south, the less experienced French buckled at the German offensive. Their armies began a retreat and the British forces were obliged to follow. The German strategy – the Schlieffen Plan – was to defeat the French before the Russians had fully mobilised their armies by pushing through Belgium and northern France. Less than a month after the outbreak of war, this plan was almost accomplished: the Germans were only thirty miles from Paris.

However, the prize of this metropolis eluded them. The French and British armies were not routed. A French counter-offensive exposed a gap between the advancing German armies: to close it, they in turn were obliged to retire. On 14 September, the German armies stopped at a fortified line on the River Aisne. Every foot soldier now took his entrenching tool to dig in. French assaults failed to break these defensive positions and so the French dug trenches in their turn.

Though it was not yet apparent to the generals, the fluid phase of the war had come to an end. The strategists of the General Staffs of both armies still aimed to outflank the enemy after breaking through their defences. On 19 October, the British Expeditionary Force attacked the German lines near the town of Ypres in Flanders. The next day, the Germans mounted a similar offensive in the same sector. The fighting continued for more than a month with neither side gaining any significant advantage: then, in November, the cold, the wet, the slaughter and the exhaustion brought that particular battle to an end.

Edward survived; more than that, he survived with distinction. Survival was simply a matter of throwing himself into a shell hole at the sound of an explosion; and of trying to kill a Boche before the Boche killed him. Otherwise, most of his duties were mundane: searching for billets for his battalion in half-ruined villages; bargaining for food with the Flemish villagers in broken French; writing letters for those of his men who could not write them for themselves; listening to their anxieties; buttressing their morale.

The first test of Edward's courage and ability came during an offensive mounted by the Germans at Ypres. His battalion was left to cover the army's retreat. Communication was chaotic: garbled voices mixed with messages in Morse came over the telephones until they were cut off by shells bursting behind the lines. Then runners came and went, conveying messages that were out of date almost as soon as they were sent and returning with orders that bore no relevance to the position they were in. Patrols from the front companies went forward into the mist of the morning to watch for the German advance. The visibility was sometimes as much as fifty yards, sometimes as little as ten. Then came the sound of rifle fire and the message came back: 'Boche in the quarry to our right' and, from another platoon, 'Machine-gun fire to the left. Request artillery support. Can see nothing.' And finally: 'Boche attacking in strength; we are firing at him but still he comes on.'

Standing by his commander, Major Collins, Edward awaited the German attack. Suddenly, from out of the mist, German soldiers could be seen stumbling towards their forward positions. They were met with rapid rifle fire, but when it became clear that the front line could not hold, the forward companies were ordered back. Now it was Edward's company, in its entrenched position, that met the enemy with a fierce fusillade. The wave of Germans faltered, then fell back behind a pile of dead. Major Collins ordered the men to cease fire: reserves of ammunition were low. The orders were his last words; a final round from a retreating Boche struck the Major in the throat.

And the retreat was merely a feint: from out of the mist now mixed with the smoke of cordite, the Germans renewed their attack. Edward sent a runner for orders from headquarters on the left flank; the runner returned to say that the dugout had been hit by a shell; the Colonel was dead. A moment later the captain commanding the right flank was dragged in, his right leg smashed by shrapnel: he was sent back to the dressing station. Edward now had no superior officer: he found himself in command.

Another runner was sent back to battalion headquarters for orders but failed to return. Seeing through his field glasses the Germans in the forward trenches massing for a new attack, Edward deployed his two machine-guns in a copse behind his position and, on his own initiative, ordered the battalion to retreat. He watched as the men climbed out of the trenches and ran back. The quick crackle of machine-gun fire came from the Germans and a number stumbled and fell. Seeing the survivors running in the wrong direction, Edward jumped out of the pit in which he was sheltering and, gesticulating with the hand that held a revolver, shouted at them to come his way.

The men tumbled into the trenches, and once more aimed their rifles at the advancing Germans; but scanning the middle distance again with his field glasses, Edward saw German soldiers creeping to outflank him and, signalling to the machine-gun unit in the copse to cover them, he ordered a further retreat.

With the remnants of the battalion, Edward reached a ruined village where he re-formed his men into companies and replenished their stocks of ammunition from a dump by the church. It was now dusk and it seemed at first to Edward that the village would be as good a place as any to make a stand. He climbed to the first floor of one of the houses and swept the countryside with his field glasses: from left to right he saw the advancing Germans; by nightfall they would be encircled. There was no choice but to continue the retreat.

A mile further back they came to a firmer line of defence manned by fresh troops. There he went for orders to a major from another regiment who shouted abuse at him for leaving his forward position. Edward was too tired to remonstrate. With his battered battalion, he staggered through the lines to safety and made for the well of a farmhouse where his men could slake their thirst. A little further on, they were then given rations of bully beef and biscuits and the men went to sleep in the village school.

Edward, scarcely able to move one foot in front of the other, walked to the *mairie* of the village, which had been requisitioned as brigade headquarters. Expecting to be berated for ordering a retreat on his own initiative, he was congratulated by the Brigadier in person: 'A commendable action, Cobb, you saved your battalion from encirclement and bought time for the brigade.'

By the end of 1914, a line of trenches and a hedge of tangled barbed wire ran for almost five hundred miles from the English Channel to the Swiss Alps. Two million armed men faced one another across the no-man's-land, taking pot shots at any head that rose above the ground but otherwise too exhausted and too short of ammunition to do more. Of the five close friends who had greeted Edward so warmly on his arrival at Rugeley Camp, only one survived. One after another, the men whom Edward had known in South Africa were either killed or maimed, some falling at his side: they were replaced by eager, untrained volunteers.

For his part in the action at Ypres, Edward was awarded the Distinguished Service Order – an exceptional decoration for one so young. In February of 1915 he returned to London for the investiture at Buckingham Palace and his first spell of home leave. For weeks he had been yearning to escape from the mud and stench of the trenches; to shed his uniform, if only for a moment; to eat at a table with a tablecloth; to soak in a bath; to sleep in clean sheets on a soft bed. Yet from the moment he stepped on to the platform at Charing Cross station, Edward felt ill-at-ease. There were Elspeth and Sylvia to greet him, Sylvia in a nurse's uniform. He embraced his wife and then his sister; how soft and warm they were, how sweet they smelt. But how could they look so cheerful? How grotesque was that admiration that he read in their eyes?

Edward peered out of the cab as it drove them into the Strand and across Trafalgar Square towards Belgravia. He moved his lips in the semblance of a smile but in his mind there was only incredulity that people were walking along the pavements just as they had done before. 'Oh, Eddie, we're so proud of you,' Sylvia said, leaning forward from the back-facing seat of the taxi-cab to squeeze her brother's hand.

Edward looked back at her, puzzled. 'Proud of what?'

'The decoration, of course, silly. And the promotion. Aren't you Captain Cobb now?'

Edward frowned. 'It doesn't mean much, a promotion, when so many are being killed.'

'But a DSO means a great deal,' said Elspeth. 'Letters have been pouring in.'

'It could have gone the other way.'

'How do you mean?'

What did he mean? That with hindsight it had been right to retreat but if it had turned out differently he might have been branded a coward because he did not hold his ground. He turned to Elspeth, who had a puzzled look on her face. He wanted to explain to her that there had been nothing admirable in what he had done because in close combat one did not premeditate, one simply reacted. He opened his mouth to speak, but before he could muster the words to say what he meant, Sylvia leaned forward again and said: 'Could you bear to say something at a dinner for the Belgian appeal?'

'The Belgian appeal?'

'For the Belgian refugees,' said Elspeth. 'We have thirty of them staying at Castle Desche and, really, they're pathetic. Some of them escaped with just a suitcase.'

'Of course.'

'And there's a lunch tomorrow at Eaton Place,' said Sylvia. 'Muriel Paget's coming to squeeze some money out of Father for a field hospital for the Russians. Apparently the condition of the wounded there is quite unspeakable.'

Edward turned to Elspeth. 'Whatever you say.'

For Edward, what followed was an ordeal that demanded a self-mastery greater than he had had to exercise under fire. The investiture at Buckingham Palace; the speech at the Belgian appeal; the warm congratulations from his family and friends; the lunch with the two busybody aristocratic women, Lady

Muriel Paget and Lady Sybil Grey, whom Sylvia was determined to join on their Russian venture; his father's bellicose talk of 'smashing the Hun'; his father-in-law's amateur strategy; his mother's complacent satisfaction at his DSO – her look which said, 'What else would you expect from a son of mine?' or his mother-in-law's matching look which said, 'What else would you expect from the man chosen by my daughter?' And, most trying of all, Elspeth's great satisfaction at *her* hero's return.

To play this role so ill-fitted to his feelings, Edward fell back on the lifetime's training in doing the done thing. As he received his decoration, as he spoke to the Belgian appeal, as he listened to his family's views on the war, no twitch or grimace gave away his gloomy thought that it was a matter of chance whether one turned out a hero, a coward, a cripple or a corpse. He accepted that they could not be blamed for failing to understand; indeed, he was sustained in his duplicity by a sense that he and his comrades back in the trenches had, through the horror of their suffering, learned truths inaccessible to the civilian population. The social bonds of kinship and friendship that meant so much to his family were feeble twigs compared to the steel bonds formed among the soldiers in the trenches.

But what of the bond of marriage? When Edward had embraced Elspeth on the station platform, and felt her bosom pressed against his chest, he had to his dismay experienced no twinge of desire. He was dismayed because, in the trenches, she had played so constant a role in the pleasant reveries of home. Yet now he felt almost repelled by this soft and scented being and it was only through the exercise of will that he embraced her and did not shake her off.

They had gone from Charing Cross to Deverall House: their own house in Lord North Street was not yet ready. As they changed for dinner that evening, they talked about the things she had attended to in his absence – constituency business, money matters, and his correspondence, much of it in reply to letters he had written from the trenches to the mothers and sisters of dead friends. Before dinner Edward drank two cocktails, and at dinner he emptied his wine glass almost as soon as it was filled. The glass for port he refilled himself from the decanter as, after the women had withdrawn, it was passed around the table. But the alcohol did not raise his spirits; it only seemed to increase his melancholy and make more onerous the role he knew he had to play.

With Elspeth, Edward retired early: he said with some conviction that he was tired. When he joined his wife in bed and embraced her, she sighed and said: 'Oh, Eddie...' stretching languorously as his right hand moved under her nightdress and over the warm skin of her body. 'Oh, Eddie,' she said again, her breathing quickening, her arms drawing his body over her: and Edward, though feeling smothered by her softness and almost choking on her rich scent, willed himself to make to love with her but found that the will was not enough. His body did not respond; even as he caressed her and she murmured endearments in a tone of growing rapture, his loins remained dead.

'You must be tired ... poor Eddie,' said Elspeth.

'Yes.'

'Would you rather sleep in the dressing room?'

'Of course not, no.'

But Edward could not sleep on the bed either; for an hour, and then another, he lay awake in the unaccustomed softness, and with the unaccustomed sound of Elspeth's breathing, and some time between three and four he did move into the dressing room, not to sleep in the single bed but, under the bed's sheets and blankets, on the carpeted floor.

The following night Edward again slept in the dressing room and did not respond to the puzzled look from his wife. He made no reference to his peculiar behaviour because he could think of nothing to say. He could not understand why his body would not function as it should in the arms of this beautiful woman whom he loved.

Worse still, he found that she irritated him with almost everything she said. In particular, he was exasperated by her preoccupation with their house in Lord North Street. She seemed to have decided that his inhibitions came from the fact that they were staying in her parents' house. Thus, though there was no bed in Lord North Street on which to test her theory, it nevertheless seemed to Elspeth to be the place where, some time in the future, their marriage would be repaired.

She therefore insisted on taking Edward on a tour of the empty house, complaining as she did so about the difficulty of getting anything done. 'All the men are away at the war. You can't get a carpenter for love or money.'

'They're cutting props for the dugouts and laying duck-boards in the trenches.'

'I know, I know.' Elspeth ignored his acid tone of voice. 'But you'd think there'd be some decorators left in London. You can't need them in the trenches.'

'When it comes to cannon fodder, anyone will do.'

'Luckily,' said Elspeth, 'Father has promised to send down some of the men from Castle Desche. Otherwise nothing will get done at all.'

As they walked on the bare floorboards around the echoing rooms, Elspeth alternated between asking Edward for advice on wallpaper and curtains and giving him advice on the moves he should make now to place himself at an advantage when he resumed his career after the war. She had not been idle in his absence: the ground for his future was being prepared, and now that the Conservatives had joined the Liberals in a coalition government, she was better placed than ever to tell him what was going on. She was confident that the war would soon be over. 'Winston' himself had told her of his plan to knock Turkey out of the war with an attack on the Dardanelles. This would enable the Entente to supply the Russians through the Black Sea and send an army to help the Serbs against the Austrians. The attack on Turkey would break the stalemate in France.

After an armistice there would be an election and the Conservatives were sure to do well. The scandal over the shortage of munitions still rankled with the voters: it was quite possible that the Conservatives might gain a majority and form a ministry. And if they did, it was more than likely that Edward would be offered a post. That was why their house in Lord

North Street should be ready: in Elspeth's mind, there was a necessary connection between the curtains going up in the long sash windows and a job in the government for the new Member for Knapley.

'It seems unlikely,' Edward told her as they walked out of the empty house into Lord North Street, 'that, even if we take the straits, the war will come to an end.'

'But when it does...' said Elspeth.

'When it does, I may well be dead.'

'Don't say that.'

'And even if I'm alive...' He hesitated as if taken aback by what he was about to say. 'Even if I am alive,' he repeated, 'I don't think I'll go on in politics.'

Elspeth stopped and turned to him, dumbfounded. 'Not go on? But why ever not?'

The two stared at one another with mutual incredulity.

'It seems to me...' Edward searched for the words to express his feelings. 'It seems to me that politicians are, well, no use.'

'No use?'

'The death ... the slaughter of so many ... they couldn't prevent it. The best minds – men like Asquith and Grey – all the power that they had in their hands ... yet they were helpless. All that diplomacy was ... a waste of time.'

'They were not helpless,' said Elspeth, a note of irritation now creeping into her tone. 'They could have caved in to the Kaiser.'

'Yes, yes, of course. But in the end, as the Germans realised, it's a matter of blood and steel. Our future isn't in the hands of the Asquiths and Poincarés and Bethmann-Hollwegs, or even the Haigs and Joffres and Falkenhayns. It's in the hands of the Boche and the Tommy in the trenches and it always will be ... and so if I survive the war I won't stand for Parliament...'

'You won't stand?'

'No.'

'Then what will you do?'

'I shall ... I shall remain a soldier. I shall stay in the army.'

Elspeth said nothing. She took hold of her husband's arm

and led him off towards Parliament Square, chatting to him kindly as if her Eddie was suffering from a dose of 'shell shock' and when he recovered would certainly change his mind.

During the days which followed – those precious days of his leave – Edward still found himself unable to make love to his wife. This failure was a source of both anguish and mystification. The Edward Cobb who had been raised to do the done thing was now mocked by another Edward Cobb who dismissed everything he did as a sham. The voice was insistent; he could not shut it out even as he continued to play to perfection the role of loving husband and military hero. The Edward Cobb who looked so fine in his dress uniform as he received his medal from the King; who spoke so movingly at the Belgian appeal about the justness of the cause for which so many of his friends had lost their lives: this Edward Cobb listened with dismay to the one who sneered at the pomp of the court; who felt contempt for the guests eating guinea fowl at the dinner for the Belgian appeal; who thought the patriotic hurrahs of the people who applauded him were claptrap.

Above all, Edward Cobb, the dutiful husband, was shocked at the repugnance his alter ego seemed to feel for his wife. Those even features which seemed so lovely to the one were dismissed by the other as dreary and bland. The luminous eyes were cold and calculating; and the thick golden hair, raised in a bun, looked like the stuffing of a burst cushion. Even Elspeth's figure, so admired by men and envied by women, might be all very well in high-waisted dresses, but they should see her naked, with her large wobbling breasts.

Edward had heard crude talk in the barracks and trenches, and it now seemed as if some part of him had become infected with mental lice. Had the cruelty of the war made him cruel? No, insisted the good Edward Cobb, because he suffered at his inability to make love to his wife. He saw how Elspeth's disappointment on the night of his return from France changed to bafflement and then to self-doubt. She looked at him with a puzzled frown, as if to ask what it was about her that put him off. Was she repugnant? Or was it something she had said?

'Neither,' said the conscientious husband. 'Both,' said the evil alter ego, and it was the evil alter ego that seemed to control the flow of his blood.

For the last night of his leave, Edward took a suite in Claridges Hotel. He and Elspeth dined there alone, showing every sign of tenderness; and when, in their bedroom, Edward remained impotent as before, they lay peacefully and almost contentedly in one another's arms, assuring each other of their love and talking freely about this unforeseen consequence of the dreadful war.

Three

The mood expressed by this chaste embrace in Claridges Hotel continued until Elspeth saw Edward off on the troop train from Charing Cross. It was mixed with melancholy, as it was bound to be; they were aware that this might be their last parting; and the seeming sincerity of their feelings might have been taken as a triumph of the good Edward Cobb over his cynical alter ego had it not been for one thing: Edward had not told Elspeth that, when meeting with the Cobbs's solicitor in Lincoln's Inn, he had put a private and delicate matter into his hands. He had asked him to find out – if necessary by engaging a private detective – the address of Mr and Mrs Maurice Fry in France.

Edward's reasons for doing this – or so he told himself as the train passed through the rain-sodden countryside of Kent – were honourable enough. A man who faces death daily in the trenches has good reason to examine his conscience and, where possible, put right what he has done wrong. Edward was not notably pious; he was a member of the Church of England and had on innumerable occasions recited the Apostles' Creed: but it was not until his own death had become likely that he asked himself what might be meant about Christ judging the living and the dead. Was there an afterlife? Was there a Heaven and a Hell? He did not know, but there were enough God-fearing men around him in the trenches to persuade him that, at the very least, he should hedge his bets by repenting of his sins.

What were his sins? Since his inability to make love to Elspeth was involuntary, only one pressed uncomfortably on his conscience and that was his treatment of Alice Fry. He had loved her, he had asked her to marry him and then, when it became apparent that she would hamper his political career, he had dismissed her and, with relief, seen her pass out of his life. He had never enquired about what had happened to her; he had followed the trial of her father, noted his conviction, and had read in a gossip column that he had gone to live in France. Edward had assumed that his wife and daughter had gone with him and had felt only relief that the English Channel now separated him from an unfortunate episode in his past.

But now that Edward was returning to France, very likely to die in the trenches on the other side of the English Channel, it seemed appropriate that, should he have a chance, he should find Alice and her parents and do what he could to make amends. Quite how he would do this, he did not know. His overtures might be rejected; but he would die with an easier conscience if he had made the attempt.

Edward returned to his regiment, now near Arras, with a sense of relief. Nonsensical as it seemed, he felt more at home in the uncomfortable billets – the brigade was being held in reserve behind the lines – than in the luxury of Deverall House; and more at ease with his fellow-soldiers in the trenches than with the coterie of admirers in London. He listened almost with envy to their account of the action they had seen in his absence; he could not bear to think that he had missed anything important; and he came to regret both the DSO and his promotion to captain that made him 'different' to those who had been his comrades before.

In due course, the battalion went back to the front where it was prevented by the shortage of ammunition from taking any offensive action. The Boche, too, seemed dormant; it was a matter of making oneself as comfortable as possible among the rats and lice in the dug-outs and on tours of inspection in the mud.

Letters came from home and letters were written home. The

good Edward Cobb expressed all the sentiments that might be expected of him in his letters to Elspeth, his parents and Sylvia; those sentiments were returned with news about money raised by the Belgian appeal and for the Anglo-Russian hospital, which, wrote Sylvia, she hoped to join as a nursing volunteer. There were also letters to be read to the men who could not read for themselves, and letters to be written for those who could not write.

Dear old pal,

Just a line hoping as how you are in the pink of condition as this leaves me at present. Well, old pal, we're out of the line last week, billeted in a ruined village. The beer is rotten.

Edward also read books – whatever fell into his hands – and copies of *The New Age* that he had bought in London – 'radical trash' in the view of his colonel, but tolerated reading for a decorated officer. And, with a young lieutenant who had studied German, he read a letter found on the body of a German killed by a British sniper in no-man's-land – a youth of nineteen or twenty years old – and dragged back into the trenches so as to identify his unit by his markings.

Dearest Father and Mother,

I hope that a trusty comrade will not have to send this letter to you, for it is a farewell letter. If it comes into your hands, you will know that I have died for my Kaiser, for my Fatherland and for you all.

There is going to be a terrible battle and it is radiant, enchanting springtime! I dream so often of you. Then I see our house in the moonlight. In the sitting room a light is burning. Round the table I see your dear heads: Uncle Lau is reading; Mum is knitting her stockings; Dad is smoking his long pipe and holding forth about the war. I know you are all thinking of me.

Along with my comrades, I often wonder what this war is for. Is it a question of the continued existence of the German Empire, of Germany's position as a World Power, or have not our enemies long since abandoned the idea of the destruction of Germany, and are they not fighting now only for an unattainable ideal (like the French); or in the desperate endeavour to uphold their world supremacy (like the English); or to prevent utter defeat (like the Russians)?

I have nothing more to tell you, for I have had no secrets. You know how I thank you all three for all your goodness to me, how I thank you for all the sunshine and happiness in my life. If I am to die, I shall do so joyfully, gratefully and happily! This is just another message of purest love to you all and to all who love me. I shall carry this last greeting with me till the last. Then it will be sent to you by my faithful comrades and I shall be with you in spirit. May the great and gracious God protect and bless you and my German Fatherland.

In tenderest love,

Your devoted,

Walter

For some days Edward and the young lieutenant brooded over this letter; both were determined that it should somehow be posted and reach its destination but neither knew how. To read in the careful, almost childish German script of the young man's home and family – his uncle Lau reading, his mum knitting, his dad smoking his pipe – gave a painful humanity to the Boche that any moment now they would be called upon to kill. And what was the cause? What was the truth? How disturbing to see in the letter how things were seen by the enemy: the Russians fighting simply to avoid defeat, the French for a high ideal, and the British to uphold their world supremacy. Was that the fruit of German propaganda? Or was there a kernel of truth? Was Edward simply fighting so that the British could continue to rule over half the world?

Four

A month after Edward's return to the front, a letter arrived from his solicitor giving the address of Maurice and Françoise Fry in Bourges. A week after that, Edward was due a five-day leave and, with a fellow officer, a young lieutenant, Andrew

Moon, he set out for Bourges. They rose at five in the morning, reached Amiens by midday and sat down to an enormous lunch, cheerful as two schoolboys playing truant from school. At two they found seats in the third-class compartment of a train to Paris. Moon, the son of a farmer in the North Riding of Yorkshire, with a round, open face and pale blond hair, muttered, in his soft Yorkshire accent: 'We treat our cattle better than this.'

They reached Paris that night and, after another heavy meal, put up in a cheap hotel. The next morning they took a train from the Gare d'Austerlitz – this time their status as officers got them seats in a first-class compartment – and by early afternoon, after changing at Vierzon, they arrived in Bourges. Here they took rooms in a small hotel near the cathedral where Edward wrote a note addressed to 'Madame Fry' to say that he was in the city for twenty-four hours and would be glad if he could pay a call.

With the note in his pocket, and leaving his friend Moon to scout out the best-looking restaurant for dinner, Edward went in search of the rue de la Chappe where the Frys were said to live. It was now dusk; the air was cold and damp. The few people who remained in the centre of the city, now that the offices and shops had closed, looked surprised to see a uniformed British officer so far behind the lines. Most met his eyes with a nod or a smile; one old man said, '*Bravo*,' and another, '*Vive l'Entente*.'

As he walked away from the cathedral towards the river, following the map that had been given to him at the hotel, Edward encountered fewer people, and when he reached the rue de la Chappe it was quite empty. There was a row of terraced houses but, towards the end, a larger detached stone house, its garden enclosed by steel railings – the kind of house that might have been built at the turn of the century for a doctor or *notaire*. Seeing from its number that this was the home of the Frys, Edward stopped at the gates and peered through at the single lighted window on the ground floor.

The curtains had not yet been drawn and Edward imagined that, at any moment, he might see Alice as if on a stage. All at once strong feelings which he was unable to define or classify – and which until now his phlegmatic temperament had kept under control – made him choke with the effort to hold back tears. The thought of that lovely, lively girl living in this dank provincial backwater appalled him and he bitterly regretted that he had so abandoned her, not just as a lover but also as a friend.

A figure did now appear to stand up from a chair that must have been by the window and, opening the window, lean out to close the shutters that were clipped back against the walls. It was not Alice; it was her mother; and only now did Edward remind himself that Alice was unlikely to be living with her parents; that she would almost certainly have gone to Paris or to work as a nurse at the front. The object of his mission was precisely to find out where she was and, in the process, convey to her parents something of his regret.

'*Est-ce que je peux vous aider?*' a voice asked behind him in an unmistakably English accent.

Edward turned and recognised Maurice Fry. He was standing wearing a hat and overcoat, holding a dog – a small pug – on a lead. Maurice Fry recognised him and said: 'Oh dear.'

'I had wanted . . .' Edward began, proffering the letter that he had taken from his pocket, 'I had wanted simply to let you know . . .'

'Please come in,' said Maurice, opening the tall gate to his property. 'I was just walking the dog.'

Edward held back. Maurice waited; he had to close the gate. Edward came in; the gate was closed; they walked up the leaf-strewn driveway to the front door. As they came into the hall, he was struck by the smell of Frenchness. The tiles on the floor, the metal banisters to the stone staircase with a brass knob at the base – these too were decidedly French. There was nothing of the atmosphere Edward remembered from the house in Markham Square.

In the dim yellowish light that came from the single bulb in the hallway, Edward could see how much Maurice Fry had aged. His hair was grey; his figure stooped. His face had little expression; he could well have been a doctor or a lawyer admitting a client to his office. He took off his hat and coat, set the pug free from the lead, and opened the door into the room that Edward had watched from the street.

'We have a visitor,' said Maurice Fry to his wife, who, sitting by the fire, now rose to her feet.

'I am sorry to appear like this unannounced,' said Edward. 'I had meant to leave a note.'

Françoise, too, looked older, and, seeing Edward, her face became momentarily contorted with a look of fury. But it took only a moment for her to regain her composure. 'You have been in the war,' she said, seeing him in his uniform.

'Of course.'

'Yes, you were a soldier. I remember.'

Françoise showed Edward to a chair; Maurice offered to give him something to drink but Edward declined.

'How did you find us?' asked Françoise.

'I . . . I had someone in London make enquiries.'

'We weren't in hiding, were we?' said Maurice to his wife.

'No, dear, of course not. But it was not as if, after everything . . .' She did not finish her sentence but looked at Edward. 'You have suffered too, I can see that. This terrible war.'

'The war . . .' said Edward. 'It is terrible, certainly, but it has made one see . . . to understand . . . things that, before, one had perhaps . . . misunderstood . . . got wrong.'

Although he felt himself to be incoherent, Françoise Fry seem to understand what he was trying to convey. 'We read that you married.'

'Yes, I married.'

'Things don't turn out as one expects,' said Maurice, 'but one has to make the best of it.' He sniffed.

'Poor Maurice . . . he misses London.'

'Of course, there are things to do here in Bourges,' said Maurice. 'The French are resourceful. The summer's very jolly with all their fêtes – the atheists with their *quatorze juillet*, the Catholics with their *quinze août*; and there are two cinemas, now, and of course the theatre.'

'And we go up to Paris,' said Françoise, 'every now and then.'

'But not to England?'

'No, not to England,' said Maurice. 'We had a bad time, you know, over that damned book.'

'I know, and I was sorry, and I am sorry now that I didn't say so at the time. And there are other things ... that one regrets ...'

Maurice and Françoise Fry said nothing.

'I wanted very much to see Alice,' said Edward. 'I wondered whether you could tell me where I could get hold of her.'

Maurice and Françoise exchanged glances.

'Is she here in Bourges?'

'No, no,' said Françoise emphatically.

'Is she in Paris, perhaps? And has she ... has she married?'

Again, the Frys exchanged uncomfortable glances.

'Is she ill?' asked Edward. 'Has something happened to her?'

'No, she is well,' said Maurice, 'but she is not here in Bourges nor in Paris.'

'She has a new life,' said Françoise, 'somewhere else.'

'Our difficulty is this,' said Maurice. 'Alice made us promise not to tell anyone where she is living. Even her friends who sometimes write to her have to send their letters here.'

Edward leaned forward, resting his elbows on his knees and shaking his head. 'Of course, she must have felt ... after all that ... a new life ... I can understand that. A break with the past.'

'She is not unhappy,' said Françoise.

'Ah, good. I'm glad.'

'We miss her acutely.'

'And,' said Maurice, 'we have never seen ...'

'The war,' Françoise interrupted. 'The war has made it hard to travel.'

'Of course,' said Edward.

'When it is over, we hope to see her.'

'And the ...' began Maurice.

'In her new surroundings,' Françoise interrupted.

'But she isn't married?' asked Edward.

The mother and father exchanged glances; then Françoise said, 'No, she is not married. Not so far as we know.'

Edward returned to the hotel to find Moon and together they went out to eat as much as they could manage in the restaurant that Moon, on his reconnoitre, had decided was the best in town. Sensing that Edward was preoccupied with thoughts he could not share, Moon was happy enough to eat in silence, working his way through five courses and methodically drinking his way through two bottles of wine. Every now and then they would chat about farming or racing – Moon, a keen point-to-pointer, spoke of the Nester stud with a certain awe; but in general he was happy to munch away quietly, leaving his superior officer to his own melancholy thoughts.

Those thoughts were contradictory and confused. There was a sense in which Edward felt thwarted at failing to see Alice and express his remorse to her face to face, but there was also a sense in which he felt relieved. He had left her parents with a promise that they would forward a letter should he write to her; but it would be a damnably difficult letter to write. If he had seen her he might have read in her expression or in what she had said ... Read what? What had he expected? Forgiveness? Or a residue of love? And if, failing that face-to-face encounter, he was still in the dark about her state of mind, was not his own equally obscure?

The next morning, Edward wrote a letter to Alice and a covering note to her parents.

Bourges, 8 June 1916

My dear Alice,

I came to Bourges to see your parents in the hope that they would tell me where you are now living. This they say they cannot do but they have agreed to forward this letter. I wish only to say that you have been in my thoughts and on my conscience. I do not want to die, as I may, without saying that I look back on the way I treated you with bitter regret. I am now married and so cannot honourably say more. I pray that you are now happy – happier than I could have made you. If you feel able to forgive me, I would be grateful. I return to the trenches tomorrow. A letter would reach me if sent to Nester.

Edward

Rather than trust the hotel to deliver it, he himself posted it through the box at the gate to their house while Moon waited in the taxi that was taking them to the station. Neither said much on the train to Paris. Lieutenant Moon stared out of the window while Edward continued to pester himself with questions he could not answer. Why had he sought out the Frys? Why had he gone to Bourges? Had it been simply to satisfy his conscience by apologising to Alice? Or had he hoped that on seeing Alice . . . ? That what? That he might make amends with an embrace. With an embrace? No, more. That he would see in her eyes that he might recover the love he had thought he was relieved to have lost.

In Paris, Edward took Moon to a brothel – not the elegant establishment where he had gone in his youth whose address he could not remember, but to somewhere chosen haphazardly in Montmartre. Moon was bashfully enthusiastic – he had never slept with a woman before; Edward was gloomily determined to test his potency on a whore. He passed the test. They then had dinner, Moon looking immensely pleased with himself and getting drunk yet again, Edward also drinking, but in despair and self-disgust. He was a man again after that bestial fuck; but what kind of man? A sham hero who had ruined the lives of two women – Elspeth whom he now realised he had never loved and Alice whom he still adored.

Three weeks after Edward's return to the front, an offensive was planned against the Germans by the British forces in France. An attack was to be made from the villages of Festubert and Fromelles against the enemy entrenched on the Aubers ridge north of Lens. The aim was to break through German defences, take the railway lines on the Douai plain and thereby choke off the flow of supplies from Germany to the front.

Prior to the assault it was important to find out which German units faced the British forces. The call went out for volunteers to mount a raid into enemy lines to capture a prisoner. Edward was the first to volunteer. His commander, Colonel Mount, tried to dissuade him: this was not a task for an officer of his experience and seniority who had already won a DSO. Edward insisted, and since the only other officer to come forward, a young lieutenant, Adrian Hart, was too raw to take command, Edward was given the assignment and a fortnight to prepare for the escapade with a sergeant, Benson, and thirty privates, all of them volunteers.

With Hart and Benson, Edward toured the trenches to find weak points in the German lines. At times, at dusk, they would crawl over the parapet of the trenches into no-man's-land to plan a route to the slip trenches through the banks of tangled barbed wire. As they laid their plans, both officers estimated the odds of the success of their mission and both realised that they were small.

This understanding had a different effect on the two men. Hart, only twenty-three, an apprentice solicitor in civilian life, began to talk plaintively to Edward about his mother and sweetheart, and when, every now and then, a shell exploded overhead, or there came the whistling crack of a rifle bullet spinning nearby, Edward could see the young man's face grow clammy and pale. Why had he volunteered? Hart was a recent conscript. No doubt he had wanted to prove himself and earn the respect of his comrades, and so had stepped forward in a moment of mad bravado. But now, as they practised crawling through the wire with blackened faces, plunging their bayonets into the backs of mock-up Boches, he had come to realise what lay in store.

Edward, too, felt fear – that mix of rational calculation of the poor odds and irrational play of the nerves; but he had, over the months of trench warfare, made up his mind to take his instincts in hand. A man could be tamed and trained like a horse: you could put blinkers on the eyes of his mind to block out both the past and the future and consider only the task at hand. And he now had something more which passed as courage: he was indifferent as to whether he lived or died.

As they approached the end of the fortnight's training behind the lines, Edward and his sergeant, Benson, assessed the performance of the different members of their troop. Three of the privates were deemed unsuitable and were dropped. But what of Lieutenant Hart?

'What do you think?' Edward asked his sergeant.

''E's in such a funk, sir,' said Benson, 'that we'd be better off without 'im.'

Edward took Hart aside and put it to him that he had lost his enthusiasm for the raid. The young man blustered but did not deny it.

'Are you afraid?' Edward asked.

Hart looked desperate. His face was pale, his eyes bloodshot from lack of sleep. 'I am, yes, of course I am.' And, with an angry look at Edward, he added: 'Even a fool would feel afraid.'

'Of course, but we have to master our fear.'

'Easier said than done,' said Hart.

Edward now went to Colonel Mount and told him that Hart's condition was such that he would be a liability and should be taken off the raid. The Colonel agreed to give it some thought, and an hour later, he recalled Edward to the dugout to say that another volunteer had come forward to replace Hart – Lieutenant Moon.

At ten at night, behind the lines, Edward and his force of men prepared for the raid. They blackened their hands and faces with burned corks; they wrapped strips of muslin around the buckles of their rifle slings and anything else that hung loose from their belts that might make a sound. At eleven they filed down into the trenches to the point Edward had chosen to creep out into no-man's-land. Each man was given a stiff dose of rum and there were whispered exchanges wishing good luck.

At midnight precisely, a prearranged barrage of artillery and trench mortars started that was to cover their sortie. Edward climbed up out of the trench, crept through the hole previously made in the barbed-wire entanglements and loped across the churned earth towards the enemy's lines. Benson followed close behind him. In the dim light of the waning moon, Edward could see the slight rise in the land where they were to wait until the barrage was lifted.

When he reached it, Edward raised his hand. Those following in Indian file crouched down. Suddenly there was silence; the guns and mortars had stopped. This was the moment to creep forward towards the German trenches. Edward could feel the thud of his heart but his mind was wholly preoccupied with the task at hand. He moved forward cautiously in the dim light, his revolver ready in his right hand. Behind him came the sergeant. The man behind the sergeant had the wire-cutters and once they reached the wire would come forward, but when Edward anticipated that they were still ten yards or so from the enemy trenches, he heard the sound of tapping to his left, then a cough, then, silhouetted against the sky to his left, two figures fumbling with what seemed to be a reel of barbed wire.

'Boches,' whispered Benson in his ear.

'Now,' said Edward. He rose and moved forward, his men behind him, but as he did so they were seen. Shots rang out, some from in front, some from behind. The Germans closest to him dropped the reel of barbed wire, unslung their rifles and raised them to fire. Edward aimed his Colt at the man on the left and pulled the trigger. He fell. A rifle shot from Benson downed the other, but behind them there were a dozen other Germans who seemed undecided as to whether they should advance or retreat. Before they made up their minds, Edward and his men were on them, firing their rifles or sticking them with their bayonets and being shot at by the Germans in their turn.

Then shell and mortar fire came from the enemy trenches; great explosions buffeted them from left and right. The men took cover but self-preservation was not Edward's objective. It was to capture a Boche; and, in the flash of a detonation to his left, he saw his quarry – a German officer – throwing himself into a shell hole to escape the effects of the blast. Edward jumped forward and was on to him. Behind Edward came Sergeant Benson, his bayonet poised to gut the Boche should he gain the advantage. But the German put up no fight. Frantic words in German came from his mouth, begging for mercy and promising surrender.

Edward had what he wanted; he ordered his men back to the

lines. Holding his prisoner by the collar of his tunic, he and Benson zigzagged back from the German positions. Bullets pursued them, and every now and then, as a shell exploded, they took shelter in dead ground. Wounded men staggered back with the help of their companions: their blackened faces made it impossible to tell which was which. In the dark they stumbled upon inert bodies in British uniform: Benson stooped to see their condition and take their tags if they were dead.

Back in the British trenches, Edward's men crowded around him excitedly to peer at the prisoner and prod him with bayonets. Edward fended them off; he had to protect his prize. As they made their way along the trenches towards the Colonel's dugout, Edward and the German spoke together in broken French. In civilian life, the officer was a schoolteacher with a wife and one child.

After delivering his prisoner, and receiving Colonel Mount's congratulations, Edward found Sergeant Benson and asked for a report on casualties. Of the thirty men, six had been wounded and had been brought back to the trenches. Five had not returned. Benson had recovered the name tags of three. The first was Private Taylor, the second Private Newman, the third Second Lieutenant Moon. ''E was a right brave lad, the Lieutenant,' said the Sergeant, 'but 'e wouldn't 'ave suffered, sir. 'E must 'ave taken a direct 'it by a mortar. 'Alf 'is 'ead was blown off.'

Five

The news of the assassination of the Archduke Ferdinand in Sarajevo took Baron Rettenberg from Soligorsk to St Petersburg. There had been a time when the whole household would move to the capital for the winter; but now Olga Pavlovna said she was too old to leave Soligorsk, and Tatyana, for reasons that were never given but Rettenberg well understood, elected to remain in the country with her daughter Nina.

As the train gently ambled across the Russian countryside,

Rettenberg sat comfortably in the spacious first-class compartment, sipping tea from a glass and reading the letters he had received from his political friends, and then, over and over again, the dispatches in the newspapers from Berlin, Vienna, Paris, London and Belgrade. His interest was not just that of a well-informed Russian whose country was in danger of being drawn into a war; Rettenberg was pricked by bad conscience because, several months before, the Foreign Minister, Sazonov, had asked him to go to Vienna – either to the Russian Embassy with an official rank, or in an unofficial capacity – to ascertain what was passing through the minds of the ministers and generals of the Austro-Hungarian Empire.

Rettenberg had refused. He had been prepared to come to St Petersburg to confer with Sazonov and his officials, giving them the benefit of his experience; but he had told him that pressing personal reasons made it imperative that he remain at Soligorsk. He had not specified that the only pressing personal reason was his fear that if he went to Vienna he might miss the moment to lay claim to his children's governess, Alice Fry.

Soon after Christmas, Rettenberg had noted, Alice had stopped suckling her child. As the winter had proceeded, the temperature far below freezing, the earth rock hard beneath a thick covering of snow, Rettenberg had seen Alice's eyes brighten and her cheeks grow pink on the freezing sleigh-rides to visit the neighbours. He had noted, with a proprietorial satisfaction, how popular she had become with the Loputkins, the Donats, the Voyeikovs and the Bieletskys; and with less satisfaction – indeed with irritation – how the husbands among his neighbours suddenly became witty and loquacious when Alice came into the room.

Had they designs on her? Had Grisha, the older son of Prince Bieletsky, or even his father, old Prince Bieletsky himself, a plan to seduce the governess from Soligorsk? Or were there plans to make her someone's wife? Rettenberg saw how Prince Bieletsky's youngest son Georg Vassilyvich, made straight for Alice at any gathering; he was unmarried but Rettenberg felt confident, from the look on Alice's face, that she was not likely to be converted either to the man or his creed. Leonid Purichievitch, the Land Captain, also danced attendance on Madame Chambon: he was a celebrated lecher, known to browbeat the wives and daughters of the peasants into his bed. Here, too, it seemed inconceivable that Alice would look favourably on his advances or that they would be tolerated by Leonid's wife, Evgenia Pavlovna, upon whom Leonid depended for both his position in society and a roof over his head.

More threatening to Rettenberg's plans for Alice was the younger brother of Maxim, the estate manager at Soligorsk, Vladimir Lvovich Markov, who had come to spend Christmas with Maxim and Sophie Kyrillovna. He was a man in much the same mould as his brother – open, honest, decent and hardworking; interested in country matters and, like Maxim, once an officer in the army, now the manager of a large estate. It was immediately apparent that he was attracted to Alice; he blushed whenever he was paired with her at games of whist, and looked ecstatic as he whirled her around the room dancing a mazurka. It was also clear that his sister-in-law, Sophie Kyrillovna, was out to engineer a match.

Did Alice take to him? Rettenberg had watched her across the card tables, or at the piano as she accompanied Vladimir Lvovich singing Schubert songs. He had a fine voice – that was incontrovertible; but did that, in the eyes of Alice, give him a sexual allure? She smiled sweetly enough when he looked at her; she responded to his friendly manner; but Rettenberg felt reasonably confident that however *nice* she found Vladimir, he was not the kind of man with whom she would fall in love.

Nor had Vladimir Lvovich any money; and Rettenberg doubted that Alice, for all her high ideals, would want to spend the rest of her life as the wife of an estate manager in the Ukraine. When Vladimir Lvovich had left Soligorsk after the New Year, Rettenberg thought he discerned a measure of relief in Alice's manner after he had gone. Nevertheless, Rettenberg had been warned. Sooner or later Alice would be looking out for another mate and it was essential that when that moment came, Rettenberg should be at Soligorsk, not in Vienna.

It was with such thoughts running through his head that

Rettenberg arrived at the Nikolaivsky station. He took a *droshky* to his house on the Fontanka Canal, now so rarely used, where the two old servants, Viktor and Dunya, had opened the shutters and removed the covers from the furniture in the few rooms he would use – his bedroom, the dining room, the library – but had left the rest of the house sombre and shrouded.

At four in the afternoon, he went to the Foreign Office and was admitted to see the Minister, Sazonov. Sazonov summarised the most recent dispatches from the western capitals. The Tsar was in personal contact with his cousin, the Kaiser, but it seemed that the Kaiser was spoiling for a war. If the Serbs rejected the Austrian ultimatum and Austria moved against Serbia, Russia would have to enter the conflict on the side of her brother Slavs. Germany would then go to war with Russia and France with Germany: but what of Britain? Would British public opinion permit the government to go to war to defend Serbia? What did Rettenberg think?

Rettenberg repeated what he had said in Paris – that the British would support the Triple Entente, not so much for the sake of Serbia but to preserve the balance of power in Europe. They then discussed the political situation in Russia itself. What line would now be taken by the right-wing members of the Duma and the Council of the Empire – people like Prince Mestchersky and Baron Rosen – who had always argued that Russia should reach an accommodation with the German Empire? And Rasputin? Which way was he influencing the Tsar and Tsarina? And what about Rasputin's friends in the government – men like Dobrovoisky and Stürmer? What was their attitude towards a war?

At six the conference came to an end and Rettenberg returned to his house to bath and change before dining with his sister Varvana and her husband Professor Dimitry Alexeyovich Sararin. Sararin was an eminent mathematician and also a member of the Duma, a Constitutional Democract, or Kadet. At one time Rettenberg had looked forward to these evenings with the Sararins – raucous disputes with their free-thinking daughters, Evgeniya and Angelica, and more sober arguments with his liberal-minded brother-in-law; but Rettenberg's daughter Ekaterina now lived with them while pursuing her studies, and since she had seen him with Vera in the summerhouse two years before, her meetings with her father had been awkward and painful for them both.

Rettenberg had been embarrassed to have been seen in compromising circumstances by his daughter, but he was also irritated by her reaction. The only person who had a right to judge his behaviour was his wife, Tatyana. But it had been clear from the moment that Rettenberg had returned to the house that afternoon at Soligorsk not only that Katya censured her father's behaviour but that she would punish him with the withdrawal of her affection and, so far as she could, her presence in his life.

The fact that Rettenberg had ended his liaison with Vera and had intimated to Katya that it was over – and that he had gone as far as he felt he could, in an oblique fashion, to express his regret at her glimpse of this side of his life – did not stem Katya's wrath. She behaved as if it was she, and not her mother, who was the woman scorned. She would not talk to him with any intimacy; she avoided his company, and when she visited Soligorsk, as she was obliged to from time to time, she behaved as if the place itself was now for ever contaminated by what had happened in the summerhouse.

That evening in St Petersburg, either because she was on neutral ground in the house of her aunt, or because the imminence of war seemed to justify a truce, Katya, though she still withheld the customary kiss when she greeted him, went so far as to look her father in the eyes. She was a thin young woman with her mother's lean face, an animated but nervous manner and, now, a deliberately careless way of dress to match that of her radical friends at university. Like many of the young – or so it seemed to Rettenberg – she was overconfident of her intellectual abilities and so too ready to give her views rather than listen to those who were older and wiser, such as her father or her uncle, Dimitry Alexeyovich. In this, she was encouraged by her cousins – Rettenberg's nieces – who liked to push Katya to say things they did not quite dare say themselves on all the usual topics, such as democracy, freedom of speech and rights for women.

Varvana, Rettenberg's sister, showed little interest in what went on beyond her family and circle of friends; but, possibly because she had been so overwhelmed in her childhood by her mother, Olga Pavlovna, she seemed to take some pleasure in the rebelliousness of her two daughters and her niece. As they sat in the dark panelled dining room that evening, Rettenberg felt as if he and his brother-in-law were two beetles trapped in a box with three grasshoppers.

'If there is to be a war,' said Katya, 'as now seems inevitable, and so many of our *young* men are to be killed, don't you think that the finger should be pointed at the *older* men who have so lamentably failed to prevent it? The so-called statesmen . . .' – she looked at her uncle – 'and of course the diplomats . . .' – she turned to her father – 'people who pretended to know what was going on but clearly didn't.'

'We live in an autocracy,' said Dimitry Alexeyovich ponderously, 'where statesmen and diplomats can only advise. They cannot decide.'

'Well, shouldn't they be held responsible for *that*?'

'For what?' asked Rettenberg.

'For living so complacently in a tyranny!'

The cousins giggled nervously.

'The Tsar is too mild to be called a tyrant,' said Dimitry Alexeyovich with a frown.

'And there are advantages to rule by an autocrat,' said Rettenberg, 'particularly in a backward country like Russia.'

'But wouldn't Russia be less backward if we were a democracy?' asked Evgeniya, the elder of Rettenberg's nieces.

'How can you have a democracy,' said Rettenberg, 'if eighty per cent of your electorate can neither read nor write? You'd end up with a coalition of special interests dominating the Duma, or a reactionary, superstitious, xenophobic party would take power – the Black Hundreds in tail coats and top hats.'

'And where would your socialist friends be then?' asked Dimitry Alexeyovich.

'At least that would be the will of the people,' said Evgeniya.

'But it wouldn't, that's just the point,' said Rettenberg. 'Parliamentary politics, by its nature, divides the people so the government is only that of the majority. The tyranny of the Tsar is replaced by the tyranny of your fifty-one per cent – or, as Voltaire put it, the lion is replaced by a majority of rats.'

'But the Tsar is not a lion,' said Angelica, the younger of Rettenberg's nieces.

'That is indisputably true,' said Dimitry Alexeyovich.

'More a kind of ox,' said Evgeniya.

'And a very clumsy ox at that,' said Angelica.

Dimitry Alexeyovich glanced at his brother-in-law and raised his eyes to the ceiling as if to say: 'The younger generation!'

'Surely,' said Katya, who had been following the conversation with a brooding concentration, 'the image preferred by the Tsar is that of the father of his people.'

'Of course,' Dimitry Alexeyovich agreed. 'The father in both a religious and civic sense, Pope and Caesar – wise, disinterested, just . . .'

'But of course he is not,' said Katya. 'It is all a pretence. He is not wise, he is a fool; everyone knows it. He is not disinterested but puts the interests of the Romanovs before the interests of the Russian people; and he is not just but uses all the means of coercion at his disposal – the army, the police and the Okhrana – to maintain a system of utter injustice with a small caste living in luxury and the great majority of his *children*' – she spat out the word – 'living in hunger and squalor.'

There was a silence around the table. 'Certainly, on the face of it,' said Rettenberg quietly, 'there is an indefensible disparity in wealth. But I think you will find that if you expropriated all the property of the rich in Russia and distributed their assets among the people, the masses would hardly be better off and indeed, with the inevitable collapse of the economy, would end up even poorer than they are now.'

'Of course, of course,' said Katya in a tone of grating sarcasm, and with an unblinking look across the table at Rettenberg. 'Fathers *always* know best. There is always some *very* good reason why things should be as they are and *they* should do just as they like.'

'The misfortune of it all,' said Dimitry Alexeyovich hastily, before Rettenberg could reply, 'is that our Tsar undoubtedly thinks that he *is* acting for the good of the people – indeed, if we are to believe what is said about the influence of Rasputin, that he is doing the will of God! And really – I think you will agree with me on this, Pavel' – he glanced at Rettenberg – 'and of course you won't, my dear' – he looked towards his wife – 'because you still cherish the belief that there is a God who intervenes in human affairs – but to believe, as does the Tsar, that this God has a particular place in his heart for Holy Russia and so that statistics about the manufacture of armaments don't really matter – that, of course, is extremely dangerous, or would appear so to free-thinkers like Pavel and me.'

'Particularly dangerous,' said Rettenberg, 'if you believe that God speaks to you through a man like Rasputin.'

'But isn't it true,' asked Angelica, 'that Rasputin has saved the Tsarevich's life?'

'Bah,' said Dimitry Alexeyovich. 'A few happy coincidences, that's all.'

'A mother will resort to anything to save her son,' said Varvana solemnly.

'Of course,' said Dimitry. 'But the mother we're talking about here isn't some peasant woman, she's a supposedly well-educated German married to the Tsar of all Russians. Imagine King George in England, or the Kaiser, for that matter, taking advice on matters of state from a degenerate monk!'

Shopping on the Nevsky Prospekt the next morning for those delicacies that were unobtainable at Soligorsk and for the gifts that he liked to bring back for the members of his family after a trip to St Petersburg, Rettenberg ran into the young wife of General Veslovsky while in Blochs, the jeweller's.

'Ah, Pavel Fedorovich!' she said. 'You're in St Petersburg. And why do you never come to see us?' The elegant young woman glanced at the black pearl necklace that Rettenberg held in his hand. 'Other preoccupations, I dare say! Or is that for

Tatyana Andreiovna?' Seeing Rettenberg's blush, she laughed. 'I thought not. Well, since you're here, you can help me choose something for my name-day. The General's far too busy to buy me a present so I have to buy his gift myself.'

'That's not what I hear,' said Rettenberg.

'Ah, what do you hear?'

Rettenberg leaned forward and whispered in her ear. 'That in the allocation of resources, the General's conjugal duties come first.'

The General's wife giggled. 'For a man of sixty-two ...'

'And are you yet thirty?'

'Don't you know, Pavel? There was a time when you knew my age to the day.'

'Thirty-one, perhaps?'

'Too old for you.'

'The prime of life.'

'But that ...' – she glanced down at the necklace now laid in a velvet box on the counter – 'is for someone younger?'

'It might be for my mother.'

'I think not, Pavel Fedorovich, nor for Tatyana, nor for Katya ...'

'She would refuse it.'

'So I'm told. Which means that there is someone else but you don't want to tell me who she is, so I won't pry, but I do wish you'd come to one of my "days". These military men are so dull. Or will you be at the Kleinmichels' this evening? Do come. Will you? Is that a promise? And in return, I'll tell no one that I caught you buying a string of black pearls!'

Rettenberg did not go to the Kleinmichels' that evening but instead dined alone at the New Club. He particularly disliked General Veslovsky, a crony of the War Minister, Sukhomlinov, himself an arch-intriguer who had gained his post through servility towards the Tsar and obsequiousness towards Rasputin. The thought that these men were now responsible for the Russian army compounded Rettenberg's pessimism about the likely outcome of a war.

Rettenberg had also felt humiliated that Veslovsky's young

wife, with whom he had flirted in the past, should have found him fingering the simple but exquisite string of black pearls that he had in mind for Alice, and had read his thoughts with such ease. The humiliation had not prevented him from buying the black pearls, as well as a ruby necklace by Bucheron for Tatyana, a pink and near colourless diamond brooch for Katya, an emerald and diamond spray brooch for Nina and two diamond-encrusted gold and enamel Fabergé cigarette cases for his two sons – all this not from a surge of generosity but from a sober calculation that, if the outcome of a war was uncertain, it was better to invest his mother's money in jewellery than leave it lying in the bank.

With these purchases carefully packed in his Gladstone bag, Rettenberg returned to Soligorsk. There he put them in a locked cupboard in his study to await a suitable occasion – a name-day or a birthday – when each could be presented as a gift. The pearls he took to the summerhouse and locked in a drawer of his desk.

At dinner that evening the talk was of war. Tatyana, who rarely read those columns in the newspapers that dealt with international affairs, had pored over the magazines that Rettenberg had brought from St Petersburg and had read passages out loud to Olga Pavlovna. At dinner the two women insisted that Rettenberg explain the terms of the Austrian ultimatum. Their anxiety, of course, was not about a war in general but of the particular war that would be fought by their son and grandson, Alexander Pavlovich, who had already been posted to the western borders of the Empire in Poland.

'But we are superior to the Austrians, surely,' Tatyana asked her husband, her face white, her eyes pleading.

'To the Austrians, yes. Certainly in numbers.'

'And the Germans?'

'The German resources will be limited if they are to fight a war on two fronts.'

'And is Sasha facing the Germans or the Austrians?' asked Olga Pavlovna.

'That, we don't know.'

'And will you be called upon to fight?' asked Olga Pavlovna, 'or are you too old?'

'I shall serve in some capacity, undoubtedly.'

The old lady shook her head. 'And our peasants? Will they have to go?'

'Almost certainly, Mother – a number of them. A partial mobilisation has already begun.'

It was a hot evening and still light. Though Rettenberg's attention throughout dinner was largely on his mother and his wife, he glanced every now and then at Alice, who, whatever her feelings about the prospect of war, kept them to herself. Her hair was pinned up on to her head; she wore a long blue skirt and a white muslin shirt with a ruffled collar. When they rose from table, Olga Pavlovna led the way out of the dining room, followed by Tatyana Andreiovna. Rettenberg, as always, stood aside to let Alice go before him, but as she passed he said: 'Madame Chambon.'

Alice stopped.

'I think,' he said in a voice quite audible to his mother and his wife, 'that we should consider your position now that war seems likely.'

'Of course.'

Rettenberg turned to Olga Pavlovna. 'Will you excuse us?'

'Excuse you? Yes. I'm going upstairs, anyway. Where's Zlata?'

'I'm here,' said Zlata who, though she did not eat with the Rettenbergs – indeed, was never seen to eat at all – always lurked in the hall to be ready when Olga Pavlovna should call for her.

After a quick questioning look at her husband, Tatyana Andreiovna followed Olga Pavlovna up the stairs. Rettenberg led Alice out into the garden and to a bench beneath a chestnut tree. He had sensed his wife's annoyance that she had been excluded from a discussion that was surely of as much interest to her as it was to him, but in his own mind he was behaving correctly. He was, after all, Alice's employer: it was he who had found her in London and brought her to Russia and it was therefore he who had a duty to discuss with her whether, in the circumstances, she should attempt to return to England or stay.

There were many things on Rettenberg's mind, ranging from the fate of the nation to the problems that would arise at Soligorsk when, in a month's time, or perhaps in a matter of days, he would be called upon to take up his commission in the army. Maxim Lvovich, too, would be called to the colours; Pytor would accompany Rettenberg; and many of the peasants would be conscripted. Only the old men and the women would be left to take care of the estate and the stud.

The list of Rettenberg's preoccupations was long but at the top of it there was Alice. Never, since he had first seen her in the Cobbs's box at Epsom, had she seemed as lovely to Rettenberg as she did that evening in the garden at Soligorsk. The drawn look to her face that had followed the birth of her baby had now gone and exposure to the sun in the course of the summer had deepened the amber hue of her skin. Her hair was thick and dark and shining; the speckling of burst blood vessels that had marred her eyes after giving birth had now cleared, leaving the whites luminous and the brown irises bright. The skin of her cheeks and her neck was flawless and smooth; and beneath the muslin bodice of her dress, her slight bosom rose and fell as she breathed in the scented air. As they walked across the garden, her skirt and petticoat rustled like poplars in a breeze and, as she sat down beside him on the bench, fell delicately over her long legs. Never before had Alice's presence and mood seemed to draw him so imperiously to embrace her – a mood so quiet, so docile, so trusting.

'Madame Chambon,' he began – since that was what she was called at Soligorsk; then, as if remembering that she was not Madame Chambon – not in fact, nor, to him, in theory – he continued: 'Alice . . .'

'Baron Rettenberg?'

Rettenberg stopped, wondering whether to see any significance in the formality of the term, then – remembering that she had never called him anything else, and considering that he might suggest that she use the more intimate 'Pavel' when circumstances had made such an intimacy appropriate – he continued: 'You understand, I think, that war is now inevitable.'

'So it would seem.'

'The terms of the Austrian ultimatum are unacceptable to a sovereign state. Serbia is bound to reject them. Austria will then go to war with Serbia; Russia will come to the defence of Serbia, Germany to the aid of Austria, and France and – almost certainly – Great Britain will keep to their commitments under the Triple Entente.'

'So there will be a war?'

'There will be a war which will divide Europe and so passage across Europe will become difficult though presumably not impossible: there will be routes through Finland and Sweden, and by boat from Archangel.'

'To England?'

'Precisely. But the journey could become difficult, even dangerous, so if you felt you should go back to England it might be best to go now.'

Rettenberg paused. Love was always best presented as solicitude and it was his intention that Alice should be persuaded that he had only her best interests in mind.

'Do you think I should go?'

'No.' He shook his head. 'That is, unless you want to be with your friends in England . . .'

'I have no friends in England.'

'Or with your parents.'

'In Bourges?' The way she spoke the name of the French town was enough to suggest that no one, least of all Alice, could want to go there.

'It's getting dark,' said Rettenberg. 'Would you mind if we went into the summerhouse?'

Now Alice's eyes perceptibly brightened, though for what reason Rettenberg could not be sure. She did not respond to his suggestion, but when he stood she too got to her feet and went with him across the lawn. She followed him into the summerhouse and, as he lit the lamp, said, in a matter-of-fact tone of voice, 'I've never been here before.'

'No, well, as you know, it is what the English would call "out of bounds".' Rettenberg sat down on the scuffed leather button-backed sofa and signified that Alice should sit next to him. After the slightest of hesitations she did so – sitting upright with her back propped against the arm of the sofa facing him.

Rettenberg, too, sat upright, then leaned forward, resting his elbows on his knees. 'If you did want to return, then of course we would do all that we could to make it possible, and I have no doubt that it could be done. President Poincaré is at this moment paying a state visit to Russia; there is a French battleship in St Petersburg; and were I to ask him, I dare say that the ambassador, Monsieur Paleologue, could secure you a berth for its return.'

'I have no wish to go to France.'

'And I have no wish for you to leave.'

'I am very happy here at Soligorsk...'

'And we are all happy, I know, that you should stay.' Rettenberg sat up and took hold of her hand. 'And of all of us, I am the happiest, as I think you must know.'

Alice gently withdrew her hand. 'Happier than Nina?'

'Happy in a different way if...' He took hold of her hand again.

'If what, Baron Rettenberg?'

'Above all...' He moved towards her.

'Above all?'

Rettenberg kissed her. Her body grew rigid; her lips did not move. The scent of her skin, which he had so often imagined, he now drew deliriously into his lungs. He drew her closer but then, like a jack-in-the-box, Alice jumped to her feet.

'Above all, if I would be your mistress. Is that what you mean to say?'

Rettenberg had expected this, or something of the kind. 'From the very first time I saw you...' he began.

'You had this in mind?' Her eyes gleamed in the dim light of the lamp and the look on her face was one of triumph.

'From the first time I saw you, I thought you were the most beautiful woman I had ever seen.'

'And you have seen many women, haven't you? So you feel I should be flattered that I should find favour with a ... connoisseur.'

'What I feel is ... sincere,' said Rettenberg, holding out his hand to draw her back on to the sofa.

'I don't doubt it. As it was with Vera, no doubt.'

'Vera could never be described as beautiful.'

'But attractive enough at the time.'

Rettenberg sat back on the sofa. 'What I felt for Vera bears no comparison with what I feel for you.'

'I am most flattered. And Mam'selle?'

Rettenberg sat back. 'What about her?'

'She, surely, bears comparison since she was your governess. And perhaps you feel I am under the same obligation to acknowledge your *droit de seigneur*?'

'You are under no obligation. Nor was she. And though she too was a governess, she bears no comparison ... to you.'

'Again, I am flattered. The connoisseur should know.'

Alice stood by the door but she did not leave. She faced Rettenberg with shining eyes and – or did he imagine it in the dusky light – flaring nostrils, as if this was a scene she had rehearsed many times in her mind.

'Clearly,' said Rettenberg, 'if you have no feelings of any kind ...' He now got to his feet. 'And why should you? I am an older man. But I had thought that, well, you were at least free of the normal prejudices and conventions; that you would not be outraged, as I see you are, that a man should be drawn to more than one woman, and to women other than his wife.'

'I do not feel outraged,' said Alice, speaking more calmly.

Rettenberg shrugged. 'Shocked, disgusted ... whatever term you like to use.'

Alice opened her mouth to say something further but Rettenberg, looking down at his clasped hands, did not notice and continued: 'But though it is now more than a year since I first met you, I have waited until now – until the moment when your child was weaned, you had regained your strength, and were free to leave your dependent position here at Soligorsk, so that I could present myself on some terms of equality ...' His voice faltered.

'I was told,' said Alice acidly, 'that you are a man who bides his time.'

'Vera...' said Rettenberg wearily. 'Vera has turned you against me.'

'On the contrary,' said Alice. 'You did not *ravish* her, I understand, and so she has only herself to blame.' A smirk appeared on Alice's face as she used the word 'ravish'.

'I have never ravished anyone,' said Rettenberg.

'How reassuring,' said Alice, 'for a woman alone with a man in a summerhouse at night.'

Rettenberg looked up at her, his expression now as weary as his words. 'In a few weeks there will be a war and I shall leave Soligorsk, perhaps for months, perhaps for years. I didn't want to leave without showing you ... telling you that I ... was captivated by you; and I had hoped to take with me the proof that, to some degree, you cared for me. Now I see that I have quite idiotically misread your feelings. That happens in love...' He smiled sourly. 'It is hard to believe that such a strong feeling is not returned. But it would be easier for me, and kind of you, if I had proof of another kind – proof that you do not ... that you will never ... that what I have imagined and hoped for is ... absurd.'

Alice turned towards the lamp. Rettenberg could see that suddenly the gleam had gone from her eye and the smirk from her face. She was silent.

'Alice...'

'Yes?'

'It isn't much to ask.'

A slightly mischievous look had returned to her face. 'Should I be sincere?'

'Of course.'

'Should I say what I *truly* feel?'

'I'd be glad if you did.'

'Very well. I feel very tired. I should like to go to bed.'

Rettenberg sighed. 'Yes. I too am tired. And tomorrow ... there will be a lot to do.' He blew out the lamp.

Side by side, in the dark, they walked back across the lawn to the house, parting in the hall. 'Good night, Baron Rettenberg,' said Alice, to which Rettenberg replied: 'Good night, Madame Chambon.'

Six

The Easter of 1915, the second that Alice had spent in Russia, brought back memories of the first and in the process impressed upon her how in those twelve months things had changed. She said 'things' in these silent ruminations but readily acknowledged that among those things she could count herself. *Then*, the year before, she had been the widowed governess, Madame Chambon, nursing her baby and teaching lessons to Fedor and Nina. *Then*, she had observed the hustle and bustle in the kitchens and bakeries at Soligorsk as the household prepared for the great Christian feast, watching as an outside observer as the mounds of flour were spread on the boards, scores of eggs broken, packet after packet of sugar opened, everything mixed together with almonds, raisins, saffron and nutmeg – all this by cheerful women who, for the past forty days or so, had harshly fasted, eating no meat or cheese and drinking no milk.

Olga Pavlovna herself had supervised these great preparations, walking from bakehouse to larder to kitchen with Zlata as her orderly and Tatyana Andreiovna her aide-de-camp. It was quite clear that Easter at Soligorsk had to be finer than Easter at any of the neighbouring houses and it was, as Olga Pavlovna kept repeating to Alice, '*très Russe, très Russe*'; by which she seemed to mean that it was something that the Russians did better than the English or the French. She insisted that Alice should observe the baking of a *kulich*, the raised round cake made with flour, raisins, peel and eggs and flavoured with cardamom; and, when it was baked, iced and decorated with the first letters of the words 'Christ is Risen'. And despite the fast, join her in tasting that unique white, pasty substance, *pashka* – a concoction of curds, beaten butter, whipped cream, sugar and vanilla mixed with a long pole in a large wooden tub until it reached a texture that satisfied Olga Pavlovna, whereupon it was poured into muslin moulds and stored in the larder.

Then, towards the end of Holy Week 1914, with the baby

Claude in a basket on the floor, Alice had sat with Fedor, Nina, Katya, old Zlata and the kitchen maids painting Easter eggs – covering them with bright and intricate patterns, chatting and giggling while they worked. *Then*, at Rettenberg's suggestion, she had gone with the family to midnight mass, standing for four hours in the packed church, growing dizzy from the mixed smell of guttering candles, incense and unwashed bodies, yet put in a strange trance by the dirge of the choir, the chant of the priests and the triumphant cries of the congregation, 'Christ is Risen, He is Risen Indeed.'

Then, she had walked back to the house with the Rettenbergs – the Baron breaking the spell with his dismissive remarks about pagan ceremonies in Christian guise – 'The egg, as you know, is an age-old symbol of fertility – and the *rising* of Christ, the rising of plants, the rising of dough, also phallic, of course . . .'; and his *sotto voce* contempt for his mother's friend, Father Boris, and the bearded *sviatchenik*, the village priest – 'Little better than a witch doctor, really, and a parasite, exploiting the peasants' superstition, trading in baptisms, marriages and funerals as rapaciously as any Jew.' And, when they reached the house, breaking the long fast at tables laden with sausages and sucking pig, cream cheese, pies, cakes, the *kulich*, rum babas, and of course the *pashka* – festivities which lasted until dawn.

How different it was *now*, a year later – the Easter of 1915. Soligorsk had become a hospital – its larger rooms serving as wards, one for officers, another for the men. Tatyana, together with Alice, Sophie Kyrillovna, Vera the schoolteacher and Dora Loputkin, were all now trained nurses. Dr Schimpfel, who had fled to Soligorsk to escape from the anti-German hooliganism in Morsansk at the outbreak of war, worked alongside two army surgeons and a number of *sanitars* or medical orderlies.

The first tangible effect of the war had been the sudden absence of horses and men. All but the finest racehorses in the stud had been sent by Baron Rettenberg for use by the cavalry. Most of the men in the village, having at one time or another served in the army, were called up during the general mobilisation. Rettenberg himself was summoned by General Alexeyev to his headquarters on the south-western front. Sasha was able to pay a brief visit to Soligorsk with two friends on his way to their regiment, stationed in Warsaw, and – Alice was now embarrassed to remember it – the presence of these dashing young officers, their irrepressible enthusiasm for the fight, created an atmosphere of festivity. Alice confined herself to a general admiration for the three young men, remarking on the elegance of the Russian uniform – the tilted cap, the belted grey-green *rubashka*, the tight breeches and shining boots: but she took trouble to make herself look attractive on the night of their stay, and when they rode off the next morning, she had felt, to her own surprise, the mix of pride and apprehension found in the simplest women when their menfolk set off for the war.

Once hostilities had started, Alice had followed the progress of the war with the same absorption as Tatyana Andreiovna, Olga Pavlovna and Sophie Kyrillovna, whose husband, Maxim, was serving with the Guards on the Galician front. The copy of *Ruskoe Slovo*, which reached Soligorsk a day late, was always taken to Olga Pavlovna in her boudoir on the first floor. Since the old lady's eyes were now failing, and Zlata could hardly read, Tatyana was sent for to read the day's news out loud and it became accepted that Alice and even Sophie might join them without a particular invitation. Since Rettenberg was fighting the Austro-Hungarians in Galicia, and Sasha and Maxim were with Rennenkampf's First Army moving against the Germans in East Prussia, both fronts had to be given their due.

At first the news was good. The German Schlieffen Plan – to knock out the French before the Russians had time to mobilise their huge army – foundered on the resilience of the French and their British allies, and the speed with which the Russians were able to put an army in the field. Acutely conscious that they must go into action against the Germans to relieve the pressure on the French, the Russian Commander-in-Chief, the Grand Duke Nicholas, had ordered an attack by the First and Second Armies on the north-western front. At first they seemed to have the Germans on the run but the two armies became separated, and in early September, it became apparent from guarded reports in *Ruskoe Slovo* that Samsonov's Second Army had been encircled and had suffered a costly defeat, with more than ninety thousand taken prisoner and fifty thousand killed or wounded.

It was after this battle, which the Germans called Tannenberg – a gloating reference to the defeat of the Teutonic Knights in 1410 by the Slavs – that the request was made by the Russian Red Cross that Soligorsk should serve as a hospital. Olga Pavlovna consented; indeed, she immediately ordered the servants to clear the salon and dining room and store the furniture in the attics; and, rather than wait for government funds, she had used her own money to buy blankets and beds. A matron arrived to supervise the operation and with the help of two Red Cross sisters gave a rapid training to volunteer nurses, first on dummy patients, but soon after on the all-too-real victims of the war.

Soligorsk had been chosen because of its proximity to a station with a direct rail link to the front. The state of the wounded soldiers – officers as well as men – gave Alice an idea of conditions in the field hospitals: often the patients who arrived from the station lying on straw in open carts had received only the most cursory treatment before being dis-patched to the rear. Bandages and dressings were stiff from dried pus and blood; in some instances, the first flies of the season were feasting on open wounds, the wretched soldiers too weak to wave them off.

Tatyana Andreiovna had not the stomach to cope with demands of this kind; at the first sight and smell of blood, she turned pale, went off to be sick and thereafter worked in the dispensary meting out the paltry supply of drugs. Sophie Kyrillovna, who had dealt with sick and mangy horses, slipped quickly and easily into the nurse's role; and Alice, to her own surprise, found that, after an initial wave of nausea induced by the stench of rotting flesh, she could detach herself sufficiently to cut away the caked dressings, disinfect the wounds, wash the soldiers' battered bodies, deal with their urine and faeces, and comfort them as best she could.

That she was, supposedly, French made her particularly popular among both the officers and the men. In the officers, the strong emotions of gratitude towards the ally who had come to support them in this struggle between Teutons and Slavs found expression in a devotion to this attractive embodiment of Marianne. To the ordinary soldiers, too – the *moujiks* in uniform or, more properly, *moujiks* in hospital smocks – she was the solution to a mystery: few of them had ever come across anyone French. One young soldier who had lost a leg would, each morning, put a question to her about France and spend the whole day pondering on Alice's answer: Was France larger or smaller than Russia? Were the French Christians like the Russians? Did they have a Tsar? Why were the French fighting this war? And why were the Russians? He had been told that it was to recover Constantinople – Tsargrad – for the Holy Orthodox Church, but he did not know where Tsargrad was. Could Alice perhaps show him on a map?

In her work with patients in the soldiers' ward, Alice now came to know the kind of peasants who, at Soligorsk, she had seen as she rode through the village or only encountered as servants in the house. She was astonished at their docility, their lack of resentment, their resignation to their fate. It did not seem to occur to them to ask why they were suffering or whether that suffering could have been avoided. With a faith the depth of which she only now began to fathom, they seemed to relate their wounds to those of Christ on the Cross. There was no outrage, but an acceptance that pain and wretchedness were part of the human condition.

That second Easter, therefore, made a wholly different impression on Alice to that of the year before. First of all, she no longer felt detached from the community at Soligorsk and so did not look upon the preparation of the *pashka* or the painting of eggs with the curiosity of a visitor from abroad, but joined in as one of the household. And during the long liturgy of the Easter Vigil, in the church packed not just with the villagers, but also with the walking wounded from the house, she did not feel the 'enlightened' superiority to the superstitions of the peasantry that she had shared with Baron Rettenberg the year before.

Quite to the contrary, the faith and hope that animated the candlelit faces struck her as more real and so, in a sense, more true than the sneer of the sceptic; it was as if the stone gargoyles or wooden carvings from the Middle Ages had come to life, drawing her into the certainties of an age of faith. For the first time the idea that the patient *moujik*, destitute in peacetime and cannon fodder in war, should look forward to some consolation did not seem absurd. How could the concept of justice be so deeply embedded in humanity, she wondered, if there was no recompense beyond the grave?

It was not that Alice was converted to the Christian faith: the inner voice of reason, though it no longer sneered, asked questions but did not give answers. In the face of the suffering that she witnessed, day after day, she lost the certainties of that rational outlook in which she had been raised. The progress which, the year before, had seemed to offer an infinite amelioration of the human condition had, in the form of the trench mortar and the machine-gun, shown that its potential for evil was quite equal to its potential for good.

There was little opportunity, at Soligorsk, for Alice to discuss her developing ideas because everyone was too busy, particularly Alice herself. In this respect, she missed the company of Baron Rettenberg; she would have liked to have confronted him with her doubts. Tatyana and Sophie showed no interest in such philosophical speculations, and Vera, though she qualified as a member of Russia's intelligentsia, showed all the short-comings of that intelligentsia – fixed positions based upon emotion rather than reason.

However, in the course of the summer of 1915, Alice found an intellectual companion in a new batch of wounded officers sent to replace those who had either gone home or returned to the front. Up until now, the patients in the officers' ward had been of two kinds: one the rather dull middle-ranking professional officer, the other the charming, dashing young captains and lieutenants from the smarter regiments – flirta-tious despite their often dire condition. Some blinded, some maimed, these begged the nurses to linger at their bedsides so that they could talk to them of their homes, their families, their sorrows, their ambitions. Their greatest consoler was Tatyana who, unable to face the less palatable aspects of nursing, and imagining that any one of these young men might be Sasha, was readiest to find the time to listen. But there were also those who liked to show off to Alice their fluency in French or even English, talking in those languages even though Alice's Russian was now good.

There gradually appeared, however, a third type of officer, former university students who, until October 1914, had been exempted from military service until they had completed their studies; but who, to make up the great losses in the early campaigns, had been called upon to serve in the army and, after six months' training, were commissioned as second lieutenants.

It was one of these, Leonid Sergeiovich Solovyov, who came to be Alice's particular friend. He had been hit by machine-gun fire on the Galician front; one lung was lost, and when he first reached Soligorsk, neither the army surgeon nor Dr Schimpfel gave him long to live. However, he had a strong, lean body and, to judge from his eyes, an angry determination to decide his own fate. Little by little, as the pus was drained out of his chest through a tube, he recovered his strength – first enough to be fed by the nurses, then to feed himself.

Lieutenant Solovyov was not an easy patient. He clearly felt humiliated by his dependence on the nurses, insisting – as soon as he was in a position to insist – that he should be helped to the lavatory only by one of the male *sanitars*. He was gruff with the volunteer nurses, even rude to Tatyana Andreiovna and Sophie Kyrillovna: on one occasion, when Sophie was sponging his body, he said: 'You're not used to this sort of thing, I dare say. Makes a change from powdering your nose'; to which Sophie had replied, 'It makes little change, as it happens, from sticking my hand up a horse's bottom.' Vera he called 'inept': his wound had reopened as she was changing his dressing: 'Isn't there a real nurse around?' he said to the matron as she was passing. After this, the volunteer nurses avoided him because of his barbed remarks, and the *sanitars* because he was not, in their view, a 'proper' officer.

Alice was spared Solovyov's disgruntlement because, being French, she could not be placed in any of the many categories which he so despised in his fellow countrymen. He talked to her in Russian – he spoke little French – and gradually she learned that he was the son of an archdeacon in Tula, a student of philosophy at Moscow University who paid his way by writing freelance articles for the radical press. He had a sister with whom he corresponded; he had not seen his parents for two years. 'And now, from my own stupidity, I've lost a lung fighting in this futile, imperialist war.'

Solovyov confided to Alice that he was a revolutionary: his knowledge of French was not so poor that he could not sing the words of the first verse of the Marseillaise. He asked Alice to teach him the words to the second, which, to his astonishment and her embarrassment, she did not know. Like Alice, he had read a smattering of Proudhon and Sorel but neither of them was quite sure which of them had written: 'All property is theft.'

'I like that, don't you?' he whispered to Alice. 'Like "Workers of the World Unite, you have nothing to lose but your chains."'

Solovyov felt able to express such sentiments to Alice because, by now, she had told him something about herself – not that she was English and an unmarried mother, of course, but that her father had published radical, even revolutionary, tracts. Like Vera, Solovyov was flabbergasted to learn that he was being tended by the daughter of a man who had met Friedrich Engels. He listened, enthralled, as Alice told him how her father had contributed to the costs of the Russian Socialist Congress in London in 1903, had met Gorky, one of the delegates, and later published one of Gorky's stories. Together, in lowered voices, they discussed the writings of Engels and Marx; and Solovyov told Alice about Russian socialist thinkers such as Plekhanov and Lenin. Alice gained the impression that he had read widely rather than deeply: 'One has "a nose" for the truth, don't you think?' he once said to her. 'One doesn't need to read every word of it. One gets the idea. And that's enough.'

A third slogan that appealed to Solovyov was Marx's 'Religion is the opium of the people.' 'I would have said arsenic myself, but I would have been wrong, because you see the way it intoxicates the people – all the chanting and incense and promises of justice in the world to come. And all those fat priests who know it's rubbish play on the credulity of the peasants because they know they're on to a good thing.'

'I have to say,' said Alice, 'that I was rather moved by the service at Easter.'

'Oh, you can be moved. I don't mind you being moved as you might be by a symphony or a poem. Just as long as you don't think all that claptrap is true.'

'No,' said Alice hesitantly. 'At least, I don't know how you can be sure it is true...'

'You can be sure it is false. Believe me. "By your fruits shall you judge them" – isn't that what Jesus said? And what are the fruits here in "Holy" Russia? The most oppressive tyranny that the world has ever known.'

Alice opened her mouth to mention Genghis Khan but, taking his point that brotherly love among the Russian aristocracy did not seem to extend to the peasants, she merely said: 'I suppose they would explain that away with the notion of sin.'

'Of course. Highly convenient. Particularly when those who forgive sins – for a fee – are the greatest sinners, and can forgive one another *gratis*: I should know. My father was a priest.'

'Yet the peasants believe,' said Alice.

'Maybe not as much as you think. They're waking up. The Tsar's banned vodka, which has forced them to be sober, and now he's dragged them out of the cosy rut of their villages into the deeper rut of the trenches, which makes them more sober still.'

'And more religious, perhaps,' said Alice.

'Not when they're sent into battle without rifles, hoping to pick one up from a companion who's dead. Not when they're ordered out of the trenches with no artillery to back them up because the guns have run out of shells. Not when they realise that the war's being directed by our German Tsarina on the advice of a dissipated monk!'

For all the ferocity of his views, Alice noticed that Solovyov preferred to express them out of the hearing of his fellow officers – when, for example, during that summer of 1915 he was able to take walks in the gardens of Soligorsk leaning on Alice's arm. She also remarked that he made no attempt to propagate his revolutionary views in the soldiers' ward. Nor, when Alice told him that he might find a soulmate in Vera, did he seem particularly pleased. His contempt for the aristocratic volunteer nurses was not matched by an affinity for a provincial schoolteacher.

Solovyov was touchy and, Alice was to discover, his sense of irony did not extend to himself. 'There once was a revolutionary agitator,' she told him, 'who spat on an icon to prove to the peasants that there was no God to strike him dead. The peasants, to prove that there was, killed him with their pitchforks. They saw themselves as the agents of divine wrath.'

'What nonsense,' said Solvyov. 'That's the sort of story they tell around the dinner table in houses like this.'

'Another agitator,' said Alice, in a mildly mocking manner, 'tried to incite a peasant to evict a landlord from a big house . . . like this. But the peasant said that would be unjust because his landlord was used to being rich and would suffer from being poor, whereas he, the peasant, was used to poverty and so suffered less. A truly Christian attitude, don't you think, Leonid Sergeiovich?'

'A good example, yes, of the opium of the people.'

As summer changed to autumn, and Lieutenant Solovyov reached the last stages of his convalescence, it became increasingly clear that this irascible but handsome young man – generally known among the doctors and volunteers as 'Alice's Bazarov' after the nihilist hero of Turgenev's *Fathers and Sons* – had fallen in love with his companionable nurse. Alice had realised that this might happen but, since it was quite common for patients to develop a dependency on their nurses, and since none of the other nurses wanted to take him on, she had felt that so long as she knew what she was doing, no harm would be done. She took advice from Tatyana Andreiovna, an older and supposedly wiser woman who was also, notionally, her employer, and Tatyana agreed that so long as Alice did not encourage any false expectations, a sentimental attachment might aid his recovery by raising his morale.

Tatyana had placed no particular emphasis on the idea of 'false expectations' because Solovyov, though an officer, was not the kind of man that 'a woman of breeding' could fall in love with; and Alice, though she appreciated Tatyana's assumption that she too would regard Solovyov as beyond the pale, found that she quite enjoyed the effect she had on a man who was both intelligent and good-looking. She had, inevitably, grown familiar with his body – almost as familiar as she had been with the body of Edward Cobb; and there had been moments when, in changing his dressing, she had felt impelled to run her hand over his white stomach and through the thick black hair on his chest.

By the late summer the wound had healed and there were no glimpses of Solovyov's naked flesh, until once, with a group of other convalescent officers, he went swimming in the carp pond at the bottom of the garden. The nurses sat on the grass to watch their charges, some of whom were only now discovering whether they could still swim with a missing arm or leg. Some had to be helped out of the pond; none was a pretty sight; and Solovyov, when he came to sit beside Alice, lay back on the grass in the hot sun with a miserable look on his face.

'We're a lot of freaks,' he said. 'Good for a circus. That's about all.'

'What nonsense,' said Alice, looking at the cavity and livid scars on the right side of his torso.

'There, you see,' said Solovyov, seeing the direction of her glance. 'What woman's going to want me looking like this?'

'Women don't love men just for their bodies,' said Alice.

'But bodies come into it, don't they?' asked Solovyov.

'Of course,' said Alice quietly, 'but yours . . .' She stopped and did what she had earlier imagined doing – she ran her fingers up his stomach to his chest, whispering: 'Yours is fine.'

Solovyov took her hand and held it. 'Alice . . .'

Alice looked around uncomfortably; they were lying only a few yards from other groups of soldiers and nurses. No one seemed to have noticed what had taken place. She turned back towards Solovyov, noting as she did so the effect of her caress – something which the Lieutenant, wearing only bathing trunks, could hardly conceal.

'Alice . . .' he began again.

'No,' she interrupted sharply, withdrawing her hand. 'I should not have done that. I only meant to say . . . to show you . . . that your wound would be no impediment to a woman who loved you also finding you attractive. That's all I meant, and anything else . . .' She looked at him almost severely to make sure that he understood her. 'Anything else must wait.'

'Wait? Wait for what?'

'For you to get better. For me to stop being a nurse and you a patient. For the war to end and life to get back to normal . . . Now please get up, Leonid Sergeiovich, and put on some clothes. It's not as warm as you think; you'll catch cold; and then pneumonia, which, with only one lung, will finish you off.'

Around a month later, Lieutenant Solovyov was declared well enough to return to non-combatant duties in Moscow. During his last few weeks at Soligorsk, he did not allude to the incident by the carp pool, or suggest by so much as a glance that his bond with Alice was anything more than that of patient and nurse. Alice still attended to him; they had their discussions about politics, art and religion; they went for strolls in the garden; but Solovyov seemed to have accepted her judgement that any feelings deeper than friendship should be suspended until the end of the war.

More than that, the Lieutenant seemed to have come to accept what Alice had implied: that his feelings for her were artificial, a response to her sympathy and care. It seemed unlikely that in normal circumstances the widowed French governess, used to the comforts of a bourgeois life, would want

267

to commit herself to the care of a penniless student of philosophy; or, for that matter, that the student of philosophy, who had hoped to dedicate himself, whatever the cost, to the overthrow of the Tsarist autocracy, would want to encumber himself with a widowed French governess and her young child.

When they parted, therefore, it was as friends who were unlikely to come across one another again. 'May I come to see you if I come to Moscow?' Alice asked. 'Of course,' he replied. He said he would send his address to Soligorsk, though both knew that these polite exchanges were merely a matter of form. Then, at the very last moment, as he was about to climb into the motorised ambulance that was to take him to the station, Solovyov took hold of her hand and said: 'I shall always be grateful, Alice. I would never have recovered without you. My body, perhaps, but not my mind.' He then kissed her hand and was gone.

Seven

The void in Alice's daily routine created by Solovyov's absence was quickly filled by the needs of new patients for care and consolation. There were also the imperative demands of little Claude who, although dandled, tickled, teased and played with by Nina, the Markov children and the numerous women in the kitchen, nonetheless distinguished between them and his natural mother. When he saw her, he ran to her and clung to her skirts, and Alice, in turn, liked to look after her own child; she loved to hug him, kiss him, to stroke his hair and nibble his ears. However distracted and agitated by her duties as a nurse, she always insisted on giving him his bath at night and reading him a story before he went to bed.

Alice also found the time to give Nina lessons for an hour after lunch – English conversation on Tuesdays and Thursdays, French conversation on Wednesdays and Fridays; French dictation and comprehension on Saturdays; English dictation and comprehension on Sundays; while the hour on Mondays was reserved for mathematics. Tatyana Andreiovna herself gave

Nina lessons in Russian grammar and literature; she accepted that she had less to contribute to the running of the hospital than Alice; indeed, besides assisting at the dispensary, and comforting the patients in the officers' ward, her principal role was mediating in the bitter disputes that arose over the most trivial things between the Red Cross matron and her mother-in-law, Olga Pavlovna.

Alice, though busy and preoccupied, could nevertheless *think* as she emptied a chamber pot, changed a dressing, or spoon-fed a soldier who had lost the use of both arms. She thought in particular about the incident by the carp pond; about the good side of Solovyov's body, his long white legs, his powerful arms, and that swelling beneath his trunks. And as she had these thoughts her body, too, showed symptoms of sexual desire; symptoms which returned when she lay in bed at night, free to think and imagine what she liked, symptoms that grew acute as she moved her limbs languorously beneath the sheets and, in a state of semi-somnolence, dreamed that she was in the arms of a lover: not Solovyov – she gave a shudder – and not her first and only lover, Eddie Cobb, whose slim, hard body she remembered so well. No, not him, not that insipid traitor, nor the charming, handsome Sasha, but another mysterious, powerful man whom she resisted but could not resist, a body strong and unfamiliar, but a face she knew – the face, surely not, the face, yes, the face of Baron Rettenberg!

When Alice awoke the next morning, she purged herself of the slight shame and embarrassment induced by the memory of what she had imagined with the thought that the content of dreams was merely the effluent left by thoughts and emotions. But the part played by Rettenberg was not so easily explained away. She found, for example, at that daily reading of *Ruskoe Slovo* in the boudoir of Olga Pavlovna, that she paid particular attention to the news from the south-western front. She also noted, to her irritation, that she grew slightly breathless when she heard Tatyana exclaim, after opening a letter, that Rettenberg might soon return on leave.

More compromising still was the way in which memories of the young lieutenant by the carp pool were now discarded in her ruminations in favour of a rerun of the scene in the summerhouse with Rettenberg. Biting her lower lip as she remembered it, Alice wondered whether she had not perhaps been precipitate in such an outright rejection. Had she not been acting simply on hearsay and *against* her own convictions? Had she not got it so firmly into her mind that she must thwart this serial seducer, and had she not rehearsed her lines as an outraged innocent so well, that when the moment had come she had played a part to perfection that had not been true to her feelings? Or to her own professed convictions? Had she not told Vera that 'seduce' was now a word without any meaning? If she had in fact wanted to give herself to Rettenberg, should she have refused to follow her own inclinations only because she was the governess, or because he was said to have slept with a number of other women before? It was always assumed that it was the man who took advantage of a woman, but why should not a woman take advantage of a man?

But why Rettenberg? He was a good twenty years older than she was – perhaps more; his appearance was striking but he was not obviously handsome – certainly less handsome than his son Sasha, or even Solovyov, or half a dozen of the young officers who hobbled around the ward. If Alice had wanted to choose a lover simply for his appearance, she felt she could do better than her employer. Was she simply responding to his desire for her? She had heard of cases where women with no initial interest in a man were won over by the energy of their attentions – the extravagant entertainments, the barrage of roses. But here there had been no barrage of roses; no extravagant entertainment – only a certain measure of comfort at the Hotel St James and Albany in Paris and in a first-class compartment on the Nord Express.

Alice thought back to her first meeting with Rettenberg at the Derby. She had hardly noticed his appearance: she would not have recognised him had she passed him in the street the next morning. It had been no different at the ball at the St Gileses' or on the Golden Arrow or in Paris. Her thoughts were then only for Eddie Cobb; Rettenberg was a mere convenience.

It was only in the dining car of the Nord Express, when he had so delicately revealed that he knew she was pregnant, and had concocted an incognito for her with such insouciance, that she had had the first inkling that he was not quite what he seemed. And if then, as he had later told her, he already wanted to possess her, well, she must surely give him credit for his fidelity over the many months when she was nurturing, bearing and nursing Claude.

But why Rettenberg? She asked herself the question a second time. Was there an element of snobbery in her selection? Was it really just a coincidence that her first lover was the son of a baronet and her second a baron? Was it perhaps Solovyov's *class* that placed him out of contention? Was it edifying to prefer to be yet another mistress of a Russian aristocrat than the life's companion of a student of philosophy and dedicated revolutionary? Had she not, for all her high ideals, become so attached to the elegance and comfort of the aristocratic life that she would rather secure it on a sofa in a summerhouse rather than lose it on the marriage bed of her own humble home?

One loves whom one loves, Alice retorted to this sceptical inner voice; and then was pulled up short to hear herself use the word love. Did she really *love* Rettenberg? Was that why she now found herself keeping the company of Vera and Tatyana, who also loved Rettenberg, and less so that of Sophie Markov, who did not? How odd, thought Alice, that women who love the same man should become friends. Vera, it was clear to Alice, for all her outrage at her 'seduction', was still obsessed with Rettenberg and would have gone back to the summer-house at a flick of his fingers, and Tatyana Andreiovna too, though she must have known why Rettenberg had brought Alice to Soligorsk, and had surely assumed that if he had not yet slept with her, he undoubtedly would, now treated Alice not just as an indispensable member of the household but a confidante and friend. Stranger still was the change in Tatyana's attitude towards Vera Mikhailovna who, before the war, she would not have in the house. Now, working in the hospital as a volunteer nurse, Vera would be asked by Tatyana to join the family for tea or for supper as a matter of course. Olga Pavlovna referred to her as the 'stray cat'.

Excluded from this sorority was Sophie Markov who until then had been Alice's closest friend. Alice knew that if Sophie even suspected that she had taken a fancy to the Baron – if she thought that Alice could now contemplate adding her name to the long list of his conquests – she would not only despise her but spread the news round the province in a flash. She had already remarked, with scorn, on the way Vera had been accepted by Tatyana; she called them 'the two Penelopes waiting for their Ulysses to return'; and Alice, knowing the intensity of Sophie's curiosity and the power of her intuition, became afraid that some word, some look, some blush might give her away, and so avoided talking to her *tête-à-tête*.

Alice came close to being discovered by Sophie Kyrillovna in February 1916, shortly before Rettenberg was due to return to Soligorsk for his much-delayed leave. It happened after Tatyana received a letter from a cousin, Princess Irina Ivanovna, also a lady-in-waiting to the Tsar's aunt, the Grand Duchess Vladimir. The receipt of this letter caused great excitement in Olga Pavlovna's boudoir and it was read aloud, at Olga Pavlovna's insistence, even before the day's news from *Ruskoe Slovo*.

Chère Cousine,

Is it true that you have a French governess at Soligorsk who also speaks English and is now working as a nurse? Could you spare her for a month or so as a favour to her Royal Highness but also the nation? As you may have heard, the Grand Duke Dimitri Pavlovich has given over the *piano nobile* of the Dimitri Palace for an Anglo-Russian hospital. Two formidable grande dames from London, Lady Muriel Paget and Lady Sybil Grey, have raised funds in London to provide it with medicines, medical staff and equipment. You do not need to be told how valuable these are when so many of our brave men are suffering atrociously because of shortages at the front. The English doctors and nurses have now arrived by way of Archangel and the hospital was opened by the Dowager Empress last week. Incidentally – and this is *entre nous* – Her Royal Highness at first said she could not do it because she had lumbago and my Grand Duchess was asked to step in, but then the Dowager Empress changed her mind which, as you can probably imagine, put my Grand Duchess into a very poor mood, but luckily she adores Sir George Buchanan the British Ambassador, and will do, or not do, anything he asks.

The hospital, then, has admitted its first patients but because almost none of the English doctors or nurses can speak a word of Russian, it is a Tower of Babel. That is why I am asking if you could send your governess to help, if only for a month. It really would make all the difference.

This letter particularly delighted Olga Pavlovna because it showed that Soligorsk, far from being a forgotten provincial backwater, had actually been a topic of conversation in royal circles. Also the confidential tone of the letter – the '*entre nous*' – though it was addressed to Tatyana, not Olga Pavlovna, seemed to endorse the elevated social status of the Rettenbergs that had been behind the marriage of Pavel Fedorovich to Tatyana. Olga doubted that even the Bieletskys knew of the tiff between the Dowager Empress and the Grand Duchess Vladimir. 'We must send a note to the Bieletskys,' she said to Tatyana as soon as Tatyana had finished reading the letter, 'to ask them over for lunch.'

Tatyana's eyes, however, were on Alice, who, as the letter had proceeded, had betrayed its effect by first a slight and then a deeper blush. Assuming, no doubt, that Alice was offended by the tone of the letter, and to show that she was sensitive to Alice's feelings, Tatyana gave a forced laugh and said: 'Really, the silly old trout talks as if Alice were one of our serfs.'

Olga Pavlovna frowned. 'What silly old trout?'

'Irina Nikolovna.'

'I hardly think it suitable to call a lady-in-waiting to the Grand Duchess Vladimir a silly old trout, even if she is your cousin.'

'But really, Maman,' said Tatyana, 'Alice is not a package to be *sent* to Petrograd.'

273

'But I am sure,' said Olga Pavlovna, turning to Alice, 'that she will feel honoured by such a call. Not every governess, after all, is talked about at court.'

'Of course,' said Alice. 'I do indeed feel honoured. But . . . well, I am so happy here at Soligorsk.'

'And we are happy to have you here, my dear,' said Olga Pavlovna imperiously. 'But there are times when happiness must be sacrificed to duty.'

'There is Nina,' said Alice.

'She can have her lessons with the Donats' children.'

'And of course there is Claude.'

'You can leave him here, or he can go with you. You can take . . .' She turned to Zlata. 'What's that silly girl called – the one who burned the tablecloth with the iron?'

'Marya.'

'You can take Marya. She'll do as a nurse. And you can stay in the house. God knows what servants are left there, but there'd be room for the three of you.'

'You're very kind.'

Olga Pavlovna turned to Tatyana. 'How did they know, I wonder, about our governess? Who can have told them?'

'Aunt Elisaveta, perhaps?'

'Yes, of course. She knows the Grand Duchess, doesn't she? Yes, it must have been her.'

Although Olga Pavlovna would have liked to have sent an immediate and affirmative answer to Tatyana's illustrious kinswoman – indeed, had she had a stamp and a label at hand, she would have posted Alice to Petrograd that very day – Tatyana was able to procrastinate on Alice's behalf. 'We must consider the practicalities,' she said. 'We must ask Matron if she can spare Alice and, well, in the end it is for Alice to decide.'

Alice had already decided: she would not go. But she realised that it would be politic to appear to agonise over the decision. She knew that if Olga Pavlovna was sufficiently enraged she might dismiss her, and nothing was more likely to enrage Olga

Pavlovna than what she might perceive as a social humiliation. It was all the more awkward because Alice could not give any of the reasons why she could not go to Petrograd.

First of all, there was the risk that she might run into someone who knew her among the British in the city. Though Rettenberg had obtained papers for herself and Claude in the name of Chambon that would suffice for internal travel, her British passport remained in the name of Alice Fry. To be discovered might not be the end of the world; Alice now felt so detached from her past that it seemed scarcely to matter if it became known that she was living in Russia. Who was there in England who would care? But there was a second, insurmountable objection to leaving for Petrograd: Alice would not see Rettenberg when he came home on leave. But, even more than her false identity, this was not a reason she could give to Tatyana Andreiovna or Olga Pavlovna, though Tatyana might quite possibly suspect it. Later in the day, after the reading of the letter, she said to Alice: 'It is a pity that Pavel Fedorovich isn't here to advise you.' Later still: 'Perhaps we should write to him to ask what he thinks.'

'Isn't he due back on leave?' asked Alice.

'Yes, he is, although he has put it off so often before.'

'I would feel,' said Alice, choosing her words carefully, 'that it would be . . . inappropriate for me to leave Soligorsk without his consent. It was he, after all, who brought me here.'

'Yes,' said Tatyana with a rare, wry smile. 'You are his package, after all, not Olga Pavlovna's.'

This, then, was the decision that was conveyed by Tatyana to her mother-in-law, and which led the old woman to send Alice to Coventry for the next five days. Her anger waned after Prince and Princess Bieletsky had been to lunch and, on being told of the Grand Duchess's request, had learned about the tiff between the Grand Duchess and the Dowager Empress. Princess Bieletsky, to Olga Pavlovna's great satisfaction, looked suitably impressed – and chagrined.

The person most astonished and even outraged at Alice's reluctance to go to Petrograd was Sophie Kyrillovna Markov. 'I simply can't believe it,' she said one evening when Alice walked over the squeaking snow to dine in her house. 'Here you are given a chance to escape from this backwater to St Petersburg – I mean, Petrograd – and you turn it down? You've no idea what fun it would be. I know it's not the same as it was because of the war, but from all I hear it's not that different. In fact, the parties are wilder and, working in the English hospital, you'd be in with the embassy crowd. Really, if I were you, I'd leave on the next train.'

'I'm so happy here,' said Alice lamely. 'And then there's Claude.'

'Oh, babies don't much mind where they are. You could leave him here; he wouldn't miss you for a month or so; or you could take a girl from here to look after him. Weren't you offered Marya? She'd drive you mad, but that rather pretty girl, Shura, would go like a shot and they'd let you take her, I know. She's clever too. Go, Alice, go. You must go.'

'I would feel intimidated,' said Alice. 'I've got used to country life.'

'What nonsense,' said Sophie. 'You've lived in Paris, haven't you? Well, Petrograd's the next best thing. I'd give my eyes to spend a month in Petrograd, I really would.'

'I feel so fond of you all . . .'

'But you'd come back. Or you'd find a husband in Petrograd – certainly a better one than you're likely to find here.'

'I don't know that I want a husband,' said Alice.

'Oh, come off it. We all saw what went on with that ghastly Lieutenant Solovyov. If you can even think about him for a moment, then you must be desperate. I don't blame you. I miss Maxim terribly and those brief leaves, well, they're better than nothing, but it's just as well that some of our better-looking officers are still so weak . . .'

'Sophie!' Alice pretended to be shocked.

'Oh, come on, Alice. You've been married. You know what I mean. Wouldn't you like another husband, or at least a lover? It's been, what, over two years since you lost your Claude? You can't mourn him for ever, and although you're still young enough, I suppose, you aren't getting any younger. And think of Claude. Doesn't he need a father?'

'Yes, but . . .'

'But nothing. Go. You must go. You've got a *crise de confiance*, that's all. Unless . . .' And now the thought that Alice had dreaded entered Sophie's head. 'Unless there's someone here that I don't know about.' She directed at Alice a lingering and penetrating glance. 'Not Captain Sandbert, surely? Or Kolya Pissarev? I can't believe you'd seriously consider either of them. Sandbert's married, anyway, and Pissarev's too languid for words.'

'Of course not,' said Alice, blushing. 'It's neither of them. It's no one.' She could see Sophie's intuition whirring furiously and, to her dismay, edging towards the truth.

'Perhaps . . . perhaps . . . you're waiting for someone. Not Sasha, surely? No, he's not your type. And not . . . no, it can't be . . . not . . .'

'Sophie,' said Alice quickly, 'there is something I haven't told you, but I think that, perhaps, you should know now.'

Sophie waited, her sharp face poised like a lizard about to pounce on a fly.

'You will, I know, keep it to yourself.'

'Of course.'

'I was not actually . . . married to Claude Chambon.'

'Ah!'

'If I went to Petrograd, this might become apparent and . . . well, you can imagine.'

The fly had buzzed off. Sophie looked disappointed. 'Do the Rettenbergs know?' she asked.

Alice shook her head. 'Of course not, no.'

'I can see, yes, that that might be awkward . . . if word reached Soligorsk.'

'I'm so happy here. I would hate to be sent away.'

'But do you want to stay here for ever?'

'Until Claude is a little older, that's all.'

Sophie thought for a moment. 'But if they don't know here, how would they find out in Petrograd?'

'My passport is in my maiden name. And then I would inevitably meet people who were French.'

Sophie nodded. 'I can see that.' Then she looked at Alice and smiled. 'So you're a fallen woman? Who would have thought it? Well, you can trust me, I won't tell anyone – not, at any rate, if you promise to tell me just what happened. Was Claude's father really killed in Morocco or is he still around?'

And Alice, relieved to have deflected Sophie's curiosity, now told her about the faithless young French aristocrat who had led her astray.

Eight

In March 1916, Rettenberg returned on leave after more than eighteen months on the south-western front. The day of his arrival had been uncertain and then suddenly he was there, stretched out on the sofa in his mother's boudoir, his boots scuffed, his breeches streaked with mud, and dust like a powder in his thick hair. He was laughing when Alice first glimpsed him. She had been in the soldiers' ward when told that he had returned, but even if she had not been told, she would have sensed it by the sudden bustle and animation in the household.

Coming into the hall, she had seen his cap on the brass knob at the bottom of the banisters. Pretending that she had some business on the first floor where medicines and bandages were stored, Alice had passed the open door to the boudoir, but, not presuming to go in, simply glimpsed him chatting volubly to his mother and his wife. Every now and then he laughed. His clothes were loose on his body: he had grown thin.

Alice only came face to face with Rettenberg as she crossed the hall to go into dinner, which, since the dining room had been commandeered by the matron, was served in the billiard room – the billiard table pushed back against the wall. She looked cautiously into his eyes.

Rettenberg smiled. 'Madame Chambon,' he said with a slight, ironic bow.

'Baron Rettenberg,' she replied, with an equally ironic inflection from the waist.

'Things have changed,' he said, 'since we were last here.' His look meant that by 'here' he meant the hall, and the inclusion of Alice in this observation made the reference to their last parting quite clear.

'Your home is now a hospital,' said Alice.

'And my governess a nurse.'

Rettenberg stood back to let her walk before him down the passage towards the billiard room. 'The library is now the matron's office,' he said with a sigh. 'But at least they've left Mother her boudoir.'

'We've lost the nursery,' said Alice. 'It's now the dispensary. Dr Schimpfel and the army surgeon have two of the bedrooms. The Red Cross nurses sleep in the attics.'

'But they haven't turned you out of your bedroom?'

'No. I still sleep there with Claude.'

Rettenberg asked after Claude and congratulated Alice on the progress Nina seemed to have made in her lessons. 'I spoke to her in English just now and she replied just like a girl from Cheltenham Ladies' College. Then we changed to French and that too seems to have greatly improved.'

'I would be ashamed if it hadn't,' said Alice. 'You've been away a long time.'

Rettenberg's leave was to last for two weeks. The first passed without Alice finding any opportunity to talk to him alone. His wife, his mother, his daughter all clamoured for any time he had to spare. After such a long absence, and with Maxim Markov also away at the front, there was a long list of decisions to be made about the stud and the estate. News of his return brought a crowd of petitioners, many of whom were dissatisfied with the way their grievances had already been dealt with by Olga Pavlovna or Tatyana Andreiovna. Peasant women from the village came to ask if Rettenberg had news of their sons: no letters could be exchanged between those who could neither read nor write. They had little doubt but that Rettenberg, their 'little father', would have kept an eye on their Mitya or Kolya from Soligorsk.

With growing alarm, Alice came to realise that the opportunity might not arise to convey to Rettenberg her change of heart. That she now loved him was now beyond doubt. From brief glances at him down the table at dinner or as they sat around the samovar in his mother's boudoir, she could see that over the past eighteen months Rettenberg had changed. The sardonic, world-weary expression had been replaced by a perturbed and melancholy look. He was not just thinner – the skin now tight over his jaw and cheekbones – he was also nervy. Gone was the languor of the sensuous connoisseur.

But this new Rettenberg attracted her more powerfully than the old one had ever done. The change had no doubt been effected by the suffering he had witnessed at the front; and it was clear that even as he attended to his mother, his wife and his children, part of his mind was on other things. Alice sensed that the war had uncovered a depth to Rettenberg's character that hitherto his self-indulgent hedonism had obscured; and as the days passed and her time ran out, she became afraid that she might be a casualty of this new gravity: that the idea of a dalliance with his children's governess might be something that the new Rettenberg abhorred.

Two days before Rettenberg's leave was to come to an end, and he was to leave for Mogilev to take up a new post at the Stavka, the Russian High Command, Alice was giving her Tuesday lesson in English conversation to Nina when the door to the schoolroom opened and the Baron came in. Nina jumped up; her father gestured to her to sit down and, for the next ten minutes or so, sat on the arm of the sofa in silence.

When the lesson ended, Nina took hold of her father's arm. Alice was about to leave but Rettenberg invited her to accompany them out into the garden. It was an unusually warm day – the kind which presages the start of a short spring. Alice stood saying little while Rettenberg pushed Nina to and fro on the swing on the chestnut tree and then, giving her a hug, told her to leave him for a while because he had things he had to discuss with Madame Chambon.

Nina frowned and looked up at her father. 'She's *not* going to Petrograd,' she said. 'We need to have her and Claude *here*.' And then, having delivered this imperious command, she turned and went back to the house.

Alice followed Rettenberg further into the garden towards a bench under a rose arbour, the weaving branches still black and wet. The bench was damp; they walked on towards the carp pond.

'That is what I thought we should discuss,' said Rettenberg. 'I read the letter with the Grand Duchess Vladimir's request.'

'More like a command,' said Alice.

'It's a habit they find it hard to break.'

'I didn't want to give an answer,' said Alice, 'until I'd talked to you.'

Rettenberg frowned. 'Yes. There are complications, but if you wanted to go, they could be overcome.'

'I'm very happy here,' said Alice.

Rettenberg looked around him. 'Yes. So was I.'

'No longer?' she asked in a tentative tone.

'It can never be the same.'

Alice waited for him to go on. 'This war . . . the suffering . . . the *unnecessary* suffering caused by complacency and incompetence . . . these are things the people will not and should not forgive.'

'The people?'

Rettenberg gave a sardonic laugh. 'Yes, I never used to use the term . . .'

'You said there were only people, not "the people".'

'Well, the war's brought me to change my mind. It's as good a term as any to describe the great mass of Russians whose sons are dying by the million because of the incompetence of the Tsar.'

'You sound almost . . . revolutionary.'

'No, I'm not a revolutionary. It's too late to change sides. But how is one to feel when that weak, ineffective man takes personal command of the army and then sends soldiers into

281

battle with no rifles, and batteries of artillery with no ammunition?'

'Is it his fault that Russia was unprepared? The French and the British also ran short of shells. No one envisaged a war that would last so long.'

'No. No, indeed. Perhaps it wasn't the fault of the Tsar or, if it was his fault, only in his choice of ministers – men like Sukhomlinov who now, it seems, was in the pay of the Germans all along.'

'That seems unlikely.'

'Everyone believes it.'

'That makes it even less likely . . .'

Rettenberg laughed, another joyless croak. 'Ah, Alice, I've missed our talks together.'

'And we've . . . I've missed you.'

Did the tone of voice with which Alice said this get through to Rettenberg? If so, he took no notice of it but said: 'The thing is this. If you want to go to Petrograd, you must go. But if you want to stay at Soligorsk, then stay. So far as I am concerned, this is your home, and while I'm alive, no one will turn you out of it.'

'Does anyone want to turn me out of it?'

'My mother would like to oblige the Grand Duchess, that's all.'

'I will do whatever *you* advise. Madame Chambon is, after all, your creation.'

Rettenberg frowned. 'I don't know what to advise. I would have been most disappointed if I hadn't found you here, but I can see that your particular talents – your knowledge of languages – are perhaps wasted at Soligorsk. And also . . .' He looked away from her. 'You must think of your future. You should find a husband and you're unlikely to find one here.'

Alice said nothing.

'Do you still pine for young Cobb?' asked Rettenberg.

'Most certainly not.'

'So your emotions are no longer engaged?'

'They are engaged,' she said quietly, 'but not to *him*.'

'Ah, well, I won't pry into your private affairs by asking who.'

His voice was brisk once again. 'I think I've said all I wanted to say, but there is something ... Would you mind coming to the summerhouse for a moment?'

'Of course not.'

They turned away from the carp pond and walked back towards the house. 'If you would rather wait here...' said Rettenberg when they reached the door to the summerhouse.

'No,' said Alice firmly. 'I would like to come in.'

It was unchanged – the tattered leather sofa, the books, the desk. Though a stove had been lit and it was warm, there was a lingering smell of damp. 'Some time ago,' said Rettenberg, going to the desk and talking in a brisk, businesslike tone of voice, 'I wanted to give you something as a token ...' He took a key from his pocket and unlocked a drawer of the desk. 'In England, don't they give gold watches to the drivers of locomotives?' he said with a smile, taking a flat leather case from the drawer. He turned to Alice. 'Well, perhaps you should look on this as a token of appreciation of your loyal service to my family.' He held out the case to Alice.

Alice took it but did not open it.

'Don't you want to see what it is?'

Slowly but deliberately, Alice leaned past Rettenberg and put the leather box, unopened, on the top of the desk. Then, turning back to him, she said: 'Before I do, I want to give you something as a token ...' She raised herself on her toes, put her hands on Rettenberg's shoulders, and kissed him.

Rettenberg neither moved forward nor back and, when Alice drew back, said simply: 'Alice ...'

The tone in which he said it was enough. Alice now brought her lips back to his and moved her arms further round to embrace him.

'Why?' he asked. 'I thought ...'

'I didn't know, then ... ' She hesitated.

'What?'

'That I loved you.'

'Alice.' Now it was Rettenberg's turn to take hold of her and kiss her once, and then again, and then take a deep breath as if he could somehow inhale all that she was into his lungs.

'Of course . . .' She leaned back and looked at him with a trace of mockery in her expression.

'What?'

'If you've lost interest in me.'

'I've thought of no one else.'

'There are surely women at the front? Camp followers?'

'There are women at the front, and time and again I've cursed you for making them unpalatable . . . impossible . . .'

'I was so stupid,' she murmured.

'No, you were wise,' he said. 'You weren't to know, well, that you weren't just one among many . . .'

'Another Vera?'

'Don't mention her name.'

'I wouldn't mind if I was . . . if I am.'

'You're not,' said Rettenberg. 'There has been no one . . .'

Alice stopped his words with her lips; then, drawing back, whispered: 'You don't need to say that . . . or anything.'

'I would so like to convince you . . .'

Alice glanced over his shoulder at the box on the desk. 'With a token?'

'No, that, it was simply that before . . . I hadn't realised . . .'

Alice moved aside and opened the box to find the exquisite string of black pearls.

'Don't think,' said Rettenberg, 'that this means . . . They were something I wanted you to have when I thought I might be killed, and now, well, I'm going to be so far behind the lines that it seems unlikely. But take them, please, unless you feel offended.'

'I'll take them on one condition,' said Alice.

'Whatever you like.'

'I'll take them if I can come back to collect them, here, at midnight.'

Rettenberg stepped back, still holding her hand, and looked with amused astonishment into her eyes. 'You drive a hard bargain, Madame Chambon, but if you absolutely insist, I shall be here.'

Could Alice conceal her happiness? That was her main

preoccupation when she returned to the ward. She avoided Sophie and Vera and busied herself with the most menial jobs, as if the stench of pus and faeces would anchor in reality a mind floating up into the ether of rapture. She was happy not just because she felt she was loved by Rettenberg; doubtless many of his countless conquests had felt the same; but rather because she felt so confident in her love for him. She did not rewrite her own history and pretend that she had not loved Edward Cobb; quite to the contrary, it had been the memory of the intensity of her feelings for him that had made her fear that such love came only once in a lifetime. Now she knew that that fear was groundless; she was in love once again.

Eating dinner with the family was difficult; Alice dared not look in Rettenberg's direction. As always, he sat between his mother and his wife. Had his behaviour changed? Would he give them away? She hazarded a glance and saw that, while he looked preoccupied, there was nothing in his manner that might seem strange. Her glance lasted for no more than a second; she did not want him to think that she was trying to catch his eye; but that second was enough to provoke a churning in her entrails as she thought what was to happen later that night.

As they rose from dinner, one of the *sanitars* came in with a telegram that had been brought to the house for the Baron. Rettenberg opened it, read it as if it could not be of much consequence, then read it again. In the dim electric light, Alice could not make out the effect of what he had read on his expression. Again, she did not like to look at him for too long.

'Come upstairs,' said Olga Pavlovna. 'Come, Tatyana, we'll play some cards, perhaps. And you, Madame Chambon, you can't always be working in the wards.'

Alice walked out after Olga Pavlovna and Tatyana Andreiovna, and as she passed Rettenberg glanced into his eyes. They were devoid of expression. He did not seem to see her or anyone else but followed his mother, his wife, his daughter and his daughter's governess up the stairs.

On the landing of the first floor, however, he called to Tatyana and, with a mere inflection of his head, directed her away from his mother's boudoir towards her bedroom. Some ten minutes later he came to the boudoir without his wife. Looking at Alice with a strange expression in his eyes that she could not decipher, he said: 'I wonder if you would very kindly take Nina to bed. There is something I must ... discuss with my mother.'

'Of course.'

Alice felt disturbed that, so soon after his protestations of love, he was treating her as no more than a governess; but then, clearly, in front of his mother, he could hardly treat her in any other way. Nina complained; Rettenberg insisted in a tone that silenced her and made her take hold of Alice's hand. They went to the bathroom. Alice waited as her charge washed and changed into her nightdress and put on a dressing gown. Then the two of them went on their nightly ritual of looking in on little Claude. That done, they went back to Nina's bedroom. Nina knelt to say her prayers, climbed into bed, listened to a story and, after a last hug, the two said good night.

Alice returned to her own room and tried to read a book. It was a quarter past ten. There was time before her assignation to take a bath and change ... into what? What was appropriate for a tryst of this kind? Her clothes must be clean and elegant and simple and not too difficult to take off and put on. But even as she was planning these preparations, and imagining herself naked, perhaps wearing only the black pearls, other thoughts followed a parallel course. What had been in that telegram? Why had he taken Tatyana Andreiovna aside? Then sent Nina to bed? Could there be anything in it that would jeopardise his plans for later that night?

There was a knock on her door. She went to open it. Rettenberg came in. At first he said nothing, but looked down at Claude asleep in his cot. Then he took Alice's hand and looked up at her. 'Sasha is dead,' he said. 'He has been killed ...' He took the telegram out of his pocket and gave it to her to read. 'It's just an official notification,' he went on. 'We'll find out later how and where. I'm sure he died bravely. He had courage ...' And now Alice saw, in the light of the lamp, that Rettenberg was weeping.

'I am so sorry,' she said.

'You hardly knew him, of course,' said Rettenberg. 'But he was the finest son a man could hope to have.' He sniffed and wiped away the tears with his hand. 'But you will understand that tonight I must stay with Tatyana, and with my mother ...'

'Of course.'

Rettenberg went towards the door but then turned back to Alice. 'Everything I said ... this afternoon ... was true. I have thought of you ... constantly ... over this past year. But there are times when others ...'

'I understand.'

'Will you go to Petrograd?'

'I haven't decided.'

'I think you should. And perhaps Tatyana and Nina should go with you. Soligorsk will now become a gloomy place.'

Part Four

One

Lady Elspeth Cobb to Miss Sylvia Cobb, c/o The British Embassy, Petrograd.

13 May 1916

Dearest Sylvia,

It is quite horrible saying what I have to say in a letter but I wanted you to know the sad news before you heard it from gossip: Eddie and I are going to divorce. It is very sad but I think you had an inkling before you left that our marriage hadn't been a great success. Of course, this ghastly war didn't help, and everyone – Mother especially – assumes that it is Eddie's being away that is to blame. She is so angry that she has shut herself up in her room, particularly as Eddie is such a hero: did you know that he now has an MC as well as his DSO? But the fact is that things were wrong from the start: even our honeymoon was a flop. Eddie never really loved me. He thought he did but I think he was always hankering after the dusky seducer. And I don't think I really loved him – now that I know what it's like to be in love. You see – don't laugh – I've fallen for Hal Dormer; he was back on leave and declared himself and, since I knew that he might never come back, everything happened all at once, and though I felt terrible about deceiving Eddie, one night with Hal was really an eye-opener and, well, that was that.

I dreaded telling Eddie but by some miracle (wrong word; no more than a coincidence, I suppose) Eddie got it in first. He said that he felt that our marriage had been a mistake; that he'd made such a mess of things that he'd actually tried to get himself killed going on a raid but got himself another medal instead. When I told him about Hal, he seemed actually relieved. I don't think he thinks much of Hal. 'So he's our next Prime Minister but one,' he said rather scornfully; and it is true, of course, that Hal won't make much of a politician. In fact, he won't make a politician at all. But I don't care. And that's how you know you're in love: when everything you thought you wanted in a man seems by the way.

Oh Sylvia: I now know that one of the main reasons for thinking that I loved Eddie was that I so wanted to be married to your brother. Please go on being my closest, closest friend. Write to me when you can. Is it awful in Russia? We hear stories of terrible shortages, even of food.

With all my love,

Elspeth

PS Lord Cheylesmore and your committee have been very busy raising funds; there are girls in Russian costumes collecting money in Piccadilly; there is to be a matinée at the Empire in the presence of Queen Alexandra with Russian peasant dancers, the Palace Girls, and a speech by Mr David Lloyd George. In the country there have been fêtes and whist drives with people paying a penny to throw darts at a picture of the Kaiser!

Miss Sylvia Cobb to Lady Elspeth Deverall, Deverall House, Belgrave Square, London SW.

15 May 1916

Dearest Elspeth,

It really is most extraordinary here. I don't know where to begin. Did you get my letter describing the frightful voyage on the *Calypso*? I was seasick all the way. I now learn that we were lucky to get to Archangel; ours was the last boat over before the sea froze. We were given a wonderful welcome by the Guards – dinners and dances – but then were told that there was no room on the trains to Petrograd. Luckily, the British jute agent who is known as 'the King of Archangel' soon sorted them out and we only had to wait for three days.

Nothing was ready when we got to Petrograd. We were put up in a girls' boarding school, the Smolny Institute, though now we've moved into a former merchants' club – not a bit like White's or Brooks's, I can tell you! – but comfortable enough. The hospital itself has taken over all the grand rooms in the Dimitri Palace. It's on the Nevsky Prospekt and used to belong to the Grand Duke Sergey. Its present owner, the

Grand Duke Dimitri Pavlovich, has kept the smaller ground-floor rooms for his own use. I've met him once or twice – he pops up to see us when he's on leave – good-looking but not husband material – they say he's dissipated and goes to orgies organised by Prince Yusupov.

Anyway, I'm not here to find a husband but to work, and work I do, along with the others, in pretty dreadful conditions. The drains are primitive, there is no running hot water, and very inadequate heating – this winter was unbelievably cold. But we put up with it largely because our patients – ordinary Russian soldiers, not officers – are so extraordinarily brave. The poor fellows have had such bad treatment in their own hospitals and so are enormously grateful for what we are doing for them. That makes the whole thing worthwhile.

Our main entertainment is the constant rows between Lady Sybil, Lady Muriel and Lady Georgiana, the Ambassador's wife. He's sweet – Sir George – tall, always smartly dressed, a moustache, a monocle – the perfect Englishman abroad. She's a battleaxe – she means well, of course, but she has her own hospital, the British Colony Hospital, and so her nose has been put out of joint by ours. Meriel Buchanan is totally crushed by her mother but has become something of a friend. I've dined once or twice at the embassy – Lady Georgiana came out with Mother – and also at the French Embassy. M. Paleologue, the ambassador, is a real charmer. But our most regular excursion outside the hospital is to the Berlitz Language School, where we try to learn Russian. It's unbelievably difficult. I've only just begun to cope with the Cyrillic script.

Which brings me to the main point of this letter. Because of the language problem we were promised a volunteer nurse who could speak English as well as Russian and French: she had been the governess to some grand country house – Madame Chambon, the widow of a French officer. She arrived last week; I was introduced to her in the staff common room. And who do you think it was? Alice Fry! We recognised one another instantly. She didn't look at all pleased and has been avoiding me ever since. It turns out that she went to Russia as the governess to the family of our old friend Baron Rettenberg – the man who bought Saladin – and pretended to be a widow because she was expecting a child. At first I thought the child was probably the Baron's – you know his reputation; but it appears that the little boy is now two and a half, which means he was conceived some time before she left England. Poor Eddie – he mustn't know. And I don't think he will because she's keen to remain incognito. She apparently lives with the Baroness Rettenberg in their house here in Petrograd, which is very comfortable and up to date so Miss Fry doesn't have to worry about running hot water!

Sooner or later, I suppose, Eddie will find out about the child but I really do think it would be best not to tell him until you have had a baby. You know what men are like about their sons. Apparently the boy's called Claude!

Dearest Elspeth – I do hope you're as happy as you can be with Eddie away at the front and so many of those we love being mown down in such a terrible way. You must be terribly proud, as I am, of his DSO, but I sometimes wish that he wasn't quite so brave and would keep his head down below the parapet a little more.

How lovely our life was before the dreadful Kaiser ruined it all. Please tell everyone in England that the Russians really are doing all they can to attack the Germans and so relieve pressure on the Western Front. There's some resentment here at stories in the papers that the Russians aren't pulling their weight.

Please write. I'll write again.

Your loving sister-in-law,

Sylvia

Madame Claude Chambon to Monsieur et Madame Maurice Fry, 12 rue de la Chappe, Bourges, France.

Petrograd, 3 October 1916

Dearest Mother and Father,

You cannot imagine how my life has changed since coming to Petrograd. As you will know from my last letter, I live with the Rettenbergs in their town house on the Fontanka Canal and take a tram (painted red as they are in London!) to work as a nurse in the Anglo-Russian hospital in the Dimitri Palace.

The Rettenbergs' house is very comfortable, with electric light and central heating. It was built in the Dutch style in the eighteenth century, and although not one of the largest is one of the prettiest, with an internal courtyard and the stucco painted yellow. Before the war, there were half a dozen servants; now there is only the old butler, Viktor, and his wife Dunya, the cook. Katya, the Rettenbergs' elder daughter, has come to live here to be with her mother: Baroness Rettenberg has not really recovered from the death of Sasha. She was always passive and apathetic and has now sunk into a fatalistic torpor. Perhaps it is just as well; a more active person might not be able to bear it. Katya does her best to raise her spirits; and there is their younger son, Fedor, who is a cadet at the Corps des Pages.

First things first – you will want news of your grandson Claude! Here is the monthly report. 1. Perambulation. He runs at great speed around the house followed by Nina, who acts as his Guardian Angel or, in Claude's view, as his slave. Since the house is filled with so many beautiful things, I live in daily terror that he will smash some priceless vase. There have been one or two 'incidents' but fortunately Tatyana Andreiovna is indifferent to material things and Katya thinks 'all property is theft'. Dunya sweeps up the evidence, whispering: 'Better not tell the Baron.' The Baron, in fact, is rarely here and when he is has other things on his mind. Dunya also takes Claude on walks in Peter the Great's summer gardens, which run by the side of the canal. 2. Speech. Claude never stops talking but, I am afraid to say, is a diminutive Tower of Babel, mixing up Russian, French and even English; he will grow up speaking three languages, all of them badly. It would probably have been best to speak only Russian but I have got used to speaking in French to Tatyana Andreiovna, English to Nina (since that was my brief) and, of course, Russian to Viktor and Dunya, so no wonder Claude is confused.

I am relieved to hear that you have enough food in France.

Here it is in short supply. Fortunately, the butchers and grocers who have traditionally· supplied the Rettenbergs continue to do so – they have an eye to their custom after the war; and we can afford to pay their exorbitant prices. But it is dreadful to think of the difficulty faced by the poorer people in the working-class districts where they have to queue for hours for a loaf of bread. And then, as often as not, the baker closes before they reach the head of the queue. All this, quite naturally, is making the government most unpopular. 'An army marches on its stomach' but so does a factory, and the food shortages have led to a number of strikes.

I told you, I think, that Sylvia Cobb is working as a nurse in the hospital. She told me that Eddie had won a medal for being brave. Well, better late than never, I suppose. How glad I am that I am not married to him! Some of those snobbish English women in the hospital remind me of the ghastliness of the English upper classes. To give her her due, Lady Muriel is *hors catégorie*: she treats the wounded *moujik* in just the same way as she does Prince Yusupov or the Grand Duke Dimitri Pavlovich, and it is a joy to watch her plough through the obstacles put in her way by the Russian bureaucracy with her grande dame manner. I also like the Scots surgeons but the English army officers and the younger diplomats are all of a type: stuffy, snobbish and unsure whether to treat me as a respectable widow or a *demi-mondaine*. The Russians, needless to say, don't bother to make the distinction; I may not be *persona grata* with Lady Georgiana Buchanan but I am an *habituée* of some of the best Petrograd salons, am constantly at the ballet, could dine out every night if I chose to, and am to be found at the most fashionable *thés dansants* on my afternoons off. All this, as you can imagine, makes a change from life at Soligorsk.

Will I marry a Russian? Well, if you want the unvarnished truth, *chers parents*, I have a number of suitors but some of them are already married and those that are unmarried may not have strictly honourable intentions. However, I do love the Russians. They're so unlike the English – idle, extravagant, indulgent, pious, wildly generous, easily bored, desperate for distraction, yet invariably disillusioned. They are always ringing me when they have nothing to say and paying pointless calls. Fortunately, Tatyana Andreiovna, thanks to her valerian drops, hardly notices who troops in and out of her drawing room. Old Viktor serves them vodka and Dunya brings up trays of those wonderful titbits that you get in Russia, and Katya's admirers, who are all mad revolutionaries, sit glaring at my *beaux* who they regard as capitalists even if most of their capital is long since spent.

Did you read about the murder of Rasputin? Our Grand Duke Dimitri Pavlovich was deeply involved and Prince Yusupov who shot Rasputin came to hide out in the Grand Duke's apartments on the ground floor of the Dimitri Palace On the day after the body was found under the ice in the Neva, the Chief of Police, General Maximovich, came to place Prince Yusupov under house arrest.

Later in the day, a group of Russians came to the hospital, pretending to visit one of the patients. We became suspicious when they asked one of the nurses which door led to the staircase that went down to the Grand Duke's apartments. We called for Lady Sybil and she called for the guard. A sentry was put on the door; Rasputin's friends left in a rage; the key to the door to the staircase remained with Lady Sybil.

So, as you can see, your daughter is at the heart of all these dramatic events; but she still thinks constantly of her dear, dear parents and longs for the day when she will see them and introduce them to their grandson, Claude.

Petrograd, 2 March 1917

Dearest Father and Mother,

The Tsar has abdicated! To all intents and purposes, Russia is now a republic. And I saw it all, as it were, from the dress circle because our hospital looks out on the Nevsky Prospekt and we could see the crowds pouring across the bridges, the Cossacks waiting on their horses and in front of the Cossacks a line of police trying to hold the line by slashing out with the flats of their swords. The crowd was like a river which burst its banks. People climbed down on to the embankment and crossed on the ice. They were shouting, 'Give us bread' and

'We want peace.' Then there was some firing and Petrograd was put under martial law. Our nurses had to be taken to the merchants' club in an ambulance. Since Claude was safe with Dunya, I stayed at the hospital. The crowd returned to the Nevsky Prospekt the next morning. There were further volleys from the police; the crowd dispersed and then re-formed. We were trapped in the Dimitri Palace and took in casualties from among the demonstrators. At one point, a group of armed civilians burst into the hospital saying that there was a machine-gun firing on the crowd from our roof. The officer commanding our guard denied it and they went away. Later, a group of sixteen soldiers with fixed bayonets burst in demanding twenty-five vests and a pair of drawers. We thought it best to oblige but after that we started to make flags displaying the Red Cross to hang from the windows, using old sheets and a red cloak that had been used as a costume for Father Christmas.

And then, on the Friday morning, came the news that the Tsar had abdicated. The police withdrew. A Red Flag was raised on the Winter Palace. The crowd sang the Marseillaise. It started to snow. I was able to go home.

You can imagine, I am sure, how exhilarating it was to have witnessed such momentous events at close hand. How I wish you were here, *chers parents* – you especially, Father, to see the triumph of your ideals! I kept thinking of Wordsworth and the French Revolution: 'Bliss was it in that dawn to be alive, and to be young was very heaven!' Certainly it was bliss for me to think of all those wretched, down-trodden people freed from their own sense of subjection to an autocrat and the self-serving *barins*; but for Katya, the Rettenbergs' daughter, it really was 'very heaven'. She is now in a permanent state of exaltation. Of course, to her this is just the beginning. On to the proletarian revolution! Although, it has to be said, she is a little muddled about how soon we should expect it because she is what is called a Menshevik, that is a strict Marxist, and until recently took the line that Russia had to move from the feudal to the capitalist phase to create a proletariat, and that, of course, could take a hundred years.

Now, I think, she's changing her views under the influence of a young man she met in the crowd – a Bolshevik journalist who writes for Pravda and who is a protégé of Gorky. He's Jewish, which her parents won't like, but Katya won't mind that. In fact, she'll be delighted. She still hates her father and gets quite cross with me when I try to defend him. She once caught him in flagrante delicto with the village schoolteacher and has never forgiven him. I point out that a liberated woman should have the courage of her convictions; that it is inconsistent for her to dismiss marriage as a bourgeois institution and then condemn her father because he strays. But her animosity is all muddled up with her political convictions; she gives the Baron no credit for his attempts at reform in his youth. To her, he's a reactionary and perhaps he is. He never argues with Katya; but with Fedor she has the most ferocious disputes. His views are reactionary and of course he knows, as brothers do, how to needle her. He mocks Katya, calling her 'a bourgeois if ever I saw one', or says, 'You're a woman, you wouldn't understand.' Katya calls him 'fossil', stamps her foot and walks out.

The Baron came to Petrograd for a brief visit: he was at the army headquarters at Mogilev during the crisis and described how Tsar Nicholas went on playing dominoes as reports came in of the riots. A totally ineffectual man. The Baron's attitude towards the revolution is 'wait and see'. What concerns him is a directive issued by the Petrograd Soviet called Order Number One. It states that from now on the soldiers are to elect delegates to the Soviet, that when off duty they no longer need salute officers in the street and that officers should address them as '*vous*', not '*tu*', which is apparently an age-old grievance since '*tu*' is used for animals and children, and formerly for serfs. To me, the decree seems quite reasonable but the Baron thinks it will mean that what discipline remains in the army will now collapse.

Petrograd, 20 May 1917

... The Bolshevik leaders have returned to Russia. Apparently they travelled in sealed coaches provided by the German General Staff. Fedor says this proves that they are in the pay of the Germans, who hope that the Bolsheviks will create such chaos that Russia will be knocked out of the war. Katya denies that they are German agents but, in her new hard Bolshevik pose, insists that revolutionaries must be pragmatic. Should Lenin have waited in Zurich until he was sent a ticket and a reservation by Thomas Cook? She went with her *beau*, Kirchbaum, to join the crowd which gathered to meet Lenin at the Finland station. Then they followed him back to the Bolshevik headquarters at the house of the ballerina Kshesin-skaya. Lenin spoke to the crowd demanding peace without annexations or reparations, which seems to me to be reasonable enough. The crowd apparently cheered him to the skies but Lady Muriel says that the ordinary people don't understand a word of what he says. 'They think that *aneksiy* is the daughter of Tsar Nicholas and *contributsiy* is a town near Archangel occupied by British troops.'

We have had some distinguished visitors from England at the hospital – a Cabinet Minister, Arthur Henderson, and Mrs Emmeline Pankhurst. There was a time which you will well remember when I would have fallen to the ground to kiss the hem of her dress; but I have to say that when I was presented to her, I felt nothing. That gives you an idea, perhaps, of how I have changed.

I have a new admirer – a young man from the American Embassy called Jamie Burke. I met him at a reception at the US Embassy to which some of us nurses were invited. The Ambassador is a rich businessman from Missouri called David R. Francis. He has a negro valet. Jamie is a second secretary, aged around thirty, from some highly respectable family in Philadelphia and educated at Princeton. He is good company, and reasonably attractive, but I think he's out for an adventure, not marriage to a 'French' widow with a three-year-old son.

We are to go to Soligorsk in August. Lady Muriel has given me leave because of Claude. If it wasn't for him, I would stay in Petrograd. You cannot imagine the beauty of the skies during the summer solstice nights. The other evening I went out to the islands with Tatyana Andreiovna and we walked in the gardens marvelling at the constantly changing colours, and it wasn't until eleven at night that the colours slowly faded with the light.

Soligorsk, 20 August 1917

... We are now at Soligorsk once again – all greatly relieved to escape from Petrograd in the great heat. The hospital is still here but half of the beds are empty. There are some wounded from Kerensky's June offensive but, as you probably know, it achieved little and now the soldiers refuse to go on the attack and there is a flood of desertions. We also feel somewhat safer here than we did in Petrograd: in July the Bolsheviks attempted to take over the government; from the hospital we could see a mass of workers – men and women – and soldiers from the 1st Machine Gun Regiment shouting, 'Down with the government' and 'All power to the Soviets.' It looked at one moment as if they were going to attack the British Embassy – or so I was told by Meriel Buchanan – but they got no support from the Petrograd garrison and the Cossacks fired at them, so they dispersed in panic, stopping only to loot the wine shops and tobacconists on the Nevsky Prospekt.

Because there are fewer patients here, the matron had no need of an extra nurse so I have reverted to my role as a governess – except, of course, that it is the holidays so my duties consist of supervising Nina and Claude as they splash around in the carp pond. It is wonderful for Claude to be able to run around in the garden. And I have time on my own, which is a boon after the hustle and bustle of Petrograd. I particularly like to go to read in the summerhouse. We all miss the Baron but he cannot escape from his duties at Mogilev. He, certainly, hasn't given up on the war and is a great admirer of the new Commander-in-Chief, General Kornilov.

On the face of it, little here has changed. Olga Pavlovna presides over the samovar in her boudoir with Zlata, her old retainer, beside her. Elizaveta, the cook, produces the same delicious borscht and wonderful pastries. But terrible things have taken place close by. Prince Bieletsky who was here for dinner says that the peasants are stealing wood and refuse to pay their rent. And, of course, nothing is done. Leonid Purichievitch, the local Land Captain, now daren't leave his house. He went to remonstrate with some peasants and was given a beating and chased away. He summoned the police. They refused to come. So now he has locked himself up in his house and drinks.

Olga Pavlovna's friend, Father Boris, who also came to dinner (but not with the Bieletskys!), had an equally awful experience. A group of deserters spent the night in his church. They drank all the altar wine and used the vestments as bedclothes. When he went there the next day he found that they had defecated behind the iconostasis and used three ancient icons as kindling for their fire. And no one from the village would come to help clear up the mess.

Things could be worse. Some landowners have been murdered and their houses burned down. Sophie Kyrillovna, my greatest friend here – she's the wife of Maxim Markov who manages the Rettenbergs' stud and estate – well, Sophie thinks that Soligorsk has been spared because it is being used as a hospital, or perhaps the peasants are frightened of Olga Pavlovna: or it may have been the moderating influence of the village schoolteacher, Vera, who was the secretary of the local Soviet until she went as an SR delegate to Moscow.

And I have had some intimation that things are *not* the same. For example – this may sound petty but it will give you an idea of what I mean – I noticed that the chamber pot in my room had not been emptied. I pointed this out to one of the maids – she is called Shura, an intelligent girl who might have come with me to Petrograd. With a look of sullen rage, Shura took the pot, but when she reached the door she turned and said: 'It won't be long now, will it, before you have to empty it for yourself!'

Of course, I was angered by her insolence but also mortified because what she said hit home. Why should she clear up my mess? Because she is paid to do so by Olga

Pavlovna, of course, but wasn't that the product of an unjust distribution of wealth? I can tell you, dear Papa, that it is very awkward to find the comforts one has taken for granted called into question by one's own progressive ideas.

The fact is that all the old assumptions about a social hierarchy have been swept away by the February Revolution. The propaganda of the social revolutionaries and Bolsheviks has finally got through to the peasants and finds fertile ground in their minds – perhaps because of centuries of Christian preaching damning the rich and blessing the poor. This was brought home to me not just by the incident with Shura over the chamber pot, but also by a talk I had with one of the old peasants from the village. I was taking Claude for a walk to the stud; he loves the horses and I like to take a lump of sugar to Saladin, my fellow exile from England. At the paddock, we found this old man Yusef painting the wooden fence with pitch. We stood beside him – a great mistake because he was smelly and repulsive-looking with greasy, matted hair and bristles on his neck – but once there I could hardly move away. I picked up Claude so that he could stroke Saladin on the silken patch on his nose and remarked to Yusef that Saladin seemed in good form. 'Yes, indeed,' Yusef replied. '*He* always has enough to eat.' 'And don't you?' I asked. '*I* do, yes,' said Yusef. 'Surely no one goes short here,' I said. 'No one's *starving*,' he said, 'but some get more than others.' Then he looked up at Saladin. 'And who will get this one, I wonder, when the time comes for things to be shared out?' I was dumbfounded. 'Surely,' I said, 'Saladin belongs to Baron Rettenberg.' 'Only as long as the government says so,' Yusef replied. 'At least, that's what we've been told.'

Petrograd, 8 September 1917.

... We have returned to Petrograd despite the political uncertainty. Things are quite clearly getting worse. You can tell it by the rude way we 'bourgeois' are treated on the trains. Our main fear now is that the Baron may be implicated in General Kornilov's attempted coup and so be in danger of arrest. The whole episode reflects badly on Kerensky and he has lost support on all sides: it is thought that he encouraged General Kornilov – whom *he*, after all, had appointed Commander-in-Chief – to move reliable units of the army to Petrograd because the present garrison has been so thoroughly Bolshevised. Then Kerensky became alarmed that Kornilov would use his troops to take power so he roused the Soviets. The train carrying the 1st Don Cossack Division was stopped by the railway workers; the Red Guards and the Kronstadt sailors took up arms 'to defend the revolution' and the whole thing collapsed. Kerensky ordered the arrest of the generals who had backed Kornilov and they are now being held in the Bykhov monastery.

Another development – Katya has left us to live with her Bolshevik young man. This has upset me more than Tatyana Andreiovna, whose apathy and fatalism seem to leave her numb. When Katya told her that she was leaving home, Tatyana thought she meant she was returning to live with the Sararins. Katya said no, she was going to live with a friend. 'Do we know her?' Tatyana asked. 'He's a man, Mother. He's my lover.' And all Tatyana Andreiovna could say to that was: 'Your lover? Oh dear. Your father might not like it.' To which Katya replied in her usual aggressive manner: 'I don't care whether he likes it or not.' Her trousseau, by the way, was made up of the dirtiest, roughest clothes she could find. She is determined not to be taken for a bourgeois.

We have just had a telephone call from Baron Rettenberg. He has not been arrested. Apparently, General Alexeyev is once again Commander-in-Chief. He says that the front is so fragile that a determined push by the Germans would give them Petrograd. He promises to warn us when the time comes if he feels we should return to Soligorsk.

Petrograd, 23 October 1917

Dearest parents,

I hope you got my telegram in reply to yours. Do not be concerned for our safety. It is quite possible that this second revolution sounds more terrifying in stories in the newspapers than it really is. Most of the population of Petrograd goes about its daily life just as it did before. The shops, the cafés, the theatres, the restaurants remain open.

Of course I long to see you again, and if I had only to consider myself and Claude, I would take the train to Murmansk and from there a boat to England. However, I am still needed here. The hospital could perhaps do without me (though few of the English nurses have learned much Russian, Sylvia Cobb least of all!) but the Rettenbergs have come to depend on me and it would seem wrong to abandon them after the kindness they have shown, at least until the Baron returns. With Katya gone, Tatyana Andreiovna still paralysed by her dejection, and Fedor too young, it is left to me to take charge. Grim things are taking place: the Bolsheviks arrest rich bourgeois, as they call them, on the most spurious charges and hold them until they are ransomed by their families. There are also groups of so-called Red Guards who are permanently drunk and therefore dangerous, but they still respect the nurse's uniform and my British passport carries some weight.

During the siege of the Winter Palace, I was at the opera with my American friend, Jamie Burke – Chaliapin singing in Verdi's *Otello*! Until then, our main fear was that the Germans would take Petrograd. The western embassies were preparing to leave. When we came out on to the Nevsky Prospekt after the opera, we heard the sound of gunfire coming from the river. We knew that it couldn't be the Germans, and when we got to the restaurant, we were told that it was the Bolsheviks up to their tricks again.

A friend of Jamie's, a journalist, Brad Burlingame, came to join us and told us that the Reds were besieging the Winter Palace. Kerensky had gone to the front to try and raise some loyal troops: he had to 'borrow' a Renault from the American Embassy and fill it with petrol from the English hospital! That gives you an idea of how powerless he had become. All the other ministers remained in the Winter Palace guarded by some Cossacks, military cadets and two hundred women from the Shock Battalion of Death. Apparently, the Cossacks felt humiliated at fighting with women and the women panicked as soon as the first shell was fired from the *Aurora* and ran down to the basement.

My biggest worry was that Fedor might have been among the military cadets, but since there was nothing I could do at the moment, we continued the evening as planned – going on from Cubat's to listen to the gypsies on the islands. It was so intoxicating that we forgot about the revolution.

The next day we heard that Fedor had indeed been among the cadets at the Winter Palace, that he had been wounded and taken to a hospital by the Red Guards but had escaped by shinning down a drainpipe, despite one of his arms being in a sling! He went into hiding – I don't know where – but sent a message to Tatyana Andreiovna to say that he was well. The poor woman: she doesn't really know what is going on and once again apathy saves her from worry.

The Baron paid a brief visit to Petrograd a week after the Bolshevik coup. It was bizarre to see him wearing shabby civilian clothes but anyone seen in the streets smartly dressed or in the uniform of an officer is likely to be abused, robbed or worse. He had good news: Fedor managed to reach Mogilev and is now being treated in a military hospital as a casualty from the front. Otherwise, he was in a grim mood. He advised me to go back to England while there was still time. But it was clear that he hoped that I would *not* take that advice because he had to return to Mogilev – he could not desert his post while there was still fighting at the front. He thinks that we should remain in Petrograd while the hospital is still functioning and there are still the embassies of the Entente.

If the embassies leave, then we will go to Soligorsk, though Pavel had heard that there were difficulties there. Before he left, he gave me gold sovereigns which he said we were to conceal somehow in our belongings. We should be ready to leave at a moment's notice.

So, as you can see, dear parents, we are living through dramatic times but for the time being anyway your daughter and grandson are warm, well-fed and surrounded by friends.

Alice

PS Since our new rulers are quite capable of opening and reading letters and arresting anyone who makes disparaging remarks about them, I shall send this from the hospital via the diplomatic bag.

Petrograd, 25 November 1917

Dearest parents,

We may not remain in Petrograd much longer. Two days ago, the Bolsheviks came to the house looking for the Baron – five were soldiers from the Latvian Rifle Brigade led by some kind of commissar wearing a black leather jacket, which seems to be their uniform. They searched the house. Their hobnailed boots made terrible marks on the parquet floor.

The Sararins have left for Dimitry Alexeyovich's estate near Tambov. Yesterday, Varvana Fedorovna came by with Evgeniya and Angelica to say goodbye. She said that Dimitry Alexeyovich has been in hiding for the past ten days, sleeping in the homes of his former students. She showed us how to conceal jewellery in our clothing. We chose the drabbest clothes, closest to those that might be worn by a working woman: Varvana stitched a ruby necklace and two diamond rings into a blue pleated dress and two diamond necklaces into the cuffs of a blouse. Some of the less valuable pieces were left on Tatyana Andreiovna's dressing table to allay suspicion. I unstitched the hem of a dress and put in a necklace that the Rettenbergs were kind enough to give me and concealed the gold sovereigns behind the lining of an old sewing basket I found in the attic. The paper money I have hidden beneath the inner soles of my shoes.

It was just as well, because the same group of Bolsheviks returned today to search the house more thoroughly, and this time they took what valuables they could find. The commissar said that he was acting under orders from the Soviet to expropriate superfluous wealth 'for the needs of the people'. He wrote out a receipt listing the items taken – a bureaucratic thief! But the sting was in the tail: as he was leaving he said that four other families would be moving into the house. We

307

have been allocated two rooms on the first floor – Tatyana's bedroom and the Baron's dressing room. The kitchen and bathrooms are to be shared! Poor Tatyana Andreiovna; she has no idea of what awaits her.

Petrograd, 2 December 1917

Dearest parents,

This may be the last you hear from me for some time. The hospital's funds have been frozen: it is to be handed over to the Russians and the British personnel are to go home. The embassies of the Entente are leaving Petrograd and so the moment has come for us to leave as well. The last month has been grim. There is no food and no fuel: we shiver in our two rooms. The 'proletarian' families who now live in the house subject us to constant abuse. They have stripped the rooms of everything that can be sold on the street – beautiful china, silver and works of art. What we managed to hide, we too have to barter for food. It is almost unobtainable except, of course, to Party members. Katya drops by every now and then with some supplies. She is clearly upset to see her mother and sister suffer but still feels that it is 'bliss' to witness the birth of a new world.

I live in constant fear, not for myself but for Baron Rettenberg and Tatyana Andreiovna. Lenin has founded a Bolshevik Okhrana, called the All-Russian Extraordinary Commission for Struggle against Counter-Revolution and Sabotage – Cheka for short – which appears to exercise the power of life and death over anyone they deem counter-revolutionary. It is quite possible that they will arrest Tatyana and Nina and hold them as hostages against the Baron's good behaviour. The Baron, of course, cannot come near us: there is no doubt that our new 'neighbours' act as spies for the Cheka. That is why we must return to Soligorsk, but we too are watched so it will not be easy. I feel sorry to leave the loyal Viktor and Dunya but they may be relieved. If Dunya is caught washing the Baroness's clothes, she is called 'a bourgeois lackey and class traitor' by the vile harridans who have taken over the kitchen. Their husbands are invariably drunk, having 'expropriated' the wine in the Baron's cellar. Their verminous children play hopscotch on the Aubusson carpet and the portrait of the Baron by Lazlo is used as a dartboard. It is a new barbarian invasion that will take Russia back to the dark ages.

Dear parents – do not worry if you do not hear from me for some time. I fear the normal postal services no longer function, and even if they did, it would be too dangerous to write anything but high praise for the new order of things.

Two

Careful plans were laid for the escape from Petrograd. The day was fixed; the tickets were purchased and the necessary permits obtained by Katya, whose enjoyment of the revolution was being spoiled by the spectacle of her mother's ordeal. Despite the permits, it was thought prudent to avoid alerting their new neighbours. Viktor and Dunya therefore smuggled the travellers' clothes out of the house over a number of days, leaving them in the house of the local priest. On the morning of their flight, Tatyana and Nina left early with their prayer books as if going to mass. Later, Alice went out with Claude as if taking him for a stroll. At the priest's house there was a painful parting with Viktor and Dunya, after which, laden with their baggage, they took a tram to the Nikolaivsky station.

With a vigour she had not thought she possessed, Alice barged through the crowds on the platform, carrying Claude in one arm, holding her suitcase with the other, with Tatyana Andreiovna and Nina following behind. They clambered on to the train. All the seats were taken and the corridors were packed tight with silent and shifty men and women – hungry workers going to the country to scavenge for food, deserting soldiers passing through Petrograd on their way back to their villages; and one could tell from the furtive look or some give-away trait – a pair of pince-nez or a too-clean handkerchief – other *burzhoois* on the run.

One of these, sitting hunched in a corner, risked exposing

himself with a chivalrous gesture: seeing Alice burdened with Claude, he rose and offered her his seat. Their eyes met but only for a moment: a brief look that said all. The middle-aged man then squeezed out into the corridor. Alice did not see him again.

It took twelve hours for the train to reach Morsansk. There was no food to be bought on the platform, and though an attendant struggled down the corridor with glasses of tea, there were no trays of *pirozhkis* and *vatrishkis* that before could be bought on Russian trains. Bread, cheese, apples and sausage that they had brought from Petrograd were sufficient to sustain them during the long journey.

No car awaited them at Morsansk: Alice had feared that a telegram announcing their arrival might give them away. There were *droshkys* and, after close bargaining, one of the drivers agreed to take them to Soligorsk. A dank mist lay over the dirty snow: inside the *droshky* it was acutely cold. Nina wriggled close to her mother; Claude slept enveloped in Alice's coat. It grew dark. The driver, not knowing the way, had to stop to ask directions. Finally they came to the crest of the hill where, four and a half years before, Rettenberg had stopped to show Alice the view of his childhood home. From here she knew the way – down the hill, along the valley, and into the avenue of poplars that led to Soligorsk.

Alice slept. Once or twice she was awoken by an anxious thought about Claude; or by one of those dreams that draw on such recent experience that it takes a moment for the mind to decide whether or not they are dreams. The snarling, mocking faces of the Bolshevik women; the struggle through the packed mass on the platform of the Nikolaivsky station; the strange, defeated look of the chivalrous stranger; the rocking and clatter of the train – all were relived in her semi-conscious mind until she half awoke and felt herself deep and warm in her old bed; and saw the dim winter light at the edge of the curtains; and heard nothing from Claude's bed – then she swooned back into sleep and remained unconscious until once again she was jolted awake by another dream.

Alice rose, finally, at eleven in the morning. Claude was not in his bed, but since they were at Soligorsk, this did not seem a reason to worry. When she came downstairs, Alice found her little son in the kitchen with Nina and Elizaveta, the cook.

The hospital had gone. With Nina and Claude, Alice went into the large and once-lovely rooms, looking at the debris that had been left behind. 'Why haven't they cleaned up, I wonder,' she said to Nina.

'The maids have all gone,' said Nina.

'Gone where?'

'Back to the village.'

'Shura? Marya? Lydia?'

'All of them. There's just Elizaveta and Zinaida and old Nikifor. Even Zlata's gone. Come and see Babushka. She'll tell you what's happened.'

Olga Pavlovna sat in her accustomed place in her velvet button-backed chair, but she was alone: there was no Zlata hovering behind her. 'Ah, Madame Chambon,' she said. 'Come and sit down. Is Tatyana still sleeping? How very tired you must all have been. Nina tells me that you travelled in a third-class compartment. Can that be true?'

Alice sat down on the sofa facing Olga Pavlovna. 'We were lucky to get on the train at all.'

'Well, I can imagine that if they've stolen my house in Petrograd they've also reserved the first-class compartments for themselves. And they've taken my house *furnished*, have they? Well, one mustn't care too much about one's material possessions.'

'I see that the hospital has gone,' said Alice.

'Yes. A week ago. Or was it longer? I can't remember. When was it, Zlata?' Olga Pavlovna turned to the companion who was not there. 'No, of course, Zlata has gone too. The old fool. Her nephew put her up to it. Did you ever meet him? I don't suppose so. He kept away from the village. Nasty, crafty, even as a boy. Quite bright. He learned to read and write and I paid for his studies in Moscow. Deserted from the army, of course.

They say he and his friends shot their officers after being filled with devilish ideas by Bolsheviks.'

'What has happened to the farm and the stud?' asked Alice.

'There, we've been fortunate. Maxim has returned. He's kept things more or less in order. The peasants respect him. Or, at least, they did. And you . . . you're back. That is good. Pavel wrote to me and said that you could have left for England but that you chose to stay.' The old lady raised her head and looked at Alice with a piercing scrutiny. 'Are you in love with him? Well, never mind. You don't have to answer. The fact is that Pavel's gone off with those generals, leaving no one to take care of his family but you. Tatyana was never one to bear hardship, and Sasha's death, well, that would drive the strongest woman to despair. And Katya. Is it true that she has gone to live with a Bolshevik?'

'Yes,' said Alice.

'I blame Pavel. It's all the fault of his liberal ideas. "As you sow, so shall you reap." You didn't know him when he was young, of course, but he was all for placating the peasants. But it was quite clear to me that if you gave *anything* away, they'd come back for more and never be satisfied until they had it all. Well, they won't get anything from me. I've told Maxim Lvovich that he can make some concessions – give them more of the harvest if that's what they want – but they shall not have my land and they shall not touch my horses. I'm quite implacable on that.'

Wrapped up against the cold, Alice took Nina and Claude to visit Sophie Kyrillovna. 'Oh thank God,' said Sophie, embracing Alice at the door. 'I've longed for you to come back. We feel so beleaguered here. We daren't ride off the estate. Did you hear that Leonid Purichievitch was killed? The stupid man. He knew that they were out to get him – they have it in for all the former Land Captains – and he'd been lying low at home, drinking. But he went to visit one of his peasant girls. She had a child he thought was his. He got into an argument with her family so they simply killed him. Stuck him with a pitchfork. Called it revolutionary justice and so nothing was done.'

Alice asked after the other neighbours and for each family Sophie had some grim anecdote. The Milyukins' manor house had been plundered; they were now living with relatives in Perm. The Bieletskys had fled to Kiev and in their absence their house, too, had been ransacked and then burned. 'The peasants are so stupid. They took the silver, of course, because they could see the use of forks and knives and candelabra; and they took the bed-linen. The curtains they tore down to make themselves dresses; but they thought the Bouchers were indecent and of course the furniture wouldn't fit into their hovels so they burned it. Priceless things went up in smoke.'

'And here?' asked Alice.

'So far so good. But it can't last. Maxim's done what he can to calm them down. He's offered them this and that – far more than Olga Pavlovna realises.'

At four in the afternoon, Maxim Lvovich came in from the stud. Alice had not seen him for two or three years but, from his appearance, she would have thought it ten. His fair hair had receded, his figure was stooped and, in the few seconds before he realised that she was in the room, Alice saw that his face, once so open, so cheerful, so naïve, was fixed in an expression of despondence and worry. When he did become aware of the visitors, the old geniality returned. He embraced Alice, marvelled at Claude, kissed Nina and asked after Tatyana Andreiovna. Then, drawing Alice aside, out of earshot of the children, he said: 'I wonder if it was wise for you to come back here.' The look of anxiety returned to his face.

'I thought it best,' said Alice. She told Maxim what had happened in Petrograd and Maxim agreed, or pretended to agree, that they had had no alternative but to leave. 'The only advantage of Petrograd,' said Maxim, 'is that one could, if the worst came to the worst, run to ground. Here everyone knows who you are for miles around.'

'But surely,' said Alice, 'they won't turn Olga Pavlovna out of her house.'

'She was safe enough while it was used as a hospital but now, I don't know . . . They aren't rational about these things. They want revenge.'

'For what?'

'For the centuries of injustice, or what they see as injustice. They not only want to share out the land; they want to punish the landowners.'

'But they won't act without authority, will they?' said Sophie.

'Oh, authority is easy to come by,' said Maxim with a laugh. 'There's a village Soviet now, and that wretch Yakov, Zlata's nephew, has been elected as secretary. He's clever enough. I saw him this afternoon in the school where he's established an office. I explained about economies of scale – how, if the farm was divided into small holdings, there would be no surplus to sell and so no money to buy seeds and machinery. I also told him that the racehorses could be of no possible use to the peasants: they might pull a cart but they couldn't pull a plough. He understood this: I could see. He put up no argument against me but simply said: "These are things for the people to decide. They are our masters now."'

'So what do they want?' asked Sophie. 'The land? The horses? The house?'

'We shall find out tomorrow. They're sending a deputation at midday to present their demands to Olga Pavlovna.'

'Would you like me to warn her?' asked Alice, rising. It was getting dark and she thought the time had come to return.

'If you wouldn't mind waiting,' said Maxim, 'then we will come with you.' He turned to Sophie. 'I think it might be prudent if we went to sleep in the big house tonight.'

'I won't leave my home,' said Sophie.

'Just for tonight,' said Maxim. 'I heard, this afternoon, that the Boborokins' daughter ... a band of deserters broke into their house ...' He glanced at the children and held back what he had meant to say.

'God help us,' said Sophie, and with no further protest, she went to pack a suitcase with overnight clothes.

The deputation that came the next day was not a group of the elders, nor even the members of the newly constituted village Soviet, but almost the entire population of the village – around one hundred and twenty men and women with forty or fifty children – the younger ones staying by their mothers, the adolescents running around on their own.

The peasants came up the drive to the front door. Previously, when a group from the village had come to present a petition, they had come through the courtyard to the door by the kitchen at the back of the house. At the head of the column were the village elders – five old men with huge beards, matted hair, lined, weatherbeaten faces and inscrutable expressions in their eyes. To their right was Yakov Grigorivich, Zlata's nephew, and towards the back of the column was Zlata herself. Among the peasants were men in army uniform – some deserters who had been given shelter, others young men from the village who had survived the war.

Maxim admitted them into the hall and then, standing on the third step of the staircase, he welcomed them on behalf of Olga Pavlovna but regretted that she was unable to come to talk to them because she was indisposed.

In fact, as Alice had witnessed, Olga Pavlovna was perfectly well, but she had been put into an uncontrollable rage by the arrival of the peasants at the front door. 'What insolence! Do they think they are the nobility now? And all of them – the entire village? Do they think they can intimidate me? Send the elders round to the back door, Maxim, and send the rest of them away.'

Maxim advised her, coaxed her and finally begged Olga Pavlovna to come down to meet the villagers in the hall. He turned to Tatyana for support: Tatyana looked back at him as if she was a bemused spectator at a game whose rules she did not understand.

'It would surely save time, Olga Pavlovna, if you saw them now,' said Sophie Kyrillovna.

'I have plenty of time,' replied Olga Pavlovna.

'A kind word would win them over,' said Maxim.

'A kind word! They come to steal my property and I'm to greet them with a kind word?'

'It might be best . . .' began Alice.

'If you minded your own business, Madame Chambon. It's you French who started all this nonsense with your revolution.'

'If you don't come down,' said Maxim in desperation, 'they may force themselves upstairs.'

Fire flashed from the eyes of Olga Pavlovna. 'Let them try!'

The news that Olga Pavlovna was indisposed seemed to confuse the villagers. 'Then who should we speak to?' asked one of the elders.

'Where is the Baron?' The second elder turned to Tatyana Andreiovna, who stood with Alice and Sophie by the door to the drawing room.

Tatyana turned to Alice. 'Where is Pavel, do you know?'

'He's still with the army,' said Maxim.

'That's not what we hear,' said one of the men in a military tunic.

'We hear he's joined Kornilov and the counter-revolution,' said Zlata's nephew, Yakov.

'Then you are better informed than I am,' said Maxim.

'He should be here,' said the first elder.

'The war isn't over,' said Maxim.

'It is for us,' said the soldier with a guffaw.

'Listen, good people,' said Maxim, looking over the heads of the elders to speak to the villagers, 'I would ask you into the drawing room but there's nowhere to sit down. The beds have gone and the furniture is still stored away.'

'Not for long,' said a voice.

Maxim smiled weakly.

'Friends . . .' said Maxim patiently.

'We're not your friends,' said the same coarse voice.

Maxim ignored him. 'If you would present your ideas, and if your ideas are ratified by the Soviet, then Olga Pavlovna, I know, will do what she can to accommodate you.'

'She won't have any choice,' came another anonymous voice.

'We have our proposals here,' said Yakov with a sly look on his thin face. He was wearing civilian trousers but a soldier's tunic. He took a sheet of paper from his pocket and, after glancing at the village elders for their approval, began to read:

316

'By the decree of the Soligorsk Soviet dated the seventh of December 1917, all the land, buildings and chattels of the Soligorsk estate are hereby expropriated and belong henceforth to the commune. No compensation is to be paid. The former owners are to be held in custody pending the investigation of charges.' Yakov read this edict in a flat tone of voice but it nonetheless provoked a roar of approval from the crowd crammed into the confines of the hall.

'What charges?' Maxim seemed at his wits' end.

'For one,' said Yakov with a look of delight on his face, 'the charge is exploitation, namely that my aunt Zlata, who, perhaps you know, worked all her life for Olga Pavlovna and never received a wage.'

'That ... that ...' Maxim looked confused. 'That is something I know nothing about. It's for Olga Pavlovna to answer that charge.'

'Then bring her down,' shouted one of the soldiers.

'Yes, bring her down,' echoed another.

'Or we'll fetch her down,' said a third.

'Yes, fetch her down,' came the clamour from the crowd. A surge from the back pushed the front row forward on to the first step of the stairs.

'No,' said Maxim. 'You will stay where you are.'

'And who's going to stop us?' said the first soldier, taking his rifle from his shoulder.

'I appeal to you ...' said Maxim, his arms outstretched to bar the way.

There was the sound of a shot. A look of shock came on to Maxim's face. He staggered back, then fell. Sophie ran forward but so did the crowd – trampling over Maxim's body as they advanced up the stairs. Then suddenly those in front stopped. The roar faded. There was complete silence except for the tap of an old lady's stick. Olga Pavlovna had appeared at the top of the staircase and, clasping the banister with one hand and her stick with the other, started to descend.

The elders, together with Yakov, retreated in front of her, pushing back on to those behind, their heads lowered to avoid meeting Olga Pavlovna's eyes. Like a receding wave, they passed back over the inanimate body of Maxim.

'Well?' said Olga Pavlovna, pointing her stick at Sophie, who had run forward with Alice to her husband's body. 'Is no one going to help Sophie Kyrillovna take Maxim Lvovich to a bed? You, Marya, didn't we nurse your children in our dispensary when they had diphtheria? And you, Yusef. Didn't I pay for Dr Schimpfel to treat you? And didn't I pay for those expensive drugs from Germany which saved your life?'

Yusef, followed by Marya, and then two or three others who, no doubt, wished to pre-empt a reminder of their debt to Olga Pavlovna, came forward to carry Maxim's body across the hall.

'And you, Tolya, you rascal. You'd be dead if I hadn't sent for Dr Schimpfel when you had appendicitis, so you go for him now. Take a horse – one of my horses – and be sure you bring it back.'

A boy – one of the adolescents who had been hovering on the edge of the crowd – slipped away to do what he was told.

'Now,' said Olga Pavlovna, coming to a halt near the foot of the stairs and staring fixedly at the lowered heads of the village elders, 'you've come for my land, have you, and my horses, and to arrest me, is that correct?'

None of the old men raised his head.

'Come, speak up. You, Timofey. We've known each other long enough. Say what you have to say.'

The old man looked up. 'It's the government's orders, Olga Pavlovna, your excellency. We're to expropriate the expropriators.'

'Expropriate the expropriators! Good heavens, Timofey. You can't even pronounce the words properly, let alone tell me what they mean.'

'God bless you, Olga Pavlovna. We never meant any wrong.'

'You don't know what you meant, you silly old man. If the Baron was here, you wouldn't be so brave!'

The elder lowered his head: the others remained mute. The young man who stood beside them, Yakov Grigorivich, Zlata's nephew, raised his head and, staring insolently at Olga

Pavlovna, said: 'All the same, if I may say so, there is the decree of the Soligorsk Soviet . . .'

'Nonsense!'

'And there are the charges, namely that you wilfully exploited the worker . . .' Yakov now lapsed into his 'clerical' tone of voice.

'I heard you, young man. I exploited your aunt Zlata, did I? I never paid her a wage? That's true enough, isn't it, Zlata? Stop hiding behind Timofey. You're the chief witness for the prosecution, after all.'

Cautiously, her head lowered, Zlata moved from the cover of the broad-backed peasant in front of her. 'I never meant no harm,' she croaked.

'I dare say you didn't,' said Olga Pavlovna, 'but you've been complaining, as always, I dare say.'

'I only mentioned,' said Zlata, 'that I was never paid a wage.'

'Of course you weren't paid a wage,' said Olga Pavlovna. 'You weren't a worker. You were my companion and, as I thought, my friend. Did you not live in my home? Did you not sleep in a bed? Eat at my table? Wear the clothes off my back? Drink tea from my samovar? Go wherever I went? Did you not come with the family to France, to Italy and to Karlsbad? What *wage*, may I ask, would ever have paid for what you enjoyed?'

Zlata was silent.

'Nonetheless,' began Yakov, sounding less confident, 'my aunt worked for you . . .'

'She never *worked* for me, you young idiot,' interrupted Olga Pavlovna. 'She shared my life. And she shared it by choice. There was never a moment when she was not free to return to the village. But she did not go. She chose to stay.'

Yakov was silent.

'Am I speaking the truth, Zlata, or am I not?'

Zlata was silent, but since the villagers all looked to her for an answer, she said, in a pitiful voice: 'Yes, Olga Pavlovna, what you say is true.'

'And is it not also true, Zlata, that you told me, time and time again, that your nephew Yakov was a rascal and a

319

good-for-nothing? Didn't you tell me that he always put his friends up to pranks and left them to take the blame?'

Again, Zlata was silent, but her expression was enough to persuade a number of villagers that this too was true.

'He was always no good,' said one.

'I never trusted him,' said another – and with a cowed murmur the peasants at the back of the hall started to shuffle out through the door.

'I am calumniated . . .' began Yakov.

'Olga Pavlovna,' said the first elder, interrupting him, 'most gracious Olga Pavlovna, if you could see your way to overlooking this intrusion, and the unfortunate accident that has befallen Maxim Lvovich – it was not our doing, I beg you to believe me, the culprit will be punished . . .'

'Abject lackeys!' said Yakov, turning contemptuously from the elders and striding to the door.

'I will talk to you tomorrow,' said Olga Pavlovna. 'To you, the elders. Not the whole village.'

Bowing, the elders backed away.

'Come at noon,' she said, and then added in a venomous tone, 'And this time, come to the *kitchen* door.'

The bullet fired at Maxim Lvovich had struck the side of his body. Alice, as she tended him with Sophie, using bandages and dressings left by the hospital, judged that it had shattered a rib but had not penetrated the lung: Maxim was not coughing up blood. They disinfected the wound and stopped the flow of blood. Maxim was conscious but in great pain. With no morphine, Alice could do little to alleviate his suffering. Dr Schimpfel arrived at two in the afternoon. He gave Maxim an injection of morphine and then, with Alice to assist him, probed the wound to extract the bullet.

The operation completed, Dr Schimpfel proposed that he should take Maxim back with him to town. 'It is most important that he should have proper care. It would also be safer. I have made it quite clear to the Soviet that the class war stops at the door to my clinic.' He advised Sophie and her children to go with him. 'You can stay with us. We have a large house.'

Sophie agreed. She returned to her own home to collect some more belongings and at four the Markov family set off with Dr Schimpfel in his buggy. Though it was not yet dark, Alice and the faithful Nikifor and Elizaveta went around closing the shutters to the windows on the ground floor. 'That Yakov will be back,' said Nikifor. 'He'll be out for revenge.'

Olga Pavlovna would not alter her routine. At five, she presided over the samovar in her boudoir and at eight came down to dine in the billiard room as before. With no oil for the generator, the rooms were lit by candles. 'If those scoundrels would bestir themselves,' said Olga Pavlovna, 'we could bring the furniture down from the attics and use the dining room once more.' Olga Pavlovna's mood was triumphant; unlike Elizaveta, she felt she had won not just a battle but a war.

After dinner they returned to Olga Pavlovna's boudoir – Tatyana to pore over her jigsaw puzzle, Olga and Nina to play cards. Alice, having been to see Claude, joined the card game and at nine rose to take Nina off to bed. As Nina was kissing her mother good night, they heard a banging on the ground floor. Tatyana looked up, alarmed. 'Is that a loose shutter, I wonder?'

They listened in silence. There was another rhythmic banging, not the sound of a flapping shutter but of someone hammering on the front door.

Alice went down the stairs holding a candle and met Nikifor in the hall. 'Should we open it?' she whispered, as if she felt it might be better to pretend that they were not there.

There was a further hammering. Alice went to the door. 'Who's there?'

'It's me, Rettenberg,' came a voice which, though muffled by the thickness of the wood, she recognised at once. She drew back the heavy bolts and opened the door. There stood two men in soldiers' greatcoats. One, only his eyes showing between his fur hat and the high collar of his coat, was Rettenberg; the other Pytor.

'Thank God you're safe,' said Rettenberg. He removed his

gloves, then his hat. Elizaveta came forward to take his coat. 'Ah, Nikifor, Elizaveta, you're both still here.'

'Of course we're still here, Pavel Fedorovich. Where else should we be?' the old man said.

'God will reward you,' said Rettenberg. He turned to Elizaveta. 'Now, can you find something for us to eat? Take Pytor into the kitchen. I'll join you in a moment.' He turned to Alice. 'Are they all upstairs?'

'With your mother.'

'Where else?' With Alice he started up the stairs. 'I ran into Schimpfel and poor Maxim and heard about this morning's drama.'

'Maxim was heroic.'

'I knew I could rely upon him but, all the same, we asked too much.'

Nina, who had heard her father's voice, threw herself into his arms when Rettenberg reached the top of the stairs. He carried her into the boudoir and, while Nina still clung to him, embraced his mother, then his wife.

'Where have you been?' Olga Pavlovna asked him in a reproving tone of voice. 'The peasants have been most tiresome. You should have been here.'

'I couldn't leave Mogilev while we were still fighting a war. But now that the Bolsheviks have asked for an armistice – which amounts to a surrender – I'm free to leave.'

'And Fedor?' asked Tatyana.

'He's gone south with two of his friends.'

'You can speak to the elders,' said Olga Pavlovna. 'They're coming back tomorrow at noon.'

'They mustn't find us here,' said Rettenberg.

'How do you mean?' His mother frowned.

'It won't be the elders, Mother. It will be Yakov with a gang of murderers calling themselves Red Guards.'

'But where are we to go?' asked Tatyana Andreiovna in a plaintive voice.

'South to the Don,' said Rettenberg. 'Alexeyev is already at Novocherkassk. Kornilov set off last week with the Tekintzy

Regiment. Romanovsky, Denikin and Lukomsky are all travelling as civilians. Fedor and his friends are on their way to Odessa pretending to be students. I have been travelling as a private soldier with Pytor; if we are questioned, Pytor does the speaking . . .'

'But can you trust Pytor?' asked Tatyana Andreiovna.

'With my life,' said Rettenberg.

Olga Pavlovna said nothing.

Rettenberg turned to Alice. 'Will you come with us?'

'Of course.'

Three

The preparations for the long journey began at once. Rettenberg had brought passports and travel documents made up at Mogilev which he hoped would suffice to get them through. He thought it too dangerous for Alice to take her British passport: if it was discovered, she might be shot as a spy. Packing took little time. They were not just obliged to travel light – there would be no porters to carry their trunks – but also the clothes they took with them would have to be the shabbiest they could find. All the things they had valued – the silver-backed hairbrushes, the bottles of scent and eau de Cologne – were to be jettisoned and replaced with crude combs retrieved from the maids' bedrooms and rough soap from the bath house.

To Nina, the search for their oldest clothes, and taking boots and dresses that the maids had left behind, was like rummaging in the dressing-up drawer for a fancy-dress party. As in Petrograd, Alice, with the help of Elizaveta, sewed pieces of Olga Pavlovna's jewellery into her clothes. Olga Pavlovna remained aloof: she would not choose what to take with her, but when Alice suggested some garment or necklace would say: 'Yes, why not?' Tatyana, having disguised herself for the journey from Petrograd, knew what to take and what to discard; but it was clear to Alice that she had become painfully agitated at the thought of leaving her home.

At two in the morning, they slept. At six, Rettenberg roused them again. Olga Pavlovna had tea served in her bedroom: the others ate breakfast in the kitchen, Elizaveta weeping as she served them because she had chosen to stay. 'But you'll be back, you'll be back,' she said to Nina, who, seeing the cook cry, had caught her dejection. 'It'll only be for a while, you'll see. God will strike these devils down.'

Rettenberg came in from the yard and sat down next to Alice at the kitchen table. 'Pytor has harnessed Saladin to the cart. He has put a saddle in the back, and when he's dropped us at the station, he'll ride Saladin to Novocherkassk.'

'But that must be a thousand miles,' said Alice.

'It's possible, if he takes his time.'

The moment came to depart. Alice and Tatyana went up with Rettenberg to fetch Olga Pavlovna. She sat, fully dressed, in her usual chair. 'You are leaving?' she said to Rettenberg.

'Everything is ready,' said Rettenberg.

Olga Pavlovna turned her face aside as if to receive a filial embrace.

'Are you ready?' asked Rettenberg.

'I have decided to stay.'

'You cannot stay, Mother. It isn't safe.'

'Nikifor and Elizaveta are staying. They will look after me.'

'They can go to the village, Mother. They won't be harmed. But they won't be so kind to you.'

'I'm not afraid of that wretched Yakov . . .'

'He'll be back with soldiers. They will rob you and burn the house.'

'They wouldn't dare!'

'Mother, they are drunkards and murderers. They have already killed Purichievitch . . .'

'Then let them kill me,' said Olga Pavlovna. 'I would rather die in my own home than . . . out there.' She nodded to the window through which a pale light had just now appeared.

Rettenberg turned to his wife. Tatyana came forward. 'There is no time to argue, Mother,' said Rettenberg. 'I cannot leave you here. You must come.' Son and daughter-in-law each took hold of one of the old lady's arms and lifted her out of her chair. Frog-marched in this way, she stumbled out of the room, across the landing and down the stairs. At the foot of the stairs, Rettenberg let go of her to take up her coat. With a quick twist of her arm, Olga Pavlovna broke free from Tatyana, took hold of the banisters and started to pull herself back up the stairs. Rettenberg leaped after her. 'Mother, you must come...' Tatyana and Alice came to his aid. Half-falling, Olga Pavlovna clung on to the balustrade. She said nothing but her face was fixed in an expression of black determination. One by one, her fingers had to be prised open before she could be brought down to the hall, bundled up in her coat, covered with a scarf and taken out into the waiting cart. The Russian custom of sitting quietly for a moment before starting a journey was forgotten: the other members of the Rettenberg family embraced Nikifor and Elizaveta and climbed into the cart. Baron Rettenberg got up beside Pytor. Pytor twitched the reins and, with a sudden lurch from the racehorse in harness, they set off.

Passing through the villages on the way to Morsansk, a number of peasants remarked upon the disparity between the majestic qualities of Saladin and the wretched condition of the cart. To any questions Pytor cheerfully answered: 'Expropriate the expropriators, comrades,' or, even, quite brazenly: 'He's from the stud at Soligorsk. Put to work at last.' Since both he and Rettenberg had red cockades in their soldiers' caps, and since the women and children in the cart passed as peasants in the dim light of the cold morning, the spectacle seemed plausible given the chaotic nature of the times.

Saladin was very unhappy in harness, pulling the cart in short bursts, then stopping and pulling from side to side. When they came to a hill, Pytor would climb down from the driver's seat and lead Saladin by the bridle; and then, as they reached the crest, jump up again and pull the brake as Saladin, with a lighter load, tried to sprint to the finish. But by eleven they were in the outskirts of Morsansk and by twelve they were at the station.

When they were on the pavement with their luggage, Alice saw Rettenberg and Pytor exchange a glance which, like that of the chivalrous stranger in the train, said more than words. They then turned away – Pytor to ride away from the station, Rettenberg to lead his family towards the ticket office and from there on to the train.

There were seats on the train which took them on the first leg of their journey, and because it was going towards Moscow, the Red Guards in the corridor showed little interest in the passengers, who seemed to be, in the most part, Muscovites returning with food from the country. Bundles tied with sack cloth were stuffed on to the luggage racks and there was the smell and the cackle of poultry in boxes and cages. No one attempted to talk to anyone else; the passengers avoided one another's eyes. Both Tatyana and Olga Pavlovna looked vacantly into mid-air; Nina played the game to perfection and Claude either slept or stared wide-eyed out of the window.

In Tula they had to change on to a train going south, and from the moment their train drew into the platform, it was clear that this would be the most testing part of their journey. The station was like an ant-hill; a solid mass of people surged and jostled on the platform, the uniformed station master at one moment raising his head to shout some inaudible announcement, at another lowering it to listen to some importunate traveller. Rettenberg led his family through the crowd, clutching his mother by her arm. Behind him came Tatyana with Nina, and Alice, holding Claude with one hand and her suitcase in the other, brought up the rear.

Compounding the crush was the bottleneck caused by a group of Red Guards checking the papers of those making for the trains going to destinations outside Bolshevik control. Watching Rettenberg push his way through the crowd, Alice feared that he would give himself away with his commanding manner. They reached the barrier; Rettenberg presented the papers and passports that had been drawn up at Mogilev. These were scrutinised by two men in leather jackets, clearly members of the recently instituted Cheka.

'Andrei Lozovsky?'

'Yes,' Rettenberg replied.

'What is the purpose of your journey?'

'I am taking my mother to my family in Rostov.'

'And you will return?'

'Of course. As you will see, I have been given leave of absence by the factory Soviet.'

'I am quite able to read.'

The Chekist handed Rettenberg back his papers but told him to wait while he examined the passports of the others. Alice could not bear to watch or to listen as Olga Pavlovna came under their scrutiny; though she had been told time and again on the journey to Tula who she was supposed to be, it was quite possible that she would either forget or, in a fit of fury, treat the Chekists in the same way as she had Yakov.

She said nothing. Tatyana and Nina, too, seemed to pass scrutiny. The commissar then came to Alice who, in her forged passport, was described as a seamstress and, because her accent might betray her, had been given a German name.

'And why are you travelling to Rostov?'

'I have an offer of employment, comrade.' Again she showed him the letter inviting her to work in a clothes factory and the requisite stamps from the Bolshevik authorities in Perm.

'Are you travelling with this family?'

'We met on the other train.'

The Chekist handed Alice back her papers and was about to wave her through when Claude pointed to the hissing locomotive and, turning to Nina, said in a delighted voice: '*Regarde, Nina, encore un choo-choo.*'

The Chekist snatched back the passport. 'So, you are German but your son speaks French.'

Alice blushed. 'I have been trying to teach him French.'

'I don't like the look of it – or of them.' He pointed out the Rettenbergs to the soldiers. 'Arrest them.'

'But they are not with me,' pleaded Alice. 'I only met them on the train.'

The Chekist paid no attention; the Rettenbergs were grabbed and, with Alice, led to a car waiting by the entrance to the station. The Chekist came with them, leaving his colleague at the barrier. His face had a look of muted triumph; Rettenberg's was without expression. Olga Pavlovna seemed indifferent as to whether she was being bundled one way or another and Tatyana simply looked bewildered.

They were driven fast and erratically to a building in the centre of the city. On the wall outside, it had the plaques of commercial enterprises – insurance companies and the like. They were taken into an office on the ground floor which had been requisitioned by the Cheka. Here Rettenberg was separated from the women and children: Alice saw him dragged down a flight of stairs by two soldiers and for the first time she realised the danger they were in. It would not take long for the Chekists to find out that Rettenberg was not an engineer from Moscow, that his papers were forged, and from this deduce that he was a Tsarist officer on his way to join the counter-revolutionaries on the Don. And what would they make of her? What if they found out that she was British? Was not Tula a centre for the manufacture of armaments? Might she not be taken for a spy?

Alice, Claude and the Rettenbergs were taken to a large, dimly lit room at the back of the building in which around two dozen other women were sitting, mainly on the floor. It had been used for storage; there were tall wooden cupboards along one wall and small windows high on the other. The women were silent: most seemed to be, like Alice and the Rettenbergs, bourgeois dressed up as proletarians; but no one dared say anything for fear either that their speech would give them away or that one of their number might be an informer. The room was airless; there was little ventilation and the only lavatory was a bucket behind a screen in the corner.

Since Alice was the chief suspect, she was the first to be summoned to appear before the commission. There was some difference between the two soldiers as to whether or not she should be allowed to bring Claude; the softer-hearted had his way and she was escorted up the stairs with her child. There she was thrust into a hot, crowded room and taken before a man in the ubiquitous black leather jacket: the Cheka commissar. She lowered her eyes in a posture of submission.

'So, Comrade Kaufmann. You are a seamstress from Perm?' The commissar's tone of voice was amused. Alice looked up and at once recognised Leonid Sergeiovich Solovyov, her patient from the hospital at Soligorsk. She opened her mouth to cry out his name, then thought better of it but gave a fleeting smile of recognition.

Solovyov turned to the Chekist who had arrested Alice at the station. 'Do you know who we have here, comrade?'

The Chekist looked blank.

'We have here the daughter of the publisher of Engels. Am I not right, Comrade Kaufmann?'

'Yes,' said Alice.

'Not just the publisher of Engels, but of Gorky, and a man who gave money to our socialist comrades in exile. When was that, Comrade Kaufmann?'

'In 1907.'

'Ten years ago, in their darkest days.' Solovyov turned to the Chekist. 'Of course, you were not to know this . . .'

'Comrade, I . . .'

'But it is a grave error all the same.'

'Indeed.'

'If I hadn't been acquainted with Comrade Kaufmann . . .'

'It is a grave error, but . . . the child spoke French.'

Solovyov looked at Claude, then at the Chekist. 'Is that grounds for suspicion?'

'I only thought that if the mother was German . . .'

'We are internationalists, comrade. Would you have arrested Vladimir llyich Lenin if you had heard him speak in French?'

'No, of course not.'

'Or Marx if you had heard him speak English?'

'Indeed not, comrade.'

Solovyov looked down at the notes. 'I see that Comrade Kaufmann is travelling with some companions.'

'Yes, comrade, all bourgeois, and one – the man – we have reason to believe is an officer on his way to the Don.'

'Yet they were travelling with Comrade Kaufmann?'

'Yes. They say they met on the train.'

'Do you think that Comrade Kaufmann, whose father published the work of Friedrich Engels, would have counter-revolutionaries among her friends?'

'I don't know if they were friends.'

'Were they your friends?' Solovyov asked Alice.

Alice nodded. 'Yes.'

'There you are,' he said to the Chekist. 'This woman is our comrade – that I can vouch for – and they are her comrades – that *she* can vouch for.'

'Of course.'

'Go and see that they are released.'

The Chekist hesitated. 'The engineer has been ... interrogated.'

'And has he confessed?'

'Not as yet.'

'Then please inform our comrades that he should be released.'

The Chekist left the room.

'Leonid Sergeiovich ...' Alice began.

Solovyov held up his hand. 'Do you remember, perhaps, a conversation in a garden by a carp pond ... Comrade Kaufmann?'

'I do.'

'Your parables about the peasants who wouldn't spit on the icon or turn their landlord out of his house?'

Alice hung her head.

'Things have changed, I think.'

'They have.'

'The people have been weaned from their opium.'

Alice nodded. 'So it would seem.'

'And the landlords are being evicted from their manors.'

'Yes.'

'And are perhaps going to join the generals in the south?'

Alice looked up and met his eyes. 'No doubt.'

Solovyov looked down at his notes. 'You are with one man, two women and two children?'

'Yes.'

'They are your friends?'

'More than friends.'

Solovyov thought for a moment, then said: 'Well, one man won't change the course of history.' He wrote a note on a piece

330

of paper. 'You must show this to the clerk in the hall. He will issue you with the requisite *laissez-passer* and make sure you are given seats on the train.'

Alice took the piece of paper. 'Are you . . . quite recovered?' she asked timidly.

'Quite recovered, yes.' He stood to take her to the door. 'I had excellent treatment, you see. The nursing in particular was first class. And now . . . to witness the revolution. To play a part. That is the best tonic of all.'

They reached the door. Solovyov lowered his head to whisper in her ear. 'Don't linger,' he said. 'Take the next train.' He then raised her hand to his lips and kissed it. '*Bon voyage*, Comrade Kaufmann.'

The Chekists who had arrested them drove Alice and the Rettenbergs back to the station. There they were ushered through the barrier and on to the first-class coach reserved for the Bolshevik *nomenclatura*. They were allocated two compartments, each with two bunks. Rettenberg, Tatyana and Nina went into one: Alice, Claude and Olga Pavlovna into the other.

Once the train was under way, Alice joined Rettenberg in the empty corridor to smoke a cigarette. His face was bruised; in places the skin had split and was sealed by his dried blood.

'I don't understand,' he said to Alice. 'Why did they let us go?'

'The commissar had been a patient at Soligorsk,' said Alice. 'I had nursed him and . . . he was grateful.'

Rettenberg frowned. 'There must have been more to it than that.'

'He became a friend,' said Alice.

Rettenberg looked at her sharply. 'Just a friend?'

Alice smiled. 'Are you jealous, Baron Rettenberg?'

Rettenberg blushed and looked away.

'If I had bartered my body for your life,' she said, 'you should be grateful, not angry.'

Rettenberg encircled her with his left arm and hissed into her ear: 'You *are* my life.' They then stood there, their bodies touching, staring out of the window at the dark landscape with points of light where oil lamps burned in the peasants' huts.

The train trundled south, passing through Orel and Kharkov, and making a number of unscheduled stops along the line. Every now and then, Red Guards would come through to inspect the passengers' papers, but since Alice and the Rettenbergs were travelling in a coach reserved for Bolshevik commissars and had a *laissez-passer* heavily embroidered with the official stamps of the Tula Soviet, they were treated with a measure of respect.

Reaching the southern edge of the industrialised Don basin, they stopped at a small station, where the Red Guards disembarked. The railway inspector, looking uneasy, came to tell Rettenberg that they were passing from territory held by the Reds to areas occupied by the Whites and might be attacked by either side. At the junction at Sachty, White soldiers climbed on to the train, and two hours later it drew into the station at Novocherkassk, the capital of the Cossack state of the Don.

As she stepped on to the platform, Alice felt giddy with relief. Here, in the station, mixing with the colourful costumes of the Cossack women, were men in the uniforms of officers in the Imperial Army. Gone were the leather-jacketed commissars with pistols stuffed into their belts and the soldiers whose unbuttoned tunics and caps set at a jaunty angle proclaimed their contempt for the old hierarchy of the Tsarist state. The terror had ended. They were safe.

It took time for Rettenberg to find his friends among the generals and for those generals to find a place for the Baron and his family to stay. In the end, it was less their influence than Rettenberg's gold that found them a small house in the outskirts of the city. They were driven there in a *droshky* and, thanks to the money they had at hand, were quickly provided by their landlord with food, bed-linen, a cook and a maid.

There was a pleasant sitting room with a wicker sofa and chairs and an icon stand in the corner; a dining room that opened out on to a veranda; and three bedrooms – one for

Olga Pavlovna, one for the Rettenbergs and a third for Alice and the two children. Once he had established his family, Rettenberg left to enrol in the volunteer army. It was left to Alice to organise the household: Tatyana Andreiovna watched from the sofa as the baggage was unpacked, while Olga Pavlovna withdrew into her room and went to bed.

When Olga Pavlovna was asked if she wanted some soup – the first cooked food any of them had had for four days – she sent Nina back to say that she was not hungry. She had scarcely eaten on the train, and Alice had assumed this was from a disdain for their supplies – black bread, cheese, apples. Now, however, she realised that there was more to Olga Pavlovna's fast. The old lady was angry and determined not to do anything to oblige her persecutors – by which she meant not the Bolsheviks but her own family, in particular her son Pavel. When he returned that evening – cold and tired – and sat down with his family to a simple supper, he asked after Olga Pavlovna and was told by Alice that she wished to stay in her room.

'But she has to eat,' said Rettenberg, rising and going to fetch his mother from her room.

Olga Pavlovna came to the table, but to thwart her son, she did not eat. Nor would she join in the conversation. When offered a plate of borscht, she said: 'It does not appeal to me.'

'You must eat something,' said Rettenberg.

'I will do as I please.'

'Are you comfortable in your room?'

'In a *chambre de bonne*? What do you think?'

'We are lucky to have lodging at all.'

'And how long are we to stay in this . . . lodging?' he was asked by his mother.

Rettenberg shook his head. 'I don't know.'

That evening, after Olga Pavlovna had returned to her room, Rettenberg explained to Tatyana and Alice – essentially he was addressing only Alice, since Tatyana showed no interest in what he said – the condition of the volunteer army. 'Nothing has turned out as we had hoped,' he said. 'Kaledin shot himself last week. The Germans have moved into the Ukraine. There are

Red armies moving against us from Kharkov. The generals are preparing to move all of us across the steppes to the Kuban.'

'Will we go with them?' asked Alice.

Rettenberg shrugged. 'I see no alternative. We have some good men but not enough to hold Rostov and Novocherkassk.' And then he added: 'Here we are to go under the name of Zagoskin. There are Bolshevik spies everywhere and it would be dangerous for my friends in the areas under Red control – in particular for the Sararins and even for Katya – if it were to be known that I had joined Kornilov.'

Olga Pavlovna fell ill. As the city continued in a state of confusion, detachments of Cossacks clattering down the street and the small volunteer army, composed largely of officers and military cadets, paraded in front of their generals, Olga Pavlovna turned her face to the wall. She ate nothing, drank little and so grew thin and feeble, the skin hanging loosely from her arms. Only when Rettenberg came to the house did her eyes show any life: they stared at him angrily, either from across the table to which he carried her, or from beneath the covers of her bed. Alice, who would accompany Rettenberg into Olga Pavlovna's bedroom in her role as her nurse, occasionally intercepted the hard glances from eyes sinking into their sockets. 'Why did you bring me here? Why did you not leave me in my home? What death could be more miserable than this in a *chambre de bonne*?'

A doctor was sent for and he came – another worthy German. His diagnosis was old age. 'These are terrible times for the old, Herr Baron. They die because they do not want to live – and who can blame them?'

Tatyana Andreiovna watched, perplexed, as her mother-in-law declined. Nina came at times to talk to her grandmother but her chatter went unanswered. Alice, as the old lady grew weaker, tried to get her to drink; but whenever she tried to raise her body in the bed, Olga Pavlovna went rigid, and when Alice held a cup to her mouth, she pursed her lips and clenched her teeth. When Rettenberg took on this duty, she was equally recalcitrant, again glaring at her son with a look of mute reproach.

Rettenberg, burdened by administrative duties that had been thrust upon him by the commander of the volunteer army, General Kornilov, begged his mother to eat or drink until there came a point when rational arguments no longer penetrated into her mind. Her gaze became imprecise; her brow puckered as she struggled to remember quite what it was she was so determined to do. 'Where is Fedor?' she asked Alice. 'Is he in London?'

'Fedor Pavlovich is in Odessa.'

'Not Fedor Pavlovich, you stupid woman,' said Olga Pavlovna. 'Fedor Mikhailovich, my husband. Where is he? Will you send for him?'

'He is in Heaven,' said Tatyana Andreiovna, who was with Alice at her mother-in-law's side.

'In Heaven?' Once again the old woman looked perplexed. 'You say he's in Heaven? Is he there with another woman?'

'No, Olga Pavlovna,' said Tatyana. 'He is waiting for you to join him.'

The next evening Rettenberg returned with a priest. 'Ah, Father Boris,' murmured Olga Pavlovna. 'Have you come to lunch? And is Aroadna Mikhailovna with you?' She tried to pull herself up from the bed. 'You must have a glass of vodka. Zlata! Where is Zlata? Ah, there you are . . .' She was looking at Alice. 'Bring the reverend father some vodka. It is so cold, so cold . . .'

The family gathered round the bed as the priest administered the last sacrament to Olga Pavlovna. Her eyes were open but uncomprehending; her face so emaciated that it already seemed to be that of a corpse. But whatever she did or did not understand, the rite seemed to calm her. 'Ah, Pavel,' she said, looking without anger at Rettenberg, who sat by her bed. 'Do you think he will manage the journey?'

'Who?'

'Pytor. Will he find us here with the horse?'

'He may do, Mother. I hope he will.'

'Yes.' She sighed. 'It would be good to have something from Soligorsk . . .'

'We have ... everything from Soligorsk that matters with us here,' said Rettenberg, holding his mother's frail hand to his breast.

'Yes, that's true,' said Olga Pavlovna slowly. 'They can't take that away, can they? That happiness ... the past.'

Olga Pavlovna died that night. She was buried in haste early the next morning after a short funeral in the nearby church: General Kornilov had ordered the evacuation of Novocherkassk.

Four

Rettenberg, holding his horse by its bridle, walked with General Kornilov and his staff at the head of the column that set out over the thawing ice of the River Don. Kornilov was also on foot, a short, thin man wearing a goatskin coat with a haversack slung over his shoulder. Behind them marched the volunteer army – a pitifully small body of men made up of military cadets and former officers of the Imperial Army, many of them now serving as ordinary soldiers. Looking back, Rettenberg could see – as any Bolshevik spy could see – how paltry were their armaments, how few the field guns and machine-guns they had with them.

Behind the soldiers came the camp followers, mostly women and children, some walking, others lucky enough to ride on carts, many wearing only the thin clothes they had brought from their homes in the cities. Before leaving Novocherkassk, Rettenberg had bought a horse and cart at exorbitant cost. Nina, who had grown into a good horsewoman, took the reins; while Tatyana, Alice and Claude sat on bags filled with straw. They were better clothed than most but did they know what lay ahead? Did he know himself? Though there were sound reasons for the retreat into the Kuban, Rettenberg wondered whether the heterogeneous detachments that marched behind him could ever be forged into an effective army.

He kept these doubts to himself. To his fellow soldiers – and to his family, whom he joined every evening either in a makeshift tent, or, if they were fortunate, in the outbuildings of a Cossack *stanitsa* – he presented a cheerful and optimistic façade. It became increasingly difficult to sustain their morale: the grim march continued for week after week, the soldiers and civilians walking through the slush and mud, their clothes soaked by rain and sleet, sleeping rough in the *stanitsas*, fording rivers in flood, fighting skirmishes with Bolshevik partisans, eating little and sometimes nothing for days at a time, with the weak falling ill and, every morning, a hurried ceremony to bury those who had died during the night: but never once did Rettenberg reveal his misgivings about the ultimate triumph of their cause.

The moments when Rettenberg believed his own propaganda were few. The zeal of the volunteers, their extraordinary courage, and the superiority of their discipline and training all made them as effective as an army ten times the size. But Rettenberg could not escape the fear that they were fighting for something that was irretrievably lost. His pessimism came from his own experience: now that they had witnessed the enmity of the peasants, how could they ever return to Soligorsk? And would he want to return to Soligorsk without his mother?

The death of Olga Pavlovna had affected Rettenberg more than he could ever have envisaged. Whenever, in the course of his past life, he had asked himself who he was and what he was to become, it had been his mother who had furnished the answer. He was her son and heir, the fusion of her husband's pedigree and her wealth; the star pupil in the Ecole des Pages, the officer in the Chevalier Garde, the member of the Jockey Club, the diplomatic dabbler, the lover of fashionable women – all of these had been her creation.

Like Russia itself, Rettenberg had lost one identity and could not envisage another. Nor could he shed the sense of remorse that accompanied his grief at his mother's death. He was haunted by her implacable fury at being forcibly taken from Soligorsk and remembered with anguish prising her fingers from the banisters. Why had he not left her as she had asked? How much better to have let her take her chances with the

Bolsheviks than die miserably in a housemaid's bedroom in Novocherkassk.

Rettenberg also felt responsible for the present suffering of Nina and Tatyana Andreiovna. They too might have been better off remaining at Soligorsk instead of accompanying him on this quixotic adventure. He felt responsible for the terrible privations they now endured. Though Nina never complained, Rettenberg saw how her hands had become red and swollen from holding the reins in the biting cold, and there were chilblains on her ears and nose. With Tatyana Andreiovna it was worse: the figure she presented filled Rettenberg with a mixture of shame and disgust. The beautiful woman he had married was now thin and filthy, old beyond her years. As the weeks passed with little opportunity to take baths or wash clothes, let alone apply powder or rouge, Rettenberg noticed an ever-widening band of grey where Tatyana's brown hair grew from the scalp: he had not known that she had dyed her hair.

What disillusion life had brought her. And who had been the prime agent of that disillusion? The man who had chosen her like a statue to please his mother, and had then left her in an empty niche at Soligorsk while he chased after other women. And now? There was no Soligorsk. And there was no Olga Pavlovna. The stage upon which Rettenberg had played his life had been demolished and the author who had created his character had put down her pen.

Rettenberg was saved from his despondency by Alice, and as the campaign proceeded, it was she who enabled him to become the cheerful and courageous man of his pretence. Despite the vile conditions, Alice remained beautiful and she became strong. She took charge of Rettenberg's Nina and Tatyana as well as caring for her own Claude. It was Alice who, when they took refuge in a *stanitsa*, found them bales of straw to sleep on and placed them in a corner out of the wind. It was Alice who bargained over bread with the Cossack peasants and cajoled the successful scavengers among the soldiers to give them some of their food.

Rettenberg watched with a jealous eye the devotion Alice inspired among the men. After the first engagements with Red partisans, there were casualties, and there was constant praise for the foreign *sisteritsa* who helped care for the wounded. It was known that Alice was part of Rettenberg's household; but this did not seem a reason for a number of the young officers not to pay court to her, and some of the older ones as well.

Alice, in the looks Rettenberg intercepted, and the small intimacies of touch and tone of voice that they were able to exchange, made it plain that he had nothing to fear from these younger rivals; nevertheless, Rettenberg felt jealous and became impatient to stake his claim. Hitherto he had hoped to avoid humiliating Tatyana Andreiovna by conducting an affair under her nose; but his resolve faded as the trek over the freezing steppes tore away every vestige of civilised life. The lack of soap and water and the scant privacy, far from dousing Rettenberg's desire, enhanced the attraction; and the elemental instincts grew stronger with death so close.

Kornilov's objective was Ekaterinodar, the capital of the Kuban. As the volunteer army moved closer, it became more vulnerable to attack by Bolshevik forces sent up from Tsarytsyn or from the Black Sea on armoured trains. On a number of occasions, detachments of volunteers were ambushed by the Reds in the deep fords or narrow gorges, but always their superior training and the courage that came from desperation saved them from defeat. In early April, the *stanitsa* of Novo-Dmitrovskaya in the approaches to Ekaterinodar was captured and secured as a shelter for the camp followers. The army moved forward for an assault on the city, and in anticipation of casualties a medical unit went with them, with Alice, the foreign *sisteritsa*, on its staff.

Alice volunteered, confident that Claude could be safely left at Novo-Dmitrovskaya in the care of Nina, because there was a great need for her skills as a nurse; but there was also a less altruistic motive behind her gesture – she did not want to be parted from Rettenberg. If he was to be wounded, she must be there to tend him; and if he was to risk his life, then she would risk hers too.

Alice had been too preoccupied with the day-to-day business of survival to analyse her feelings for Rettenberg, but the very severity of the conditions that they had encountered together had forged a bond far stronger than anything she might have anticipated in a civilised state. All those things which might have led to repugnance – the smell, the filth, the pain, the hunger, the fear – had in fact enhanced her love with the comradeship that comes with shared privations.

She had also come to know him better than she ever could have done in a more settled life. She had seen his grief after the death of his mother and his anguish at his impotence to save Tatyana and Nina from their present ordeal. She had seen how, despite this inner desolation, he had remained good-humoured and raised everyone's morale. Rettenberg also looked handsome on his horse, and her heart trembled when, every evening, she saw him walking towards her through the mist and smoke from the camp fires, his long greatcoat swirling around his ankles, his head bowed in thought. She treasured those rare moments when, in the dark of night, he would reach out from where he lay to take hold of her hand and sometimes reach under her rough blankets to lay it gently on her chest. The smell, the filth, the pain, the hunger, the fear – all weighed lightly in the balance against the joy of moments such as these.

On 8 April, the medical unit to which Alice was attached reached the ferry across the River Kuban close to Ekaterinodar. The day before, Red Guards had attacked the vanguard of the volunteer army as it had made the crossing but after ferocious fighting had been driven back into the town. There were a number of casualties from the previous day's engagement and the field hospital was set up by a barn close to the ferry. Knowing that Rettenberg had taken leave of absence from Kornilov's staff to fight with Kasanovich's White partisans, Alice searched for him among the wounded. He was not there.

On 10 April Kornilov ordered a frontal assault on Ekaterinodar, and a further flow of wounded soldiers were brought back to the ferry. Scraps of information came with them: Markov's regiment of White officers had taken an artillery barracks in the outskirts of Ekaterinodar; General Kasanovich's partisans had broken through the Red defences and had reached the Haymarket in the centre of the town. Was Rettenberg with them? She did not know; but all the while, as she washed the most terrible wounds and bandaged them up as best she could; as she used soft words where there was no morphine to try to alleviate the agony of some young soldier; Alice thought only of Rettenberg and what had happened to him.

In the early evening of the 11th, after a lull in the fighting, Alice sat outside the barn on a tree trunk with two of the doctors, drinking tea. The weather was now warmer and it was still light. The three were tired and spoke sporadically; the sounds that puncuated the silence were the snorts and neighing of horses, the bark of a far-off command and the call of a bird of prey.

Then, suddenly, Rettenberg was there standing in front of her, his uniform filthy, his boots caked with mud. There was something menacing about his manner, but beneath the peak of his cap were smiling eyes.

'Have you a moment?'

Alice placed her metal mug on the ground and slipped off the tree trunk without a word. Rettenberg took her hand and they walked slowly up a track that led away from the barn alongside the river. 'We've been down at the ferry picking up supplies,' he said.

'Is the town taken?' asked Alice. 'Have we won?'

Rettenberg shook his head. 'No. We got into the centre but we couldn't hold it. We were only two hundred and fifty men. They outnumbered us ten to one.'

'So what will happen?'

Rettenberg shrugged. 'We'll regroup and try again.'

The track, following a bend in the river, had taken them out of sight of the hospital and the ferry. Between the track and the river there was a band of willow trees and impenetrable undergrowth, broken every now and then by a small path to allow fishermen to reach the river bank. Alice followed

Rettenberg down one of these paths to a small glade by the river. The light was now fading. Rettenberg laid his greatcoat on the ground. All was quiet and they were alone. Still standing, Rettenberg embraced her, and she clung to him. Neither spoke, but his kisses were like whispers and she heard, as if it was a cry of a bird, a whimper rise from her throat. Her legs grew weak; she could not stand; but as she sank to the ground she felt herself caught and gently laid on the greatcoat. The many months of yearning had finally come to an end.

Five

Edward Cobb returned to London from France in January 1919. After the armistice with Germany the previous November, conscripted officers had been impatient to be demobilised and get on with their civilian life. Edward, who had elected to remain in the army, was given the task of reorganising his battalion in readiness for a further push towards Germany should the Germans refuse to accept the terms of the Entente.

When he did return on leave, Edward was fêted as a hero. Two grand dinners were given at Nester – one with beer and roast beef for the tenants and estate workers, another with champagne, lobster thermidor and *tournedos aux morilles* for the neighbours and family friends. In London, too, there were dinners at private houses, and reunions with comrades from the trenches; while eminent members of the Conservative Party did their best over lunch at their clubs to persuade him to resign his commission and resume his political career.

Edward accepted the laurels placed on his brow with modesty and grace. He did so because this was expected of him, but he found the festivities quite as much an ordeal as the war. He did not feel a hero; he did not want to stand out from the crowd. It pained him acutely to see how the attitude of his comrades from the trenches, often conscripts from modest backgrounds, changed as they came to appreciate Edward's elevated station in civilian life. His decorations had already set him apart but they were a distinction they could esteem; not so the accoutrements of social ascendancy – the titled relatives, the chauffeur-driven car, the butler who answered the telephone.

These things were now also alien to him, but how could he shake them off? As he sat at the candlelit tables of his family and friends eating rarefied dishes off delicate porcelain, he hankered for the bully beef and beans on tin plates in the dugouts; and as he listened to the gay chit-chat of elegant women, or the ponderous discourse of his political friends, he longed to be back among soldiers with no ambition but to beat the Boche and no pleasure beyond waking each morning to find oneself alive.

After five years spent in dugouts or transitory billets sleeping on palliasses laid on planks, Edward felt uncomfortable in his parents' house in Eaton Place. The soft mattresses, linen sheets and fluffy blankets stifled him. He was determined to move out. He now owned a house of his own in Lord North Street – the house, bought with his money, where he was to have lived with Elspeth; but there was no staff to run it and the furnishing was incomplete. Edward therefore moved from Eaton Place to the small flat in Duke Street whose lease he had bought in 1913. It was, he told his mother, handy for White's and Pratt's, clubs that could cater for a bachelor without an establishment of his own. Edward did not tell his mother that, besides its convenience, the flat also held some of the few memories that he treasured from his pre-war life.

Much had changed since he had last lived in England – most notably the death in the trenches of so many of his friends. Most of the calls Edward paid while he was in London were to their parents – painful encounters in which he felt almost embarrassed that he should have survived. His decorations proved that he had not dodged his duty, but that hardly consoled the grieving mothers and fathers. Even as they thanked Edward for his condolences, they could not conceal an expression of resentment in their eyes. There was also the matter of his divorce: it was generally known that Edward was the innocent party, but this did not altogether save him from a measure of stigma.

Edward's parents had aged; his younger brother and sister

were now in their last years at school. Sylvia, who had returned to England from Russia eight months before, was now married to a Scottish baronet: Harry Baxter had been killed in the war. She came south to Nester for the weekend of celebrations to mark her brother's return, and there told him of her adventures in Russia – the drama of the October Revolution, the evacuation of the British staff from the Anglo-Russian hospital, the long journey from Moscow to Vladivostock on the trans-Siberian railway. From Vladivostock she had sailed with Lady Muriel to Japan and from Japan to the United States. She had spent a week in Washington with Lady Muriel before sailing back to England from New York.

Sylvia told her story well, and on the face of it she was the same as before: yet Edward sensed a certain reticence in her manner; she seemed to be choosing her words carefully when before, with her brother, she had said whatever came into her head. In some way difficult to define, Sylvia had changed. Was this the consequence of her marriage? Or the death of Harry? Or the trauma of her ordeal in Russia? Edward could not tell.

Sylvia had news of Elspeth. She was now married to Hal Dormer, and as soon as he was demobilised they had sailed for Kenya, where the Earl of St Giles had bought them a thousand-acre farm. 'Hal thinks that Europe's finished because of Labour and that Africa's now the place.'

'Was Elspeth happy to go?'

Sylvia shrugged. 'She encountered a number of cold shoulders because of the divorce. No one approves of wives carrying on while their husbands are at war.'

Edward frowned. 'People should mind their own business.'

'Of course. And it meant a lot to Elspeth that you took it so well.'

'We should never have married.'

'Perhaps not,' said Sylvia. 'But I hope it doesn't mean that you won't marry again.'

There were some loose ends left by the divorce, and towards the end of his two months' leave, Edward went to tie them up in the chambers of the Cobbs's family solicitor in Lincoln's Inn.

Little had been disputed between the two parties: most of the arrangements over the joint property had been easily unravelled. Some of the furnishings for the house on Lord North Street had been paid for by Elspeth out of her private account: Edward agreed that these should be reimbursed. Elspeth had returned her engagement and wedding rings and the jewellery that had been given to her by the Cobbs. Only one matter remained to be settled: 'It seems that some of your personal belongings remain at Deverall House,' Ashton, the solicitor, said to Edward. 'As I understand it, you and Lady Elspeth stayed there when you were on leave?'

'That is correct.'

'Lady St Giles is willing to have them taken round to Eaton Place, but it would appear that . . . ahem . . . Mr Dormer also stayed at Deverall House and there is therefore some uncertainty about the ownership of certain items. It seems that Lady Elspeth and Mr Dormer, who are now in Kenya, left in some haste . . .'

'I understand.'

'Lady St Giles suggests that you might like to call to collect your belongings. If she should be absent, the staff have been told to admit you and you are to feel free to take whatever you wish to claim.'

Two days later, hearing that the St Gileses had gone to Castle Desche, Edward called at their house on Belgrave Square. Blunt, the butler, admitted him solemnly and, after greeting him, said how sorry he was that 'you and Lady Elspeth did not find happiness together'.

'Thank you, Blunt.'

'And all the staff feel the same.'

'I am, of course, sorry as well.'

Blunt led the way up the stairs. 'She was always an impulsive young lady, even as a child.'

'It was the war, Blunt. We were not the only ones.'

'No, sir. Indeed, sir. It made life difficult for all concerned.'

Blunt opened the door to the bedroom that Edward had shared with Elspeth and then withdrew. Edward sat for a moment on the sofa at the foot of the four-poster bed. He felt

Elspeth's brisk presence in the room and remembered the painfully chaste nights and their conversations about wallpaper, curtains and his political career. So, the woman who had seen herself as the power behind a Prime Minister was now to be the wife of a farmer in Kenya. Well, at least she was with a man she loved, whereas he, Edward, had lost not just the woman he loved but his capacity to love: after five years of the worst war in history, there was not a scratch on his body, but his heart was stone-cold dead.

He went through to the dressing room. A suitcase had been laid open on the luggage stand and Edward started to pack it with the suits in the wardrobe that had been hanging next to a thick tweed jacket that no doubt belonged to Hal Dormer. There was also a dinner jacket, some shirts, underclothes, socks and ties packed into a bottom drawer. At the bottom of the wardrobe there were two pairs of shoes and on the dresser a set of ivory brushes marked with the Cobb crest.

He returned to the bedroom. He remembered two silver-framed photographs of his parents and found them, face down, under some of Elspeth's clothes in a chest of drawers. There were also three books belonging to Edward on top of the small bookcase and some letters and accounts concerning the house on Lord North Street in the top drawer of the desk.

Where were his cuff links? Edward thought he had left two pairs – one gold with his initials, the other with a green enamel fleur-de-lis; and there had also been some silver and mother-of-pearl shirt studs. He looked through the two chests of drawers, then on Elspeth's dressing table, mildly irritated to think that Hal Dormer might have taken the studs and cuff links as well his wife. He went finally to search through the drawers of a walnut-veneer davenport by the window. Beneath the leather-topped lid there was some writing paper and a fountain pen that was his. The drawers down the side were stuffed with letters which, at first, Edward was inclined to ignore. But then he decided that if he could find them, he might recover the letters he had written to Elspeth and burn them when he got home.

Edward took a whole drawer out of the davenport and,

sitting on the sofa, placed it on his knee. He rifled through the letters, searching for any in his handwriting. He found one, then another, and then drew out a third whose hand he recognised as being that of his sister Sylvia. It was from Petrograd.

> It really is most extraordinary here. I don't know where to begin. Did you get my letter describing the frightful voyage on the *Calypso*? I was seasick all the way. I now learn that we were lucky to get to Archangel; ours was the last boat over before the sea froze ...

Edward ran his eye down the page.

> The hospital itself has taken over all the grand rooms in the Dimitri Palace ... the Grand Duke Dimitri Pavlovich ... he's dissipated and goes to orgies organised by Prince Yusupov.

He turned the page.

> I've dined once or twice at the embassy – Lady Georgiana came out with Mother – and also at the French Embassy. M. Paleologue, the ambassador, is a real charmer ...

Edward's eye now stopped at the phrase '... the main point of this letter'.

> Because of the language problem we were promised a volunteer nurse who could speak English as well as Russian and French: she had been the governess to some grand country house – the widow of a French officer called Madame Chambon. She arrived last week; I was introduced to her in the staff common room. And who do you think it was? Alice Fry!

Now, as he read on, Edward's hand started to tremble, and the letter, written in his sister's firm, pedantic hand, began to shake before his eyes. He felt a constriction in his throat and a smarting in his eyes. He tried to stop the trembling that made it difficult to read the letter but found that he could not master the powerful emotions that arose in him. Could this be true? Was Alice in Russia? Why had Sylvia kept it from him? She had left with Rettenberg? How could she have contemplated taking a post with such a scoundrel. Then he came to words that stopped his breathing.

> ... she was expecting a child. At first I thought the child was probably the Baron's – you know his reputation; but it appears that the little boy is now two and a half, which means he was conceived some time before she left England. Poor Eddie – he mustn't know.

He had a son! Edward read to the end, the words now obscured not so much by his shaking hand as by welling tears. Having finished the letter, he sat back, counting in his mind the number of years. How old would his son be now? Five – even six? His son Claude. Why Claude? Presumably to back up the pretence that Alice was French.

Edward recalled the letter he had written to Alice and now wondered whether it had reached her in Russia. Had her parents held it back? And if they had sent it, would it have reached its destination in the chaotic conditions of the war? Was she now the mistress of Baron Rettenberg? The thought of the Russian roué stopped Edward's tears and prompted him, rather, to grind his teeth. How vile to prey on vulnerable women; but then why had Alice been vulnerable? He thought back to that time when her father had been indicted and he had jilted her for fear that the scandal would blight his political career. Rettenberg might be despicable, but Edward was worse.

Edward continued to look through the letters in the first drawer. It started to get dark. After a gentle knock on the door, Blunt came in with tea and cucumber sandwiches on a silver tray. He showed no surprise at the stacks of letters on the floor: had he not been told that Edward was to take what he liked? After pouring tea and milk into a cup, Blunt withdrew. Edward went to the second drawer; he now had five or six letters from Sylvia in Petrograd but none said anything substantial about Alice. 'Madame Chambon avoids me.' 'Madame Chambon is said to run the Rettenbergs' household. She receives the Petrograd *demi-monde*.' 'Lady Muriel has taken a liking to

Mme C. which I find hard to understand.' And, in the final letter:

> Mary Dunn is furious because James Burke, a young American from the US Embassy, to whom she's taken a fancy is said to have fallen for our friend, Madame Chambon. I can't say I'm surprised. With her past *histoire*, Mme C. is a better bet for an amorous adventure than a proper girl like Mary.

Further letters from Sylvia, which Edward found in the third drawer, had been written from Nester to Elspeth in London, or from London to Elspeth at Castle Desche – telling her of Harry's death and her engagement to Sir David Gregg, and asking about her plans to live in Kenya. Edward now returned all the letters to the drawers, keeping back Sylvia's letters from Russia and his own letters to Elspeth – the first to be read and reread, the second to be burned. He put them in his pocket, closed the suitcase and, carrying it down to the hall, took his leave of Blunt and went back to his flat in a cab.

The discovery that Alice was in Russia and that he had a son radically changed the mood of melancholy detachment which for a number of years Edward had fostered to keep his more powerful emotions at bay. He had until that moment seemed to exemplify the sangfroid of an English gentleman whose one brush with passion – his affair with Alice – had been out of character, a lapse from his code. Now he understood more clearly than ever before that it had been the purest expression of his true self. That there should be a child – a son – seemed to Edward to be living proof that Alice had always been destined to be his wife. Claude embodied a union that had only been postponed. Edward's thwarted passion now turned into an obsession: he would find his wife and his son and bring them home.

For the last four days of his leave Edward refused all social invitations, devoting all his time to this new quest. He would deal with Sylvia in due course; she would not escape his wrath in Scotland; but the more urgent task was to get hold of some of those who might know what had happened to Alice

Chambon. Edward telephoned Lady Muriel Paget: she was in the country. So too was Lady Sybil Grey. He got hold of Lord Cheylesmore, the chairman of the appeal for the Anglo-Russian hospital, who gave him the names of some of those who had worked in Russia – the surgeon in chief, Herbert Waterhouse, who might be found at the Charing Cross Hospital; or the second surgeon, Douglas Harmer, at St Bartholomew's. There was the matron, Miss Robertson, who would know the whereabouts of most of the nurses, or he might try the radiologist, Dr Flavelle.

Edward immediately made appointments to see those who were in town. Since he was Sylvia Cobb's brother, all were willing to see him and each had his own reminiscences that Edward had to listen to before asking, almost casually, if they knew what had happened to the French nurse, Madame Chambon. They all remembered her; they tried to recall when, during the turbulent days that had followed the October revolution, she had last been seen at the hospital. 'She wasn't living at the merchants' club, you see,' said the matron, Miss Robertson. 'She had been a governess to the Rettenberg family and she stayed with them.'

'And do you know what became of the Rettenbergs?'

'No. I dare say they left Petrograd when it became dangerous for people like them.'

'To go to the country?'

'Quite possibly. I have no recollection. It was remiss of me, perhaps, but my first duty was the safety of the English nurses.'

'But you are sure that Madame Chambon did not leave with them?'

'Oh yes, quite certain. She was lent to us by the Russians, you see. She wasn't British. And, of course, she had a child.'

Edward could not press them too hard: many of those he spoke to seemed puzzled by his interest in Madame Chambon. In the end he invented a pretext for his investigations: he said that he was really trying to track down the Rettenbergs. The Baron had bought Saladin and now, given conditions in Russia, the Cobbs wished to make an offer to buy him back.

After two days of fruitless interviews, Edward went to the American Embassy and asked if they could give him an address for a member of their Foreign Service, James Burke. After waiting for half an hour or so, he was given an address in Philadelphia. Edward then sent a wire to Burke from White's.

ANXIOUS FOR INFORMATION ON WHEREABOUTS OF ALICE CHAMBON STOP MAJOR EDWARD COBB STOP

On the last morning of his leave, while eating breakfast at White's, the porter brought him a reply.

ALICE CHAMBON LEFT PETROGRAD WITH RETTENBERGS FOR COUNTRY ESTATE STOP NO NEWS SINCE STOP FEAR THE WORST STOP BEST HOPE THE CZECHS STOP JAMES BURKE STOP

Edward Cobb returned to France. To the bafflement of his fellow-officers, his mood had changed. Where he had seemed resigned and even content to undertake the humdrum duties of running a regiment on standby, waiting on the diplomats and statesmen in Paris negotiating a formal end to the war, Major Cobb now seemed constantly exasperated by the inaction and became irascible in the mess. He was teased by his friends. 'Got a taste for civvy life, did you? Lionised in London? Rosnay not good enough for you?' Or, 'Who is she then, Cobb? Must be quite something to have you straining at the leash to get back.'

Edward took the teasing – he knew how to play the part of 'a good sport' – and he did what he could to regain some of his composure. But that had come from the feeling that there was nothing much that he wanted out of life – that he might as well endure the antics of the regimental buffoons and listen to his colonel's theories about what had finally broken the Boche as do anything else. Now, suddenly, he knew that there was something he *did* want out of life: he wanted to find Alice and lay eyes on his son.

His son! 'You know what men are like about their sons,' Sylvia had written: how cynical but how true! Edward thought of Alice – her soft face and slender figure wafted in and out of his waking reveries; but more often he tried to imagine the little boy who was his natural child. The dormant instincts to nurture, to protect, to cherish and to teach now erupted to torment him. The sight of a small boy in the village of Rosnay where they were billeted, of around the same age as Claude, evinced an anguish that was as acute as physical pain. Edward Cobb might have come through the war without a scratch but Sylvia's letter to Elspeth had reopened a deep and gruesome wound in his soul.

What could he do? The able officer, appreciated as much by his superior officers for his administrative abilities and his common sense as for his proven valour, now thrashed around for a rational plan. The woman he loved and would always love was in Russia with his son. Russia was in turmoil and stories of Bolshevik atrocities appeared frequently in the newspapers. Edward had to find them and help them even if – the thought had wormed its way into his mind – Alice had attached herself to some other man, and that man had come to play the role of a father for Claude.

What would Edward do if he were to discover that Alice had remarried? And what if Alice, even if single, no longer felt a shred of her earlier love? There were facts to be gleaned from Sylvia's letters that gave grounds for hope. At the time of writing, Alice was not married. And she was not – or was no longer – the mistress of Baron Rettenberg, because if she had been she would not have been courted by the American diplomat, James Burke. But Alice did not love Burke, because she had left Petrograd with the Rettenbergs, not with him.

None of this meant that Alice still loved him. Edward had to face the fact that she had not replied to his letter of apology written in Bourges. Edward blushed to remember that letter – its pomposity and the way in which he had left so much unsaid. 'I am now married and so cannot honourably say more.' What was that meant to convey to Alice? That he was unhappily married? That he still loved her? Then why had he not said so in the letter? Because he had still believed sincerity was less important than convention. What should she reply to a man who could not say he loved her because it would be a breach of a code?

The day after his return to France, Edward wrote a letter to Maurice Fry in Bourges saying that he now knew that Alice had been in Russia and that he was most anxious for her safety: he did not say that he also knew that she had had his child. Ten days later he received a reply.

> Yes, indeed, she was in Russia – I would have told you if she had not specifically forbidden us to tell anyone where she was – but we have not heard from her now for over a year. We read the stories of the Bolshevik terror in Russia and fear for her safety. We have made enquiries but have learned nothing. The British Embassy say they have no record of an Alice Chambon and the Quai d'Orsay say that she was not registered at the French consulate in Petrograd, which, since she had a British passport, is undoubtedly true. We have written to the Red Cross but they too know nothing. If you can think of any way in which we could make further enquiries, I would be most grateful if you would let us know. We feel helpless here in Bourges.
>
> My wife joins me in sending our cordial regards.
>
> Maurice Fry

Added in a scrawl at the bottom of the letter was a postscript.

> You may or may not have heard that Alice has a five-year-old son. His name is Claude.

Having read this, Edward sent a wire to the Frys in Bourges.

YOUR LETTER RECEIVED STOP EVERYTHING POSSIBLE WILL BE DONE TO FIND ALICE AND CLAUDE STOP EDWARD COBB STOP

In early March, Edward Cobb returned to London on extended leave. He did not live incognito but did not report his presence to his family or his friends. All his energies were now directed towards finding Alice and his son.

He knew from reading the newspapers that the situation in Russia was chaotic, with the Reds fighting the Whites in a civil war. There was no longer any diplomatic representation with the Bolshevik government – the British Consul, Robert

Bruce-Lockhart, after being arrested, had been exchanged for the Bolshevik diplomat Litvinov; but the British had military missions to the different White armies, and had troops in the north under General Ironside that had seen action against the Red Army. However, the situation was confused and Edward, though he spent many hours in the London Library reading back numbers of *The Times*, found it difficult to make out what was going on. He therefore wrote a note to a friend at the War Office, Alan Templeton, inviting him to lunch at White's.

Templeton, a tall, stooping man with receding hair, had been a star of military intelligence on the Western Front – a don at Oxford at the outbreak of war, fluent in German and French. If he was now at the War Office, he told Edward, instead of at Balliol College, it was because he enjoyed being at the centre of things and observing the workings of government from the inside.

'What can you tell me about the situation in Russia?' asked Edward.

'Russia? A mess.'

'We're backing the Whites?'

'Yes . . . and no.'

Edward looked perplexed.

'It's a complicated story. Our policy until the armistice was clear. Russia must remain in the war. If she made a separate peace, the German divisions on the Eastern Front would be sent to France. Already we were supplying the Russians through the ports of Archangel and Murmansk. When the Bolsheviks came to power, as you will remember, they asked the Germans for an armistice and eventually got one: however, there were still elements of the Russian army prepared to fight on and these had regrouped in the south by the River Don, protected by the Cossacks, who had proclaimed an independent state.

'We were inclined to help them; so were the French, but it was difficult to know how. Then something quite unexpected occurred. We were dealt a joker in the form of the Czech Legion, a well-trained, well-equipped and highly motivated fighting force that the Russians had formed with Czechs who had been taken prisoner or had defected from the Austro-

Hungarian army. In 1917, after the Bolsheviks had made peace with the Germans at Brest-Litovsk, the Czech Legion asked to return to Europe to fight on the Western Front. Clearly they could not travel through the territory of the Central Powers so they set out to go the long way round by way of Siberia and the United States. But as they were travelling along the trans-Siberian railway, there was some altercation with Hungarian prisoners of war. The Bolsheviks tried to disarm the Czechs; the Czechs refused. Fighting broke out and within weeks the entire trans-Siberian railway was controlled by the Czechs and the Bolsheviks were cleared from Russia east of the Urals.'

Edward nodded. Much of what Templeton was telling him he already knew, but previously it had been of slight interest. Now, with Burke's telegram fresh in his mind, it was a different matter. Was Alice with the Czechs?

'Protected by the Czechs, a number of anti-Bolshevik regimes took power in Siberia and we, the Allies, got more deeply involved. You will remember – I am talking about last September – our line in the west was buckling from the German offensive. It wasn't at all clear that we were approaching the end of the war and it made sense to back those Russians who would reopen an eastern front. The Bolsheviks had put themselves beyond the pale; they had murdered Francis Cromie, our naval attaché in Petrograd, and shot five hundred hostages from what they called the capitalist classes. Both our heart and our head told us to intervene. The French agreed and sent troops to Odessa. The Japanese and Americans occupied Vladivostock. So we became involved on all three fronts in Russia – the northern front around Archangel, the eastern front in Siberia and the southern front on the Black Sea ports and the Don. And one mustn't forget the navy in the Baltic protecting the Baltic states.'

'And now?'

Templeton raised his eyes in a gesture of despair, then paused while he cut into his lamb cutlets. 'The situation now,' he said eventually, 'depends largely on where you look and who you talk to. Our minister, Winston, makes the most of every White success, and General Wilson is keen on the intervention.

The Prime Minister reluctantly supports us and the Labour lot are furious that we are fighting their Bolshevik friends.'

'The Whites never opened a second front against the Germans?' said Edward.

'No, and it was fanciful to have imagined that this might have been possible. And, of course, with the armistice everything changed. There was a strong move to end intervention and let the Russians stew in their own juice. But to Winston it's a crusade of good against evil and even Lloyd George thinks it would be dishonourable to ditch the Whites and leave them to their own devices. But things have gone badly up at Archangel – the Americans want out – and no one took up Winston's suggestion of joint Allied action against the Soviets which he made in Paris last month. Foch backed it but the conference turned it down.'

'What has happened to the Czechs?'

'They're still there, poor blighters, but by all accounts they're desperate to go home.'

'Can the Whites do without them?'

Templeton shrugged. 'Winston believes that they can but it may be wishful thinking. They have some able commanders – Admiral Kolchak in Siberia, General Denikin on the Don – but it seems unlikely that a coalition of monarchists, liberals and socialists can prevail against the utterly ruthless and determined Reds under Trotsky.'

'Could we intervene more forcefully?'

'Not a chance. Public opinion won't let us get more deeply involved. What troops we have there are close to mutiny. They want to come home.'

'So if one volunteered?'

'We'd be delighted. But why this sudden interest in Russia?'

'I'm bored in France. Could you fix a transfer?'

'To Archangel, at the drop of a hat.'

'What about Siberia?'

'Not quite as simple but I'm sure it could be arranged. General Knox would be glad to have someone with your record, and so would General Holman on the Don. But are you really sure that you want to go to Russia? The Whites are a nightmare to work with. It would be a thankless task.'

'There are personal reasons . . .' Edward began.

Templeton blushed. 'Of course.'

Before applying for a transfer that would take him to Russia, Edward had to decide whether Baron Rettenberg was more likely to be found on the eastern or southern front. He could discount Archangel – the White forces there had been recruited from the region – and had therefore to choose between Siberia and the Don. Templeton had given him the names of a number of White Russian refugees who had come to London, and through them he met others both in London and in Paris, but none had certain information of what had happened to Baron Rettenberg. Some said they had heard that he had joined the volunteer army on the Don, others that he was with Kolchak in Omsk. Through friends in the War Office, the British Military Missions in Archangel, Omsk and Novocherkassk were asked if they knew of a Baron Rettenberg fighting for the Whites: all three sent negative answers.

Then, in mid-March, came the news that Admiral Kolchak had mounted an offensive that had met with spectacular success, driving the Soviet forces back to the Urals. It seemed that he would soon link up with Denikin in the south and the Allies in the north. It now seemed to matter little which portal to Russia Edward chose and, recalling James Burke's view that Alice's best hope had been the Czechs, Edward applied for a transfer to the staff of General Knox in Siberia. Within two weeks his transfer was approved, and on 10 April he sailed from Tilbury on a troopship bound for the Far East.

On the long sea voyage to Singapore and from Singapore to Shanghai; during his wait in Shanghai for a boat to take him on to Vladivostock; during that last leg of the long voyage; and on the interminable journey on the trans-Siberian railway to Omsk, Edward felt content as never before. All the contradictions that had bedevilled his previous life were resolved. He had one clear objective – to find Alice and Claude. Quite what would happen when he found them was of course uncertain, but that was something about which he could dream.

Edward reached Omsk in the middle of July and there learned that the White forces under Admiral Kolchak had suffered a series of defeats. 'Apparently,' Edward wrote to Templeton:

> the Siberian peasants at first welcomed the Whites because of the atrocities of the Bolsheviks but now they feel they are no better off. Their horses are requisitioned and their sons conscripted so they can't plough their fields. There is little reason why they should support one regime rather than another.

Edward was welcomed by General Knox, who made use of his fluency in French to liaise with the Czechs and White Russians who spoke no English. Edward performed his duties diligently, but his reason for coming to Siberia had not been to help the Whites win the civil war. He was looking for Alice, but months of enquiries produced no results. The Czechs remembered the British nurses who had travelled to Vladivostock with their leader, Thomas Masyrk; but Edward already knew from the matron, Miss Robertson, that Alice had not been among them. A number of White officers had worked with Baron Rettenberg at Mogilev but none knew where he was. Had he joined Mannerheim in Finland? Had he gone to the Don? Or was he still in Russia? Certainly, he had not passed through Omsk on his way to Vladivostock; nor was he serving under Admiral Kolchak.

Edward lost heart. Given the turmoil in Russia, it now seemed vain to have ever imagined that he might find Alice and Claude. This pessimism persuaded him that he might as well remain in Omsk. With the other British officers, he worked hard to train the Russian troops, but when given the chance, whole contingents would desert to the Reds, taking their British equipment with them. By the end of September the White army, now made up of only fifty thousand men, had withdrawn to a line on the River Ishim, only one hundred and fifty miles from Omsk. With defeat came a collapse in morale. Conscripted soldiers slipped away, either to their villages in the *taiga*, or to join one of the many bands of marauders behind the lines. Raids on the trans-Siberian railway stopped traffic for days at a time. Debauched officers or autonomous war lords, controlling long stretches of the line, plundered the trains, raped women and executed their captives on a whim.

In November General Knox ordered the evacuation of the British Military Mission. The government in London had given up on Kolchak: because of the great distance, the scarcity of shipping and the chaotic condition of the trans-Siberian railway, future British aid was to be concentrated on General Denikin's forces in the south. As the Reds moved closer to Omsk, the British Military Mission entrained for Irkutsk, their locomotive flying the flags of the Entente. From the comfort of his compartment, Edward could see the column of wretched refugees trudging east along the track that ran alongside the railway – streams of men, women and children, some peasants, some middle class, some on crude carts but most walking, the bourgeois in tattered leather shoes, the peasants in boots made of bark. Edward scanned the faces of the younger women, tormented by the dreadful thought that somewhere in a column of such misery might be Alice and Claude.

Edward spent a month in Vladivostock, helping to wind up the British Military Mission and enjoying – in so far as he could enjoy anything – the crazed gaiety of the White Russians crammed into the city, going from party to party, drinking as much as his hosts. Handsome, melancholy, withdrawn and often tipsy, he nonetheless kept his distance from the velvety young women from the best Russian families eager to surrender themselves to an Englishman who would help them escape with their dependants to Europe or the United States. If he could not have Alice, he would have no one and, immune to illusions, he knew that tender looks were no proof of love. He was not indifferent to the plight of the Russians; he drew on his own resources to help his Russian friends: but when he finally sailed from Vladivostock to Kyoto, he was alone.

Edward did not hurry home. In England he would have to

face up to a life without Alice: while travelling he could still pretend that his quest continued. In Tokyo, Edward stayed at the embassy – the ambassador's wife was an old friend of his mother's. Here he learned that Admiral Kolchak, abandoned by the Allies, had been surrendered by the Czechs to the Bolsheviks in Irkutsk. Both he and his prime minister had been shot by the frozen river and their bodies pushed into the water through a hole in the ice.

Continuing his slow journey, Edward stayed in Shanghai with friends in the International Concession. From Shanghai he sailed to Singapore and from Singapore to Calcutta. In the huge, lugubrious palace of the Viceroy – another friend of his parents – Edward enjoyed the resplendent privileges of a member of the Empire's elite. His wealth, his war record, his social connections – even the tinge of tragedy associated with his divorce – made him a popular guest at the dinners and balls of the Raj.

In mid-February 1920, after hunting tigers with the Maharaja of Jaipur, Edward sailed from Bombay for home. The vessel, the SS *Swabia*, burst a boiler passing through the Straits of Oman and, limping up to the Suez Canal, put in for repairs at Port Said. Edward took the opportunity to go to Cairo, where he stayed at the officers' club and found another clutch of former friends.

One of these, Teddy Haddon, who had known Edward in the trenches, took it upon himself to show him around. They saw the Pyramids and the Sphinx and went to the races at Heliopolis. An enthusiast of the Turf, Haddon introduced Edward to his friends in the members' enclosure as the son of the owner of the celebrated Nester stud. One of these, a rich Greek, Andreas Papanides, invited the two English officers to visit his own stud in Alexandria. Edward at first declined this invitation but later, learning that the SS *Swabia* was still disabled, he changed his mind. It was unpleasantly hot in Cairo and Haddon promised that Papanides' house would catch the cool breezes coming in from the Mediterranean Sea.

The two officers took the train from Cairo to Alexandria, where they were met by a car sent by their host. Papanides' house, in the suburbs of the city, was as cool and comfortable as Haddon had predicted. Edward did not take a particular liking to Papanides: the man behaved as if he was enjoying some kind of private joke. Papanides' chef was good but his wife was tedious and his fifteen-year old daughter swarthy and plain. It was a toss-up, so far as Edward was concerned, whether they had made the right decision to come to Alexandria or would have been better advised to remain in Cairo.

After lunch on Saturday Papanides proposed a visit to the stud, five miles along the coast. It was set in an oasis: grass as green as that in Newmarket was shaded by palm trees which grew to the very edge of the desert. The fine Arab horses were housed in well-ventilated brick-built loose boxes – grander habitations than the houses of those who tended them. This contrast reminded Edward of Alice and made him despondent, a mood exacerbated by the joviality of Papanides and his trainer, an Irishman called Kelly.

'You'll want to see our new stallion,' said Kelly with a smirk, leading Edward to a loose box.

Edward peered in with a feigned interest. Was not one horse much like another? But the horse, as if to contradict him, gave a snort and tossed its head, and it suddenly struck Edward that the head, the neck, the colouring – all were familiar. The stallion standing before him was Saladin!

Edward turned to Papanides. 'Where did you get this horse?'

Papanides laughed: this was his joke. 'So you recognise him, Major Cobb?'

'Isn't it Saladin?'

'It is indeed. Saladin is now the pasha of his harem. He is the prize stallion in our stud.'

Edward was dumbfounded. 'But Saladin was sold to Baron Rettenberg.'

'Of course. Rettenberg sold him to a British officer in Russia who meant to take him back to England. But when I saw Saladin in Constantinople, I persuaded him to change his mind.'

'You bought him?'

'I did. A fine pedigree stallion for a most reasonable price.'

'But where did the Englishman find him?'

'In Novocherkassk. He had been ridden right across Russia from the Baron's estate.'

'So Baron Rettenberg is in Novocherkassk?' asked Edward.

'So I understand. And he was apparently short of money. He sold Saladin for just a thousand pounds!'

Edward returned to Cairo that night and the next morning secured an appointment with the Commander-in-Chief Eastern Mediterranean. He requested an attachment to the British Military Mission to the White Army on the Don. Once again, the combination of his war record and his social connections got Edward what he wanted. The orders were signed, the travel warrants issued and Edward, having recovered his luggage from the stricken SS *Swabia*, sailed on HMS *Beaver* bound for Constantinople and Novocherkassk.

Six

In the Rettenbergs' household in Novocherkassk, reoccupied by the volunteer army in the spring of 1918, plans were made to celebrate Christmas twice over – first on the anniversary kept by western Christians, and subsequently, some days later, on the day set according to the calendar used by the Russian Orthodox Church. To the 'English' Christmas were invited two officers from the British Military Mission to the White Army – Major Charteris and Captain Addis – and to the 'Russian' Christmas four of the Rettenbergs' Russian friends – General Stcheglovitov and his wife Lydia Semenovna, and Elena Konstantinova Davydoff, the widow of Colonel Yuri Davydoff, and their sixteen-year-old daughter Marina.

There was little room for guests in the small wooden house where the Rettenbergs lived but, whatever their previous experience, all now had reduced expectations and knew well how fortunate their hosts were to have a house at all. In a small provincial town, once the capital of the Don Cossacks but now serving as the metropolis of White Russia – packed with soldiers and refugees from the Red terror in the north – it was hard to find any kind of accommodation. The Rettenbergs had had the advantage of being among the pioneers of the volunteer army: Baron Rettenberg, now with the rank of general but still using the name Zagoskin, wore on his uniform a crown of thorns pierced by a dagger hanging from a red, white and blue ribbon – the decoration awarded to those who had fought in the Ice Campaign of 1918.

On their return to Novocherkassk, Rettenberg had reclaimed the house in which his mother had died. There the smallest room was kept for Fedor, who had joined them from Odessa; a larger room was shared by Alice, Nina and Claude, and the largest was for Rettenberg and his wife. However, since Fedor was mostly away at the front, Alice would escape from Nina and Claude to his single room. There, when the children were sleeping and Tatyana was dosed with her valerian drops, Rettenberg would join her. The bed was narrow but the room was out of earshot at the back of the house. In time they became careless; Rettenberg overslept in Alice's arms; they were 'caught' by Claude woken by a nightmare, and Rettenberg was later seen by Nina returning to his room.

Neither of them seemed upset. Nor did Tatyana. Rettenberg was not even sure that she was aware that he slept with Alice. Her utter lethargy made it possible that she did not. Rettenberg was therefore persuaded that none of his family was injured by his affair. As to 'public opinion' in Novocherkassk, Rettenberg knew that to the British officers, Major Charteris and Captain Addis, adultery was par for the course. Some of the British officers had taken up with Russian women and most of the White officers seemed to have mistresses, and few were as pretty and intelligent – or spoke such good English – as Madame Chambon. And the Russians, Rettenberg supposed, took a similar view. If Tatyana chose to turn a blind eye to the scandal, then so would they. Many other wives had had to suffer worse indignities at the hands of their husbands: at least Rettenberg still lived with his wife.

Nor would public opprobrium have led Rettenberg to

change his ways. All the considerations that had previously governed his behaviour were now subordinate to his love for Alice. For the first time in his pursuit of women, there had been no cooling of ardour after the kill. It was now nine months since they had first made love by the River Kuban, and his passion for Alice obsessed him more than ever before. It was as if he had always loved her, and that first glimpse of her all those years before in the Cobbs's box at Epsom had simply fired feelings latent in his mind. His view that she was simply another governess upon whom he would, if he fancied, exercise a *droit de seigneur* he now saw as a parachute to slow his fall into the chasm of irrational, uncontrollable adoration. He thought back to those earlier days and compared the jilted girl from Chelsea, the self-styled free-thinker plunging unwittingly towards the life of a *demi-mondaine*; the socialist suffragist on course to be a baronet's wife; the girl blown hither and thither by her rootless upbringing and precocious learning; the slender beauty as fine as any yearling; the girl who so bravely and recklessly spoke her mind – and saw the incubus of the composed and determined woman who now each night welcomed him into her bed.

What does a man love in a woman? Rettenberg asked himself. Was it her naked body or the look in her eyes? The first Rettenberg tried to judge objectively with the eye of an experienced roué, trailing his fingers over her slight breasts, her soft stomach, her long legs. The months of hunger in the Kuban had taken their toll: she was thin, her ribs visible beneath her skin, her hip bones protruding. Her breasts were recognisably those of a woman who had suckled a child; they did not defy gravity like a young girl's, and the pale pink nipples of a virgin were now brown nuggets of puckered skin. On her neck, the skin was loosening: she was losing the bloom of youth. Her hair was now cut short – a precaution against typhus – and its blackness showed up the appearance of the odd grey hair. Her face, too, was no longer that of a girl. Childbirth and hunger had left their marks – in certain lights and at certain times it seemed gaunt. More than that, Alice's previous expression of humorous perplexity, though it could at

times reappear, had been replaced by something more determined.

Yet these attempts to escape from his passion for Alice by
such an 'objective' assessment wholly failed. Hers was a body
like no other body and a face like no other face. The tender,
loving look from her eyes; the whispers and murmuring from
her lips; the gentle entwinement of her limbs; all taught
Rettenberg, the experienced seducer, that greater joy could be
had from making love to a woman than he had ever imagined
or had previously known.

But this enjoyment of her body was the least of it. He found
that he looked forward to returning home from army
headquarters, not simply to see his family and, at night, make
love to Alice, but to discuss the day's events with a person
whose judgement he valued and whose mind he admired.
Unlike most Russian women, Alice did not feel that a lover
should be held by feminine artifice – flirtatious looks,
sentimental sighs, stolen caresses, innuendo. She had a mind as
straight and as good as that of any man. It was far easier and
more profitable for Rettenberg to discuss with Alice the
situation at the front or his difficulties with Denikin or the
British than it was with his fellow-officers on Denikin's staff.
She had no axe to grind; she was part of no faction; and she saw
the weaknesses of the White Russians more clearly than
Rettenberg himself.

The very day after Rettenberg and Alice had first become
lovers on the banks of the Kuban, the fortunes of the volunteer
army had reached their nadir: a shell fired from Ekaterinodar
had hit the *stanitsa* housing its headquarters and General
Kornilov had been killed. General Denikin, the former
Commander-in-Chief of the Imperial Army, who had replaced
him, had decided that Ekaterinodar could not be taken. The
volunteers had withdrawn towards the Caucasus – and here the
news had reached them that the Don Cossacks had risen
against the Bolsheviks. Rostov and Novocherkassk were once
again in White hands.

The tide had turned: the volunteer army returned to the
Don. Rettenberg, recalled to the staff of General Denikin

housed in the Atman's Palace in Novocherkassk, had helped plan the second Kuban campaign that had succeeded where the first had failed in taking Ekaterinodar and the Black Sea port of Novorossisk. His knowledge of French and English had made him indispensable when, after the armistice of November 1918, and the surrender of Turkey, the Allies were able to send their military missions and supplies through the Dardanelles to the south Russian ports of Tagenrog and Novorossisk. British tanks were landed on the quays and, driven by British volunteers, joined the flamboyant White general, Baron Wrangel, in the taking of Tsarytsyn on the Volga.

Rettenberg had then argued for a push towards Siberia to link up with the forces of Admiral Kolchak; but Denikin had decided that the coal of the Donets and the corn of the Ukraine were essential to supply his growing army and a drive for Moscow vital for its morale. In the course of the summer of 1919, Poltava, Kharkov, Odessa and Kursk fell to the White forces, and on 13 October they took Orel, less than two hundred and fifty miles from Moscow.

Among Denikin's staff officers, the least excited by these dramatic victories was Rettenberg. His misgivings were not just about Denikin's military strategy but the political weaknesses behind the lines. The innate contradictions and incompatible objectives of the White coalition compared unfavourably with the Bolsheviks' single-minded determination. The Caucasians and the Cossacks wanted to be independent from Russia. Denikin and the officers of the volunteer army fought to restore the Russian Empire. Even among the volunteers there were fundamental differences: young monarchists such as Fedor wanted a Tsar; many of the more democratically minded wanted a republic. Denikin envisaged a redistribution of the land to the peasants while many of his officers who came from land-owning classes fought primarily for the restoration of their estates.

Rettenberg could see that Denikin, the grandson of a serf, was ill-at-ease in the company of the former courtiers and the aristocratic officers from regiments such as the Chevalier Garde. Rettenberg came from the same elite but his experience of a wider world – particularly his familiarity with the British – gave him a broader perspective. He saw the wisdom of Denikin's policy of leaving constitutional questions to be settled after the Bolsheviks' defeat: but to defeat them it was imperative to gain the support of the peasants in the territories held by the Whites.

To Rettenberg's dismay, however, the White officers did everything possible to alienate the peasants. Their brutal treatment of conscripts and their toasts to the Tsar and to 'Russia whole and undivided' showed that they had learned nothing from the events of 1917. While their men slept on straw, the officers lived in comfortable billets or the spacious compartments of well-furnished trains; while the wounded were jolted in open carts, the officers rode in closed carriages or cars; and while the soldiers froze in threadbare uniforms, often without tunics or boots, the officers attended balls and banquets held in the warm candlelit salons of Novocherkassk, dazzling the company with their smart uniforms, sparkling decorations, bright ceremonial swords, gold-braided epaulettes and polished boots.

On the pale bosoms of their wives and daughters were to be seen the diamond necklaces salvaged from the wreckage of their privileged lives. With an unreality that baffled Rettenberg, a replica of Petrograd high society was created in this small provincial town – with the same snobberies, the same vanities, the same disdain. Had they learned nothing from recent events? Or was it a calculated act of defiance? Many of those now living in Novocherkassk had suffered from the Bolshevik terror; some had been tortured or seen their wives and daughters raped en route; others had escaped with their lives by a whisker; most had close friends and relatives who had not. And so, rather than accept that the rich should not flaunt their wealth before the poor, the émigrés seemed determined to live the same life as before.

There had been a further reason for Rettenberg's pessimism: his mistrust of Great Britain. Denikin and the other White leaders were all military men whose only experience of politics was living under the autocracy of the Tsar. The concept of a coalition of Liberals and Conservatives of the kind led by the Liberal leader, David Lloyd George, was quite beyond their understanding. They assumed that the British Cabinet, Parliament and people shared their abhorrence of Bolshevism and must feel grateful that, while the British expended only their money, the Russians were paying with their blood.

Rettenberg, who read the English newspapers that arrived with the members of the British Military Mission, and also read some of the more confidential papers shown to him by the Mission's commanders, first General Briggs, subsequently General Holman, knew that the British government's policy on Russia was less fixed than his friends supposed. Its original objective had been to keep Russia in the war. With the armistice, that justification had become redundant. Rettenberg tried to impress upon General Denikin that Britain had no vital interest in the outcome of the civil war between Whites and Reds. It was a nation of shopkeepers and, though Churchill might be the grandson of a duke, the Prime Minister, David Lloyd George, was not. He tried to get across to Denikin and his advisers that, in a democracy like that in Britain, the view of the opposition, sympathetic to the Bolsheviks, could not be entirely discounted; and that the cost of losing trade with Bolshevik Russia, added to the direct expense of the intervention, already a hundred million pounds, could in the end outweigh in the British government's deliberations Churchill's anti-Bolshevik zeal.

Rettenberg's assessment of the fragility of British support was shared by Alice, who also read the British newspapers and the reports. It was her view that the British would support the Whites only so long as their armies were advancing. By the autumn of 1919, her hypothesis was put to the test. The northwestern army which, in October, had overlooked Petrograd from the Pulkovo Heights, was thrown back by the Bolsheviks and had retreated, a spent force, into Estonia; and on 20 October the Red Army recaptured Orel. Soon after the news reached London, on 8 November, in a speech at the Lord Mayor's banquet in London's Guildhall, the British Prime

Minister David Lloyd George told his audience that, in respect to Russia, 'we cannot, of course, afford to continue so costly an intervention in an interminable civil war'.

This measured warning was seen as a gross betrayal by the Whites and further eroded their morale. A week after Lloyd George's speech, Kolchak evacuated Omsk and Denikin's forces lost Voronezh. On 17 October it had been the turn of Kursk. Throughout November and December, the retreat of the White forces continued and the toast 'to Christmas in Moscow!' took on a hollow ring. Recriminations arose between the British Military Mission and Denikin's staff. Rettenberg was asked by Major Charteris how it was that the equipment for a two-hundred-bed hospital sent from Britain for Ekaterinodar had vanished into thin air; and why fifteen hundred nurses' uniforms had never reached the field hospitals but the skirts and stockings made for British nurses were to be seen worn by prostitutes on the streets in Novocherkassk.

What could Rettenberg answer but that the whole White hinterland was a morass of embezzlement and corruption? Not for the first time in his life, Rettenberg was tormented by the contradictions inherent in his mixed blood. His Germanic nature yearned for efficiency and order and was mortified by the dishonesty and inertia of his fellow-countrymen; but at the same time his Russian nature took a certain relish in the madness and absurdity of the White ethos that if one could not live as one had lived before then one might as well not live at all.

Equally confused in her loyalties was Alice, who, through her love of Rettenberg, had enthusiastically adopted the White cause. She worked at the hospital in Novocherkassk where, as in the Dimitri Palace in Petrograd, her knowledge of English as well as Russian and French proved vital in extracting medical supplies from the British Military Mission; and she counteracted the somewhat lackadaisical approach of the Russian medical authorities to preventative measures against typhus, supervising the unloading of casualties from the hospital trains and having them wrapped in sterilised blankets while their clothes were deloused. As many soldiers now died of typhus, which was carried by lice, as were killed by the war.

Alice also took charge of the Rettenbergs' domestic arrangements with the help of a Cossack woman who came to clean and cook. Tatyana Andreiovna could do some sewing but anything else was quite beyond her. It was Alice who went to find food, bartering in the markets, dressed simply and wearing a headscarf, her dark hair and skin making her less conspicuous than many of the Russians among the crowd of Caucasians, Armenians, Tartars, Georgians and Azerbaijanis that thronged the bazaars.

It was also Alice who, when money ran out, sold off the pieces of jewellery to the Jewish and Armenian merchants in Rostov or Novocherkassk. The financial predicament of the Rettenbergs became severe because the Baron, in the early days, had high-mindedly donated most of his money to the cause. He was paid a salary; Fedor too; but these were wholly inadequate to cover their expenses. The paper roubles lost their value, and the prices of the most basic commodities continued to rise.

First the gold coins hidden in the sewing basket, then the lesser pieces of jewellery sewn into the women's blouses and dresses, had been sold to pay for food. Alice, keeping the household accounts, saw that Rettenberg himself was a source of unnecessary expenditure. She recognised that it was difficult for a man who had been used to extravagance suddenly to become frugal, but she grew exasperated when he ordered crates of Abrau Durso, the Tsarist champagne, or bought beautiful fur coats for Alice, Tatyana and the children which Alice objected to not just because they were expensive but because they had almost certainly been looted by Mamentov's cavalry on their raids in the north.

She realised that Rettenberg, like all Russians, liked to entertain his friends and colleagues, and would have felt ashamed if he had been unable to receive the officers from the British Military Mission in the traditional Russian fashion; the goose for the 'English' Christmas dinner in 1918 had cost the equivalent of forty pounds; but by the summer of 1919, they had run out of money and their only remaining assets were

Fedor's Fabergé cigarette case, Tatyana's ruby necklace and Alice's string of black pearls.

Alice informed Rettenberg of their financial position soon after his return from a visit to the front. She saw that he was troubled and exhausted – the military position was going from bad to worse; but she had run up bills with all the merchants and had no money to buy food in the market. The supper she served up – buckwheat with scraps of chicken gizzard – would, she thought, convey the position they were in better than words. And sure enough, after eating half of what was on his plate, Rettenberg threw down his fork and said: 'Our soldiers eat better than this.'

Alice waited until the supper was over, then followed Rettenberg out on to the veranda of the house where, now that it was summer, he went out to smoke a cigar. She sat down beside him on the wicker sofa and herself lit a cigarette. 'We have no money,' she said. 'We have to sell the cigarette case, the rubies or the pearls.'

'Is there nothing else?'

'No. I've shown them to Rosen and to Nassapian.'

'And what have they offered?'

'Two hundred and fifty roubles for the rubies, one hundred and fifty for the pearls and fifty for the cigarette case.'

'But that's ridiculous. They're worth a hundred times as much.'

'In Paris, perhaps, but not in Novocherkassk.'

'Who offered most?'

'They were more or less the same.'

'The damned Jews – they're colluding.'

'Nassapian is Armenian . . .'

'They're as bad as the Jews.'

Alice was taken aback by this remark: never before had she heard Rettenberg disparage the Jews. Among other White Russians, anti-Semitic sentiments were common and peppered the conversation at almost every social occasion that Alice attended; and Tatyana Andreiovna and even Fedor had let drop remarks that reflected the general contempt for the Jews. Alice had always thought Rettenberg an exception, and now a sense of exasperation welled up in her that she could not control. She could see that Rettenberg was in a black mood, yet said irritably: 'Why say something so stupid when you don't mean it?'

Rettenberg leaped to his feet. 'Stupid? To call the Jews bad? Aren't the Bolsheviks led by the Jews? Aren't Axelrod, Deich, Martov, Kamenev, Zinoviev all Jews? Isn't Trotsky a Jew? You know what we discovered in Tagenrog – fifty cadets like Fedor promised amnesty and then thrown into a blast furnace? And in town after town the most terrible evidence of atrocities – prisoners rolled in barrels lined with nails, their skulls crushed by leather straps tightened with iron bolts, metal cages containing hungry rats fixed to their bellies, and worse, much worse.'

'Some Bolsheviks may be Jews,' said Alice quietly, 'but not all Jews are Bolsheviks.'

'But as often as not their leaders are Jews, or if they aren't Jews then they're Latvians or Armenians or Poles like Dzerzhinsky. And what do they all have in common? A hatred of Holy Russia and the Orthodox Church. Why are priests tortured and executed, nuns raped and churches burned? Were they combatants? Are they capitalists? And why did they murder not just the Tsar but the Tsarina, the Tsarevich and the Grand Duchesses? No, it's because of the Jews' age-old and implacable hatred of those who believe that Christ was the Messiah.'

'And can you blame them,' said Alice, 'after all the pogroms? What reason have they to think fondly of Holy Russia? And how are your soldiers treating them? Not all the stories we hear of Jews being slaughtered can be Bolshevik propaganda!'

'Don't underestimate Bolshevik propaganda. It's one of the things they do well. But you're right. I will admit that we did treat the Jews abominably, and old fools like my mother believed in *The Protocols of the Elders of Zion*. So too, perhaps, did the Tsar. That was why he was so determined that Beiliss should be found guilty. But remember – Beiliss was acquitted! The Tsar wasn't even given a trial!' Then, as if he could not bear to continue such a painful conversation, Rettenberg turned and went into the house.

Alice sat for a while in silence. This was the first time she had quarrelled so violently with Rettenberg. She thought of her friend, Vivien Flesch, whose parents had fled from Russia, remembering her sweet smile and twitching nose; then of Rettenberg, wondering whether, after this argument, he would stay away from her bed.

It was getting dark; the air grew colder and already a dew had dampened the dust on the road in front of the house. Lamps had been lit in the other houses; the mist mingled with the smoke from the wood fires. Far down the street, Alice saw a solitary horse and rider approaching out of the dusk. She watched their tired amble and wondered why a single cavalryman should take this back street that led nowhere.

Seeing her sitting on the veranda, the rider reined in his horse. 'I am looking for the house of His Excellency Baron Rettenberg.'

'This is the house of General Zagoskin,' she said as she had been told to say. 'I know of no Baron Rettenberg...' But even as she was speaking she recognised the voice and then the horse: it was Pytor and Saladin. 'Pytor!' she shouted. 'Pytor, Pytor, yes, it's us.' She took two steps towards him but then turned, went to the door of the house and shouted: 'Pavel, Pavel, come at once. Nina, Claude, come and see who's here.'

And all at once the whole household tumbled out on to the veranda. Rettenberg ran forward, followed by Nina, and while Nina held Saladin's bridle, and Claude stroked his neck, the Baron helped Pytor dismount. Then the two men embraced. 'We had given you up,' said Rettenberg. 'Come ... come in. You must be thirsty, hungry ... What can we give him, Alice? Have we some eggs?'

From the kitchen, where she made an omelette, Alice listened to Pytor tell of his journey – joining one cavalry contingent, then deserting to another, zigzagging across the country, at one time fighting with Budyenny against Petlura, then with Petlura against Makhno, then with Makhno against Mai-Mayevsky.

'But how did you survive?' asked Rettenberg.

'A soldier with a sabre is always welcome, your excellency,' said Pytor, taking three coloured ribbons from his pocket as he spoke. 'With the Bolsheviks I was a Red, with the partisans I was a Green and here in Novocherkassk I am a White.'

'And will remain a White, I hope,' said Rettenberg.

'Whatever your excellency prefers.'

Ten days after Pytor's return, he left to join Fedor, who was serving with the Terek Cossacks at the front. One of the British officers with the Military Mission, Colonel Cooper, a *cognoscente* of the Turf, hearing that the stallion Saladin was at Novocherkassk, offered to buy him for five hundred pounds. When Rettenberg pointed out that he had paid twenty thousand to Sir Geoffrey Cobb, Cooper countered that six years had passed during which Saladin had pulled carts, fought in battles and ridden a thousand miles across Russia. This, said Rettenberg, had no bearing on his pedigree; Saladin might be in no fit state to win races but he could still sire winners. Cooper acknowledged this but mentioned the expense of shipping Saladin back to England. Rettenberg feigned an attack of bad conscience: the cavalry was short of horses and it was perhaps his duty to put Saladin in the pool. Cooper doubled his offer to a thousand pounds. Rettenberg raged at the man's stinginess but, since there was no other buyer, eventually agreed. The money was paid; Saladin was shipped out on a British navy transport bound for Constantinople. 'And to think,' Alice said to Rettenberg at the end of the tortuous bargaining, 'Colonel Cooper is neither an Armenian nor a Jew!'

Seven

Towards the end of December, 1919, as the Red armies drew closer to Novocherkassk, Denikin asked Rettenberg to take a visiting British officer, Brigadier Clarke, on a tour of the front so that he could see for himself the critical situation faced by the retreating White forces. A train was provided, fitted to the requisite standard for a general, with a salon and kitchen in one coach, sleeping quarters in another, wagons for horses, coaches for the soldiers, and a flat wagon for a large car, a Packard.

Rettenberg's train followed in the wake of an armoured train newly fitted with British naval cannon.

The train set off from Novocherkassk in the early morning for the town of Krivoe Ozero. It stopped frequently – either because the line had been damaged by Red saboteurs or because a train further up the line had broken down. Therefore, instead of arriving at Krivoe Ozero that night, they did not reach it until seven the next morning. There, while the armoured train proceeded towards the front, Rettenberg's train drew into a siding. Though a telegram had been sent to the area commander to announce their arrival, no one was at the station to meet them. The temperature was many degrees below zero: old snow lay on the ground. Rettenberg and the English officer walked from the siding to the station and warmed themselves by the stove in the waiting room while the Packard was unloaded from the train.

It was still dark when they drove into the town. As they approached the centre, the headlights of the car picked out a body lying in the middle of the street. The driver turned to circumvent it, and as he did so, Rettenberg saw that the leg of the corpse was being gnawed by a dog. He ordered the driver to stop the car, climbed out and kicked the dog, which skulked off into a side street. Rettenberg looked down at the body: it was that of a woman, almost certainly a Jew.

Leaving Clarke in the car, Rettenberg walked on down the street, the cold mist of the morning mixing with the stench of old smoke and charred timbers. Every few yards he came across another body – in places a number were piled on top of one another – men, women and even children, none showing the signs of gunshot, but all marked with the slash of sabres and all, apparently, Jews. There were naked bodies – many of young girls – some with gaping wounds at their genitals, one with a breast cut off, its pair still hanging by a shred of flesh and skin.

Rettenberg went back to the car and told the driver, through the lowered window, to take Brigadier Clarke back to the train. Clarke remonstrated. Rettenberg insisted. 'I cannot ensure your safety. I must arrange for an escort. I will join you as soon as I can.'

The Packard turned and drove back towards the station. Rettenberg walked forward alone. He came to a shop with smashed windows and a broken door. Through the door he could see a Cossack soldier standing behind the counter. Rettenberg looked in. The man did not seem to notice him: he appeared to be totally drunk. The front of his greatcoat and also the sleeves were caked in blood. On the counter was a blue-patterned china wash bowl which the Cossack was now filling with bottles of eau de Cologne. He then plunged his stained hands into the heavily scented spirit which at once darkened, dissolving the dried blood.

'Soldier!' shouted Rettenberg. 'What is your regiment?'

The Cossack turned, his hand going to the hilt of his sabre; then, seeing a Russian officer, he stood to attention and mumbled: 'The Terek Cossacks, your excellency.'

'And where is your commander?'

'The regiment has pulled out, excellency. I was . . . I was delayed.'

Rettenberg turned and left the shop. If the regiment had pulled out, then Bolshevik forces might soon take the town. He did not care to contemplate the fate of a White or British officer found on the scene of such butchery. There was a further reason why he could not bear to remain: Fedor had been fighting with the Terek Cossacks. Rettenberg walked back to the station, ordered his escort to reload the Packard, and the train left Krivoe Ozero to return to Novocherkassk.

Though much of the money from the sale of Saladin had been spent by the end of November and the price of food was higher than ever before, Rettenberg insisted that they should once again celebrate a double Christmas – first with officers from the British Military Mission, and later with the Davydoffs and Stcheglovitovs and other Russian friends. However, two days after the Rettenbergs' celebration of their English Christmas, General Denikin ordered the evacuation of Novocherkassk and for the second time Alice had to prepare to leave a house she had come to love so well.

The Red armies were now only a two-day march from the

city and Denikin's headquarters was to move south to Ekaterinodar. Rettenberg had places reserved for himself and his family on General Denikin's train. Others were not so fortunate. Frantic refugees packed into the station, desperate to get away. Soldiers guarding the box cars filled with their booty brutally clubbed the civilians trying to get on to the trains. On the platform, distraught doctors and nurses searched for transport for their patients. As the trains drew away from the platform, women leaped on to the buffers between the coaches, dragging their children with them, while those with the strength climbed on to the roof.

Wrapped in their fur coats, and escorted by the Cossack guards of Denikin's staff, Tatyana, Nina, and Alice, holding Claude's hand, followed Rettenberg into the warm comfort of the General's train. The extreme cold had frozen the condensation on the windows, obscuring the fearful sight outside. When the train moved off, crawling out of the station, Rettenberg scratched a hole in the ice on the window to see the receding lights of Novocherkassk. Huddled men could be seen with crowbars prising open the frozen points of a siding. The lights faded: they were in open country, trundling towards Rostov and the bridge over the Don.

On 3 January 1920, Tsarytsyn fell to the Reds. Two weeks later Rettenberg, now in Ekaterinodar, received a message from Pytor that Fedor had been wounded in the subsequent retreat. Rettenberg immediately found a train going north. He disembarked at Veliko Knyazhesk where he found Pytor waiting with a spare horse. How long had he been waiting in the cold? Rettenberg did not ask. Nor did he seek to penetrate the man's silence and expressionless face. But Rettenberg had known Pytor so long and so intimately that he could tell at once from his demeanour that Fedor's condition was grave.

On entering the hospital, Rettenberg was struck by the stench. For a moment he could see little; then in the dim light he could make out the shape of a barn. Empty sacks were piled in a corner and listless men lay on bales of straw in two close-packed rows. Though bitterly cold, few had blankets: at best they were covered with their bloodstained coats. Pytor led Rettenberg between the lines of the wounded: only their murmuring groans showed that they were living. Here and there a *sanitar* could be seen stooping over a body, to give a drink of water to one man, to raise the eyelids of another to see if he was dead.

At the end of the barn were some wooden steps leading up to a granary which was now the ward reserved for the officers. The only advantage seemed to be that the floor was made of wood rather than earth. The wounded lay on bales of straw and there were no more blankets than there had been below.

Fedor lay in one corner against the wall. His eyes were closed but they opened as the two men approached his bed. 'Ah, Pytor,' he said. 'Have you found Father?'

'I am here,' said Rettenberg.

Fedor turned his head. 'Ah, good. Father ... I'm sorry ...' Then he added in English: 'Isn't it a bore?'

Rettenberg sat beside him on the edge of the bale of straw. He could see from his son's shivering, and the livid pallor of his face, that he had a fever. 'Where are you wounded?'

'In my side. A sabre slash.' A feeble hand came out from under his greatcoat and pulled it aside. 'Two came for me at once. I downed one, but the other ...'

Rettenberg was hit again by the stench of putrefaction. He looked down. Dirty black patches of cloth covered his son's ribs. Gently, Rettenberg lifted them. He could see at once that the gash had gone through Fedor's ribs and was infected. Yellow pus mingled with the clotted blood, and something wriggled in this suppuration: the wound was infected with maggots.

'Fetch the doctor,' Rettenberg said to Pytor.

Pytor left them. Rettenberg turned back to Fedor. 'When was this dressing last changed?'

Fedor frowned as if he had been asked an unanswerable question. 'The war is lost, Father,' he said.

'I know,' said Rettenberg. 'We are to be evacuated.'

'Will you go to England? Nina would love that,' he said.

'You will come with us.'

'As God wills,' he said.

'As God wills,' Rettenberg repeated.

Fedor beckoned to his father to come closer. 'Father,' he whispered, 'I am afraid.'

'We will take you away from here.'

'Not of dying, Father, but of what follows. You see, I have sinned.'

'We have all sinned,' said Rettenberg.

'Yes,' said Fedor. 'But some sins are terrible . . .' A frightened look came into his eyes. Then, in a whisper that was quieter still, he said, 'At Krivoe Ozero . . . the Jews . . . I was there.'

Rettenberg nodded. 'I saw what was done. But I cannot believe that you did such things.'

Fedor shook his head. 'No, it was the Cossacks, but we knew what they were doing and . . . were you told? The Cossack officers held a ball . . . we had to go along . . . they forced the magistrate, too, and there were whores from Kherson and an orchestra; they played music to drown the sound of the howls of pain, the cries for mercy. Father, I looked out, it was a vision of Hell – the Jews were offering money to the Cossacks to spare them but the soldiers were maddened by some terrible lust for blood. They took the money and killed them all the same – old men, children, babies even . . .' He paused and shuddered. 'I saw two little children who had been killed by bayonets strung together with a rope and left hanging from a balcony . . . And all the while we drank champagne and danced with the whores. Can God forgive that, Father? I asked the priest. He said that God would forgive me if I was sorry, and I am sorry, Father.'

'Christ died to save sinners,' said Rettenberg.

'Even the worst sinners?' asked Fedor.

'The very worst.'

Pytor returned with the army doctor – a harassed, exhausted man – who looked scornfully at the epaulettes on Rettenberg's greatcoat. 'Ah, General. Have you brought us some supplies?'

'This is my son.'

'Well, I regret, *your excellency*' – angry irony was in his tone of voice – 'that there are no bandages or disinfectant even for officers.'

'We have sent supplies.'

'So they say. But somewhere between there and here they seem to have disappeared.'

'I will look into it,' said Rettenberg.

'Please do,' said the doctor acidly.

Rettenberg stood and drew the doctor aside. 'I wish to take my son away from here.'

'That is your right. But I should warn you that, if you move him, he will die.'

'And if he stays here?'

The doctor peered past Rettenberg at Fedor, then back at Rettenberg. 'He has internal injuries. He has been vomiting blood. And his wound is infected.'

'Can you save him?'

'No.'

'So if he goes or if he stays . . .'

'He will die.'

Rettenberg sent Pytor to find a cart or some other means of transportation, and wrapping Fedor in his greatcoat he carried him down the wooden stairs from the granary into the barn. Fedor smiled. 'Do you remember, Father, at Soligorsk, how you used to carry me up to bed? Sasha was so jealous. He said that you never did that for him.'

'I remember,' said Rettenberg.

'How fine things were,' Fedor whispered. 'How fine . . .'

The same smile remained on his face as they rode in a cart found by Pytor, the son still in his father's arms. In the waiting room at the station Fedor coughed up more blood. The train drew into the station. The senior officer – a general who knew Rettenberg – invited him into his compartment with Pytor and his wounded son. While the train moved south, Fedor lay on the bunk in the general's bedroom with Rettenberg at his side, while Pytor stood like a sentinel outside the door. At the junction at Torgovya, the general's adjutant found a doctor, who changed Fedor's dressing then left, saying nothing. Fedor, too, was silent, and by the time the train reached Ekaterinodar he was dead.

*

Work, incessant work, a sequence of meetings to deal with unceasing crises, the endless demands made of the British by Denikin, and of Denikin by the British, saved Rettenberg from succumbing to grief at the death of his second son. As his train had rolled into Ekaterinodar, his first impulse had been to smuggle Fedor's body off the train and bury it secretly to save Tatyana Andreiovna the knowledge of his death; but subsequently he decided that, since it could not be kept from her indefinitely, it might be best, after all, if she was to witness the interment of her son.

Fedor was duly buried in the Orthodox cemetery at Ekaterinodar – his coffin carried by Pytor and three of Fedor's fellow cadets. There could be no wake afterwards because the Rettenbergs had no home in which to hold it; Rettenberg slept on the floor of his office, Tatyana Andreiovna shared a room with her widowed friend Elena Konstantinova Davydoff and her daughter Marina, while Alice squeezed into the attic of the same lodging house with Nina and Claude.

In Ekaterinodar, General Denikin prepared for a counter-offensive. The drunken, dissolute General Mai-Mayevsky, was dismissed as commander-in-chief. General Wrangel, appointed in his place, in turn dismissed the Don Cossack General, Mamontov. Rostov, which had fallen to the Reds on 8 January, was retaken on 20 February but lost again three days later. Now there could be no doubt that the war was lost. General Holman, commanding the British Military Mission, sent a telegram to London to say that Denikin's situation was desperate. A British High Commissioner, Halford Mackinder, arrived in Ekaterinodar with full authority from the British Cabinet to review the situation. He gave a pledge that if necessary, all White officers and their families would be evacuated by the Royal Navy, 'for almost certainly,' as he reported to London, 'all these women would be murdered if they fell into the hands of Bolsheviks . . . I need hardly add that the private soldiers run no similar risk, since they and their families could disappear into the general population.' On Mackinder's advice, Winston Churchill ordered the British Military Mission to fall back to the Black Sea port of Novorossisk.

It was Rettenberg's task to make sure that the British lived up to their commitments and to help organise an orderly evacuation of the White officers and their families. He and his British colleagues were determined that they should avoid the chaos that had accompanied the French evacuation of Odessa. Eight warships of the Royal Navy were steaming towards Novorossisk but it was already apparent that these might not be enough to evacuate the tens of thousands of refugees who were already clogging the roads leading to the Black Sea port – not just soldiers and peasants with their families but entire communities of Cossacks from the Don and Astrakhan, many of them stricken not just with panic but with disease.

Typhus, carried by lice, was widespread in the filthy huddle of humanity, and it soon became clear to Rettenberg that the compassion of the British did not extend to the victims of the disease. A telegram from London stated that 'It is impossible to evacuate refugees from Odessa or any other Russian port, for on sanitary grounds no country will receive them.' The ship *Christian Nebe*, arriving at Malta packed with refugees from Russia, some with typhus, was ordered back to the Crimea.

Under Alice's direction, the Rettenberg household, when in Novocherkassk, had taken the strictest precautions against typhus – keeping the house scrubbed clean and fumigating clothes with sulphur after any visit to public places. Her own hair Alice had cut to just below her ears, while Nina's was cropped almost as short as a boy's. Tatyana, however, had refused to permit her hair to be cut short.

Alice had been anxious about the journey to Ekaterinodar: in public trains upholstery had frequently been torn from the compartments for fear that it might be infested with lice. The salons and sleeping quarters on the train that had brought the Rettenbergs from Novocherkassk had, Alice had been assured, been thoroughly fumigated, and Alice, though normally sceptical that Russian orderlies had done what they said, felt reasonably confident in this case because it was the train of the Commander-in-Chief.

In the turmoil they had encountered in Ekaterinodar, it was impossible to take the same stringent precautions. There was no way of knowing who had slept in their rooms before. Despite the children's complaints, Alice would not let them lie on the beds until the mattresses had been fumigated, and so on their first night in Ekaterinodar they slept on the floor. She advised Tatyana Andreiovna to do the same, but the General's widow, Elena Konstantinova, who shared Tatyana's room, pooh-poohed Alice's precautions, saying to Tatyana in an audible whisper: 'I really don't understand why you allow your governess to order you around.'

Ten days later this same lady was obliged to swallow her pride and ask Alice to take a look at her daughter Marina, who had been complaining of a headache and pains in her limbs. Alice at once recognised the symptoms and sent for a doctor: the doctor confirmed her suspicions. The girl had typhus and must go to the hospital at once. Elena Konstantinova went with her, not only to care for her daughter but, no doubt, to avoid seeing Alice. Alice herself set about disinfecting the room that Tatyana Andreiovna now had to herself. Her mattress and clothes were fumigated and the floor scrubbed clean.

In the evening of 28 February, Rettenberg went to his family's lodgings to say that they should be ready to leave at a moment's notice: they were to be evacuated with the staff of General Sidorin. He returned for them later that night and, with Pytor standing on the sideboard, drove them to the station in the Vauxhall abandoned by the British Military Mission. The spectacle which met them was like that they had witnessed at Novocherkassk. The platforms were packed with wretched, demented people, desperate to find a place on a train. Soldiers who had abandoned their units, their faces black from frostbite, their feet wrapped in sacking, mingled with half-swooning victims of typhus, still dressed in hospital garb, abandoned by the doctors and nurses, wild eyes deep in their sockets, skin taut on their livid faces, shuffling, then falling and crawling forward until trampled underfoot.

Leaving his family to wait in the car, Rettenberg forced his way through the gruesome crowd to be told by a railway official that General Sidorin's train had gone north to Kushkevska and it was not known when it would be back. The Reds were advancing so fast that many trains had been taken. Others had stopped for lack of fuel. A hospital train had drawn into the station without a soul alive: doctors, nurses and patients all dead from typhus. Frozen corpses thrown from the trains were stacked in piles at the entrance to the station.

Seeing the coaches immobile, rooted to the track by the stalactites of dirty ice from the lavatories and kitchens, Rettenberg gave up the idea of waiting for the return of Sidorin's train and rejoined the family in the car. It was around one hundred kilometres to Novorossisk; the car's tank was full of petrol; he therefore decided to risk a breakdown, or an ambush, and drive. With the two women, Nina and Claude huddled on the back seat, and Pytor now beside Rettenberg with a revolver ready on his knee, they left Ekaterinodar for the Black Sea port of Novorossisk.

Their progress was slow: the road was clogged with carts and a silent file of refugees. On the dirty snow on the verge lay abandoned weapons, dead horses and broken-down cars. Huddled figures were seen hacking at the frozen ground to dig a grave for some wretch who had died on the road; more often, corpses had simply been abandoned. Emaciated peasants carried their possessions in sacks made from horse blankets slung over their shoulders, while fallen *burzhoois*, betrayed by the tattered elegance of their delicate shoes and well-cut clothes, pushed perambulators piled with hat-boxes along the rough road.

'*Ah, que j'ai mal à la tête*,' complained Tatyana Andreiovna.

Alice gave Tatyana boiled water to drink from a bottle, and passed to the children the English-style sandwiches that she had made for the journey. They ate surreptitiously, hiding the food from the people they passed.

'*Ah, ma tête, ça fait mal*,' Tatyana moaned, her head resting on Alice's shoulder.

Alice felt her forehead, then met Rettenberg's eyes in the mirror.

Finally, at four in the afternoon, they drove over a crest of hill and came in sight of the sea and, to their left, the foothills of the Caucasus. Half an hour later, in the dim light of the winter sun, the port of Novorossisk came into view with five British warships at anchor in the harbour. In the streets of the town, the car could only edge slowly through the crowds of refugees. At the headquarters of the Military Governor, all was confusion. Denikin had resigned his command, naming General Wrangel as his successor. Wrangel, however, who had been in Constantinople, was returning to continue the fight from the Crimea, not the Kuban.

No lodging had been allocated for members of Denikin's staff: even for generals, it was now a matter of *sauve qui peut*. A junior officer who had worked with Rettenberg gave him the address of a house belonging to an Armenian merchant in the heights above the town where it was conceivable that he might find a room.

As they drove up the hill, Rettenberg turned to Alice 'Shouldn't we take Tatyana to a hospital?'

'Her best chance is if we take care of her.'

'We won't get a room if they know.'

'Then don't tell them.'

Rettenberg was told by the Armenian that the house was full, and no amount of paper money could persuade him to change his mind. However, there was something in the man's manner that suggested that he was open to an offer of a different kind. Rettenberg went back to the car, opened his wife's suitcase, found the pleated blue dress, tore apart the stitching at its collar and removed Tatyana's ruby necklace. He went back to the house and showed it to the Armenian. 'Find us a room and feed us,' he said, 'and for each day you shall have one of these stones.'

The Armenian took a closer look at the necklace. 'Of course, of course, your excellency. You shall have mine,' he said. 'One for each day, you say?'

'Twelve for twelve days. If we leave before, you can keep them all.'

The deal was done. The Armenian and his family moved out of their own quarters to sleep on the floor of the kitchen. Tatyana was put to bed on a heavy mahogany *lit bateau*. Nina and Claude were fed and then curled up on cushions. Pytor slept under his greatcoat in the Vauxhall. Rettenberg made a bed with the cushions of an armchair while Alice lay down on a sofa.

Over the next two days, Tatyana's condition deteriorated. Her temperature rose to 104°, then to 106°; her eyes became congested, her lips swollen. She complained of aching limbs and a fierce headache. To ensure that none of the lice carrying the disease survived to infect others, Alice shaved Tatyana's hair. She cooled her patient's skin with a damp cloth and coaxed her to drink milk or water. On the sixth day reddish spots appeared on dark patches of skin on Tatyana's stomach and arms. On the seventh, the same rash appeared on her chest. Tatyana lapsed into delirium, moving restlessly under her blankets, murmuring incomprehensible words.

Alice remained by her side and Rettenberg left only to go down to the port and arrange the evacuation of his family. Most members of the British Military Mission had already departed and those who remained were patently unable to distinguish between one White Russian officer and another. Generals were two a penny and, since the British guarantee only applied to officers and their families, many impostors appeared in uniforms that had been stolen or stripped off the dead. Rettenberg's knowledge of English confirmed his credentials, and he was asked to help the British interrogate the desperate refugees pressing around the gangplanks that led up to the ships. Before being allowed to embark, every passenger was inspected by a British medical officer: there was no question of accepting anyone with the symptoms of typhus.

For the first time in his life, Rettenberg felt helpless. Everything material that had hitherto sustained him – his money, his title, his connections – had gone; and now the psychological blows began to take their toll. It seemed that he had failed all those who had looked to him for sustenance and protection. He was tormented by the memory of how first his mother, then Fedor, had died in his arms.

And now Tatyana was dying: this was quite clear to

Rettenberg as he sat at her bedside. To give Alice some rest, he kept vigil through part of the night, trying to calm Tatyana when, in her delirium, she started or barked out some incomprehensible word. He wiped her burning face with the damp cloth and, every now and then, held a glass of water to her dry, cracked lips. Her breath was hot and foul. The face that had once been so lovely was now sinking into the cavities of her skull, and all that was left of those flowing tresses was the grey stubble on her head.

Seven days after their arrival in Novorossisk, the Armenian took Rettenberg aside. 'Your excellency,' he said, in a fawning manner, 'I wonder if it would be possible . . . the rubies, you see . . . we must leave now, I and my family . . . not on the boats that would not be allowed – but to the mountains. The Bolsheviks are only a day away and they are merciless with merchants like me.'

'You want your seven stones?'

'It would be such a pity, your excellency, to take them from their setting. I would suggest, perhaps, that you could stay here now for at least the twelve days, beyond them if you cared to, even for ever – take the house and everything in it – in exchange for the necklace.'

'Very well.'

Rettenberg went up to Tatyana's room, took the ruby necklace and gave it to the Armenian. Within an hour their host and his family had gone.

Rettenberg knew better than the Armenian how close the Bolsheviks were to the city. The Red cavalry had been seen within ten miles of Novorossisk but the main army was still two days away. Nevertheless, on the morning following the departure of the Armenian, and finding that the house had emptied of the other refugees, Rettenberg told Alice that she too must go. 'I shall stay with Tatyana. But you and the children must leave before it is too late.'

'I will not leave without you.'

'I cannot leave without Tatyana.'

'That is clear.' Alice began to busy herself with her nurse's chores as if there was nothing more to be said.

'You must think of Claude,' said Rettenberg. 'And of Nina.'

Alice said nothing.

'Please, Alice.'

Now she turned to face him with an implacable look. 'If you want to, you could find some family to take them on a ship. But I will not leave you or Tatyana and I suspect that, if asked, Nina and Claude would also choose to stay.'

Rettenberg felt his will wilt before Alice's resolution. He went to the town in search of food, bartering his gold signet ring for a cabbage and a piece of lard. He went to the port: several boats remained on the quay and British warships were anchored offshore, their guns pointing towards the approaches to Novorossisk. He returned to the house. They cooked the cabbage and then Rettenberg played cards with Nina and Claude.

At nine that night, with the children in bed, Rettenberg came to Alice as she sat beside Tatyana. 'What is the prognosis?' he asked.

'Normally, the crisis comes on the fourteenth day. The patient either dies ... or recovers.'

'And this is the seventh day?'

'The eighth.'

At midnight, Alice went to rest on the sofa and Rettenberg took over the care of his wife. She was unconscious; her breathing was a painful rasping; her skin was hot. 'She will die,' Rettenberg thought to himself, 'but she will not die soon enough to save us.' He looked at the pillow and thought of how little strength it would take to smother her. Then he could bury her in the garden and they could escape. Would it be wrong? After all the slaughter they had witnessed, would it matter if he was to bring her death forward by a day or two and thereby save his own life and no doubt the lives of Nina, Alice and her son?

Rettenberg looked at the pillow but his hands did not move towards it. Unaccountably he felt quite unable to obey his own common sense. Perhaps it was just because he had seen so much slaughter; because Sasha had died; because Fedor had killed and then had died; that he now could not contemplate taking an innocent life. The woman who had been entrusted to him, and whom he had so mistreated, would be cared for by him until the end.

Rettenberg fell asleep in his chair. At four in the morning he awoke. He took up the damp cloth to cool Tatyana's brow but felt that it was already tepid. Her eyes were closed and her breathing had stopped. He took hold of her wrist: there was no pulse. He lifted her lids and saw that her eyes had rolled round in their sockets. Tatyana was dead. Standing, he made for the door, then – remembering a phrase from the Orthodox liturgy that he had heard so often in his youth – he returned, made the sign of the cross on her forehead and kissed her parchment cheek.

He then woke Pytor and together the two men went to dig a deep rectangular hole in the garden. When the work was done, they went to the kitchen and Pytor made tea.

'If your excellency pleases . . .' Pytor began.

'Anything,' said Rettenberg.

'You will now leave with the British?'

'If we can.'

'If your excellency will permit me,' said Pytor, 'I shall stay behind.'

'Where will you go?'

'Back to Soligorsk. My parents are there.'

'Of course. But how?'

'I will find a horse and . . .' Pytor gave one of his rare smiles. 'I still have my three tags – the white, the red and the green.'

'Yes. Well, may God go with you, Pytor.'

'And with you and Madame Chambon and your children.'

The two men then said nothing more but sat for a long time in silence, their hands cupped around their glasses of tea.

At dawn, watched by Alice, Nina and Claude, Rettenberg and Pytor lowered Tatyana's body, wrapped in a blanket, into the grave. Together, all said the Our Father in Russian; Pytor then shovelled the earth back into the grave.

As they gathered up their belongings, Rettenberg handed Pytor the Fabergé cigarette case. Pytor protested. Rettenberg insisted. They then left in the Vauxhall for the port.

The sound of guns could be heard from the hills behind Novorossisk, and heavy thuds in the air, followed a second or two later by the sound of an explosion, as the British warships returned the fire. Crowds of refugees like flotsam had collected at the waterfront, some huddling round burning piles of rubbish, others looking disconsolately towards the port. The occasional crack of a rifle could be heard from Bolshevik agents or Red Army infiltrators on the roofs. The entrance to the port itself was blocked by the most pitiful mass of humanity – the detritus of a whole civilisation now choking the only conduit through which it could escape the impending terror.

A throng of middle-class men and women, their genteel clothes now in tatters, their hair bedraggled, their faces drawn from malnutrition, mixed with groups of Kalmuk Cossacks straight from the steppe holding the bridles of their horses. In the water floated the trunks, suitcases and pieces of furniture that had been abandoned by the desperate refugees. Over the heads of the crowds, Rettenberg could see men fighting their way towards the gangplank of a Russian boat, lashing out with fists and rifle butts at men, women and children in their way. The ship, already overburdened, cast off its ropes. The gangplank, with people still clinging to it, was raised but then collapsed: a suitcase, caught on the railing, burst open; shirts, petticoats and underclothes followed their owners into sea.

Rettenberg forced a way through this dense mass of humanity for Alice, Claude and Nina with Pytor bringing up the rear. Though he wore his Imperial Army greatcoat, he shouted in English, 'make way, make way,' and this had the effect of confusing those in front of him just long enough for him to push past. Whatever sympathy Rettenberg may ever have had for others was now subordinate to his determination to save Alice and the children. Pushing, pummelling, making the most of his height, Rettenberg reached the bottom of the gangplank to the last British transport, guarded by a sergeant and soldiers of the Scots Fusiliers.

'I am General Rettenberg,' he said. 'I am to be evacuated with my family.'

The sergeant looked askance at this tall Russian speaking

fluent English but wearing a greatcoat stripped of its epaulettes and sullied by the earth from Tatyana Andreiovna's grave. 'Sorry, sir. No more Russians to be let on board. All the transports have left. Only our own military personnel.'

'Please inform General Holman that I am here.'

'General Holman's left, sir, and it was his instructions.'

'I demand to see an officer.'

'It won't do any good.'

'For God's sake, you stupid man . . .' Rettenberg pushed forward. The soldier next to the sergeant struck him savagely with the butt of his rifle and, when Rettenberg clung to the banister of the gangplank to prevent himself falling, brought the barrel of the rifle down on to his fingers, leading Rettenberg to fall face down on to the quay.

Alice stepped forward. 'Sergeant, I am a British subject and I claim the protection of the Crown.'

There was something about Alice's perfect English accent, and her archaic and melodramatic choice of words, that confused the sergeant. 'Have you a passport, ma'am?'

'No.'

'Any way of verifying your identity?'

'No.'

'Then I'm afraid there's nothing I can do.'

Alice looked round at Rettenberg as Pytor raised him from the ground. She could see from his expression that his anger had now given way to an abject despair. She turned back to the sergeant and, with a contrived smile, said: 'If you were to ask Major Charteris or Captain Addis . . .'

Again, Alice's familiarity with the names of British officers serving in the British Military Mission appeared to disconcert the sergeant but not enough to overcome his determination to prevent any Russians getting on to the boat.

'They've all left,' he said. 'And, quite honestly, ma'am, you don't look British to me. Now, if you'll kindly step aside. You're blocking the way.'

Peering over the shoulder of the soldier who had barged in front of her, Alice saw, coming towards them, four British soldiers ploughing a path through the crowd with their rifles for three officers, apparently the very last of the British Military Mission. She scanned their faces hoping that she might recognise one of the officers but they were all unfamiliar – all, that was, except the first, a major, who reminded her of Edward Cobb. Had he been younger, she would have taken him as his double. Then, as he reached the foot of the gangplank, Alice saw that the man was not a double – it was Edward himself.

She opened her mouth to cry out to him but the sound was stifled before it emerged. For some reason she did not at once understand, she felt loath to appeal to him for help. It was not the shock at his sudden appearance, or the fear that he was a phantom which, if accosted, would disappear; but a dread apprehension that to be saved again by one of her admirers would be a last, insupportable humiliation for the man she loved.

'Cobb!'

Edward turned to see who had shouted his name. For a moment he looked nonplussed. Then the furrows on his brow cleared and his eyes widened into an expression of surprise, then vindication. 'Baron Rettenberg! At last!'

The sergeant, seeing Rettenberg greeted in this way, now gestured to the private who had so brusquely pushed Alice aside to bring her forward. 'There's a lady here, Major Cobb, sir, who claims she's a British subject.'

Alice looked up and saw in Edward's eyes, as he recognised her, a look of utter astonishment and joy. 'Alice!' He stepped forward and opened his arms to embrace her. Alice stepped back. Edward lowered his arms but took hold of Alice's left hand. 'Where have you been? I've been looking for you everywhere.'

'We were here.'

'And Claude?' Edward looked down at the boy holding his mother's other hand. 'You must be Claude.'

'Yes,' said Claude in English. 'I am Claude.'

Edward, still holding Alice by the hand, led her towards the gangplank. 'Let them through,' he said to the sergeant.

Alice stopped. 'I can't leave without my friends.'

'Baron Rettenberg. Of course.'

'And his daughter Nina,' said Alice.

'Let them through.'

Alice turned to Pytor and, speaking in Russian, said, 'Farewell, dear, dear friend.' She kissed him on both his cheeks; Claude did likewise, followed by Nina.

'Take care of Soligorsk,' said Nina. 'We will be back.'

Rettenberg raised his hand in a salute 'Goodbye, Pytor Sergeivich. God be with you.'

'And with you and yours, Pavel Fedorovich.'

The two men embraced, then broke apart and, after a second and final salute, Pytor turned and slipped away into the crowd while Rettenberg followed Alice, Claude and Nina up the gangplank and on to the boat.

Eight

One of the many left behind at the port of Novorossisk was the French governess, Madame Chambon. On the voyage to Constantinople on HMS *Steadfast*, Alice was addressed by the crew as Miss Fry. She was unable to discuss the question of her identity with Edward because the Russian refugees were kept apart from the personnel of the British Military Mission. Nor did she see much of Rettenberg. The ship had been packed well beyond its capacity: the available cabins were given over to women and children; the men slept where they could, covered either by naval blankets or their greatcoats. After the horrors that had preceded their embarkation, a great lethargy had come over the Russians, who stirred only to accept, from the British sailors, plates of bully beef and mugs of tea.

The person who most regretted the loss of Madame Chambon was Alice. As she sat on the deck of *Steadfast* staring at the placid water of the Black Sea, lulled by the throbbing of the ship's engines, she looked back towards Russia with muddled feelings of relief and regret. There was no doubt but that if they had stayed Rettenberg would have been killed, and her fate and the fate of the children would have been little better. When she slept she dreamed of the terrible scenes of sickness, death, panic and despair that she had witnessed, and on waking trembled to realise that the nightmare had been real.

Yet in the little house in Novocherkassk Alice had been happy as she had never been happy before. The very collapse of the civil order that had gone on around them had enabled her to feel that she was married to the man that she loved. As she breathed in the damp sea air, she imagined the scent of smoke and tanned leather and remembered how contented she had been to find fruit and vegetables that he might like, or a fish or a chicken to take back and cook for his supper. She thought too of how she had grown to love Nina and Tatyana Andreiovna; how happy she had been to be the one who had managed their home.

Now she grappled with the paradox that, although they had been saved from the Bolshevik terror, they had also been plucked from that life in which she had been so happy and thrown back into a safer, saner but less certain world. That it had been Edward who had saved them – that he should have been there at that desperate moment had been providential, but it also intimated that perhaps she and providence were not of a like mind.

On landing at Constantinople, Alice, Baron Rettenberg and their children were taken by Edward Cobb to a villa in the suburb of Pella with large airy rooms and a walled garden already planted with sweet-smelling spring flowers. Turkish servants were there to attend to them. They dined on a feast of kebabs and salads, fruits and sticky pastries and then fell thankfully on to soft beds.

The next morning, tailors and tradesmen called to take measurements and orders for new sets of clothes. Alice then went with Edward to the British Consul to apply for a new passport with Claude appended as her child. This process, the Consul made clear to Alice, would be expedited thanks to an intervention of the British High Commissioner at the request of Major Cobb. The same influence exercised through the same connections saved Baron Rettenberg and his daughter Nina from internment in a camp for White Russian refugees.

Each morning, in the days that followed, Alice lay for an

hour or more in the sunken marble bath letting the heat draw the grime out of her body and feeling her skin softened by the scented oils. From the open window came the sound of Nina entertaining Claude in the garden; and beyond, over the wall, the cries and clatter of the street. Alice used this time to assemble her thoughts – something she did not find easy. The single-mindedness required over the past year to survive was not easily laid aside for the more complex and nuanced considerations of her present predicament.

Alice's principal anxiety now was not for Claude or Nina but for Rettenberg. It was not an unselfish solicitude, because she had no doubt but that her happiness depended on his. She suffered to see him suffer, and suffer he did – from the indignity of his position as the destitute dependant of her former lover. It was painful to see him now, shorn of his epaulettes and his decorations, his emaciated and weather-beaten face protruding from his new shirts. While in Russia – even during those last terrible days – he had been able to stave off the effect of the deaths of those he loved by the paramount need to save the others; but she could see that now, with this manly role taken out of his hands, he had become deflated: though Alice hardly liked to admit it, even to herself, Rettenberg now looked old.

Alice knew that it was the malnutrition and attrition of recent months that had given Rettenberg's features a cadaverous look. She herself, she had to acknowledge when she looked at her face in the mirror, could be taken for forty. Her body, soaking in the bath, was certainly not that of the soft, slender girl that Edward had known seven years before. Had he been taken aback by her appearance? It seemed remarkable that he had recognised her at once. Had she been taken aback by his? The passing years showed in his face, perhaps, but he still had the vigour of someone who had never wanted for food.

Alice had no doubt but that when Rettenberg had rested and been properly fed, the lines of age would soften; he would then recover his spirit and reclaim his rights as her lover. It was wholly comprehensible that, since arriving in Constantinople, he had made no attempt to come to her bed. Both were enfeebled by a cumulative exhaustion and lack of proper food. He no doubt also thought it inappropriate to make love to her under Edward Cobb's roof.

Was Edward his rival? Edward had said nothing to suggest that he still loved Alice or loved her once again. Indeed, his behaviour was baffling – or was it just English? Had Alice been in Russia for too long to be able to interpret the Englishman's obliqueness and understatement? He did look at her, it must be said, with a particular expression – a look of astonishment, even incredulity – but that was hardly proof of love.

Edward's words did not match this expression. He had a way which irritated Alice of behaving as if they had both simply been on holiday in different parts of the world. He had been to France and then to Siberia: she had been in Russia and then on the Don. He did not avoid the business of the war: he and Rettenberg talked at length about the differences between Kolchak and Denikin and the chances of Wrangel in the Crimea. Both men treated one another with great politeness; not for a moment did Edward give the impression that Rettenberg and Nina were an unwelcome burden, and Rettenberg in turn behaved as if he were a guest in a friend's country house.

But why had Edward Cobb gone to Siberia? What had he meant when he had said, on the quay at Novorossisk, 'I've been looking for you everywhere', as if they had been playing a game of hide-and-seek?

One afternoon Edward suggested a boat ride on the Bosporus. Alice, Nina and Claude accepted: Rettenberg, claiming to have a headache, declined to come.

'Do you know,' Edward said nonchalantly as they sat in the centre of the ketch, a Turkish boatman at the tiller, Nina and Claude at the prow, 'I ran into your parents in Bourges? I was on leave, you see, and thought I'd look them up.'

'Were they ... well?'

'Yes, I'd say so. I didn't see much of them.'

'I long to see them ... and for them to see Claude.'

'Claude, yes. We've all longed to see Claude.' He looked

forward to the six-year-old boy leaning over the edge of the boat while Nina kept hold of his belt to make sure he did not fall in.

Alice blushed and said nothing.

'You didn't get a letter, I suppose? I asked your parents to forward a note.'

For a moment Alice remained silent. Then: 'Yes, I did.'

'Perhaps your answer got lost in the post?'

'I didn't write an answer.'

'No. I thought perhaps you hadn't.'

'I didn't know what to say.'

'I'm glad you got it, all the same. I wanted you to know . . . that I was sorry.'

'I felt, I think,' Alice began, choosing her words carefully, 'that all that was water under the bridge.'

'Yes, of course . . .' He did not finish what he had started to say, but asked instead: 'You ran into Sylvia in Petrograd, I gather?'

'Yes. We both worked in the Anglo-Russian hospital.'

'I was never told. She thought that if I knew about Claude . . .' Again he did not finish his sentence but looked at the boy whose physiognomy had so many of the Cobb traits.

'Do you and Elspeth have children?' asked Alice.

Edward looked back at her in surprise. 'Children? No. Didn't you know? We were divorced.'

'I'm sorry,' said Alice.

Edward smiled. 'I'm not.'

'And did you remarry?'

'She did. To Hal Dormer. You won't have known him. They've gone to live in Kenya.'

'And you?'

'Did I remarry?' He laughed. 'No, I didn't remarry.'

'Why not?' she asked.

'Why not?' he repeated as if dumbfounded by her question.

'Haven't you been in love with anyone else?'

'Yes, I have been in love with someone else – before I was married, while I was married, and after I was married – but she disappeared off the face of the earth!'

Alice turned away to hide her confusion. But whether or not Edward noticed her reaction to this declaration, he did not stop. 'It was absurd to imagine, of course, that after so many years she . . . you could overlook the way you had been treated, or would not have found another . . . a better man to marry. But then, when I learned that you had not married, I started my search.'

'You've been looking for me?'

'Oh yes, for more than a year.' Edward now told Alice about how he had found Sylvia's letters to Elspeth, about his wire to James Burke, his posting to Siberia, his return via India and Egypt, the excursion to Alexandria and his recognition of Saladin in the Papanides stud. And as Alice listened to the account of this epic of modern knight errantry, she could not but be moved. She even wondered whether there was not something lovable, after all, in this correct Englishman, and she was about to reconsider the contempt she had felt for him when he broke the spell by saying that he hoped she would let him 'do something for Claude'.

'Do what?' asked Alice sharply. 'Pay his fees at Eton?'

'Not just that . . .' said Edward lamely.

'What a pity that Elspeth didn't give you a son. Then you wouldn't have had to worry about Claude.'

'I expressed myself badly,' said Edward. 'I don't want to do something for Claude. I want to do anything and everything for him and for you. I would like to make you my wife and him my heir.'

'And if there had been no Claude?' Alice asked triumphantly. 'Then, I dare say, you'd have been quite happy to let me rot in Russia.'

Instead of immediately denying this charge, Edward pondered her question as if determined to give a truthful reply. 'No. It would make no difference. I would still want you to be my wife.'

'Well, that's very good of you,' said Alice, inexplicably angry. 'And it was very good of you to have saved our lives, and the life of Nina, and the life of Baron Rettenberg, whom I happen to love. For that I shall always be grateful, but I think it is quite enough.'

Edward did not react to this rebuff, or the information it imparted about her feelings for Rettenberg. He opened his guidebook to identify the different palaces that looked out on the Bosporus; then went forward to explain to Claude and Nina that they were sailing between Europe and Asia and told them about the English poet called Lord Byron who had swum from one continent to the other. When he returned to sit by Alice, he treated her as courteously as before. It was only when they got back to the villa, and Nina and Claude had gone ahead through the front door, that he said to Alice, in a lowered voice: 'I have no wish to intrude into your life but I think I can still be of some use to you and I hope you will let me help you in any way I can.'

Alice remained annoyed. She wished, somehow, that Edward would be less courteous, less dignified, less well-behaved. She knew she had no choice but to let him help her. She was destitute. So was Rettenberg. Neither had papers of any kind. If she had been determined to be utterly independent, she could no doubt have chosen to go with Rettenberg and Nina to an internment camp and wait for her British citizenship to be verified from London. But particularly after the suffering of those last weeks in Russia, she could not bring herself to do this: she had no alternative but to swallow her pride. She therefore continued to live under Edward Cobb's roof, eat his food and wear the clothes bought with his money. She even accepted the banknotes that, with great diffidence, he gave her for 'anything that you or the Baron or the children might need'.

Rettenberg was more sanguine. While they were waiting for their papers, he and Alice often went into Pella to drink coffee in a café, or they crossed the Golden Horn into Constantinople itself to visit Hagia Sophia and the Blue Mosque. When Alice told him how humiliated she felt at their dependence on Edward, he told her to regard his help not as charity but as recompense for his past omissions. 'That's how I look on it,' he said. 'I have provided for his son, after all, for the first six years of his life.'

'*You* provided for his son?' asked Alice. '*I* provided for Claude with the wages squeezed out of a bourgeois employer.'

'Look at it as you like,' said Rettenberg. 'Cobb only did what you or I would have done in the same circumstances.'

'Did you know that he has been looking for me for over a year? He told me that he went to Siberia because he thought we were there.'

'I suspected as much.'

'He says he still loves me and would like to marry me.' Alice looked flirtatiously at her lover but her words did not provoke the reaction she expected. Rettenberg looked thoughtful. 'And what about Claude?'

'He would make him his heir.'

'I would never have thought that an Englishman could be ... so romantic.'

'He's not romantic. He's just stubborn.'

Rettenberg gazed up at the domes of Hagia Sophia. 'To think,' he said, 'that we Russians imagined that we would recover Constantinople. What vain hopes we had. What foolish ambitions.'

'You are changing the subject,' said Alice.

'Not at all,' said Rettenberg. 'Vain hopes and foolish ambitions ... But whose? That is the unanswered question.'

From Hagia Sophia, they strolled down towards the Galata Bridge, mingling with the Turks wearing fez and caftan or drab uniforms with insignia removed. Coming in sight of the Golden Horn, a figure seated in a doorway suddenly shouted out in Russian: 'Pavel Fedorovich, is that you?'

Alice turned to see an old man with one leg selling matches in the doorway. On the shoulders of his *rubashka* could be seen the marks left by epaulettes.

'Good God, Kyril Leonovich,' said Rettenberg. 'What the devil are you doing here?'

'Earning a living,' said the old man. 'It's better, I can tell you, than life in those dreadful camps.'

Rettenberg turned to Alice and presented Colonel Kyril

Leonovich Baradin of the Chevalier Garde. Alice listened as the two men discussed what had become of their comrades; then, after giving the man half of the money that Alice had received from Edward, they walked on.

They sat down at a café by the Galata Bridge. Rettenberg was pensive.

'Who was that old man?' asked Alice.

'He's not much older than I am,' said Rettenberg.

'He seemed so.'

'No doubt, he has suffered more.'

'Was he in your regiment?'

'Yes. Many years ago. Like Kornilov – the heart of a lion and the brains of a sheep.'

'Surely something can be done for him?'

'And the tens of thousands like him?' Rettenberg laughed. 'If he had two legs, he might get a job as a doorman in a nightclub in Paris or sweep the streets of Belgrade. But with only one leg, well, I imagine he'll go on selling matches or perhaps polish shoes.'

'You have two legs and you speak four languages,' said Alice firmly, sensing the direction of Rettenberg's thoughts.

'I know, I know. I'm luckier than most of the others. But . . .'

'No buts.'

'What did you say to Cobb's proposal?'

'What did I say? What do you think I said?'

'I have no idea.'

Alice reined in her exasperation. 'I said that I was grateful to him for saving my life, the lives of the children, and the life of the man I love.'

'You said that?'

'What else should I have said?'

Rettenberg shrugged. 'I don't know. A bird in the hand is worth two in the bush.'

'A bird?'

'A husband.'

'I have . . .' Alice stopped and blushed. 'I hope to have a husband.'

'Do I know him?'

401

'Very well.'

'Recently widowed?'

'Sadly, yes.'

'Has he proposed?'

'Not as yet.'

'But you think he will?'

'If he doesn't, I will.'

'And if you do, will he accept?'

Again she blushed. 'I would hope so.'

'He might not be the marrying type.'

'He was married to his first wife for thirty years.'

'And was he faithful?'

'No.'

'Would he be faithful to you?'

'I think so.'

'Why?'

'Because he loves me.'

'You're sure of that?'

'Quite sure.'

'But perhaps, even if he loves you now, he might love someone else later. Perhaps he's congenitally unfaithful, a Don Juan, who loves the chase but who, once he has caught his prey, however long it has taken him, loses interest and goes after another.'

Alice scowled, unamused. 'Perhaps.'

'Perhaps he is a snob – a baron, say, who wouldn't deign to marry a governess.'

'Perhaps,' said Alice. 'And perhaps not.'

The light was fading – the sun sinking behind the skyline of roofs and minarets. Hidden by the hood of the horse-drawn barouche which took them back across the Galata Bridge to Pella, Alice took hold of Rettenberg's hand. He turned to embrace her. They kissed. If, for a moment, his earlier words had made Alice momentarily uncertain – if, for a moment she had wondered whether he had possibly meant what he had said – the doubts were now dispelled by the touch of his lips and the look in his eyes when, eventually, they broke apart.

'You are foolish,' she whispered.

'Why?'

'To think you can escape from me.'

Rettenberg leaned back on the leather bench of the barouche. 'I thought it worth a try.'

'Why, Pavel, why?'

'Because I can offer you nothing, whereas he can give you so much.'

'Do you think I want what he can give me? To be Lady Cobb? The mistress of Nester? Part of that vile family – surrounded by cold-hearted snobs?'

'You did once.'

'And you were once a philanderer, but I like to think that we have both changed.'

'Oh, yes,' he said with a sigh. 'We have both changed.'

Alice took hold of his head and kissed him as if some of her vigour and determination could pass to him through their lips. He did not resist her; he clasped her with an almost equal strength; but again, when they broke apart, he looked at her wistfully, and asked: 'Have you considered what your choice would mean for Claude?'

Alice sat back, frowning. 'Yes, of course.' In reality, she had done her best not to consider his interests because of the possible result of such calculations.

'It is a fine thing for a son to grow up with his father.'

'You're the only father he's ever known.'

'But now . . .' Rettenberg turned to Alice. 'I love Claude but he isn't my flesh and blood and, well, it wouldn't be the same.'

'I too love Claude,' said Alice fiercely, 'but I will not sacrifice my life so that he can be a baronet with a landed estate. And he would never forgive me if I did.'

'I'm not so sure,' said Rettenberg, smiling. 'He's so clearly a Cobb.'

'We can live in France,' said Alice, 'perhaps with my parents. My father must still have some money. They'll move to Paris from Bourges. I'll get a job and so will you. We'll live in a villa near the Bois de Boulogne. I'll have your children. I know they will never replace Sasha and Fedor but they will love you, Pavel, and I will love you and we will squeeze every ounce of happiness out the rest of our lives.'

Rettenberg did not answer. Alice gripped his head again and looked into his eyes. They had a distant look which she had never seen before and, when they focused on hers, an expression of fathomless affection.

Edward Cobb was waiting for them at the villa, playing cards with Nina and Claude. With a look of great satisfaction, he brandished the passports and *laissez-passers* that had been delivered from the British Consulate that afternoon. 'Can you be ready to leave tomorrow?' he said. 'I have made reservations on the Orient Express.'

The five sat down at nine to eat their last dinner on Turkish soil. Nina, though at first slightly put out that Claude had also been allowed to stay up as a special treat, mellowed as Edward insisted that she be given a glass of wine. All the adults were cheerful – Edward exultant that he had secured the means to get his friends into England; Alice in a radiant mood, which always raised the spirits of the others; and Rettenberg apparently relaxed and benign.

At ten, Alice took Claude up to bed. Nina followed him half an hour later. Soon after that, the three adults agreed that they too should turn in. Alice led the way up the stairs. At the top Edward said good night: his room was in a different wing. Rettenberg followed Alice down the corridor towards their adjacent rooms. Coming first to the open door to Rettenberg's, Alice stopped. They kissed. Then Alice retired to her room and Rettenberg to his.

There Rettenberg remained standing by the open window, looking up at the moon and listening to the rustling sounds of the night. He felt immeasurably weary but knew it was a weariness that would not be cured by sleep. He loved Alice. Though he had puzzled for a lifetime over the exact nature of the love between a man and a woman, vacillating between the belief that it was a sublimation of crude desire and the equally base but more psychological conclusion that it was an *égoïsme à deux*, he had now discovered it as an indefinable reality – but he had discovered it too late.

Rettenberg loved Alice, but he saw with a melancholy clarity that he could neither take her on nor shake her off. He had lived his life. Hers had yet to be lived. He had staggered on as best he could under the blows that had hit him relentlessly – the loss of Katya, Sasha, Soligorsk, Olga Pavlovna, Fedor and finally Tatyana. Why had he never understood that the affections he had taken for granted were so deep-rooted? Why had he not realised that, even while strength remains in the body, the mind can wear out?

It was not just the succession of personal misfortunes that had led to Rettenberg's sense of defeat and prostration: it was also the demise of his Russia and the degrading manner of its death. He had believed, as had so many others, that the fight of the Whites had been a crusade against absolute evil; but as the civil war had progressed – as he had witnessed the venality and corruption of his own companions, and heard of the atrocities committed by the White troops – he had come to fear that justice and righteousness were not the prerogatives of either side. The scenes he had witnessed at Krivoe Ozero, and the subsequent discovery that his own son had been there – drinking and cavorting with prostitutes while Jewish children were slaughtered by the Terek Cossacks – had given Rettenberg an insight into himself. His crusade was a sham. He was and had always been a complacent impostor. He had not been fighting for liberty, justice or civilisation but for a regime that had protected his privileges with the sabre and the knout.

Rettenberg had never seen himself as someone who worried unduly about right or wrong. He had betrayed Tatyana and seduced other men's wives with an easy disregard for the Sixth Commandment; religion was for superstitious peasants and self-interested priests. Yet, though he had been happy to renounce any ambitions to sanctity, he had nevertheless been sustained by a certain belief in himself. Now that belief had gone.

A man who was merely a living cadaver could be of no use to his surviving daughter or the woman he loved. But what could such a man do if he had not the strength to escape them? Turning back into his room, Rettenberg pulled open the chest in which he had placed his laundered colonel's uniform shorn of its epaulettes. Beside it were his boots, cleaned and polished by the Turkish servants, and beneath it the service revolver that he had brought from Novorossisk. Rettenberg took out the revolver, removed the clip to make sure that it was loaded, then snapped it back into the barrel. He then went to the window and looked at the moon, waiting for the moment when it would finally pass behind the roof of the neighbouring house, extinguishing the remaining pale light and leaving the world in darkness.

Alice awoke suddenly. Had it been a sound or a dream that had roused her? She lay for only a moment; the night was silent. It had not been a sound nor a dream but a fearful thought which, like a vile worm, feeds on the swirling mess of thoughts that continue during the unconsciousness of slumber. And what was that thought? That Rettenberg would leave her; that he had somehow persuaded himself that for those he held dearest he would be better off dead.

She got out of bed and, wearing only her nightdress, crept into the corridor. The house was silent. She tiptoed to the door of Rettenberg's bedroom. There was no sound. She hesitated, afraid that if she were to wake him he would think that she was disregarding his sense that it would be improper under Edward's roof to share his bed. She turned the handle to the door quietly; if she could just see him, sleeping, it would calm her fears. She opened the door. The room was dark. She crept closer to the bed. It was empty, the covers untouched. Only then did she see a man standing in the window, his figure outlined against the dim glimmer of the still-moonlit sky.

Alice crept round the bed. She came up behind Rettenberg and saw the last of the moonlight reflected on the steel of the gun held in his dangling hand. Gently, she laid her hands on his shoulders and rested her head on his neck. Rettenberg did not move. She stood on tiptoe, raised her lips to his ear and whispered: 'I will marry him, Pavel, if that's what you want, but I cannot go on living if you are dead.'

Epilogue

In September 1920, Alice Fry married Edward Cobb at the Caxton Hall Registry Office in Westminster. In the same month, a private Act of Parliament accorded to her son Claude Chambon the name of Cobb, and all the rights and privileges of inheritance of title and property as Edward Cobb's acknowledged son and heir. Less than a year later, Sir Geoffrey Cobb died. Alice and Edward took up residence at Nester Hall. Edward's mother, Lady Joyce, went to live in a house on Sylvia's estate in Scotland. Maurice and Françoise Fry moved from Bourges to the dower house at Nester.

The new Lady Cobb became well known in the course of the 1920s as one of the most stylish and interesting of figures in London society. The drawing room of her house in Eaton Place was frequented by writers, painters and radical politicians. In Yorkshire she caused a stir by insisting that all the farm houses and cottages on the Nester estate should be fitted with bathrooms and given running hot water. She stood in the Labour interest for the constituency of Thirsk and Malton, and though she lost her deposit, she was always cheered at her political meetings.

None of Alice's escapades appeared to aggravate her husband. His devotion to her and tolerance of her eccentricities became the measure to which many other wives drew their husbands' attention. Edward himself had no eccentricities except one: he could not disguise his immoderate pride in his elder son, Claude. No father could have been more assiduous at coming to watch his son play cricket at Eton or could have taken a greater interest in the details of his academic achievements. Claude returned his father's affection and justified his pride. He turned out to be good at cricket, Greek and mathematics; a fine rider and an excellent shot.

Edward showed almost the same affection for the three children that were born to Alice after their marriage. Her elder daughter, like Claude, had the unmistakable look of a Cobb. Her second son, however, had dark eyes and high cheekbones: he was christened Alexander; and the second daughter, whom they called Olga, bore a remarkable resemblance to the Cobbs's adopted daughter, Nina.

Nina, on reaching the age of eighteen in 1921, was presented at court, and her ball was one of the finest of the season. Within a year she was married to James Hitchcock-Hardy, heir to Viscount Cawton. The wedding took place at the Brompton Oratory in London and the bride was given away by her father, Baron Rettenberg.

This was Rettenberg's first visit to England since the end of the Russian civil war. It was not, of course, the first time he had seen Nina, who had been to visit him in Paris on a number of occasions. There Baron Rettenberg lived modestly in a small flat in the rue des Saints Pères. He had obtained a minor post on the staff of the League of Nations and also wrote the odd article for the Russian émigré press. In 1928, six years after Nina's marriage, Katya came to Paris from Moscow for a Peace Congress with her husband Isaac Kirchbaum and their son Max: thanks to the influence of Kirchbaum's patron, Maxim Gorky, the whole family had been allowed to leave Soviet Russia at the same time. When the time came for them to go home, Katya claimed political asylum for herself and her son and stayed in France. Kirchbaum returned to Russia and two years later was arrested by the Cheka and, like so many others, disappeared.

Katya and Max did not live with Rettenberg: his flat was too small. Instead, they rented a larger one nearby and the Baron would dine with his daughter and grandson twice a week and have lunch with them on a Sunday. At other times he would eat in a nearby restaurant, and it was to restaurants that he would invite his French and Russian friends. Rettenberg never entertained at home. There was little more in his flat than one might find in the cell of a Russian monk – a wall of books, a sofa, an armchair, a desk and a lamp that burned in front of an icon depicting Christ, the Universal Judge.

There were two bedrooms – a single one that had been used

by Nina before she married, and his own larger room with a wide bed. On the whole he slept in this alone. Though there were a number of women – French and Russian – who set their sights on this still-handsome man, Rettenberg remained faithful over the years to one woman, who, every so often, arrived on the Golden Arrow from London, always elegantly dressed in a different outfit but wearing the same string of black pearls.

Acknowledgements

The letter from the dead German officer comes from *German Students' War Letters*, translated and arranged from the original edition of Dr Philipp Witkop by A. F. Wedd; Edward Cobb's experience in World War I is based on that of my father, Herbert Read, as described in 'In Retreat' and 'The Raid' found in *The Contrary Experience*. The workings of the Anglo-Russian Hospital in Petrograd comes from *Lady Muriel: Lady Muriel Paget, her Husband and her Philanthropic Work in Central and Eastern Europe* by Wilfred Blunt. I should also like to acknowledge *The Blaze: Reminiscences of Volhynia 1917–1919* by Sophia Kossak; *The Victor's Dilemma: Allied Intervention in the Russian Civil War* by John Silverlight; *Farewell to the Don: The Russian Revolution in the Journals of Brigadier H. N. H. Williamson*, edited by John Harris; *An Ambassador's Memoirs* by Maurice Paleologue; *On the Estate* by Mariamna Davydoff; *The House by the Dvina: A Russian Childhood* by Eugenie Fraser and *The Dissolution of an Empire* by Meriel Buchanan.